CW00377278

The Samurai Revival Trilogy (Vol. 2)

BITTER JUSTICE

To whoever is reading this book at RCH,

Wishing you a full and speedy recovery.

Rheagan Greene

Hamon Publishing

Author's note:

Although predominantly accurate geographically, this is a work of fiction. Any resemblance in this story between people or events and real life is unintended and purely coincidental. Furthermore, use of the Japanese, German and Burmese languages, and historical references, have been simplified to facilitate reading. Nevertheless, a glossary is included at the back of the book.

ISBN 978-0-9573040-2-4

1st Edition (v. 1005)

Cover concept and design by Rheagan Greene (v.21)

Printed and bound in the UK by TJ International Ltd., Padstow

Hamon Publishing
Suite 55, 28 Old Brompton Road, London, SW7 3SS, UK
www.hamonpublishing.com

Dedication:

To my mother and brother, and in fond memory of my father.
Their support made life's worst bearable and its best
something to be shared with gratitude and pride.

Acknowledgements:

My sincere thanks to all those who have encouraged me to
complete this book. Notably: Anne-Marie, Helen, Jo, Rob,
and especially Anna and my editor, Lynn Curtis.

Also, my thanks again to Simon King of Inside Japan Tours Ltd.
His knowledge of Japan and advice concerning my intricate location
requirements enabled me to travel Japan effectively and experience
first-hand much that has influenced this story.

BITTER JUSTICE

CHAPTER 1

Friday 13ᵗʰ June 2025...

Calver Cats Threaten Us All

The UNWP has finally been forced to admit that the criminal gang known as the Calver Cats poses a significant threat to world order. Originally UK-based, the gang has expanded rapidly. It now controls much of the world's illegal arms and drugs trade from operations as far-flung as Bogotá, Chicago, Shanghai and Tokyo.

The Calver name is derived from the Japanese technique of gutting fish alive, and many of the gang's victims have suffered a similar fate. British Calver Cats chief, Beauchamp Caille, was detained once, but escaped in a bloody ambush which left twelve dead. A UK-led multi-national offensive against the gang has proved inconclusive prompting calls for a different approach...   **Global Times**

Calver Cats Peacekeeper Slaughter Continues

The Calver Cats have consistently targeted International Peacekeepers in order to hamper Special Forces and dissuade new recruits. Particularly in Japan, Peacekeepers have been ruthlessly hunted down and slaughtered. It is believed only a handful of them remain active, but the secrecy surrounding these anonymous, licensed-to-kill individuals makes verification of this difficult.

Calver Cats boss, Beauchamp Caille, wants to settle some personal scores too. Not only is he hunting the UK Peacekeeper who annihilated the original London gang, but also his own sister whom he holds responsible for his temporary incarceration. However, she has not been seen in public for a long time and rumour has it that she is already dead...   **Japan News**

CHAPTER 2

In northern Cambodia…

The ancient Khmer ruins shimmered in the humid haze rising through the jungle. Five men sat around an ornately laid dinner table, having just finished an excessively bibulous feast. Two of them were English; the others Japanese.

Nearby, a Japanese woman was tied to a chair. Once proud and striking to look at with long silky black hair, she was almost unrecognisable now. Her clothes were blood-stained, her face badly bruised and misshapen from the ruthless beating to which she had been subjected. She moaned as consciousness returned painfully.

"Damn it, I know business is good!" shouted the blond-haired Englishman at the head of the table. He glowered at his prisoner and stood up angrily. He was an imposing figure, over six feet tall, fit and strong with piercing blue eyes in a heavily suntanned face. Now in his late-forties, the once-respected London lawyer was living as a fugitive; hiding in places he had barely heard of before his dramatic exposure as the boss of a criminal gang. He went behind the woman and with one hand on his sheathed knife, grabbed some of her hair and yanked back her head.

"For the last time, where is that sibling freak of mine?"

"I still don't know," hissed the woman defiantly, "and if I did, I wouldn't say."

"Really! Brave words, Peacekeeper," Beauchamp sneered.

"One day, you'll pay f…"

She didn't finish speaking. He'd already slit her throat. Her head lolled back unnaturally as the last vestiges of life flooded from the gaping wound. Beauchamp calmly walked back to the table.

"What is it with you guys?" he hissed, wiping his knife clean on the tablecloth. "You've had nine months and only brought me one know-nothing Peacekeeper! I refuse to accept that *anyone* can disappear without trace. Find the abomination! I will not ease up on you until this is resolved; preferably in front of me. I am not going to forget what happened in London, and neither should you, Bill. This blemish on my family's honour must be expunged. Surely you can manage that?"

Beauchamp always boiled over when he thought of his sister. On this occasion, he finished by slamming his fists down hard on the table, causing all the extravagant porcelain, silver cutlery and crystal glasses to bounce noisily. It could have been far worse. As he walked over to stare moodily into the wide temple moat, his friend and associate, Bill Chalmers, and the three Japanese guests exchanged glances.

"Everything is going so well," observed Fujiwara Senior. "I don't understand this obsession of his."

His sons remained silent, preferring the safer option of finishing their wine.

"Yeah well," replied Bill, in broad cockney tones, "yer own family ain't exactly all 'unky dory, is it? They've got unfinished business an' we gotta sort it. Else even Leiko wun't be able t' quiet 'im down."

CHAPTER 3

In northwest Japan...

As night embraced the historic town of Kanazawa, swarms of mosquitoes forced people indoors, compounding the unnatural stillness.

Amongst the hills to the east, around a gravelled clearing, wisps of smoke snaked skywards from stoves set within two ageing wooden houses. Close by, an imposing double-roofed gatehouse guarded an ancient stone wall encircling secret grounds. From the other side of the gatehouse, a path meandered down through the forest, over a narrow Kintai-style footbridge and on across waterlogged paddy fields. Eventually, a massive castle rampart could be seen, silhouetted in the moonlight against the starry sky.

Meticulously constructed from enormous boulders, the rampart sides were surprisingly smooth. They jutted resolutely out from the deep moat, reaching upwards at a dizzyingly steep angle to a summit which seemed curiously bare. Where there should have stood the soaring ancestral home of a once-powerful warlord, there was almost nothing.

A line of well-worn flagstones traced a path across the *honmaru* towards a towering wooden arch. They passed underneath and on through an avenue of trees, trained to slope inwards to provide shade from the summer sun. The path ended at the entrance to a courtyard fronting a fine, traditionally built Samurai house. Although big for such a dwelling, it still seemed out of proportion with a site clearly intended for a much larger structure. Five stone steps led up to a roofed gateway, the main entrance through the perimeter wall. This extended as far as the edges of the rampart, before circling round to surround both the house and its immaculate garden, the centrepiece of which was a recently watered, newly planted fragrant camellia lutchuensis.

Inside the courtyard, the trail of artfully laid stones continued. It passed between six monolithic lanterns and several covered racks containing vicious knives, shuriken and other throwing weapons.

A burgundy-coloured banner hung across the front of the house. It displayed large white logos depicting the coat of arms of the family responsible for building the rampart and house. It was a complex design comprising three Samurai swords pointing upwards with their blades crossing near the centre. Completing the design, on either side of the swords, was a large white-and-gold stylised chrysanthemum, the Imperial flower of Japan. The banner was gathered up in the middle to form an arch over the entrance to the house; wooden latticework doors had been slid aside to reveal the Audience Hall within. The occasional crackling of the dying charcoal fire was all that disturbed the silence. Two people sat cross-legged by the hearth.

Slowly, Tessa's vision began to clear. She sensed the strange tingling of the toxins she had taken to facilitate her training finally being metabolised. As her hearing returned, she noticed the *clickety-clack* of a beetle scampering across the verandah. She smiled, recognising the sublime artistry with which the Audience Hall had been built.

To her left sat a distinguished-looking Japanese man. His heavily weathered features made him look older than his years. But even so, dressed in his loose-fitting burgundy coloured tunic, he was notably fit, sharp and strong. He focused his gaze on her eyes.

"*Ohayou gozaimasu*, Nariko-san," said Matsumoto softly. "Don't move yet. Let your senses and strength return first. It will not take long now."

He proceeded to make *macha* green tea using a pristine silk cloth to clean all the utensils and a bamboo ladle to measure water into two exquisite hand-made cups. They were unmatched, but both bore his family crest. He whisked froth on to the tea and placed one cup in front of Tessa, positioning the other for himself.

After a brief silence, they bowed to each other, simultaneously lifted their cups, rotated them clockwise a quarter of a turn so that the crests faced each other, and drank the contents in three gulps.

"A *lifetime* in a moment," he sighed.

"But only a *moment* in a lifetime," she replied quietly. He smiled at her.

"That was a sad smile, Master Matsumoto."

"Nariko-san, I smile at you in many ways." He paused and took a deep breath while he chose his next words. "You have trained for nine months. There is nothing more I can teach you and your departure can be delayed no longer. However, you should know that the world to which you return is even more treacherous than when you left it. The Calver Cats gang has flourished under your brother's stewardship. Your friends Sinclair and Jones have coordinated an international action against the gang, but with only limited success. Your brother says he will not rest until you are dead. He has spies looking for you everywhere. Your paths will soon converge..."

Tessa had hoped that by the time she returned home, it would all be over. Beauchamp would have faced justice and the Calver Cats would have been exterminated. She wanted only to go back to London and pick up her relationship with her lover, David. But apparently it wasn't going to be that easy. Her expression betrayed the disappointment she felt.

"Yes, you awaken into darkness. But peace, freedom and tolerance are all worth striving for. Alas, others cannot assume this struggle on your behalf...

"Before you leave there are two things you should never forget. First, do not be over confident. Your skills are formidable, but no one is invincible. A Samurai rarely appreciates the gravity of a mistake, until it is about to kill them. Secondly, do not undertake to fight continuously for too long. Your body is trained to ignore tiredness. It will continue at the pace you demand, until completely exhausted. Then, with little warning, it will stop. You will recover in a day or two, but if you are in the middle of a battle when this happens, you will be defenceless."

Tessa bowed in proud acknowledgement. She knew he would only say such things out of concern for her. Surely that was the biggest compliment she could ever hope to receive from him.

The distant sound of birds heralding the dawn and the gentle pull of her two Samurai swords slung in her trademark style over her shoulders, brought her back to reality.

"Three months last time, nine this," mused Tessa. "And I still don't remember what I've learnt. Must I really face the Calver Cats without a full understanding of my own capabilities?"

"You know that is the way I teach my students. But many of your memories will return this time, some within hours. And if you need any more of your knowledge, it will surface for you."

He stopped speaking with what Tessa interpreted as a benign, but tired, expression on his face.

"So, what would you have me do now?" she asked.

"Nariko-san," he replied with a wry smile, "I equip the vessel and launch it. Where it goes and what it does are not for me to decide. I leave that to you and your destiny. However, in accepting an International Peacekeeper Mission against the Calver Cats, you have taken on a great burden. You have been able to evade these responsibilities for a while as your friends fought on alone. But victory has eluded them, so now you must seek it yourself... Before this story is finished, you will have to confront many adversaries, and some perhaps sooner than you think. Who ultimately remains standing will only become clear at the very last moment."

"Will we meet again, Master Matsumoto?" she asked, battling to take in everything he had said.

He sighed, lost in thought.

"Time will tell. You are as prepared now as you could ever hope to be. Nevertheless, you are going back to a cruel, harsh world where plans do not always work out as we would like. As before, if you find yourself facing what your heart tells you is an unbeatable force, then discretion is the better part of valour; it is always far wiser to live to win another day... Good luck, Nariko-san. Although I doubt it will be down to luck. Hayasaka has made all the necessary arrangements, but from now on you travel alone."

In one fluid movement, he rose to his feet and looked down at her.

"Conscience, patience, perfection," she murmured.

A smile fleetingly crossed his face. He bowed respectfully to her, turned and walked away. The fragment of a memory flashed unbidden into her mind.

"Who cleared up all those broken eggs?"

Matsumoto paused. Even though he hadn't turned back, she knew he smiled.

"You made the mess, who else but you should clean it up?"

"Hmm… and I remember, *two times*," she added, more seriously. His smile evaporated. She could tell from the set of his head.

"Yes. If you are fortunate enough to cheat death twice, you will remember everything. *Sayonara*, Nariko-san."

He disappeared along the passageway that led deep into the Samurai house. Back in his room, he gazed forlornly at the two mattresses, rolled up side by side.

"Be careful, Nariko-san," he whispered, shaking his head. "Please be careful."

In the Audience Hall only the hissing of the embers disturbed the silence. Tessa immersed herself in the civilised tranquillity that pervaded the Samurai house. She didn't want to leave this place. She turned round to check the dull glow in the east. Hayasaka would be opening the perimeter gates at dawn. She had to go.

She stood up shakily, tired muscles complaining. She had no idea what she had been doing during the last few days, but it must have been strenuous. She steadied herself, and took a deep breath. She savoured looking round the room for what she suspected would be the last time. A feeling of intense sadness and imminent emptiness engulfed her. She would miss this strange and solitary place. One part of her wanted to go home, but the rest shouted: *This is home.*

Tessa walked out of the Audience Hall, discarding her indoor sandals and continuing barefoot down the steps and across the courtyard. Invigorated by the freshness of the night, her muscle coordination returned and she quickened her pace. Completely sure-footed, despite the darkness, she started down the rampart. She had made this journey so many times she could have found the way with her eyes closed. There was a chill in the air, but she didn't notice it, and barely paused as she passed the two stone chinthes at the bottom of the stairway.

Once over the moat, she ran along the banks between the paddy fields. After her first training session with Matsumoto, she had returned along this path with newfound energy. But then it had been adolescent, unbridled power. Now it was different. Now she felt as though she had matured and her energy reserves were vast by comparison. She could release them in a calm, confident and controlled manner. No longer feeling at one with nature, she felt as though she had *merged* with the environment around her. Running on towards the Kintai-style bridge, she made hardly any noise, only a light breeze indicating she had passed by.

Finally, Tessa started zigzagging up towards the imposing gatehouse in the perimeter wall. She stopped and smiled at the stately camellia trees there, inhaling their almost intoxicating perfume. Deep in her subconscious she knew these trees held a very special meaning for her; though what it was exactly, she had no idea. She hoped that back home in London, her friend Lee's wife had been taking care of the cutting she had brought back with her last time. She entered the gatehouse, with its staggered entrance and exit, just as the first rays of sunlight shone through the trees behind her. She heard the clunk of the massive doors being unlocked and the unenthusiastic creaking as one of them was pushed back. She immediately passed through the narrow opening. The two men by the doors jumped back in surprise. They were expecting her, but had not heard her approach. Hayasaka stood a little further back. He greeted her with a smile and a bow.

"*Ohayou gozaimasu*, Hayasaka-san," said Tessa. "Have we time for breakfast?"

"It is already prepared," he replied pleasantly, adding. "There is even time for a hot shower, Nariko-san, which I think might be a good idea." He gestured hospitably towards his wooden cottage.

She grinned and walked quietly on, listening to the sound of the gatehouse door being pulled shut behind her. She wondered when and for whom the door would next be opened.

CHAPTER 4

An hour later, Tessa was sitting in the back of the familiar old black limousine en-route to Komatsu airport. She had discarded her threadbare tunic and now wore a smart blue business suit with a red silk blouse. Her small roll-on bag was in the boot of the car; her double sword case always stayed with her.

She removed her black leather gloves and studied her hands. They were bruised, but nowhere near as battered as they had been after her first training session in Japan. She smiled. It seemed such a long time since this saga had started and changed her life forever.

It had all begun when various political, economic and religious upheavals spawned popular Internet petitions, forcing politicians to ban all guns, explosives and weapons of mass destruction. A new society with secular government had evolved in which freedom of religion was guaranteed and extremism, evangelism and social prejudice were all outlawed. To help keep the peace, independent Samurai sword-wielding marshals were established; and, reluctantly, Tessa had become one of them, operating under the codename, Nariko.

To qualify as an International Peacekeeper and merit a licence to kill, candidates had to endure rigorous training and intense character assessment, finally needing to be proposed by two countries, each of which provided a Guardian for day-to-day monitoring and communication.

But criminal gangs had adapted quickly to the new status quo, also arming themselves with swords, and the worst of them, the Calver Cats, had been formed by Tessa's own brother Beauchamp. Outwardly a reputable London lawyer, he was secretly experimenting with a clandestine career in organised crime. Eventually, as a favour to a close business colleague, he'd ordered the murder of Penny Reid, Tessa's best friend. Sinclair and Jones, two high-up members of the

UK Special Forces, had helped Tessa expose this and her brother had been apprehended. However, Beauchamp soon managed to escape and publicly swore vengeance against his sister. Because of these threats, she had been persuaded to return to the safety of Matsumoto Castle for further training as a sword-fighter. Everyone, including Tessa, had thought that by the time she returned, Beauchamp would be safely behind bars…

Tessa kept having to remind herself that she was returning home. To where she spoke English, not Japanese, and was called Dr Tessa Pennington. Her surname used to be Caille, but she had decided to change her name when she made some fundamental changes in her life … ones that had earned her the undying enmity of her brother and his family. However, as a Peacekeeper, she would still be addressed by her Samurai name, Nariko.

She was looking forward to meeting Sinclair again, her UK Peacekeeper Guardian. He was a good man; she liked and respected him. However, the prospect of having to use her sword more, even in the pursuit of justice, filled her with foreboding. She still hadn't come to terms with the violence she could inflict with it. But the Calver Cats had to be stopped, and she was going to play her part, irrespective of her personal feelings.

In leaving the UK, Tessa had also left behind her new partner David, Lord Kensington. He had a large ancestral estate in Orkney, but spent most of his time in London, like her. Because of the changes she'd made to her life, their relationship had got off to a bumpy start, but they had since grown very close. Now, all she wanted was to be in his arms again.

It was barely light as the car sped southwest. Occasionally, Tessa saw the sea breaking against sea defences not far to her right. But then more memories from her past nine months here started to return. So she relaxed and let one in particular engulf her.

She had learnt during her previous visit that Master Matsumoto's teaching technique relied initially on exhausting a student; mentally, physically and emotionally. After this he would induce a trance-like state in them by having the person eat some remarkably colourful but disgustingly flavoured fish, laden with carefully selected toxins. Only then would training begin in earnest. In an attempt to derail this

19

process, Tessa had prepared herself particularly arduously. So, when Matsumoto gave her horrendous challenges to wear her out, she had grown weary but remained mentally and emotionally strong. By mid-afternoon he was perplexed.

"Well, Nariko," he'd said, grinning. "I'm impressed... and not sure what to ask you to do next."

"Thank you," she'd replied, bowing, grateful for the respite.

He walked to the edge of the rampart and looked down through one of the archery slots in the wall.

"So, do you swim well?" he called to her. Tessa didn't reply; he'd zeroed-in on the one thing that truly scared her. "Ah! Silence speaks louder than words, doesn't it, Nariko-san?"

"I can swim, but I have a big problem with water."

"Really? You must tell me about it..."

Tessa gathered herself to describe how, many years ago, her brother had assaulted her and then tortured her in the bath. He'd nearly drowned her afterwards to coerce her into keeping quiet, and she'd been terrified of water ever since.

"Well..." she started.

"Oh, not now," interjected Matsumoto, "later. Let me show you the back door, you'll enjoy the view."

Tessa sighed and bowed. He led her through the Samurai house and on across the garden. Eventually, they stopped by a door in the perimeter wall; he pulled it open. From it extended a narrow wooden plank jutting out a remarkably long way over the moat a hundred feet below.

"This is easy compared to everything else you have done," said Matsumoto. "Gravity does all the work; you simply step off. The challenge is to enter the water making as little noise and as few waves as possible. After that, swim round the rampart and return ... spending as much time as you can underwater."

Tessa paused and looked at the plank, and then at the moat far below. She swallowed.

"Couldn't we talk about my phobia first?" she pleaded. "It is serious."

Matsumoto smiled.

"I daresay, but don't worry; the water is more than deep enough."

"Oh, good," she groaned. She kicked off her sandals and stepped on to the plank.

"I recommend going right to the end," he continued lightly.

She walked slowly forward as the plank started to bend and bounce. However, that didn't worry her anywhere near as much as the thought of swimming underwater. She reached the end and curled her toes over the edge of the plank. The view was indeed magnificent.

"No time for that now!" said Matsumoto, stamping on the other end. It flexed violently, and threw her off.

"Oh, shiiiiii…" exclaimed Tessa as she plunged down.

"Don't swear!" shouted Matsumoto, calmly walking to the end of the plank to keep an eye on her.

"…sorry!" echoed back.

He watched her enter the water, surface and start swimming. Then he smiled and went back to make himself some tea.

When she returned, still dripping, he simply nodded, and Tessa went and jumped into the moat again, and again, and again. She sighed remembering how her fear of drowning had been her undoing…

Hayasaka turned to face her.

"We're nearly there… It won't be the same without you."

She smiled.

"I'd love to stay, but I have things to attend to."

"I know. People to find, debts to settle, wrongs to right. I wish you success in your endeavours, Nariko-san. Here are your tickets. Your flight to London departs at two-thirty this afternoon. Even allowing for another diversion at Ueno, you should be in Narita at least three hours early." He grinned. "Be careful, be righteous, and may you be victorious."

"That sounds ominous, Hayasaka-san."

"Indeed. We worry that you will have to confront many dangers, and much depends on the outcome."

"Yes, but good always triumphs in the end. I read that somewhere," replied Tessa, trying to lighten the atmosphere. "I must simply remain firmly on the side of right."

"But the boundary between right and wrong is not always clear, and many righteous people meet their end before the final act… However, you should not pay too much attention to the ramblings of an old man. Do your best, and promise you'll come back one day?"

"I promise. In fact, you'll have difficulty keeping me away." The limousine came to a gentle halt in the airport drop-off area. "Don't get out, Hayasaka-san," she continued. "It is better if we are not seen together. Besides, I have never enjoyed goodbyes. I cannot thank you enough for everything you and Master Matsumoto have done for me. I remain in your debt on many counts, not least for your loyalty and friendship." She bowed to him and asked the driver to get her bag out of the boot. "Don't worry, Hayasaka-san. I will be fine."

He tried to conceal his concern behind a weak smile.

"Nariko-san, do not underestimate the hatred of your brother; nor the skill and cruelty of those who accompany him. Family feuds are deep and dangerous things. Your brother will stop at nothing to destroy you."

"If he finds me, I will be ready. And, if he doesn't find me soon, I will find him."

Hayasaka forced another smile, nodded and bowed.

"*Sayonara*, Nariko-san," he said, turning away.

She bowed back and eased herself out of the car and slung her double sword case over her shoulder. The driver passed her the handle of her carry-on bag and stepped back, bowing deeply.

As Tessa entered the crowded check-in area, the babble of conversation stopped immediately. People were curious to see her, and nervous. Her being an immaculately dressed Caucasian didn't concern them; nor her neat blonde hair, steely blue-grey eyes, tanned complexion and healthy physique. It was her double sword case displaying the gold OCL emblem that every eye fixed upon. Few people were licensed to carry a cased Samurai sword; even fewer had the right to carry a sword in the open. Only International Peacekeepers could do that. The *Open Carrying Licence* logo on her sword case meant that she was one of them, with a licence to kill.

Tessa joined the check-in queue. But as soon as people saw her behind them, they bowed respectfully and moved aside. Normally she wouldn't have taken advantage of her Peacekeeper status, but today she felt very tired. So, bowing and thanking them in Japanese, she moved forward and handed her ticket to the young man behind the desk.

"Ah, yes ... er ... Nariko. Have you any bags to check in?" he stammered, visibly trembling as he studied her OCL Identity Card.

"No, only hand baggage," she replied with a disarmingly pleasant smile.

"OK." Unsure what to do he looked round, prompting his manager, a smart looking woman called Suzuki, to come over. She gave him some instructions, but he kept fumbling. Brusquely, she nudged him off the chair and completed the check-in procedure herself.

Tessa asked for a seat at the front, so Suzuki blocked out the entire first row. They both knew nobody would want to sit next to her anyway. She handed Tessa her Boarding Pass, and, scowling at the cowering check-in clerk, apologised for the delay.

Tessa passed through security and sat down in the cavernous Departure Lounge. She considered ways to while away the time. Another memory rose from her subconscious, so she leant back and closed her eyes...

It was evening and she was sitting opposite Matsumoto in the Audience Hall. The atmosphere between them was amicable, warm and relaxed. She asked whether he could tell her the history of the Samurai house. Why had it been built on such a large rampart?

"That's a long story, Nariko-san," replied Matsumoto thoughtfully. "But maybe you should know... One of the most important events in Japan's history was the Meiji Restoration of the late-1860s. It marked the end of many years of civil war, bloodshed and betrayal. Japan had become polarised into two rival factions. On one side, the Matsumoto and Amakuni families marshalled the Satcho Alliance to support the Emperor. Against them, the Fujiwara and Amafuji families plotted with the Tokugawa Shogunate. Eventually, the Satcho Alliance was victorious, thus ending the two hundred and fifty years of the Edo period. The Emperor never forgot that his victory owed much to the combination of the fighting prowess and influence of the Matsumoto, and the superiority of Amakuni weapons. He rewarded our families handsomely, while those who had supported the Shogunate paid dearly for their treachery. Many Fujiwara and Amafuji were ordered to commit *seppuku*. Those who remained were disgraced and their estates forfeited.

"The Matsumoto had built two impressive castles to secure their extensive lands. The biggest was here, it was nearly as large as the castle at Himeji. The smaller one still stands today, over the mountains past Hida-Takayama." He paused to drink some green tea.

"The Crow Castle," interjected Tessa in awe, beginning to understand. "I've been there, it's very beautiful."

"Yes, I think so too," agreed Matsumoto with a nod of his head. "Anyway, while our forces were supporting the Emperor in Kōchi and Karatsu, the Fujiwara attacked our castle here. Eventually it fell and the Fujiwara slaughtered many of my relatives. The castle was razed to the ground. But within weeks the Fujiwara were driven out, and their fall from grace was final and complete. Those who survived turned to a life of crime. Racked with hatred and jealousy, they swore to end the Matsumoto line and started a feud between our two clans which still continues today.

"In 1692, the Emperor established the Chrysanthemum League. It was for clans who swore to uphold the law and support the Imperial blood line. It had two clan members, the Matsumoto and the Amakuni, and was never expanded further. So, only we are permitted to incorporate the Imperial chrysanthemum within our family crests. Even now our two clans have special rights, and obligations. Those who carry the chrysanthemum mark are revered throughout Japan. You have seen the mark within the family crest on this house, and on your Amakuni sword. It is also here…"

Matsumoto pulled up his sleeve, revealing a neat chrysanthemum tattoo on his wrist.

"The Emperor alone decides who from our clan should receive the mark of the chrysanthemum. However, with this sign comes the responsibility to remain righteous and loyal, and, if asked, to support the Emperor in ensuring Japan is a just and peaceful place. The identity of those who carry this mark is known only to a few, and is never divulged to the public or even most of the Japanese state administration. The lands contained within this castle's perimeter wall will belong to the Matsumoto for ever. The same applies to the Amakuni's valley near Iga Ueno. The locations of both are kept secret. The Emperor instituted a brutal purge to ensure that, something which I never really understood. But ever since, to trespass on these lands, or to mention their whereabouts to others, are crimes punishable by death. Not even the police may enter unannounced; that right belongs only to the Emperor's private guard, who also wear the chrysanthemum mark.

"After the land here had been retaken, my family decided not to rebuild the castle as the time for such buildings had passed. Instead they constructed this beautiful Samurai house, and, when it was completed, they presented the Crow Castle to the Emperor. Then, in a bid to ensure continued peace, they swore never to take up arms against the Fujiwara to end the feud."

"What happened to them?" asked Tessa.

"Oh, they proved to be highly successful as criminals. The remaining Amafuji made them weapons, and together they forged a dark new existence. And so started the Yakuza, the source of all organised crime in Japan…"

He paused for a moment, apparently unsure whether to continue.

"Hayato Fujiwara is the current head of the family. He has two sons, Ryota and Ryuu, neither of whom has children. Ryota married a long time ago, but it didn't last. So, the future of the Fujiwara rests on these three people. Meanwhile, even though I am not the eldest of the surviving Matsumoto, I am the head of the family; which is why I live here. Neither I nor my brother has any offspring either… The other things you should know is that for centuries the Hayasaka have been a loyal part of the Matsumoto clan. It started as a master/servant relationship, but has progressed far beyond that."

"Amazing," said Tessa. "But I am not surprised to hear what you say of Hayasaka. Thank you for telling me this, it helps put things in perspective."

"Does it? Well, I hope you remain grateful," replied Matsumoto with a curious smile. "Anyway, enough of history, you have work to do. You may start by fetching…"

"…a camellia sprig?" interjected Tessa.

Matsumoto smiled and produced a stop-watch.

Tessa bowed and left to run to the camellia trees by the castle wall. It was his standard work-out for her. She always had to get back in a faster time than the one before…

Back in the Departure Lounge, Tessa was pleased to have these memories of her time with Matsumoto. It had been so strange before, being with him for ten weeks, but hardly remembering any of it. Nevertheless, she sensed that many of these current revelations were as troublesome as they were intriguing. Why had Matsumoto wanted her to retain these images? More importantly, why did she now have a chrysanthemum tattooed on her own wrist? She had only noticed when she showered, and had hidden it under her watch…

Curious to find out what was happening in the world, she went to the newspaper rack and took copies of the *Global Times* and *Japan News*. A moment later, her eyes widened in amazement as she read the lead articles; *'Calver Cats Threaten Us All'* and *'Calver Cats Peacekeeper Slaughter Continues'*.

"Wow, Beauchamp, you have been busy!" she muttered.

However, it was good he didn't know where she was, or that she was the Peacekeeper who had killed so many of his people in London. But the Calver Cats' rapid expansion would make it even more difficult to detain him. No wonder Matsumoto and Hayasaka said she had work to do. What had happened to her brother: the gregarious if somewhat arrogant London lawyer? She tried to imagine what his immaculately groomed, social-climbing, wife Caprice thought of it all…

Tessa's flight was called and people formed an orderly queue to board the plane. She knew it would be better to get on last, as that would avoid her having to put up with the nervous stares of people filing past her. When boarding completed, she walked forward and fed her ticket into the automated reader.

"Have a nice flight," said the clerk in broken English.

"*Arigato gozaimas*," replied Tessa, without thinking.

She sat down and wrapped the sword case strap around her wrist. As soon as the plane took off, she sat relaxed back in her seat and closed her eyes. She wanted to sleep, but felt it wiser to hover close enough to sleep for it to be restful, while sufficiently awake to remain aware of her surroundings.

An hour later, Tessa eyes were jolted open by the bump of the plane landing at Tokyo's Haneda airport. As it taxied to a jet-way, she grinned remembering the trouble she had managed to get into last time she'd traversed Tokyo. She had become embroiled in a scuffle at Ueno station. It hadn't been her fault, but she had been obliged to overcome five Japanese attackers, albeit without seriously injuring any of them. It had taken a long meeting with Inspector Maeda before she had been allowed to leave Japan with her record unblemished.

As the door opened, she stood up, but to her surprise, nobody else did. Usually, when domestic flights landed in Japan, they immediately became a heaving mass of people jostling to get out. But everyone was waiting for her. She grabbed her carry-on bag and hoisted her sword case on to one shoulder. Then she turned to face the passengers and bowed. They looked bemused by her politeness and, in unison, bowed back.

At the end of the jet-way, she quickly mingled with the crowds heading for the exit. She wanted as few people as possible to know she had just arrived from Komatsu. In the Main Terminal, she headed for the exit by the taxi rank. But then she noticed a well-dressed man sitting alone in a row of seats. He looked at her, and smiled. She went over to him.

"*Konichiwa*, Inspector Maeda."

The man stood up and bowed. He was in his early-fifties, slim and clean-shaven with a friendly, intelligent face.

"*Konichiwa*, Nariko-san. How nice to see you again. You are looking well … very well, in fact. I hoped we would bump into each other."

Tessa raised her eyebrows. He shouldn't have known she'd be here. The movements of Peacekeepers were meant to be secret.

"Well, you've found me now, so what can I do for you?"

"You can join me for tea. I have transport."

"Thank you, that is most kind. But I'm afraid I don't have long before my flight from Narita."

"Oh, there's plenty of time before that. Surely a short chat will be possible? After all, I am one of your Guardians," replied Maeda smoothly, cocking his head inquisitively. "And by the way, it's Chief Inspector now."

Nodding, Tessa sighed.

"Congratulations, Chief Inspector…"

Two months earlier, Beauchamp had also been in Tokyo, enjoying an excellent teppanyaki lunch with Hayato Fujiwara. Their relationship had developed considerably over the past year and they'd become

27

friends.

"Business is very good here," remarked Fujiwara, using his chopsticks expertly to select a piece of freshly cooked Kobe steak from the decorative plate in front of him. "Profits are high, and increasing."

"I agree, it all looks very promising," replied Beauchamp with a smile. "We're both doing well. But you still haven't made any progress with those other tasks I set you and Bill."

"You mean finding the woman Nariko, and your sibling?" Fujiwara had learnt to be careful when describing Beauchamp's sister. Everyone knew Beauchamp hated her far too much for any more direct reference.

Beauchamp nodded, drinking another glass of hot sake; only to have it quickly refilled by the obsequious silk-clad geisha beside him.

"Well, I still don't think either of them is in Japan, and our spies in China haven't come up with anything... After your detention, I can understand why you want to get even with your sibling. But what has this Nariko done?"

"Oh, I thought you knew? She's a Peacekeeper about whom nobody seems to know anything. We suspect she single-handedly wiped out the original Calver Cats at the Rippleside Industrial Estate in London. That was the night Bryani died. Bill and I were there when she arrived..." Beauchamp paused, trying to decide what to eat next. "A couple of Special Forces guys had just been downed, but Bryani was handling it, so we left. We caught a glimpse of the lone Peacekeeper; but she was wearing a balaclava, so we don't know what she looks like. By a process of elimination, we think it must have been Nariko; although I suppose it would be as well to confirm that before she dies."

"Well, Bryani was highly skilled, losing her was a surprise. No doubt her husband will be after her killer too," replied Fujiwara with a provocative smirk. Beauchamp declined to take the bait. He knew Bryani had married an Asian man a long time ago, but she had never spoken about it to him. "Mind you, asking questions of, or about, a Peacekeeper is never easy, and this one sounds a challenge. But it's usually easy enough to track them down. One simply follows the wake! Although not knowing what she looks like doesn't make it any easier... Have neither of your inside sources been able to find out anything?"

Beauchamp shook his head.

"Hmm. Shame. And both so well connected too. Anyway, is this sibling of yours likely to be difficult to handle?"

"Oh, I don't think so," replied Beauchamp, chuckling, "she's studied karate and Kenjutsu, and has taken up the sword, but she's far too much of a wimp to be any good at it. She's terrified of water, for God's sake."

"Hah! Well, we'll do our best."

"Good. I'd better be on my way. Bill will continue to handle Southeast Asia for now. He's enjoying himself in Burma and generating some useful contacts..."

Fujiwara nodded. Like most people, he didn't particularly like Bill Chalmers. Some of his sexual preferences were distasteful and dishonourable. However, everyone knew that he and Beauchamp went back a long way.

"...Eventually though, I shall want you to assume responsibility for all the Calver Cats' Far Eastern operations, not just here, China and Taiwan."

"When you're ready, it would certainly make sense. But there's no rush, we've plenty to do."

He gestured to his son Ryota to settle the bill. "So, we'll meet next in Cambodia?"

"Yes, in four weeks," replied Beauchamp as the geisha fussed over his bib.

"OK. Give my regards to Ryuu... And Leiko, of course."

CHAPTER 5

As Tessa peered out from the back of the unmarked police car, she reflected on how the Calver Cats had changed her life. A successful business career had left her embarrassingly rich and looking forward to enjoying herself. But then her friend Penny had been murdered, and Tessa inherited everything of hers. This included an incredibly valuable sword which Penny had especially commissioned for Tessa as a surprise birthday present. Forged by master sword-maker Kimi Amakuni, it could do remarkable things. Not only did the folded steel blade ring when held by its true owner, but it possessed two cutting surfaces. The front edge was designed to cut through flesh and bone, while the back edge could shatter other swords and stone.

Perhaps bizarrely for a Peacekeeper, Tessa abhorred violence. Nevertheless, having found the sword, and knowing that it had been especially commissioned for her by her much-loved friend, Tessa felt honour bound to learn how to use it. To her surprise, she not only found she was extremely gifted with it, but also that she enjoyed wielding it. Initially she had been taught by Master Lee at South Kensington Samurai, or SKS as it was known, and then, on his recommendation, by Master Matsumoto in Japan.

Although her new skills troubled her greatly, they had proved useful. Penny's killers had been tracked by the UK Special Forces to the Calver Cats' training ground in East London. Tessa went and confronted the gang. In the battle that ensued, she was victorious as well as saving her Special Forces contacts, Sinclair and Jones, who had both been badly wounded. But Bryani, the gang's teacher, was shot by one of her own people in order to stop her talking. However, before she died, she bequeathed her own Amafuji sword to Tessa. It wasn't as good as her Amakuni weapon, but very nearly. Swords made by these two families were accepted as the best in the world. Now Tessa carried both swords in a unique harness that she had invented in order to be able to wear and draw the swords over her shoulders, ready for action in a split second whenever danger threatened.

Eventually, the car arrived in Asakusa. Tessa knew and liked this bustling north-eastern suburb of Tokyo. She revelled in the confident atmosphere indicative of its long and chequered history. Once famous for its brothels and *sashimono* carpenters, it now boasted many other attractions including the Senso-ji temple and numerous excellent bath houses. Asakusa also had a reputation for narrow unmarked streets in which one could easily get lost or pass unnoticed. So it came as no surprise to her when their car turned into just such a street, devoid of cars, bicycles or people, and not overlooked by any other buildings. After a while, the car slowed and to their right two solid metal gates moved apart. The car glided through and the gates began to close. They had entered a surprisingly large cobbled courtyard fronting a wonderful old wooden house. As the car stopped, latticework panels slid aside. A woman clad in a beautiful yellow chrysanthemum-design silk kimono bowed to greet them.

"Here we are," said Maeda genially.

Tessa got out with her sword case and followed the inspector up the three wooden steps, replacing her shoes with the slippers placed in front of her by the kimono-clad woman. Then, the woman led them along a corridor floored with fine tatami mats. Eventually they entered a lounge furnished with items representative of the epitome of Japanese artistry. At one end was a decorative alcove with a large hand-painted blue vase containing freshly picked chrysanthemums. Hanging above it was a scroll inscribed with Zen calligraphy saying *'May all your endeavours be righteous and successful'*. A delightful aroma of sandalwood pervaded the room. In the middle of it stood a low black lacquer table.

"This is lovely," observed Tessa. "Is it your home, Maeda-san?"

"Hah! I wish it were!" he replied. "This is a government house, used for special guests who wish to maintain a low profile while staying in Tokyo."

"Well, it certainly is a very pleasant place to come for such a short meeting."

He smiled and beckoned her to sit. Tessa laid her sword case down and gracefully lowered herself onto the nearby *zabuton*.

They sat in silence. First, Tessa admired the magnificent table, beautifully inlaid with a dragon design in mother-of-pearl. Then she turned her attention to the Japanese garden on to which the room looked. It had been wonderfully laid out with a pond stocked with koi, and a waterfall. But she was growing impatient.

"Maeda-san, delightful as this is, I would like to know why you have brought me here."

Before he could answer, the partition door slid open and the kimono-clad woman carried in a lacquerware tray with a pot of green tea and two beautiful hand-painted porcelain cups on it. She knelt down at the head of the table and placed a cup in front of both of them, on circular wooden mats. Then she poured some tea, leaving the pot on the tray at the end of the table. Without having said a word, she reversed out of the room, knelt in the hall, bowed and slid the door closed.

"Yes, of course," replied Maeda, glancing at Tessa's sword case and picking up his cup. "However, I can assure you, we are perfectly safe here. Also, our conversation will only ever be known to the two of us."

Tessa said nothing, she simply sipped her tea.

"I don't know whether you've been keeping up with the news where you have been, but a lot has been happening; most has been bad and most of that has been instigated by the Calver Cats. They are everywhere now, including here in Japan and we have borne the brunt of their strategy to eliminate Peacekeepers. Regrettably it has proved highly effective and has left my country vulnerable. We have only three fully qualified Peacekeepers left. One of these is wounded, another is in Okinawa. We have some being trained, but none is ready for active service. All eyes are on us to see how we handle this challenge."

He paused and poured Tessa some more green tea, but still she said nothing.

"We don't believe it was a coincidence that this campaign of elimination started here. It began in Japan to clear the way for the Far Eastern expansion of the Calver Cats. We recently discovered that most of their Asian operations are soon to be managed from Tokyo. Together with the remaining South American operations, these make up the core of their international drugs supply chain. Afghanistan was important, but opium production there has now all but ceased following concerted UNWP efforts to purchase the poppy harvests and fund crop replacement programs.

"A year ago, an old-established Japanese crime syndicate joined forces with the Calver Cats. It is led by Hayato Fujiwara. Apparently the partnership stems from a private meeting held between him and Beauchamp Caille. I hate to think what deal was struck, but the outcome has been a rapid increase in the influence of the Fujiwara within the Calver Cats. It is Fujiwara who masterminded the Peacekeeper killings. He is a particularly nasty piece of work … his family has been involved in crime for seven generations now."

"I see," said Tessa, drinking some more tea. "Quite a big family is it?"

"Not any more. There's only the old man and his two sons, Ryota and Ryuu. They're effectively their father's left- and right-hand men. They're easily recognised, they're big guys for Japanese as apparently their mother was an American though she's dead now. Anyway, people have been trying to stop the Fujiwara for more than a century. Although Hayato Fujiwara has been convicted and sentenced to death several times, he has always managed to evade justice on some technicality or other." Maeda paused to sip his tea. "By chance, we found out Fujiwara has convened a meeting of his people tonight. I had almost given up hope of finding you in time but fate smiled on us…"

"You think so?" interjected Tessa dryly, pouring more tea for both of them.

"Hmm. We even found out the place and time of their meeting … admittedly suspiciously easily. Fujiwara probably hopes to eliminate any remaining threat the Peacekeepers represent in Japan. He must know Hachiro is the only active Japanese Peacekeeper left. If Hachiro is killed, Japan will be helpless, and a terrible message about Peacekeeper vulnerability will have been sent world-wide."

Tessa shifted her position uncomfortably; it was obvious what he wanted.

"Hachiro is a very experienced Peacekeeper. He has been fighting Fujiwara for years. I have worked with him for a long time and trust him completely. Fujiwara knows Hachiro will come, but he won't want to take risks. He will have more people than one man can handle, even Hachiro. But now we have a wild card with which Fujiwara will not have reckoned, since we are sure the Calver Cats do not know you are in Japan. So, as I daresay you have deduced, Nariko-san, I would like you to consider going with Hachiro to confront Fujiwara. Of course, Hachiro would lead."

"Of course," replied Tessa with a rueful smile. "Tonight?"

Maeda nodded sheepishly.

Tessa desperately wanted to find an excuse not to get involved. But she needed a more substantial excuse than her burning desire to go home and be reunited with David.

"I'm afraid it is not permissible without signed letters of authority from my Guardians," she said. "I daresay you can soon prepare yours, but what about Sinclair in the UK?"

"I have both here," replied Maeda smoothly. He produced an envelope from which he removed a fax. It was typed on UK Special Forces notepaper and had been signed by Sinclair. Tessa quickly scanned the typically concise text. Conveniently for her, it said that if she wished to participate in what Maeda proposed, the UK had no objections. Then Maeda slid another envelope across the table in which she found his letter of authorisation, signed on behalf of Japan. She took a deep breath.

"Maeda-san, as you see, I am under no obligation to do this and to be quite frank I just want to go home. I have been away a long time and I am weary."

"I understand, Nariko-san. But you are our only hope. Without your intervention, I believe Hachiro will die tonight. No matter what you may think, I take the fact that you surfaced today as a good omen. I am sorry to have to ask this of you, but it is very important. Not only to Japan, but also for the Mission you accepted to defeat the Calver Cats."

Unimpressed, Tessa tried to look as reluctant as she felt.

"This is a unique opportunity to stop Fujiwara," pleaded Maeda, "and to deal a serious blow to the Calver Cats. They have suffered setbacks, but continue to expand in Southeast Asia. However, tonight they will have prepared to outnumber only one Peacekeeper. Your presence is likely to tilt the balance in our favour. Nariko-san, will you do it … will you go with Hachiro?"

For a while, the only sound was the splashing of the nearby waterfall.

"I'm not ready for more killing," sighed Tessa, eventually. "I am tired and I do not want to earn a reputation as a harbinger of death, even as a Peacekeeper. Yes, I want to see the Calver Cats defeated and Beauchamp Caille brought to justice. But in pursuit of this, I have already killed many who perhaps did not deserve to pay the ultimate price."

"But presumably you have just spent nine months honing your skills. To what end if not to prevent the sort of crime for which Fujiwara is responsible?"

"Yes, I know," she replied disconsolately. "But it makes more sense if one is familiar with the build-up to a conflict, with all its twists and turns. In this instance, I feel neither informed nor prepared."

"I understand," continued Maeda, "but this desperately needs to be done, from many perspectives including your own. Alas, we do not have the luxury of choosing when and where events such as these take place. You knew that when you agreed to become a Peacekeeper. I have brought some files describing the Fujiwaras' crimes, but they only support what I have already told you. I accept this cannot be a good time for you. But precisely because of that we will have the advantage. No one need even know it is you…"

Tessa finished her tea and took the files he offered; she scanned their contents. Fujiwara Senior seemed to be a most unpleasant man who had perpetrated many brutal crimes. Violence against innocent people, particularly in the pursuit of riches or in the name of religion, had always infuriated her. She soon found his sons were at least as bad.

"Of course, Nariko-san, I would understand if you said no, and you do have that right. If Sinclair had not given it to you, then I would. Make no mistake, if you go with Hachiro tonight your life will be as exposed as his, and the odds are unlikely to be in your favour. No one will think less of you if you decline this invitation."

"And what will Hachiro do if I refuse?"

"Well, he doesn't even know you exist. He is expecting to go alone and says he will try to take Fujiwara down before he falls himself. But that is no concern of yours. He will do his duty, just as you would. But

35

you are not from Japan, and you had no warning of this. You must make your own decision."

As Maeda waited, he became convinced it would be both logical and sensible for Tessa to demur.

Meanwhile she was slowly making her decision. To turn down a chance to deal the Calver Cats a severe blow would be foolish; especially given the fact that she might be able to avoid becoming associated with the event by name. However, her memories of Matsumoto describing his family's feud with the Fujiwara made this all smack of something more than serendipity... But so be it. She already owed her life to what Matsumoto had taught her, so perhaps she should do this for him.

"Maeda-san, I accept," she said resolutely. "I will fight tonight under Hachiro's leadership and help him bring Fujiwara back to face justice."

Surprised, relieved and elated, Maeda bowed.

"Thank you, Nariko-san. I am very grateful and many others will be too. You can meet Hachiro later in my office, I am sure he also will be delighted."

"That remains to be seen. At some point you will have to tell him I am not a man."

"Oh, I'm sure that won't be a problem."

"Really? I thought Japan was still near the bottom of the World Gender Equality League?"

"Regrettably so, but Japan is continually modernising ... and Hachiro is a very emancipated man. I think."

"Well, you know what they say, beggars can't be choosers," mused Tessa.

"Indeed. Anyway, please treat this house as your own. I think it would be wise if you did not go out so if there is anything you need, do not hesitate to ask for it. A suite is prepared, and I can recommend the hot spring bath at the end of the corridor. I will send a limousine to collect you at ten with the constables you just met. They will bring you to Special Forces headquarters, not far from the Imperial Palace. Oh, and Sinclair-san asked me to give you this. I believe it's hair dye."

Tessa opened the small package he passed her; it contained a note and two bottles.

Dear Nariko-san,

Thank you for accepting Maeda's invitation. These bottles contain hair dye/remover. I would recommend using them. They provide a simple and effective disguise which will help conceal your identity. The bottle with the black label turns your hair black. Guess what the other does… Good luck.

Sinclair

"Hmm. I'll need some camellia oil as well," added Tessa quietly.

"What?"

"Camellia oil. It was used extensively during the Edo period for maintaining swords. I use it too."

"Oh, right, no problem. I will arrange it…"

After the metal gates had closed behind Maeda, the kimono-clad woman led Tessa back down the corridor. They passed the lounge where the meeting had taken place. The tea paraphernalia had already been cleared away and a screen drawn to protect the room from the sun. She was shown into a very comfortable room with an en-suite bathroom. A screen had been opened along one wall to reveal another view of the garden. As the woman started to reverse out, Tessa addressed her in Japanese.

"I shall bathe first, but then I would like to eat, please. Miso soup, mixed sashimi, rice and fruit with some more green tea and a large bottle of still mineral water."

The woman bowed and the door panel slid quietly closed.

A few minutes later Tessa gently lowered herself into the hot bubbling spring bath. She looked down … and burst out laughing.

"You're bonkers!" she exclaimed, shaking her head in disbelief. "As if dying violently wasn't scary enough already!"

Back in her room, she enjoyed a superb meal and settled down to get some sleep. As her consciousness drifted, another recollection from her time with Matsumoto invaded her thoughts. She was back at the castle and had just surfaced from his drug-induced trance. She was standing by a thick plank of wood lodged between two stone pillars, with a sack of wet sand hanging in front of it. She looked at him and smiled.

"Ah! I thought we should talk," said her sensei warmly. "Don't worry about the wood; the challenge is to break it without bursting the sack. You won't be able to do it yet, but perhaps we'll return to it later. Come and sit down."

He gestured towards a stone bench not far away. It was a glorious afternoon and the view from the top of the Castle rampart was magnificent.

"Nariko-san, before we continue your training it is important you understand, and consciously accept, how this will affect you. What you learn now will not simply complement your present skills; it will change you, and your life, for ever. If you develop your God-given gifts to their fullest extent, you will become a true Samurai Peacekeeper. Not just a person wandering the World assisting Special Forces to uphold the law, but someone who lives and breathes this honourable, all-embracing righteous art. There are many benefits, but you will be forced to make sacrifices too. From here on, there is no going back. Are you ready and willing to forgo the many other things that life, Western materialism and the world can offer?"

"Hmm, nothing too complicated for such a beautiful afternoon then?" observed Tessa sarcastically. "You know I always want to be as good as I can at anything I choose to do. However, this doesn't sound particularly enticing."

"Oh, but it is. You are on the threshold of a life far more fulfilling than you could ever imagine. Yes, it replaces much of what you now think you might miss. But in its place, you will find something of considerably greater value; more demanding, more satisfying and more virtuous. But this is a decision which you alone must make."

"I think I understand what you mean… May I have some time to consider it? The sun will be setting soon. Perhaps I could watch it go down first?"

"Of course," replied Matsumoto. "I will make some tea to accompany your deliberations."

Tessa gazed westward, admiring the panorama of lush green countryside framed by distant mountains. It was wonderful and she revelled in the chance to relax and think while enjoying the fresh warm air.

She drank the cup of green tea Matsumoto placed on the bench beside her and marvelled at the scene playing out beneath the waning sun. As the mountains became hazy purple shadows, the forest changed from shades of green to fiery orange. Clouds of insects rose above the trees, tiny black specks tempting a nearby congress of starlings to swoop down on them in a series of dazzling aerobatics. It was an intoxicating sight, enhanced by the sounds of rustling trees, birdsong and the distant river. It all seemed so tranquil. Yet she had to decide whether further training would, in the name of justice, make her a destroyer of such peace, or a protector of it. And even with such a noble goal in mind, would that justify the sacrifices she would have to make?

Tessa had always felt that if one had been born with a skill, it would be selfish and wasteful not to develop it to its fullest extent, not least since such skills were surely an integral part of one's destiny. On that basis surely she should continue learning as much as she could? But Matsumoto had made it clear that if she did, many other things would be lost to her. Presumably close relationships, friends, family and her own safety. Well, following her brother's treachery, her family had already disintegrated, so she didn't seem to have much to lose from that perspective. But what effect would all this have on her love life? Even if David had stayed true to her in London, would he be able to accept her Peacekeeper status, which, so far, she had managed to keep secret from him? She smiled, realising she already knew the answer to that one.

She slowly came to the conclusion that she didn't have much to lose by continuing, and possibly a lot to gain. If what she learnt did give her life a proper purpose, to the benefit others, then surely she had a responsibility to go ahead?

As the sun finally set, she finished her tea and smiled at Matsumoto, sitting patiently nearby on another bench. Then she stood up and walked over to the plank. Without pausing, she punched the bag of sand with all her strength. The impact was so powerful and abrupt that the centre of the plank exploded in a cloud of splinters. However, the bag barely moved and the depression she'd made soon disappeared.

Matsumoto raised his eyebrows.

"So be it, Nariko-san. And with that little demonstration, you have earned the right to try learning something which generally I do not teach others. It is a very difficult technique, and different from everything else you have mastered. But it may one day be useful for you to remember you have learnt it, so we will do it now."

He led her across the courtyard to a covered equipment rack she had not used before.

"This technique," said Matsumoto, "is *up close and personal*, as our American friends would say. It is as brutal as it is difficult to learn. No weapons are required; your hands and your eyes are all you need. Few are sufficiently skilled even to attempt it."

She looked at him questioningly.

"But what circumstances would lead me to require such knowledge?"

"Well, if we only learnt what we expected to need, schooling would be over rather quickly, wouldn't it?"

She smiled.

"*Harmonic Induced Cardiac Arrest* is essentially a series of three sharp punches, like the one you just so ably performed. The first is to the chest of the target. It must be powerful enough both to wind and to stun and will probably break several ribs. If delivered correctly, it will expel all the air from the target's lungs and initiate an harmonic wave within the chest cavity sufficient to disrupt the normal heart rhythm. After air has been expelled so quickly, the autonomic response is immediately to breathe in deeply. Combined with the stunning, this response is entirely involuntary and will only stop when the lungs are completely refilled.

"Now, if you look carefully," he continued, pointing to his neck, "you can see the pulsations in my carotid arteries as my heart pumps blood to my brain. Synchronised with the pulse in the target's carotid artery, the second punch is delivered to the front of the target's neck, just below the Adam's apple, which is less pronounced in females. This will thrust the soft palate and false vocal cords abruptly backwards, temporarily blocking the windpipe, preventing the lungs from emptying. The target's heart is now tightly constrained between the fully inflated lungs. With the next arterial pulse, the third and final punch is delivered upwards into the diaphragm. Timed correctly, it will coincide with the maximum intensity of the harmonic wave generated by the first punch. This will ensure the maximum compressive force is directed into the target's heart. The shock will stop their heart beating, possibly rupturing it, and the target will have been killed. The timing and strength of these punches is critical. All should be delivered in less than two seconds. The first blow alone will stun and injure, but not kill…"

Matsumoto pulled the cover off the rack to reveal a model of the human torso. It seemed to be made of a translucent silicon material. But Tessa could see an egg had been placed where the heart should be.

"This dummy will respond in a sufficiently life-like manner for you to accurately judge the force and timing of your punches. If the blows are applied correctly, the egg will break shortly after the third punch has been delivered. You will have mastered the technique when the egg has broken correctly twenty times consecutively. Watch."

Matsumoto stepped up to the dummy and punched it hard below where the egg was positioned, but the egg didn't break. Tessa could see the chest cavity flexing and a pulse seemed to appear momentarily in the dummy's neck. Then Matsumoto punched the dummy a second time, and then a third. Shortly afterwards the egg broke.

Tessa was shocked and astonished. The procedure was so brutal she wanted to refuse; defeating an opponent who was attacking with a sword seemed almost justifiable by comparison. But she knew she'd just relinquished any right to object. She took a deep breath and glanced at the ominously large basket of eggs nearby. Then she approached the dummy and punched it. The egg broke immediately and the dummy fell over…

She continued practising throughout the night, frequently amending her technique in response to Matsumoto's patient coaching. Judging the strength and timing of the blows was proving incredibly difficult. Being able to deliver the punches without thinking made it all the more difficult. But Matsumoto was adamant; for the technique to work under stress, it had to be automatic. Soon her right hand was bruised and throbbing painfully, but she refused to give up.

Just after dawn, she started to achieve the consistency required and, much to her surprise, the egg was breaking shortly after she delivered the final punch. Gradually her successes became more frequent.

With the sun high in the sky, she managed a run of seventeen successful attacks. Despite being exhausted, with a raw and bleeding hand, she did it again, and again. One more time and she would have her run of twenty. Matsumoto gave her a wry smile and nodded.

She bowed, turned and without thinking, hit the dummy perfectly. Shortly afterwards, the egg burst.

Matsumoto stood up.

"Very good. Now do it another five times while I prepare some food."

Ten minutes later she joined him in the Audience Hall. Waiting for her was a plate of the trance-inducing fish. She ate it quickly and sat back, ready for the flash of light and thunder crack in her head which she knew would herald her return to oblivion…

It was early-evening when Tessa woke in the government hideaway, feeling surprisingly refreshed. The sword-cleaning equipment was delivered so she spent the next hour and a half carefully cleaning and oiling her weapons. While doing this she was amazed to find both her blades now rang when drawn. Although her Kimi sword always rang when she drew it, its note had become louder and clearer. However, her Amafuji sword, which previously didn't ring at all, now had a deep throbbing note too. It seemed likely that during the past nine months Kimi Amakuni had done some work on both weapons, as blades ringing when drawn by a specific user was uniquely an Amakuni trademark.

After she'd finished, Tessa decided to have another hot bath and to dye her hair black. The colourant proved extremely effective. Then she ordered some more food and waited patiently in the lounge, sitting in the lotus position, contemplating what the evening might hold.

Eventually she went back to her room to change. She put on the dark bluish-purple leather cat-suit which Kono had made for her in London. Then she slung her double sword harness over her shoulders. Unusually, the harness held her swords across her back, one hilt protruding over each shoulder. Her mechanism securing the sheaths, enabled her to draw the swords quickly despite their length prohibiting this with a conventional harness. The highly innovative system not only gave her a speed advantage, it also surprised anyone who had not seen it in action before. She checked the contents of her waist bag in which she kept various medicinal herbs, and put it on. Then she glanced round at her belongings; neatly folded, but not put away; confirmation of her intention to collect them later. The alternative didn't bear considering.

Following a gentle knocking at the door, the panel slid aside to reveal the kimono-clad woman, kneeling by the doorway. Without reacting in the slightest to Tessa's transformation, she bowed and announced that the car had arrived.

Tessa followed her down the corridor to the latticework door. There, she slipped off her sandals and put on her boots, making sure they were tied comfortably. She nodded to the woman, and the door slid open…

CHAPTER 6

"*Konichiwa*, Hachiro-san," said Maeda, looking up from his desk, "punctual as ever."

Hachiro was in his mid-forties and a big man, especially for someone born in Japan; at just over six foot tall, he towered over his compatriots. He had a chiselled, suntanned face and his watchful brown eyes shone brightly. His head was shaven from the top of his forehead to just behind the crown. The rest of his hair had been allowed to grow long enough to be tied at the back. He was dressed in traditional-looking, but actually modern, Samurai armour and carried a similarly advanced perfumed helmet, historically indicative of his preparation for battle. He wore two fine swords, one long and one short; both slung conventionally through a wide waist belt. He looked both proud and threatening, if a little old-fashioned.

"Yes," boomed Hachiro, "even for my own funeral. So, Maeda-san, am I doing this alone? Or have you found some other foolhardy Peacekeepers to accompany me?"

Maeda took a deep breath.

"Well, as you know, there are no Japanese Peacekeepers available. However, there are other Peacekeepers courageous enough to join you in battle tonight. But I doubt they would be pleased to hear you call them foolhardy."

"Hah! Well, I'm surprised anyone is willing to accept this challenge," roared Hachiro. "How many are there? We need lots, but four should suffice!"

"Well, actually there's only the one. But that halves the odds, doesn't it? Also, on the basis of my own experience, I know you couldn't ask for better. You are lucky I found one."

"Yes, I suppose so. What nationality is this Peacekeeper?"

"British," said Maeda. "That's not a problem, is it?"

"No, I suppose not. It just makes communication more difficult. I would have preferred Asian if not Japanese; it's more ingrained in our culture in this part of the world. But you say he's good?"

"Oh yes," said Maeda, "very good indeed. But I never said the Peacekeeper was a man. In fact, she's quite definitely a woman."

Visibly shocked, Hachiro paused to digest this revelation.

"Maeda-san, a British female Peacekeeper! I can't go into battle with a woman! I need to be concentrating on slaying our enemies, not protecting a woman. I expect to rescue women, not to have them dying dramatically by my side. Please, tell me you are joking?"

"I am most certainly not," retorted Maeda. "And, as I said, she is excellent. She also comes highly recommended by her UK Guardian, whom I trust and respect. She will not let you down. Furthermore, I would suggest you don't make any stereotypical chauvinist remarks to her. You need all the help you can get."

"Oh, no," groaned Hachiro, "you mean she's a feminist too?"

"Really, Hachiro-san. Don't be ridiculous!"

Just then the lift doors to the twenty-third floor opened. Bemused, Tessa peered into the large open-plan workplace. Having taken care to avoid the gaze of the security cameras, she now had to walk the gauntlet of an office packed with extremely curious people. At her bidding the two constables led the way to Maeda's suite of rooms. The cacophony of conversation faded as everyone turned to look at her. They were expecting a female Peacekeeper, but the spectacle that met their eyes exceeded their wildest dreams. Tessa cut a formidable figure in her leather cat-suit with neat black hair and two swords slung over her shoulders.

As the office outside went quiet, Maeda looked at Hachiro.

"That's probably her now."

Hachiro nodded and moved back into a corner which could not easily be seen by someone entering the office. Maeda shook his head in exasperation.

When Tessa arrived at Maeda's office, a constable opened the door for her. She paused briefly by the entrance, smiled, and approached Maeda's desk. She addressed him in English, with a fixed gaze.

"Good evening, Chief Inspector. Is everything ready?"

"Er, yes," replied Maeda, wondering what would happen next.

"Hmm, I seem to remember you saying once that you liked Gilbert & Sullivan," she continued. "Perhaps you remember the Duke of

Plaza-Toro, from *The Gondoliers*?"

Maeda thought for a moment and then burst into laughter.

"Hachiro," said Tessa quietly, still looking at Maeda, "if you are to lead tonight, wouldn't it be better if you were standing in front now?"

Maeda grinned and Hachiro coughed and came forward.

"Indeed. Who's the Duke of… Oh, never mind. I will lead tonight, but not a fashion show!"

Tessa turned to Hachiro and looked him up and down.

"Hmm, sorry, I don't do Kabuki."

"Serves you right for trying to play tricks on her," interjected Maeda quickly as he saw Hachiro's eyes widen in anger. "Now, please, you two, stop provoking each other!"

Tessa and Hachiro sized each other up. They looked equally intimidating, albeit at absolute extremes in terms of style. Then she smiled and bowed; Hachiro returned the greeting.

"I am sorry if my participation comes as a surprise, Hachiro-san," continued Tessa, trying to sound conciliatory. "But this is not going to be easy for either of us, is it? I presume we will be outnumbered, and we have not even seen each other with swords before, never mind guarded each other's back. You don't know whether you can trust me, and I don't know whether I can trust you."

Unfortunately, her comments did not have the desired effect. Hachiro virtually exploded, addressing a torrent of not terribly polite Japanese at Maeda.

"It's no good, Maeda-san. I can't take this *woman* with me," he said. "Look at her. Was she watching Kill Bill before she came here? And now this British female, with a couple of swords across her pretty little back, has the audacity to question whether she can trust me! I was probably exterminating Japan's enemies before she was even born."

Maeda flopped back into his armchair. It seemed all his efforts to persuade them to fight as comrades had been in vain. But then Tessa addressed Hachiro in perfect Japanese.

"Hachiro-san, before I came here I was not watching films, I was preparing my swords. We don't know whether we can trust each other, that is the truth. Tonight is tonight, what we have both done before is in the past. Your comments just now were discourteous and based on traditional prejudice and ignorance; not mature, sensible or honourable. If you do not wish me to accompany you tonight, then say so. I will not be insulted, and no harm will have been done. But if you would like me to go with you, I will do everything within my power to protect your back, and I expect you to do the same for me. The choice is yours."

Hachiro's face went red. He said nothing, and seemingly for ages he and Tessa simply glared at each other. Then he broke the silence with a booming laugh.

"You are right," he said with a deep bow, "please accept my apologies. I didn't even know you spoke Japanese."

"Apology accepted," replied Tessa, bowing back. "There is much about me you do not know, and vice versa. But let us leave all that until later. Tonight I am honoured to fight under your leadership. When we return, we will both laugh about this first meeting."

Maeda sighed with relief.

There was a knock at the door and a nervous young constable entered. He hurried over to Maeda and handed him a piece of paper. He turned, looked at Hachiro and then Tessa, swallowed and quickly retreated, looking scared.

Maeda read the note.

"This will be even more difficult than we thought," he said. "There are already more than twenty waiting for Fujiwara, and it is still early. More will surely come."

"So be it," said Hachiro shrugging his shoulders, "plenty for both of us. We will wait until Fujiwara has arrived before we leave. What shall I call you?" he asked Tessa.

"Nariko."

"Well, Nariko-san, you spoke well just now, but coming back will not be as easy as going. Of that I am sure."

"It never is," she mused.

Hachiro looked at her swords and grunted in awe.

"A Kimi Amakuni sword," he whispered in a reverential tone, "and a beautiful one it is too. And you have an Amafuji sword too! This is remarkable, Maeda-san. It is seldom that one sees an Amakuni weapon, and almost as seldom one sees one from Amafuji. To see someone carrying both is quite unheard of!"

Maeda winked at her and unfurled a map.

"The meeting is taking place on an industrial estate in Kawasaki-ku. We will need about an hour to drive there. It is almost due south of where we are now, not far from the Tama estuary. Here…"

Maeda pointed to a square on the map and placed a more detailed plan over it.

"I have had the area reconnoitred," he continued. "It is essentially an enclosed courtyard between high factory walls, with no windows. One of the two vehicle accesses had already been blocked this afternoon. The other is easily closed with a pair of high metal gates. We must assume Fujiwara will lock these once he has entered. The only other way in is across a wooden footbridge and up a narrow alleyway."

Hachiro sighed.

"Challenging indeed," he acknowledged with a sardonic smile. "The alleyway it is. But with dignity. Yes?"

"Absolutely," replied Tessa, "they will be as trapped as us. I suggest we come out the same way … with dignity."

"Hah!" boomed Hachiro. "Good idea!"

Maeda's phone rang and, as he answered it, his demeanour changed palpably. Tessa turned quizzically to Hachiro; he shrugged.

"How odd," said Maeda, putting the phone down, "we have all been summoned to a meeting. Would you come with me, please?"

They followed him through a door at the back of his office into a dimly lit conference room. Two smartly dressed men sat at a large elliptical rosewood table. Hachiro looked at one of them, sucked in his breath, and bowed. The man was dressed in what Tessa felt was the archetypal civil service uniform; black pin-stripe suit, white shirt and blue-striped tie. The other man wore a dark grey suit, white shirt and a plain burgundy-coloured silk tie.

Maeda led them to the three chairs which had been positioned opposite the two men. Hachiro was on the left, nearly opposite the man in the pin-stripe suit; Maeda in the middle and Tessa on his right, almost opposite the other man. She was convinced the man on her far left was a government official, but she had no idea at all about the man opposite. He had a completely different air about him. He looked confident and extremely fit but slightly uncomfortable, as though he preferred to be in the background rather than at a meeting table.

"May we speak Japanese?" asked the man in the pin-stripe suit, looking at Tessa.

"Of course," she replied.

The man smiled and continued.

"Good evening. We apologise for interrupting your preparations. My name is Dr Miyazaki. I am responsible for Homeland Security in Japan. My colleague, General … er, has a special position of authority."

Tessa was surprised not to be introduced to the second man by name.

"On behalf of Japan, we would like to thank you both for agreeing to undertake this difficult venture. We are sorry there are so few of you, but we particularly appreciate the support of the UK in this matter..."

He looked at Tessa. She bowed in acknowledgment, but said nothing.

"During the past few hours the Fujiwara history and this affair have been discussed at the very highest of levels. It has been decided that some rather unusual measures should be adopted. Put simply, we would prefer you not to take any prisoners. Of course, we can only request this as it is you, Hachiro, who must decide how the battle is fought. But we feel it is important to send a clear message…"

Although they were primarily addressing Hachiro, Tessa considered how furious she would have been if anything like that had been said to her.

"To put it another way," continued Dr Miyazaki, "it would be *convenient* if there were no survivors. None at all."

Both men looked at Hachiro expectantly, and he shifted uneasily in his chair.

"Gentlemen," he said, gathering himself. "With respect I am sure you appreciate that this is political intervention, no matter how politely presented. As you have already intimated, it is up to the Peacekeepers involved to decide how the battle should be fought. Furthermore, it is normal practice for every effort to be made to bring the leader of any gang back to face trial. Surely that is message enough?"

"We fully understand your unease. However, our request comes from the highest levels of government, and on behalf of Imperial Japan…"

At the mention of Imperial Japan, a cold shiver ran down Tessa's back.

"Therefore this *suggestion* also applies to Hayato Fujiwara. As you know, he has been sentenced to death on several occasions. It is these legitimate judgements that are to be meted out to him tonight. But…," Dr Miyazaki took a deep breath before continuing, "…we wish the verdict of the Courts to be implemented by someone who is not Japanese."

Tessa's eyes widened and, throwing protocol to the wind, she intervened angrily.

"Maeda-san, did you know of this?"

"No," he exclaimed, defensively. "This is the first I have heard of it!"

"Dr Miyazaki," continued Tessa, "have I understood correctly? In one breath you wish to thank me for risking my life on your behalf while in the next requesting I implement the death penalty brought down on Fujiwara, in your Courts?"

"Yes, that's right. Naturally, you will need clearance from the relevant UK authorities, signed by your Guardian. Here it is," he said, sliding a piece of paper across the table.

Tessa breathed out noisily and scanned the document with considerable distaste. It seemed Sinclair had been signing a lot of letters recently. She only wished he were there!

"And here is an equivalent letter from Japan. Chief Inspector, perhaps you would complete it?" Maeda quickly read it and signed. "Also, since the sentence will be delivered at a place of … convenience … you will require authority from our Head of State, the Emperor. This is that authority, together with the words you should recite, if time permits before … well, before the conclusion."

A sheet of paper and a fine envelope were passed to Tessa. She scanned the sheet, and then broke the seal to open the hand-made envelope. Hachiro and Maeda strained to see, but she kept it to herself. The letter was of ornate hand-painted Japanese calligraphy; its beauty was mesmerising, albeit with a cold hard message. It appeared to have been sealed by the Emperor himself although she had no idea what his seal looked like.

Tessa shook her head. She hadn't been as angry since Penny was murdered. Admittedly she'd agreed to help Maeda, and support Hachiro; but taking advantage of her presence to rid Japan of a local problem seemed to her to be outrageous. However, could she really refuse a request from the Emperor of Japan? People had probably lost their heads for less.

"Why must this be done by a non-Japanese national?" she rasped. "Why can't you do your own dirty work? Especially if there are to be no witnesses."

"It is inevitable that eventually rumours of tonight's conflict will circulate," continued Dr Miyazaki smoothly. "For reasons we cannot divulge, it is important that we are able to say that no one from Japan killed Hayato Fujiwara. By the nature of your Peacekeeper status you have immunity and guaranteed anonymity, even from those around this table. Of course, we fully accept that events may not develop as we would like, but if the opportunity arises, then this is what we would like to happen."

"Oh, you mean we might ruin your plan by getting ourselves killed too soon!"

This last response of hers prompted an awkward pause.

"This is most … *unconventional*," declared Hachiro. "I feel as leader that I must speak up on behalf of Nariko. The odds of either of us coming back tonight are not high, and now, in return for her generosity in putting her life at Japan's disposal, you ask this of her? It is just not appropriate … in my humble opinion, of course."

Tessa smiled at Hachiro's somewhat uncertain attempt at a diplomatic intervention. But then a surprisingly animated discussion broke out between Maeda, Hachiro and Dr Miyazaki. Tessa glanced at the taciturn man sitting opposite her. Briefly their eyes met and a wisp of a smile crossed his face. His right hand twitched and, with remarkable speed, he produced a matt grey business card from inside his sleeve. It matched the colour of his suit perfectly and would have been difficult for the others to see. He quickly flipped it over, before pushing it back up his sleeve. The other side of the card was burgundy-coloured with a gold chrysanthemum logo; exactly the same as the one tattooed on her wrist. She pursed her lips, sat back in her chair and sighed.

Now I'm really screwed, thought Tessa as she marvelled at the man's manual dexterity. Matsumoto-san, what have you done to me!

"…You are right," continued Dr Miyazaki, unaware of his

companion's actions, "and we regret the circumstances. However, this is how it is Hachiro. So, Nariko, are you willing to do this for us, er, please?"

Suddenly all eyes were on her. Still considering her wretched situation, she said nothing.

"No, she isn't," interjected Hachiro. "Maeda-san, I will not tolerate this level of political interference. It is not fair on either of us, and especially Nariko. It is out of the question."

Dr Miyazaki smiled at Hachiro, and looked back at Tessa.

"Nariko, do you understand what we are asking?"

"Yes, of course," she replied sharply. "I'm just a little surprised that this madness has been sprung on us now, and that my Guardian here has not objected."

Maeda coughed uncomfortably.

"We understand your disquiet," continued Miyazaki, "but let me assure you, it is far from madness. This has been considered very carefully, and our conclusion was unanimous. So, will you do it?"

She bowed her head, partly in disbelief and partly out of frustration.

"No, she won't," repeated Hachiro, this time clenching both his fists on the table.

"Yes, she will," mumbled Tessa, "sort of."

Hachiro and Maeda looked at her in amazement. Dr Miyazaki smiled.

"Sort of?" he queried.

"Yes. If Hayato Fujiwara can be persuaded to tell all he knows to the authorities, including everything about the Calver Cats, then I would like to have the option of bringing him in alive."

For a moment Dr Miyazaki seemed unsure what to do. But the man opposite Tessa smiled, turned and leant towards him. He whispered something and then looked back at Tessa. Dr Miyazaki chuckled.

"We agree … sort of," he said, bringing a smile to Tessa's face. "It is agreed that you may bring Fujiwara in alive if he is willing to talk. However, you must secure his full co-operation before he knows you are empowered to implement his execution order."

Tessa considered this for a moment. Unfortunately, their suggestion was logical, and probably as good as she was likely to get. If Fujiwara agreed to talk only to save his life, then once he had been detained and she had left, he could change his mind. But presumably they thought it unlikely that he would agree to co-operate anyway.

"Distasteful though it remains to me, I accept. However, I would like your assurance that copies of all these documents will be sent to the UK for inclusion within my Peacekeeper file." Dr Miyazaki nodded. "I will keep these originals. So, is there anything else?"

"No, that is all," replied Dr Miyazaki with a surprisingly sympathetic smile. "Thank you for agreeing to do this. Japan will be in your debt. We wish you good fortune in your endeavours."

Tessa scooped up the papers and put them in her waist bag. Then she looked at Hachiro, effectively signalling her desire to leave. He stood up, prompting everyone to follow suit. They all bowed to each other across the table and the Peacekeepers and Maeda went back to the inspector's office.

"Well, excuse my Japanese," said Tessa angrily, "but this is pretty shitty. While we'll be hard pressed to survive, your *friends* have the gall to ask me to do things Japan doesn't want to do itself."

"She's right," agreed Hachiro. " Maeda-san, this stinks! If anyone is to do this, it should be me!"

"I am sorry," Maeda spluttered, visibly taken aback. "I really don't know what to say … I had no idea."

"Hmm. Come on, Hachiro-san," said Tessa. "Let's just get on with it."

An uneasy silence followed as Tessa and he studied the maps. Their deliberations were interrupted by an uncertain knock at the door. A nervous young female constable entered and handed another piece of paper to Maeda.

"Hayato Fujiwara will be there shortly. His son Ryota is with him."

Hachiro looked at Tessa.

"Are you sure you want to go through with this?"

"Put it this way," she replied resignedly, "let's go before I change my mind."

They checked their swords and Maeda picked up his phone.

"Your transport is ready," he said. "I will come with you."

As they left the office, Maeda led the small convoy. Hachiro followed and Tessa brought up the rear. The open-plan office seemed even fuller than before, but was completely quiet. In the basement, a blue-grey armoured van was waiting for them. The seats were all individual with space around them to accommodate swords. Tessa sat opposite Hachiro. As the van moved off, they both started flexing their muscles to warm them.

CHAPTER 7

Hayato Fujiwara was a portly man. Once slim and fit, he had spent the last 10 years concentrating on strategy and enjoying the fruits of his successful career in crime as his two sons assumed responsibility for the day-to-day running of the family business. Tonight, he was wearing an elaborately patterned dark grey *dôbuku sugata* with a vermilion neck scarf. He had left Yokohama earlier that evening in an armoured limousine with Ryota, the younger of his sons.

"We have secured the area," reported Ryota confidently. "No one will disturb us. As you suggested, we will leave the limo outside and walk in through the main gates. It's not far and I will lock the gates behind us." He motioned towards a large key dangling from his belt. "Hachiro will be forced to use the only other way in. It's a tiny footbridge with a narrow alleyway leading into the courtyard. Our people will block it after he has passed. We checked again; Hachiro is the only Peacekeeper in Japan capable of responding tonight. He is too proud to ignore this invitation, so, as you planned, he will have to come alone."

Fujiwara looked at him and smiled.

"Good, my son, you have done well. I am sure we will all have an interesting meeting. Even you may be surprised! With our actions tonight, I believe we will set Peacekeepers back many years. Beauchamp will be pleased, and I am rather looking forward to meeting Hachiro again. We are about to send a powerful and unexpected message to Chief Inspector Maeda!"

Their limousine drove into the industrial estate and stopped. As soon as Fujiwara and Ryota entered the courtyard, they were greeted by a tumultuous uproar from the gathered throng. Fujiwara smiled and, with almost presidential pomp, walked over to a shallow podium. In the middle stood a luxurious rococo armchair, beautifully upholstered in thick vermilion-coloured velvet, the Fujiwara family colour. He sat down and raised his hand to quell the noise. The ensuing silence was broken only by the sound of the gates clanging shut. Once they were locked, Ryota returned the key to the chain dangling from his belt, and took up position by his father's side.

Fujiwara started a long diatribe addressing his people in a loud, defiant voice.

Finally, the Special Forces van reached the industrial estate. It reversed a short distance and the rhythmic vibrations from the engine ceased. The cabin's fluorescent lighting dulled to a doleful red glow.

"Hmm," observed Tessa, "I suppose that means the boring part is over?"

Hachiro nodded and started to stand up.

"I will check it is safe."

"Hachiro-san," interjected Tessa, "that is my job. You are the leader of our small but select army. But I don't need to look to tell you it won't be safe."

She stood up and took a deep breath.

"If I knock twice, come out. Anything different and I'm afraid you might be on your own after all."

Maeda switched off the light to ensure she wouldn't be silhouetted in the open doorway. Tessa paused for her eyes to adjust, then eased the door open and stepped out...

Lovely! she thought, looking round. And to think I could have been relaxing in a First Class seat en-route to London.

A single street lamp cast a dim apologetic light over the area. The van had stopped just short of the footbridge. It comprised three planks side by side; on the left was a thin rusty handrail, with a wire slung loosely beneath to form a rudimentary balustrade. The stream was about ten feet wide and eighteen inches deep, with water flowing quickly over a bed of large smooth stones. The banks were made from irregularly hewn stone blocks which sloped down steeply.

On the opposite bank, either side of the footbridge, were groups of thugs, most armed with swords. They were clearly surprised to see Tessa. She scanned the buildings and stood in silence for a moment. Then she knocked twice on the van door. Hachiro appeared and looked at the bridge.

"Care for a dance," he murmured.

"Love to," she replied, "lead on."

Hachiro set off at a slow but deliberate pace; she followed a short distance behind. Everyone heard the eerie clunk of the van door closing, after which only the sound of water bubbling over the rocks disturbed the silence. They were on their own now; the way it was meant to be these days.

Hachiro crossed the footbridge purposely loudly to emphasise his arrival. She walked silently with her eyes scanning the buildings and the two groups of thugs. Whispering, she and Hachiro exchanged observations about the disposition of the people. As they approached the alleyway, the two groups backed away. Hachiro could see the light from the courtyard, but Tessa wasn't looking. She was watching what was happening behind them, and started walking with her back to Hachiro.

The alleyway comprised worn flagstones, bordered by two rows of cobbles. The flagstones sloped into the centre slightly, forming a shallow gutter.

"Exit blocked," she whispered.

Hachiro grunted, and entered the courtyard. She followed, still facing backwards. Curious, she quickly glanced round; they were completely surrounded. Not far away, on a makeshift podium, Fujiwara Senior was sitting in a gaudy rococo armchair. Silence fell across the courtyard.

"*Konichiwa*, Hachiro-san," greeted Fujiwara, "you're late. I was beginning to wonder if... But, what's this? I see you've found someone to hold your hand? How thoughtful to bring us a present. She's prettier than the last one we came across. I do hope she lasts a little longer."

"Fujiwara-san, you do me a great injustice before all these people. You knew I would come. As for my colleague ... well, you should know by now never to underestimate something you do not understand. Suffice to say, my purpose here is unaltered, and we both know what that is, don't we?"

Hachiro paused for a moment to look round, Tessa knew he was counting.

"Thirty-five," he whispered to her.

"Thirty-six," she whispered back.

"So, Fujiwara-san," continued Hachiro, "is it really necessary for so many to die tonight? Why don't you and I just settle this on our own? Or are you scared?"

Tessa gently reversed into Hachiro. He knew what she meant; this tactic had not been discussed.

"What do you expect," he whispered, "we have to respond to the situation as it develops."

"We should be so lucky," she muttered.

Fujiwara thought about Hachiro's challenge, and then laughed.

"Clever! I suppose you and I could fight … but as you know, it is Ryuu who carries the family sword now. I stopped duelling many years ago so it would hardly be a fair contest. However, I will nominate a champion, my son Ryota, to fight your champion."

Fujiwara looked at Ryota who bowed and stepped forward.

"I, Ryota, son of Fujiwara, am honoured to be my father's champion. I challenge yours, Hachiro… But since you are only two, I presume your champion is the Caucasian in the catchy leather number. Not that she'll be so pretty after I've finished with her."

He laughed, as did many others. Only Hachiro looked serious.

"Oops," he whispered to Tessa. She smiled.

"So, are you also scared to fight me?" continued Hachiro.

"Oh, no," replied Ryota, "I want you to see this presumptuous whore die first, then I will kill you."

At this point Tessa, whispered to Hachiro. "It's OK, I don't mind fighting him."

"He's quite … substantial. I understand he's handy with a blade, too."

"The bigger they are, the harder they fall."

Hachiro smiled.

"My champion accepts."

Tessa turned round and studied her opponent. He was very well built, over six foot tall and thick-set; nearly as big as Hachiro. He looked to be extremely fit. He leered at Tessa, who smiled back as sweetly as she could.

"He is a big boy, isn't he?" she whispered to Hachiro.

As Tessa moved left a space cleared in front of her. Ryota moved forwards. They stopped a few feet apart in the centre of a circular area. Thugs surrounded them completely, except for gaps through which Hachiro and Fujiwara could watch.

"You really are quite pretty for a Caucasian slut," said Ryota adjusting his vermilion neck scarf. "Leather suits you. I shall enjoy fucking you before you die. Maybe that will be the last thing you'll ever feel. Aren't you the lucky one?"

Tessa laughed.

"Well, I doubt you're man enough for the job. But we'll soon see what you're really packing."

"Brave words, bitch. So, how long have you been playing with swords?"

"I don't have time to play with them," Tessa replied with a bored lilt to her voice, "I'm too busy ridding the world of scum like you."

He laughed.

"Well, your swords look good, if stupid, hung over your shoulders like that. They'll make fine trophies."

"My swords will never be owned by such a one as you. So, stop babbling like a child and try to take them!"

"Like candy from a baby."

He roared and went for his sword.

He was remarkably fast and had soon drawn his sword several inches. But compared to Tessa it was all happening in slow motion. As her right hand moved upwards, she rolled her shoulder. The sword sheath shot down and the hilt catapulted up into her waiting hand. The confident ringing of her Kimi sword speeding through the air momentarily interrupted the silence before it struck Ryota's neck. She had aimed with consummate precision and sensed from the vibrations of the sword how deeply and through what she was cutting. Ryota died almost instantaneously, but she'd wanted to make sure that most of his nervous system continued to work, at least for a short while. It was an extraordinarily difficult manoeuvre and a feat of sheer artistry if performed correctly. If successful, his muscles would stay tensed, and he would remain standing. Finally, she felt she had done enough and carefully withdrew her blade. Ryota's nerveless fingers released their grip on his sword, but he continued to stand bolt upright.

Tessa flicked his blood off her sword, turned it over, and with the back of the blade pulled Ryota's sword out of its sheath and flicked it into the air. As it came down, she caught the hilt neatly in her left hand. Then she noticed a large key fastened to his belt, and smiled.

The stunned silence was broken by Hachiro, slapping his knee and bellowing with laughter.

"Bravo!" he yelled. "Text book accuracy for a near-impossible stroke … and done with lightning speed! Very impressive."

Tessa turned her head towards him, winked and mouthed, "Thirty-five".

Hachiro bowed to her.

They both knew it would not be long before Ryota collapsed. Hachiro turned back to Fujiwara. He had to think quickly.

"Fujiwara-san, it seems my champion has won … even the best-laid plans must be changed sometimes. Perhaps you'd better come with me after all. Or…?"

Hachiro nodded to Tessa. She stepped forward and gently pushed Ryota over. The dull thump of his body hitting the ground echoed round the courtyard and his head lolled at an unnatural angle to his torso.

"My son is dead! You bastard!" yelled Fujiwara, trembling with rage. He glared at his people. "Kill Hachiro! Then kill her."

Shrieking, the gang drew their swords and descended on Hachiro and Tessa. They were both swamped in a seething mêlée of attacking ruffians. The fast and ferocious battle for survival had begun.

For a while, Tessa lost sight of Hachiro. This concerned her since she still felt obligated to watch his back. So she used her Kimi sword in her right hand and the rather heavier sword she had taken from Ryota in her left to slowly force her way towards him. It seemed Fujiwara's people were indeed concentrating their efforts on him. Hachiro was completely surrounded and there was a concerted effort to keep him so occupied in front that he could be approached from behind. If Hachiro sensed the danger, he was powerless to do anything about it.

Tessa increased the reach of her sword swings to clear a space and buy her some time. Then she spun round quickly to her left, squatting down to avoid the blades above. As she turned, she took careful aim and let go of Ryota's sword. Like a javelin it flew towards the two men who were creeping up on Hachiro. The blade passed straight through the neck of the first and the point buried itself in the temple of the second, instantly killing both. For a moment Hachiro's eyes met hers, but then they were fighting again.

Tessa drew Bryani's sword, immediately revelling in its superior quality. The fight continued for nearly twenty minutes as the two circles of conflict slowly edged their way towards the podium. Eventually the odds changed in favour of Tessa and Hachiro. Fujiwara's confident smirk evaporated. The battle had nearly been lost and the only key to the gates remained chained to Ryota.

The conflict continued unabated with Tessa and Hachiro fighting feverishly. The vehemence and finality of the struggle was clear. Their sword strokes were not intended to immobilise, they silenced permanently. It soon became a desperate fight to the death…

Then, suddenly, with two final cries, the conflict was over. The sounds of clashing swords and groans of anguish were replaced by a tomblike stillness.

"Phew," exclaimed Tessa looking round. "So many dead," she added sadly.

"Indeed," replied Hachiro, nodding.

Still seated on the podium, Fujiwara started a slow hand-clap.

"You should have surrendered, Fujiwara-san," declared Hachiro. "All of this could have been avoided."

"Postponed perhaps," mused Fujiwara, "but, I suspect, not avoided. Events would have followed a very different course if this woman had not been here. How did you persuade her to join you?"

"I make my own decisions," interjected Tessa. "People like you must be stopped."

She flicked the blood off her swords and nonchalantly returned them to their sheaths. She walked forward and stepped on to the podium, stopping a few feet in front of Fujiwara, slightly to his right. Hachiro also moved forward but stayed well back from the podium.

Fujiwara was both amused and slightly intimidated by Tessa's proximity and aggressive stance. He was also puzzled by Hachiro's distancing himself.

"You don't really think you can stop me, do you?" he sneered, eyeing Tessa with disdain. "I have always got away before, and I will do this time too. I probably won't even spend twenty-four hours in jail before my lawyers get me out. I'm too influential."

"That's not the impression I get," retorted Tessa. "You've spent too much time with the Calver Cats. You're as arrogant as Beauchamp... How is he these days, by the way? Missing England, his wife, the family?"

"Ah! So, you want to know about Beauchamp, do you? I met him recently. He's fine and good fun to be with. He has the *gift of the gab*, as you English would say. I doubt he's missing much from his past. He's found himself a Japanese girl-friend who tends to his every need."

"Really? She must be a truly remarkable woman."

"Oh, she is. She likes swords too. So, how do you know Beauchamp?"

"Our paths have crossed," she replied evasively.

"Well, you clearly haven't stopped him, have you?"

"It's not going so badly," chimed Tessa, glancing at the bodies strewn throughout the courtyard. "So, where is he? I'd like to renew our acquaintanceship."

"Would you now ... and why should I tell you?"

"Well, one very good reason comes to mind. I might spare your life."

Out of the corner of her eye, she saw Hachiro stiffen in surprise.

"My life is not yours to take. And I do not bargain with women; especially foul-smelling foreigners. You are nothing. But it is with *my* assistance, the Calver Cats have become the most successful criminal gang of all time."

"The Calver Cats gang is nothing more than a pitiful house of cards. It will soon come tumbling down. Tell me where Beauchamp is and I can help you."

Fujiwara laughed.

"Hachiro-san, she speaks confidently but I'm bored with her drivel. It's time for a chat with Maeda."

Hachiro said nothing, and Tessa's eyes encouraged Fujiwara to continue.

"Hmm. OK, I'll throw you a crumb. Beauchamp is in Southeast Asia. Europe has become a little too hot for him, and he doesn't like America. But I'm not saying anything more. Hachiro-san, let's go. I need to phone my lawyer."

He made as though to stand, but Tessa gestured him to stay seated. Fujiwara stopped smiling.

"Tell me precisely where I can find him," she pressed. "We don't have much time."

"Tell me your name first?"

Tessa smiled.

"Nariko."

"Really!" exclaimed Fujiwara, laughing. "Beauchamp is looking for you too."

"In which case, he'll be pleased if you facilitate a meeting."

"Sorry to disappoint, but I just don't need to," replied Fujiwara chuckling. "You see, I always get away."

"Not this time," she replied quietly.

"Yes, every time! You presumptuous harlot," he snarled. "You don't understand how things work here. I have had enough, I wish to leave."

Tessa moved closer and whispered to him so that Hachiro couldn't hear.

"Surely Beauchamp would want his sister to know where he is?"

Fujiwara exploded into laughter. He laughed so much, his eyes started watering. When he eventually stopped he replied equally quietly, in order that only Tessa would hear.

"So, Nariko, you are his sibling freak. That really is the best joke I've heard in a long time! If Beauchamp knew, he would be even more angry, if that's possible. Now, my innocent one, you listen to me. I have seen many things in my life, but nothing so convoluted as the plot which entwines us all. You are just a pawn and clearly do not see the whole game! However, some of us intend to preserve our honour, even when the odds are stacked against us in these deceitful times."

Tessa was curious. The look in Fujiwara's eyes convinced her he knew something important.

"Carry on."

He looked up at her, but said nothing. She sighed.

"Please, we're running out of time. Just tell me where I can find Beauchamp?"

"Find him yourself, bitch. Shame on you, Hachiro-san! I'm not surprised you don't dare speak."

"Is that your final word?" pleaded Tessa.

Fujiwara nodded.

She glanced at Hachiro. But he turned away, annoyed not to have heard all the conversation.

"Hayato Fujiwara," said Tessa firmly, "you were born on the

thirteenth of April 1959 in Karatsu, Saga Prefecture, Kyūshū. On three occasions in Japan you have been tried in absentia by a Court of Law, and found guilty of crimes for which you were sentenced to death. Are you aware of this?"

"Of course. I thought it was four actually, but I daresay you are right. Do I really have to listen to a history lesson, now?"

"I am in possession of a decree signed today by the Emperor of Japan, instructing me to implement the death sentence as passed by the Courts of Law in Japan."

"What! That's an Imperial execution order!" exclaimed Fujiwara, wide-eyed. "I don't believe it. One of those hasn't been issued for over a century. Hachiro-san, what is this nonsense?"

"It is out of my hands," he replied quietly. "You have had many chances to save yourself, and turned them all down."

Fujiwara looked in terror at Tessa standing impassively in front of him.

"You have destroyed many people's lives," she continued. "Now you must pay the penalty."

He responded by plunging his hand into his dôbuku sugata. Totally relaxed, Tessa watched as he pulled out a knife. For a moment she thought he wanted to commit *seppuku*, which she would have allowed, but then it became clear he wanted to kill Hachiro and she could delay no longer. She drew her Kimi sword and swung it hard and fast from right to left. The ringing of the blade was interrupted with a brief ping as it passed through his neck. Such was the force of the blow that his head shot into the air, eventually falling a few feet away with a loud thump. Lifeless, his twitching body keeled over in the chair.

Tessa cleaned her sword and returned it to its sheath.

"Come, Nariko-san," said Hachiro, "this place reeks of death. It is time to go home."

He turned and started walking. In silence, she followed and they picked their way through the bodies across the courtyard. As they entered the narrow alleyway, Hachiro stopped and turned to Tessa.

"You saved my life. Thank you. I am honour bound to return the favour."

Tessa smiled.

"You're welcome. It was my duty. Besides, I wasn't sure I could handle them all on my own."

"Who knows? One does what one has to do," replied Hachiro. "But to think even in that last moment he wanted to kill you... Anyway, what was it he said to you?"

"Oh, nothing of consequence."

In fact, what Fujiwara had said worried Tessa greatly, but she wanted to keep it to herself. The two of them walked to the end of the alleyway. The shallow gutter in the flagstones now ran red with warm blood; steaming and filling the air with a sickly-sweet metallic smell. As Hachiro approached the back of the van, the doors swung open. Looking very relieved, Maeda stood silhouetted against the red light.

"It is done," said Hachiro, climbing into the van.

Tessa turned back to the bridge to check that all remained quiet. As she scanned the opposite bank she heard Maeda issuing orders. She took a deep breath of fresh air and climbed into the van. She and Hachiro sat down and Maeda closed the door. He picked up a flask and in silence poured them both some green tea. A few minutes later the van moved off. Eventually, Maeda could contain himself no longer.

"So, what happened?"

"Well," said Hachiro looking at Tessa, "we won, and they lost. We had to kill many people tonight, Maeda-san. Hayato Fujiwara and his son Ryota are both dead at Nariko's hand."

"I see," said Maeda glancing uncomfortably at her. "Well, thank you, both. Of course you will need to prepare reports, and I am sure there will be a number of officials who will wish to express Japan's gratitude for what you have done…"

"Maeda-san," interrupted Tessa, "I'll prepare my report, but then, if you don't mind, I would prefer just to slip away quietly and go home. Please could you book me on the first flight to London? I don't wish to offend, but I have already been away too long."

"Er, if you insist," he replied. "I will explain the situation to those concerned. Maybe next time."

"Indeed," said Tessa gratefully. "Besides, Hachiro led."

When they arrived back at the Special Forces Headquarters building, Hachiro and Tessa showered and their clothes were taken away to be cleaned. Then, dressed in tracksuits they were led to separate rooms to dictate their reports of the night's proceedings. They next all met at

3 a.m. in Maeda's office. He looked at them and smiled.

"I have just received the preliminary report from Kawasaki-ku," he announced in awe. "There were indeed a very large number of them. I don't know what to say. You achieved a phenomenal feat."

"We fought like a team which had been together for years," replied Hachiro proudly.

Maeda smiled and turned to Tessa.

"A reservation in First Class has been made on tomorrow's JAL flight to London. I will send a car to collect you at nine a.m., if that would be convenient?"

"Perfect. Thank you, Maeda-san."

Finally alone in her room in Asakusa, Tessa didn't feel like sleeping. She cleaned her swords, returned her hair to its natural blonde colour and dozed for an hour before going for a run, much to the disapproval of the house guardians. After she had bathed again, she packed; deciding to wear her more discreet executive suit for the journey home. In the lounge, she quickly ate some fruit and drank green tea. Then the kimono-clad woman knocked and announced that the car had come.

Ninety minutes later, Tessa arrived at Narita to find both Maeda and Hachiro waiting for her. Dressed casually in black denim, Hachiro looked very different today, and quite handsome; but slung from a black belt were both his swords.

Maeda bowed deeply to her.

"Nariko-san, I have been asked formally to express Japan's gratitude to you. The many officials concerned fully understand your desire to go home, and wish you well in the future, as indeed do I. You will always be welcome in Japan, and if we can be of assistance, you need only ask."

He took a respectful step back and bowed again.

"Maeda-san, I am honoured to have been of service, and grateful for your colleagues' generous understanding. Until next time."

"Hah!" boomed Hachiro. "No such lofty words from me, I'm afraid. I only came to make sure you really go. It's too exciting for me when you're here, even your hair keeps changing colour! Besides, I thought you might need a personal guard."

Tessa laughed and bowed. Eventually Maeda bade his farewells, apologising that he had to get back to his office while two nervous constables rushed off to complete the booking formalities. Tessa and Hachiro walked slowly towards the security gates.

"Are you hungry?" asked Tessa.

"Yes, I am actually," replied Hachiro. "I had a busy night and didn't have time for breakfast."

"Me too, let's have lunch. I know an excellent restaurant here."

Tessa led the way through the Duty Free shopping area to a small restaurant hidden behind the escalator leading up to the observation deck. When she entered, the owner-chef greeted her warmly as a returning customer, a process which increased in fervour when Hachiro appeared wearing his swords. They sat at a corner table next to an ornamental pool in which some koi were gliding. Tessa and Hachiro were soon enjoying an extensive meal, consuming a vast amount of sushi, sashimi and hot sake.

They had been eating and drinking for nearly two hours when one of the constables came over to Tessa. He bowed deeply and addressed her obsequiously.

"I apologise most sincerely for this interruption, but your flight has nearly finished boarding. It would be most convenient for the airline schedule if you could join the other passengers soon."

Tessa looked at her watch, and surveyed the wreckage on the table.

"Hachiro-san, he's right, we've been here ages!"

Tessa quickly pulled out some cash to settle the bill. Initially, the owner declined payment, saying it had been an honour to serve them. But she insisted, assuring him they had enjoyed themselves so much, neither of them wanted to feel they had not paid for their meal. Tessa and Hachiro walked out of the restaurant to find an airport buggy waiting for them.

"Oh, now that's a good idea," said Tessa in a slightly slurred voice. "I wasn't looking forward to trying to walk in a straight line all the way to the plane."

"Yes indeed," replied Hachiro, clearly having to concentrate on what he was saying. Then he belched loudly. "Oh, sorry, that just slipped out."

The buggy set off with them on it, both laughing uproariously.

Eventually, it stopped at the end of the jet-way leading to the First Class section of her flight to London. Tessa lightly swung her sword case on to her shoulder as one of the constables handed her carry-on bag to a flight attendant.

"*Sayonara*, Hachiro-san."

"*Sayonara*, Nariko-san. I am sure we will meet again."

"I shall look forward to that possibility with pleasure and anticipation."

"Likewise," replied Hachiro, "and thank you for lunch, it was excellent."

"You're welcome. But just for the record, Hachiro-san, you can drink an awful lot of sake."

He laughed.

"Trust me, Nariko-san, so can you!"

Smiling, they both bowed deeply to each other. Then she walked up the gangway to the plane, while he returned to the buggy. Neither of them looked back. That was not the done thing.

CHAPTER 8

Tessa's flight to London proved blissfully peaceful. The front section of the First Class area had been cordoned off for her and, although embarrassed that this marked her out as someone special, she appreciated the privacy.

After drinking a vast amount of water she dozed off, but didn't sleep well. She was haunted by gruesome images of the Kawasaki-ku conflict and also what Fujiwara had said. Why had he wanted to kill Hachiro rather than her? After all, she had killed his son and was about to kill him? What did he mean by saying she was simply a pawn in a convoluted game which she didn't understand? Even the way he'd spoken unsettled her. She believed he'd been telling the truth.

Two hours from London, she got up, washed and enjoyed an excellent Japanese breakfast. To her surprise, she felt refreshed if still very angry about how her involvement at Kawasaki-ku had come about. The plane landed and all the other passengers were held back while she got off. When she reached the top of the jet-way, she found two men waiting for her.

"Good morning," greeted Sinclair, "pleasant flight?"

"Yes, thank you," replied Tessa tersely, continuing past them.

Jones raised his eyebrows as he and his boss turned to follow her.

Sinclair, Head of UK Special Forces, was a complex man; cultured, taciturn and with a sharp intellect. Just turned sixty, his complexion was tanned and weather beaten. As usual, he was wearing a dark collarless suit with his white hair gathered into a tight ponytail at the back. He also sported a small neatly trimmed beard. Tessa had never been a fan of men with ponytails, but his definitely suited him. He had a distinguished, confident look about him, almost oriental. She had always liked his caring eyes, and his Scottish accent added to his attraction. Normally.

Jones, his right hand-man, was in his late-forties. He had an open and pleasant face, not suntanned but still healthy-looking. He was fit

69

and strong with short black hair. He had bright eyes which darted continuously, watching everyone. Very different from Sinclair, he was nevertheless a likeable man, with his Welsh accent and enormous hands which added to his well-earned reputation for being somewhat clumsy.

"Er ... Nariko," said Sinclair, pointedly using her Peacekeeper name to which, since he was one of her Guardians, she had no choice but to respond.

Tessa pursed her lips and stopped, but didn't turn round. She simply waited for them to catch her up.

"Whether you like it or not," he continued, "you're famous in high circles now. There was considerable excitement when Japan requested your services. It raised your profile somewhat. There are some high ranking politicians who'd like to meet you, and express their appreciation."

"Sinclair, as far as I'm concerned, you can tell them to..." she replied with such vehemence that people looked round, noticing this, she continued more quietly. "...get lost. Next time your politician friends can risk their own lives ridding the world of its scum. Have you any idea what it's like to fight so many for so long, with orders not to take prisoners? Have you any idea what it's like to be asked by a foreign government to implement an execution order? Now, if you don't mind, I intend to go home and get on with my real life. Have a nice day!"

"Um ... we have a car," interjected Jones hesitantly.

"Well, congratulations!" she retorted sarcastically, walking away.

Sinclair smiled at his second-in-command.

"She's good, isn't she? I'd better help her vent some more steam. I somehow doubt I'll be long."

"OK. Shall I get the discreet protective cordon re-established round her place?"

"Not just yet. She'll be safe for a while."

"Really?" replied Jones incredulously.

Sinclair winked, and hurried after Tessa. He caught up with her in the queue for Passport Control. Everyone was nervously eyeing her and her sword case.

"You don't need to wait here," he said. "You'll only attract attention.

Come with me."

She breathed out noisily. But he flashed his pass and they were immediately waved through. However, as they were leaving Passport Control, Sinclair went to a door marked "Staff only". He punched a code on the keypad and beckoned her to go inside. They entered a sparsely furnished, brightly lit office. He closed the door and they stood facing each other.

"I'm sorry. You have every right to be angry," he said contritely. "I can guess only too well what it was like at Kawasaki-ku. I do know how such events simultaneously assail one's senses: sight, sound and smell. I understand how one's conscience feels afterwards too even if you know what you did was right. It is unfortunate that you found yourself in such a situation so quickly."

Tessa looked at him in silence for a moment.

"Well, sorry is just not good enough! I trusted you, and look what happened."

"Now steady on," objected Sinclair, "I haven't betrayed your trust. I specifically left you a way out, but you decided to accept. And I can't believe you did so for my benefit. The Execution Order surprised us all. I couldn't do much about that."

"Really? Let's start from the beginning and put this all in perspective. I allowed you to persuade me to put my life on hold and go to Japan because you, Lee and Matsumoto wanted me to. I left David because you said it would be safer for him. You assured me that while I was away, you would stop the Calver Cats and get Beauchamp back behind bars. Yes?"

Sinclair nodded.

"OK, let's review progress, shall we? Am I any happier about losing what has turned out to be, nine months of my life? *No!* Am I happier about having learnt to hurt people more effectively? *No!* Is my relationship with David likely to be stronger as a result of this? *No!* Have you stopped the Calver Cats? *No!* Have you got Beauchamp back behind bars? *No!* Not going too well, is it? Then, when I do finally surface and try to make my way quietly back to London, what happens? I fortuitously bump into Maeda at the airport and get whisked off to a safe house. There, he asks me to help save the only active Peacekeeper in Japan from almost certain death.

"I was tired, Sinclair. I only wanted to go home. But while I was considering the options in as balanced a way as I could, letters of authority were slid across the table which you and Maeda had already signed. And if that weren't bad enough, the same thing happens while I'm being asked by a career diplomat, and some other mysterious-looking guy, to chop Fujiwara's head off because they've failed to do it themselves! Sinclair, we had difficulty walking out of the courtyard because there were so many bodies and … and, daft as it may sound, I still detest violence, and violent people!"

Tessa's eyes flashed with fury.

Sinclair sighed and dropped his shoulders. He pulled up a chair by the small table and gestured Tessa to sit down opposite him, which, reluctantly, she did.

"Daft as it may sound, so do I. But we are the few tasked with stopping the violent ones. What you said is all true. But what can I say apart from *sorry?* I really am. I have failed to deliver what we all hoped, and expected, would be possible. But don't think it was for want of trying. Let me tell you what has been happening in your absence. Would you like some tea or something?"

"No! I'd like to go home. In fact, in five minutes, I definitely will."

"Fair enough. After you left I started working in three directions. First, I canvassed international support to apprehend Beauchamp and his sidekick, Bill Chalmers. Secondly, I used these discussions as an opportunity to form an international alliance to combat organised crime, and in particular the Calver Cats. Thirdly, I secured backing for a targeted campaign to detain or eliminate senior Calver Cats people."

"Decapitation," interjected Tessa pointedly.

"Indeed, occasionally an unpleasantly accurate term. Anyway, eventually, I received support for the lot, which was good. However, even our collective efforts to apprehend Beauchamp and Chalmers proved unsuccessful. Not that they disappeared underground, they just moved around so fast we could never get to them in time. They went everywhere: South America, Afghanistan, *Irabya* in the Middle East and, of course, Japan. Anyway, at first our strategy to target their senior people proved very effective. But inevitably they responded by targeting senior Special Forces people, and then Peacekeepers too. By the very nature of their jobs, our people were far more visible than theirs, and it was not long before we were losing a lot too. Jones and I have both had some narrow escapes, and meanwhile, as you know, the offensive against Japanese Peacekeepers proved particularly effective…

"Nevertheless, the Calver Cats' operations in Afghanistan and South America were closed down. But in response to losses in the West, they redoubled their efforts in Southeast Asia. They've established bases in Cambodia and Burma and are not unwelcome in Thailand, Laos or Vietnam. Meanwhile, their operations in China, Taiwan, Korea and Japan have grown significantly. This was almost entirely due to the ruthless efficiency of the Fujiwara. Distasteful as you may have found it, you have dealt a serious blow to the Asian aspirations of the Calver Cats. Yes, many are dead as a result of your efforts, but you have saved thousands..."

"Wonderful. May I go now?"

"No, I'm not finished yet. I promised to keep a protective eye on Lord Kensington, and I have done that. He is safe and there have been no attempts on his life. However, I warned you before you left that if we failed to deliver everything we'd hoped, it would be worse when you came back; and regrettably it is. The Calver Cats have more than blossomed since Beauchamp and Chalmers escaped. We still don't think they've connected you with Nariko, but it probably won't take long. Either way your brother will soon find out you've resurfaced, and then he'll be after you with renewed vigour…"

Tessa looked at her watch.

"Don't forget, you're a Peacekeeper on active service and you've accepted a Mission to stop the Calver Cats. You cannot shirk those responsibilities. I will do what I can to stop you from being involved for a while, but at some point it is inevitable. Your handiwork in Japan will buy you some time with Beauchamp, I suggest you enjoy it."

"Good idea. Please only contact me if you have something very important to add. I have done more than enough killing for my liking, so it will take a very persuasive argument to get me to draw my sword again. Goodbye."

Tessa stood up to go, and sighed.

"She's fading fast, Sinclair and I want her to live for as long as possible."

"What do you mean?"

"It wasn't only thugs who died in Kawasaki-ku. Tessa all but disappeared too. Soon only Nariko will be left, and I am not at all sure I want to be her, even if that is what everyone else seems to want."

"Look, this isn't something terrible which others are imposing on you. It's your destiny. As I said before, Tessa is evolving into Nariko in response to a changing world. Nariko will be just as good, or bad, as you want her to be. That will always remain under your control. I trust Nariko, and as her, I am sure you will make a good and righteous future for yourself. Anyway, please take this."

"What is it?" she asked, looking at his outstretched hand.

"It's a secure *Cloud Based Communicator*. It looks like your *cbc*, but if you dial #*[ALT] before a number, it will encrypt the call, voice, text or whatever, provided the receiver is using a similarly equipped phone. It will allow us to communicate securely, wherever we both are."

Tessa took the phone; she never could resist new gadgets.

"Also, you shouldn't use the underground or high-speed train, they're too public. Take a taxi, please."

She nodded and left, still fuming. She stomped quickly through the Baggage Claim Area; for once pleased everyone moved out of her way.

Fifty minutes later, she arrived at her house in South Kensington. Only after she had let herself in, switched off the alarm and opened all the shutters and curtains, did she begin to feel better.

"Home sweet home," she sighed. It seemed everything was in good order. Clearly Helen, her neighbour, had looked after it well. With some music playing, Tessa made some green tea and delighted in checking her gadget strewn Peacekeeper Equipment Bugatti in the garage. Buying it had been a considerable extravagance. But, following the sale of her companies, she had the money and enjoyed owning the car immensely. She was desperate to go for a drive, but decided to postpone that self-indulgence until after she'd sorted out a few other things.

She put her new *cbc* on charge, and cleaned her swords. Then she tended to the letters, her e-mails and various other chores. She had finished by mid-afternoon and decided to unwind by going for a run in Hyde Park. She didn't want to attract attention by wearing her swords, so she took a rucksack with some weights in it to stand in for them. Two hours later she returned feeling much better. She had a refreshingly hot shower and, wearing a hooded tracksuit top, walked to the sushi restaurant in Thurloe Place.

She called David on the way, but his mobile went to voicemail and only the answering machine responded from his house in Belgravia. Not being able to reach him straightaway disappointed her at first. But, on reflection, she thought it would be unreasonable of her to expect anything else after not having been in touch with him for nine months. He would have got on with his life. Then she began to worry he might have found someone else. And why not? Handsome, rich, a Peer of the Realm? However, she soon told herself to get a grip, phoned him again and left a short message.

On the way back home she put a note through the SKS letterbox telling Master Lee she would be training there the following morning. Then she went for a drive. It was wonderful. Although staying within the speed limit was a constant challenge, she checked that the car and all its Peacekeeper Equipment were functioning correctly. She even tried the car's partial and full stealth modes; not only to confirm they were working, but also to make sure that she remembered how to drive the car when it was made to look like an Audi TT and when it was barely visible. Everything seemed fine, but she thought it should be serviced after having stood idle for so long.

It was 10 p.m. when she returned home. She flopped down on the sofa and realised that apart from being tired, jet-lagged and still a little fed-up, she was pleased to be home. She went to bed feeling more happy and relaxed. Redecorating her bedroom in the style of a room in a Samurai house had cost a lot, but at times like this, it proved a worthwhile investment.

The following day she woke as usual at 4:30 a.m. and went for a long run, wearing her swords. She loved running with the park so quiet and fresh. She even stopped for a friendly exchange with the policewoman opening the park gates. It had been a long time since they had met this way and they both enjoyed the reunion.

She returned home and had breakfast. Suddenly, her *cbc* rang. Her heart started racing as she picked it up.

"Hello," she said, tentatively.

"Tessa, is that really you?"

"Yes, David, it is," she replied, choked with emotion.

"Oh, Tessa, it's so good to hear your voice. I was beginning to think something awful had happened to you." His voice trembled. "I don't know what to say..."

"Neither do I," she said, tears filling her eyes. "I'm sorry it's been so long, but I'm back now. I've missed you so much."

"Tessa, I… Never mind, where are you?"

"South Ken. You?"

"Graemeshall. I'm meant to be here for another few days, but I'll come back now. I'll catch a plane and Andrew can follow with the Rolls. Your place here is fine by the way, I've been keeping an eye on it for you."

Overcome, Tessa couldn't speak for several seconds.

"How about if I come to you? I have some catching up to do today, but I'd quite like to spend some time at *Pennysview*. It's been ages since I was there."

"Well, if you don't mind, that would be marvellous. What plane will you be on? I'll meet you at Kirkwall."

Tessa thought for a moment. If she travelled by plane, she would either have to leave her swords in London or alert lots of people, including David, to her Peacekeeper status.

"I think I'll come by car so I've something other than the moped while I'm there. The Bugatti could do with a blast, anyway."

"OK. Any idea what ferry you'll be on?"

"The first tomorrow morning, I'll drive through the night. Shall we meet for breakfast?"

"You bet! Where?"

"Balkie Hotel?"

"Perfect. I'll be there from seven-thirty. Drive carefully, won't you? Northeast Scotland's a desolate place, especially at night."

"Don't worry, I'll be fine," she replied, involuntarily thinking back to Kawasaki-ku.

"Oh, Tessa. This is wonderful, I can hardly wait! Ah, sorry, apparently I'm needed."

"I'll say! Don't worry, you go now. It's good to be back, but much better to talk to you. I'll see you tomorrow."

"Welcome back, my love!"

Finishing the call, she heaved a sigh of relief; then, ecstatic, she danced around the room. Eventually, still beaming, she made appointments to have her hair styled and her legs waxed. Then she phoned John Brown, her contact at the garage in London which dealt exclusively with Peacekeeper cars. After a brief explanation, he suggested she bring the car in for a service which could be done that day. She readily agreed, picked up her sword case and drove to the garage.

Once back in South Kensington she went straight to SKS. Lee was waiting to greet her.

"*Konichiwa*, Nariko-san," he said, bowing. "It is good to see you again. I understand from Master Matsumoto that you have learnt much."

"*Konichiwa*, Master Lee," she replied, bowing back. "Quite possibly. But I'm still not sure I want to know any of what I have learnt. Isn't that more important?"

Lee chuckled.

"It sounds very healthy to me. Let us talk. I want to hear what you have been doing. You can wear me out later."

They walked through the busy training area to Lee's Japanese-style private rooms, where he lived with his wife. The two of them sat in silence on *zabuton* either side of the fine lacquered table, listening to the sound of water gurgling over the waterfall into the koi-filled pool. Tessa admired the Japanese garden through the large picture window until Lee's wife came in. As usual, she was exquisitely dressed, this time in a hand-decorated pink kimono. She bowed and put a lacquer tray on the table with two finely decorated Japanese cups and a matching pot carefully arranged on it. She poured green tea for them both and reversed out of the room. She had never spoken to Tessa, who had long since given up trying to engage her in conversation.

Lee and Tessa talked and drank green tea. He brought her up to date with what had been happening, and she told him about Kawasaki-Ku. Eventually, Lee's wife brought in a veritable sashimi feast for lunch. Then they trained for a couple of hours, after which Lee was completely exhausted while she had barely worked up a sweat.

"You're not getting old on me, are you?" asked Tessa sarcastically.

"Hah! How nice to have you back!" he laughed. "No, I'm barely older than when you left. It is you who are faster, stronger and more skilled. We're going to have to find other ways to keep you in practice. But we'll worry about that when you get back from Orkney. Why don't we finish for now? You should go and collect your car, you have a long drive ahead."

CHAPTER 9

Tessa had a quick meal at home and set out on the 700-mile drive to the ferry terminal at Scrabster. The gloriously clear evening heightened her enjoyment of driving the Bugatti. She was also happy in the knowledge that her swords were safely, but discreetly, stowed in the car's secret compartment. In the early hours of the morning, completely alone in the highlands, she put her foot down. She briefly reached 220 m.p.h., but then decided to slow down in the interests of everyone else's safety. She arrived in Scrabster to find her favourite ship, the ageing *St. Ola*, had already berthed.

Tessa settled down in the lounge with a cup of black tea as the ferry steamed across the Pentland Firth. It had been a long time since she had spread Penny's ashes from this very ship. But every time she passed the Old Man of Hoy, she couldn't stop her mind returning to that dreadful time. She still missed her friend, and was reminded that her oath to see all those responsible for her friend's murder face justice had yet to be fulfilled. But ultimately she was determined that she would not fail to deliver lawful retribution.

After docking in Stromness, Tessa drove to Kirkwall and parked her car in Watergate. She felt sure David had already arrived. Her heart started beating more quickly in anticipation. She walked down to the harbour and turned left along the quayside to the hotel. Entering the lounge she instinctively turned to the table in the bay window where they usually sat.

He was there, Lord Kensington of Graemeshall, looking as handsome as ever, casually but smartly dressed. He was just over six foot tall, with an athletic well-toned body. He had a healthy tan and his square-cut jaw was enhanced by a crop of neatly styled jet black hair. His sideburns were neatly trimmed with just enough white hairs to make him look distinguished rather than old. His sharp, blue-green eyes glinted in the morning sun. He still represented Tessa's perfect intelligent, well-groomed male, one she found totally irresistible.

When he saw her, he stood up so quickly he nearly knocked the table over. She ran into his arms and they embraced as her eyes watered.

"Oh, David, I've missed you so much," she sobbed.

"I've missed you too, my love," he replied quietly, holding her as though he didn't want to let go.

They moved apart, still embracing, and looked into each other's eyes. They were both crying with joy. They kissed passionately and only broke apart when they realised everyone was watching them.

"Maybe we should have breakfast first," whispered Tessa, drying her tears.

"Good idea," he replied, "the *first* bit I mean."

They sat down and started the long process of catching up. She didn't want to talk much about what she had been doing, but knowing her absence had resulted from the showdown with her criminal brother, David expected that and didn't press her. Instead, he told her what had been reported concerning Beauchamp's escapades, and also how he was placing his considerable Orkney property holdings in a Trust for the Orcadians. Not having any heirs, it worried David that the eventual ownership of his family estate might be uncertain. He'd mentioned this before, but Tessa hadn't expected him to be working on it quite so soon. However, as he pointed out, forward planning seemed sensible in such troubled times. Furthermore, with them being seen together again, it would not be long before he also became a target.

Arm-in-arm, they left the Balkie Hotel mid-morning. As they walked along the harbour front, the *M.V. Shapinsay* had just finished loading. David turned to Tessa.

"Well, darling. Do you fancy a stroll round Shapinsay?"

"What a lovely idea," replied Tessa enthusiastically. "It's such a gorgeous day it seems a shame not to be out in it. Can you afford the time?"

"Hah!" he exclaimed. "It's been so long, how could I afford not to?"

They were soon aboard the small roll-on roll-off ferry and, twenty-five minutes later, were strolling round Shapinsay. They spent the next two hours walking, occasionally through lush green countryside and sometimes along the coast. They ended up at the local manor house hotel and enjoyed a hearty lunch. Back in Kirkwall they decided to go their separate ways for a few hours, and meet again that evening.

Using her *cbc*, Tessa phoned *Pennysview*, the cottage she had finished building when her friend had died and bequeathed the land to Tessa. She used the not inconsiderable home automation she had installed to switch on the heating system and prepare the garage in advance for her car. Then she went shopping before driving south to Burray. She drove over the first three Churchill Barriers, turned right along Scapa Flow and then left on to the narrow track which led up the northern side of the island. Only *Pennysview* painted on a small faded wooden sign indicated that her cottage stood further up the hill.

After driving up half the steep side of the hillside the road finally levelled out and she saw the cottage some distance in front of her. Again she phoned the house and soon all the shutters and the garage door were opening. Automation had been her profession and remained her hobby. She had really gone to town on *Pennysview*. The layout remained much as Penny had designed it, but Tessa had included a number of enhancements, as she liked to call them. It had been nearly a year since she'd last visited.

Later, satisfied the house was in order, Tessa sat outside drinking a cup of green tea and admiring the view over Scapa Flow. Her telephone rang.

"Hello," said David, "done all your chores?"

"Certainly have. I'm sitting outside with a cup of tea, waiting for you. What's the plan for tonight then?" she asked, failing completely to conceal her anticipation.

"Hmm," he replied, sensing her mood. "I suppose we'd better get something to eat, sometime?"

"Probably. How about St Margaret's Hope? Then we could come back for, er, a night cap," she said mischievously.

He raised his eyebrows and chuckled.

"Sounds … irresistible. I'll give Andrew the night off and drive myself. I'll be there by six-thirty, at the very latest."

"OK. I'll make a reservation. Don't be late!"

"Oh, I won't be."

It was 6:15 p.m. when David's Rolls drew up outside *Pennysview*. Tessa had put on an attractive summer dress. After kissing and cuddling for a few minutes, they went to the restaurant and sat outside at a quayside table. They barely noticed the chill in the air; they were too pleased to be together again. Finally, after all the other customers had left, David looked at Tessa and smiled.

"It's getting late."

"I thought you'd never notice," she replied, grinning and signalling for the bill.

Twenty minutes later the Rolls turned on to the track leading up to *Pennysview*.

"Do you want to park it in the garage? It looks as though there might be a storm tonight," she asked, taking her *cbc* out.

"Probably a good idea. Andrew would never forgive me if I brought it back chipped. But isn't the Bugatti in the garage?"

"Oh, haven't I told you about that?" said Tessa, telephoning *Pennysview*. "I could only get approval for a single garage, but eventually, with a nod and a wink, they let me build a double garage vertically; one space is under the other. So the Bugatti is safely tucked away in the basement."

"Honestly, you and your technology," laughed David, driving into the garage. "Mind you, I still haven't had a close look at this wonderful vehicle of yours. The nearest I've been allowed is a hundred yards."

"Sorry, just never quite got round to it…"

Half an hour later, with clothes strewn throughout the cottage, they curled up in bed together. Neither of them got much sleep, but they had a very enjoyable night.

In the morning, David went to make a cup of green tea for her, and some coffee for himself. Then they sat in bed and admired the extensive views towards Stromness.

"I feel better for that," she said.

"Oh, so I've made the tea right for once, have I?"

"Yes, but I wasn't talking about that," she replied, nudging closer. "But why don't you tell me about that new scar of yours?"

"Ah," he replied lightly, "nothing exciting, I had my appendix out."

She looked at him, put her cup back on the bedside cabinet and dived under the covers.

"Wow! Tessa, I'm not sure I'm ready," he exclaimed, trying not to spill his coffee. But then she reappeared.

"That's not an appendectomy scar," she observed suspiciously, "and the incision's too big."

"Really? Perhaps the surgeon couldn't find it. Strange, he came highly recommended."

"Don't be silly. What happened?" she asked, nuzzling up to him. "You are all right, aren't you?"

"Oh, yes. But it was a bit of a problem. Apparently I'd left things too long and that's why it looks more gruesome than one would expect."

Tessa looked at him doubtfully.

"Anyway," he countered, "since we're discussing bodies, let me make some observations. When I was helping the 2012 Olympic Committee, I saw a lot of extremely fit ones. But the beautiful body I'm fortunate enough to have draped over me now is in an entirely different league. Tessa, you're incredibly fit! I've never seen anyone so fit; you're only toned muscle and bone. How many times are you going to have to run round Burray to work off that excessive meal we enjoyed last night? Hmm?"

"Quite a few, I suppose," she replied ruefully. "I've been working out, that's all."

"That's a bit of an understatement!" he laughed. "How about we call a truce, and just accept the way we are?"

"Only if you swear, hand on heart, that you're OK. Now I'm back, I don't want you thinking of leaving. You're too important to me, David. I couldn't bear the thought of being without you."

Emotions welled up in Tessa, and her eyes began to water. He smiled affectionately and put his arm round her.

"Silly thing. Neither of us knows when our time will be up. Such things are decided by a higher power. One or both of us could be gone tomorrow. You know that, as well as I do. What I will say is that, for my part, I have done everything I can to ensure we both live out our allotted time together."

He kissed her fondly.

"You would tell me if there was anything seriously wrong, wouldn't you?" she asked, still concerned.

"The moment there's anything for you to worry about, you'll know."

"Hmm. OK." She retrieved her cup of green tea. "So, er, when will you be ready?"

"Well, since you ask, things are beginning to perk up…"

They eventually parted mid-afternoon, but agreed to meet that evening at David's ancestral home.

Tessa adored Burrody Castle. It had been built from local grey sandstone high on the western slope of Burrody Hill; full of character, it was always warm and cosy. The property dated back to the seventeenth century, and was surrounded by a castellated wall enclosing a large cobbled courtyard. A beautiful, albeit externally dour, three-storey Victorian house stood at one corner of the enclosure. From the top floor there were commanding views over Scapa Flow round to Kirkwall, while to the east lay Deerness with Burray to the south. In the middle of the west wall stood the solitary square watchtower. Through it passed the only vehicular entrance, an imposing arched gateway just wide enough for David's Rolls.

Tessa and he spent the next two days together, but then he had to go to Edinburgh for business. She considered going with him, but decided to stay and have a quiet day on her own. After sleeping soundly she got up early and ran numerous times round the twenty acres surrounding *Pennysview*. Afterwards she showered, had breakfast and rode into Kirkwall on her moped. She often used the moped to avoid drawing attention to the Bugatti. She bought some supplies and a selection of newspapers, and went to the Balkie Hotel for some tea. Since not many places in Orkney served green tea, she brought her own.

Sitting in the bay window, sipping her tea, she watched the ships in Kirkwall harbour. It was a wonderful day and the bright sun illuminated the rolling scenery with incredible clarity. Smiling, she picked up a prestigious broadsheet and scanned the headline, 'UK Peacekeeper Massacres Tokyo Gang'. She promptly muttered some choice expletives, and read further.

For months, Japan and the UK have been seething over the Calver Cats' murder of so many Peacekeepers, particularly in Japan. But last week, a bold counterattack was mounted. One Japanese Peacekeeper, together with another from the UK, confronted the gang at Kawasaki-ku, an industrial town near Tokyo. The two Peacekeepers faced 36 gang-members. However, precisely what happened next is not known since although the Peacekeepers emerged unscathed, not one of the gang survived! Even Hayato Fujiwara, the seventh-generation boss of the clan's extensive criminal dynasty, died that night. It is believed he was killed last, following presentation of an execution order signed by the Emperor. Japan has refused to comment officially, but apparently, Fujiwara, who had been sentenced to death several times in absentia, did not die at the hand of the Japanese Peacekeeper. Furthermore, Ryota Fujiwara, the younger of Hayato's two sons, also died that night after a duel with the UK Peacekeeper...

Suddenly the waiter interrupted her reading.

"More hot water, Madam?"

Tessa swallowed, and quickly folded the newspaper.

"Oh, er, thanks. Perhaps in a few minutes."

She picked up a tabloid. Its leader was equally sensational, albeit with a greater emphasis on bloodthirsty speculation. For once, she wasn't sure which she preferred. Fortunately, she found nothing to implicate her in either account. It seemed the media were respecting the official ban on identifying Peacekeepers.

She looked round, half-expecting people to recognise her and what she'd done. But only a couple of the other tables were occupied, and the people there were totally uninterested in her. She took out her *cbc* and dialled #*[ALT] and Sinclair's number. It rang twice and a metallic voice muttered "*Encrypted*".

"Good morning, Nariko," greeted Sinclair. "How nice to hear from you."

"Have you seen the newspapers?" she hissed.

"Yes. Congratulations! Your reputation precedes you."

"Oh, for goodness' sake, this is serious! You didn't say the action would be splashed all over the newspapers. What happens if they mention me by name?"

"Well, it's still against the law for them to do that, even if they knew it, which I doubt. But I did say some politicians wanted to meet you. Since you declined their invitation, you can hardly expect them to go out of their way to protect you."

"What!" she exclaimed. "I can't believe you said that. You're meant to be my Guardian, not my publicist! Is this what I get for doing other people's dirty work?"

"Politics is a dirty business too, and politicians are very good at it.

They're focused on their forthcoming electoral prospects. Cynical, I know, but alas more true than any of us lesser mortals would care to believe... But seriously, you do know that I'll do everything I can to protect you and your anonymity, don't you?"

"I'm not sure what I know any more. A moment ago, I thought you might be hanging me out to dry."

"Sorry. Heathrow apart, I hadn't intended to give that impression." Tessa smiled, and relaxed.

"Hmm. Maybe we should start over?" she suggested.

"What an excellent idea. Let's forget the unfortunate past, and consider where we go from here. Agreed?"

"Agreed. But I'm still not keen on pressing palms."

"Understood. Unofficially, I don't think you should, either. After all, Peacekeepers are meant to be independent. Anyway, while we're talking, why don't I tell you about a plan I've been working on to make it more difficult for people to identify you. I thought we could help protect your anonymity by using a false Peacekeeper name. That way, if, or when, Beauchamp finds out that Nariko was involved at Rippleside and Kawasaki-ku, hopefully he still won't realise it's you. Using a different name would also give you cover for practising with a sword. Beauchamp would think you're only a beginner. You could even tell Lord Kensington if you wanted. Then, if we needed to, we could leak the name Nariko. What do you think?"

"Sounds good, and it might even help flush Beauchamp out. So, how long have you been thinking about dropping this red herring?"

"Ever since I saw the newspapers and started waiting for your call. What name do you fancy?"

Tessa laughed.

"Well, how about Yoshino? It was the name Penny was given when she joined SKS, so there'll already be some paperwork in the system. It will feel a bit strange using her name, but I daresay she'd be flattered."

"Great minds, I thought of Yoshino too! I'll get on to it right away. Of course, if the name Nariko does get into circulation, Beauchamp will go after that person too."

"Yes, but that's no worse than now, is it? In some respects, I wish this whole thing would come to a head. Then maybe I could get on with my life, assuming I still have one."

"You will. So, are we friends again?"

Tessa took a deep breath; she liked and respected Sinclair too much not to be.

"Yes. I'm sorry if I blew my top at Heathrow. I was angry, and upset."

"You had every right to be; a lot of what you said was true. So, for me, it was more important to know we'd made up and moved on. Anyway, where are you?"

"Orkney."

"Oh, lucky you. I'm envious. It's wonderful there isn't it? I take it Lord Kensington is with you?"

"Well, not right now. He's gone to Edinburgh for the day, but he'll be back tonight."

"Well, you enjoy yourself. I'll take care of things here, and when you get back we can meet and bring each other up to speed. *Sayonara*, Nariko-san."

"*Sayonara*." There was a pause as she struggled to recall the Japanese name Matsumoto had given him. She felt sure she knew it. But he assumed she had finished talking and the phone clicked. She smiled; his name was so close to the surface. She would have to work on it.

She ordered some more hot water and continued reading the newspapers. But soon found her mind meandering back to wondering what Fujiwara had meant. If she was only a pawn, maybe the question was not *who* was playing but *how many*?

The following morning, David and Tessa woke up in *Pennysview*.

"By the way," said Tessa as they lay in bed, "given Beauchamp's still on the rampage, maybe I should take up some sort of defensive sport? What do you think?"

"Sounds like a good idea to me," he replied, running his hand through her hair. "Then you could guard me. What did you have in mind?"

"Well, I'm not sure, but what about the Samurai sword? Penny enjoyed it, so maybe I should find out whether I do."

"Heavens," said David, lying down and making it clear he wanted her to return her cup to the bedside cabinet and join him. "You're not going to become a Peacekeeper, are you? Did you read what happened in Japan last week?"

Tessa took the opportunity to glance away, unable to meet his eyes while she lied to him.

"I think I'd find it morally challenging being a Peacekeeper, and apparently it's very difficult to qualify anyway. But yes, I did see that stuff in the newspaper. Quite something wasn't it?"

"If you ask me, they were a pair of incredibly foolhardy, unbelievably brave, and fantastically skilled fighters. For two to take down forty with swords is quite incredible. Anyway, you do what you want, darling. You know I'll support you whatever."

"Thanks" she said, rolling on top of him and kissing his forehead. "How about having a picnic at the Brough of Birsay?"

"Anything you say," he whispered. "But first…"

Two days later, Tessa drove back to London. David followed the next day when he had booked for them to see Berlioz's *The Damnation of Faust* at Covent Garden. It was the first time they'd been seen together in public for nearly a year. Neither of them had expected this to prompt a media frenzy, but their pictures were in several morning newspapers. David laughed it off, but Tessa didn't like it. She hated publicity and took a dim view of the people behind it. Later that day, an SMS arrived from Sinclair asking whether she could meet him at Antonio's Patisserie in Brompton Road.

She went early since she knew Antonio would need some time to recover from her reappearance there. He was the larger-than-life, extremely camp Italian owner of the place, who had perfected the art of lengthy histrionic welcomes. She loved it when he veritably erupted with joy and surprise.

"*Dr Tessa!!*" he shrieked. "*Finally youa comea back to me after aller this time!*"

"Oh, Antonio, how I've missed you," she replied in her mock Italian accent. Both roaring with laughter, they embraced and he kissed her on both cheeks.

"So, your usual table?" he asked eventually. "With," then he looked round to check no one was listening, "green tea?"

"Yes, please. Two more people are coming." He blew her another kiss, and ten minutes later Sinclair and Jones arrived.

"Good afternoon, gentlemen," she said, gesturing them to sit down.

A waiter came to take their order and they exchanged pleasantries until their drinks arrived.

"Well, you certainly announced your return with a flourish," observed Sinclair with a smile, sipping his tea.

"Regrettably, it wasn't our intention," replied Tessa ruefully. "We only wanted to enjoy the opera. But David had hardly been to anything since the Guildhall show-down with Beauchamp, and nobody had seen or heard anything of me. So, when we popped up together, the media went wild. It was quite surreal. We slunk in surreptitiously and came out to a seething mass of reporters and photographers. If Beauchamp didn't know I was back, he certainly does now!"

"Not to worry," continued Sinclair. "It was bound to happen sooner or later. However, it probably means we shouldn't delay implementation of our red herring plan. But the fewer people who know about it the better, which is why we've come here today. We should revert back to Headquarters for future meetings. Anyway, as discussed, ostensibly you will take up the sword using the name Yoshino. Are you still OK with that?"

"Yes, I think so," Tessa replied. "I certainly haven't come up with anything better."

"Good. Jones has already spoken with Potter and I've approached SKS. So, everything should be in place by the end of the week. But, just so you know, it will only be the five of us who are party to this plan. You, me, Jones, Potter and Lee. Not even Maeda knows."

"Right," muttered Tessa thoughtfully.

"There's something else you should be aware of," added Sinclair. "It has the potential to be quite a nuisance. There are some high-level moves to limit Peacekeeper rights, particularly with regards to anonymity. I doubt anything will come of it, but public reaction will probably be tested during the run-up to the election."

"Good grief!" exclaimed Tessa. "That's madness. They'll never get anyone to sign up any more, and those that do will be marked people."

"I know," agreed Sinclair. "We think it's crass stupidity too and we're doing everything we can to block it. But, as I said, politicians are politicians, and that could be a vote winner."

"Yes, but the resultant upsurge in crime wouldn't be!"

"That won't worry them," interjected Jones, "they'll be in power for five years, so they'll have plenty of time to win more votes by fixing the problem before the next election."

"Heavens! I thought I was being unreasonable, harbouring cynical thoughts about politicians. It seems I massively underestimated their duplicity!"

"Who knows?" continued Sinclair. "Anyway, don't believe everything you read in the newspapers… Meanwhile, in Japan, there's a brutal power struggle going on for control of Fujiwara's Calver Cats operations."

"Who are the key protagonists?"

"Maeda's not sure. He's surprised its happening at all with one son still living."

"…And the Calver Cats are starting up in the UK again," added Jones. "They've left a few of their calling cards at crime scenes, but we don't have much information yet. We'll keep you posted."

"Sounds ominous," observed Tessa…

CHAPTER 10

After a few weeks Tessa began to feel better about life. Although always on her guard, she spent much more time smiling. She enjoyed every moment she was with David, and had seen virtually nothing of Sinclair and Jones, which pleased her no end. Also, to her considerable puzzlement, there had been no sign as yet of the Calver Cats. She couldn't understand why there had been no threats or attacks made on her.

But the political situation concerning UK Peacekeepers was in turmoil. The media was rife with suggestions that their rights ought to be curtailed and the law prohibiting the naming of Peacekeepers repealed. Fortunately, implementation of such proposals seemed unlikely since they would be in direct contravention of the International Peacekeeper Treaty. Nevertheless, publicity stunt for the General Election or not, Tessa was uneasy. Without anonymity, she would be foolish to continue as a Peacekeeper. Although she enjoyed the sword, she had always despised all forms of violence. The only way she had been able to justify what she had already done, was by convincing herself it was for the good of the peace-loving majority. However, she doubted whether she would be allowed to relinquish her Peacekeeper status whilst engaged in a Mission against the Calver Cats. Furthermore, relinquishing her status wouldn't stop the Calver Cats from coming after her and currently at least she could legally defend herself.

She continued training hard every day. Using the name Yoshino had enabled her to be more open with David about her sword-wielding hobby, although he didn't appear to take it seriously. She tried to bolster this view by always completing her practice sessions early so she could devote the rest of her time to him.

Eventually, Sinclair invited her to Special Forces Headquarters for a meeting with him and Jones.

"Now that everything's running smoothly with you using the name

Yoshino," said Sinclair, "I think we should leak that it was Nariko who was involved at Kawasaki-ku. The Calver Cats are trying to identify the UK Peacekeeper concerned and it would probably be better to feed them the name Nariko rather than risk them making a connection to Yoshino. It looks as though they know now that Nariko was responsible for Rippleside, so it shouldn't come as a big surprise if the same person was active in Japan, too."

Tessa nodded.

"This Nariko person sounds like a nasty piece of work to me. Wherever she goes, lots of people die."

"Actually, I think she's all right," interjected Jones pleasantly. "By removing all the nasty folk, she makes the world a better, safer place for everyone else."

Tessa smiled, unconvinced.

"OK, leak the name *Nariko*, but they're bound to catch up with me sooner or later."

"True," continued Sinclair. "But this way we might be able to control the process. Ideally, we want any confrontations to be on our terms, not theirs. Besides, leaking the information selectively could help us establish whether the Calver Cats are driving the media concerning the Peacekeeper rights proposals."

"Any more thoughts about whether anything will come of it?"

"I still think it will only be a nuisance until the election is over. Too many countries have invested too much in the Peacekeeper Treaty; and it's not as though Peacekeepers haven't been successful. If anything serious looks like materialising, we'll let you know…"

Meanwhile, hardly a day passed without something bad appearing in the news about the Calver Cats. But she had still seen no sign of them, which she found increasingly frustrating. While Tessa waited, her life was on hold. She wanted Beauchamp to come for her, so that one way or another the affair would end. She had told Hayasaka she would go after the Calver Cats if they didn't come soon. Would it really come to that?

One day she received an encrypted SMS from Sinclair. It read, *Urgent we meet. 1 on 1. AP today at 3? Tell no one.* It was very strangely worded for him. She considered it for a moment, thinking of all the bad things which might be about to happen, and then replied, OK.

She went home, put on jeans and a hooded tracksuit top, and walked to the patisserie. When she arrived, Antonio greeted her euphorically, as usual. But once the hugging and joking had finished, she settled at a quiet corner table with some green tea. Sinclair arrived shortly afterwards. He sat down looking uncharacteristically nervous, and while she ordered him some tea, checked whether anyone had followed him.

"Heavens Sinclair, if I'd known you were going to be this jumpy, I'd have brought my swords," she said jokingly.

"I'm glad you didn't. I don't want to attract any attention. Suffice to say, this meeting is not really happening … Nariko." She looked at him in surprise. "Yes, this is business, sort of. I have kept out of your life for as long as I can, but a piece of enticing intelligence has surfaced and I'd like you to consider something. It's incredibly risky, bordering on the foolhardy in fact, so I'll understand if you refuse. However, it is imperative that no one ever finds out we had this conversation. It is against the law for a Guardian to attempt to manipulate a Peacekeeper, and it's not exactly good for a Peacekeeper knowingly to listen to such a proposal."

Sinclair sipped his tea. Tessa thought for a moment and then sighed.

"Well, you know me … carry on."

He smiled.

"Overall, our progress against the Calver Cats in the Far East has been poor, except in Japan. We've achieved nothing of consequence concerning their operations in Burma and Cambodia, nor their satellites in Laos and Vietnam. However, we recently discovered that Bill Chalmers is in Burma. Apparently, he's having to stay there because of the chaos you caused by eliminating Fujiwara. That gives us a small window of opportunity."

"Exactly which us is this?" asked Tessa drinking some tea.

"Er, just you and me. But let me finish first. Now, although Thailand, Cambodia, Laos and Vietnam have all recently signed the Peacekeeper Treaty, it will be a while before Peacekeepers are properly accepted there. Meanwhile, Burma's decrepit Military Junta doggedly refuses even to adopt the NLD's proposal for democracy, let alone sign the Treaty. Even China has exerted some pressure on them, but they're not willing to be overly persuasive since Burma remains a big purchaser of

Chinese goods and they need Burmese raw materials and electricity. Which means any form of official intervention within Burma is out of the question. Chalmers presumably realises that and feels safe. However, he is still Beauchamp's right-hand man; Ryuu Fujiwara is certainly a rising star, but he's distracted by the situation in Japan. The wild card, almost literally, is Beauchamp's Japanese girlfriend whose identity remains a mystery. She's a nasty piece of work who, amongst other things, acts his strategic planner."

He looked round suspiciously.

"Anyway, I was wondering whether you'd consider going after Chalmers? Personally, I doubt it would be possible to get him out alive. So this would probably be another of the very type of action of which I know you are rightly unenthusiastic. But I don't think there's any other way of doing it in this case. What's more, with the Calver Cats running short of senior people, it would be a serious setback for Beauchamp if Chalmers were eliminated. I'd give you as much help as I could, unofficially, including some excellent in-country assistance from the local Special Forces. I know the man in charge there very well.

"Fortuitously, the timing is good because many Burmese are busy with the poppy harvest and the Junta is still preoccupied with moving the capital to Naypyidaw. However, if you were to go, I don't think you could risk taking your swords, and you would be completely on your own if captured. If it became known that you are a Peacekeeper, the adverse publicity would be horrendous. As for your future, well, if you were unlucky enough to survive, you would probably end up in Rangoon's Insein Prison, and the Calver Cats would surely find out. To complicate matters further, Chalmers has befriended the number two within the Burmese Military Junta which still runs the sham parliament there. His name is General Soe Gyi and he's a very influential, cruel and callous man."

Tessa raised her eyebrows.

"Yes," continued Sinclair, "it would be incredibly dangerous for you. I'm sorry to have to ask you to consider this, but you are my only hope. If you're not interested, we'll just forget this conversation ever took place. But then Chalmers will walk, and he did after all oversee Penny's murder."

Sinclair paused to make sure the gravity of what he was suggesting had sunk in. Tessa took the opportunity to signal Antonio to refill their cups.

"Who else knows we're talking about this?" she asked.

"Absolutely no one, and that's the way it's got to stay."

"Not even Jones?"

"No," replied Sinclair, shaking his head. "This is just between you and me."

"So, where in Burma is Chalmers?"

"Apparently he doesn't like the heat of the plains, so he stays at old colonial hill stations. He was at Maymyo, north of Mandalay, but now he's in a small town called Kalaw, southeast of Thazi."

"They're both very nice," replied Tessa with a smile, "but Kalaw is quieter."

"You know it?"

"Yes, when I was younger, I visited Burma several times. I love the place. It's a beautiful country with delightful people and the most despicable bunch of brutal thugs imaginable running it, illegally. I can't understand why nobody does anything about it." She spoke with a degree of vehemence that surprised Sinclair. "Anyway, Kalaw is in a mountainous region. It wouldn't be easy to get in without being noticed, never mind get out. It's a long way from anywhere by road, plus the roads are terrible. The nearest airport is Heho, but that's run by the military."

"You do know it! I doubt I could extract you from there; it would start an international incident. A low-key intervention to bump off a notorious bad guy will infuriate the Junta, but it's unlikely to bother anyone else, not even the Chinese. The Calver Cats have killed a lot of their Peacekeepers too."

"Are there still lots of spies watching foreigners?"

"Yes, but my contact will get you away from them."

"I can hardly believe we're talking about someone's death in such blasé terms."

"You think Beauchamp considers yours, or mine, any more compassionately?"

"There is that," acknowledged Tessa. "Well, I have to admit this is very creative. I said I'd need a great deal of persuading to draw my sword again, so you've found a way I can risk my life without using a sword! But Sinclair, I really would have to be mad to accept."

"Yes, you would," he agreed resignedly. "Fine, I'm sorry I mentioned it. Let's just forget all about it."

He finished his tea and prepared to leave.

"Hold on, I didn't say I wasn't mad."

He grinned.

"That was mean."

"I'm sure you deserve it for something. Anyway, I'm not definitely saying I'll go, but I'm not saying I won't either. At least not yet. Knowing the Burmese people as I do, irritating the Junta would be at least as satisfying as getting Chalmers. Tell me exactly what assistance you would be able to provide and I'll go away and think about it. Then we can meet again, say, the day after tomorrow? I'll give you my answer then."

"Fair enough."

He opened his briefcase and passed her some papers in an unmarked folder.

"Inside are copies of all the information we have, including some satellite images of the areas you'll be interested in…"

As Tessa was walking home, she suddenly realised she wanted to go. She knew it would be ludicrously dangerous, especially without her beloved swords. But dealing another blow to the Calver Cats by, hopefully, kidnapping Bill Chalmers had to be worth considering. Perhaps this would bring the affair to a head. But there again, it could just be a well-conceived trap.

During the next two days, much to Lee's surprise, Tessa spent her time at SKS practising unarmed combat and knife-throwing. At home she planned and considered ways to incapacitate and extract Chalmers. However, she soon concluded that getting out on her own would be difficult enough, never mind with a reluctant captive. So, if she went, she would have to be prepared to kill him there and then. Both Beauchamp and Chalmers had already been awarded the death penalty in absentia by a UK court, so, arguably, she could justify eliminating him as implementing a judicial sentence. But she still felt uneasy about it. Nevertheless, she developed a detailed plan, listing everything she needed. The time came to meet Sinclair again.

"This is where I'm at," she whispered, passing him her list. "I *might* be willing to do this, provided you can at least supply me with everything on that list."

Sinclair perused the lengthy list, and smiled.

"No problem. It'll take me a few days, but if you're willing to risk everything, so am I."

"OK, here's the plan," continued Tessa, handing him some more papers. She spoke for nearly an hour; he was deeply impressed.

"Wow, that's a plan and a half! What's more, I don't see why it shouldn't work. I certainly can't think of any way of improving it. And you've hidden your identity well, so hopefully Chalmers won't recognise you. But as far as we know he's never got a particularly good look at you, even at the Guildhall, and that was a long time ago. The throwing knife will probably have to be sourced in Burma. It could be difficult getting a good one, but leave that with me. As you rightly point out, the biggest challenge will be getting out safely, but I'm sure my local contact will be able to handle that. He's brilliant. However, there is one slight complication. I'm not entirely sure we can trust all our people in the UK Embassy in Thailand. I think we have a mole there; in fact, I rather suspect we have one here too. But as far as getting you back to London is concerned, I'll bypass them and handle that myself. So, if you're willing to go, I'll need about a week to get this organised."

"This is madness," muttered Tessa. "Why are we doing it?"

"It is somewhat perilous," observed Sinclair with a wry smile. "But I'm doing it because it's my job, and Beauchamp is running out of senior people. I suspect he tied up with Fujiwara because he needed him and his sons. You took two of them out. That only leaves Beauchamp himself, Chalmers, Ryuu Fujiwara and this mysterious Japanese woman. If this action deprives Beauchamp of Chalmers, we will have moved ourselves a long way towards stopping the Calver Cats. But you'll be at the sharp end – why are you doing it?"

"Well, apart from trying to kill me at Sloane Square, Chalmers organised Penny's murder. Also, the Burmese Junta is brutal and corrupt. I would be delighted if this destabilises it in some way. Finally, I've been back for quite a while now. I haven't tried to hide, and yet Beauchamp hasn't shown himself, presumably because he's busy planning something horrible of his own. So, I would prefer to go on the offensive rather than just wait for it to happen. Nevertheless, I will be acting illegally in Burma."

"I know, but if Chalmers were sheltering in a Peacekeeper country, it would be a no-brainer. So, the Junta only has itself to blame. But what I would say is that if at any time in Burma you feel it's all too difficult – for example, if you sense it's a trap – then please, just give up and come home. But if all goes well, it will enable me to provoke Beauchamp into coming after me again and hopefully then, between us, we'll be able to finish it."

"Putting your name up there with mine is inviting trouble."

"It's probably there already. Besides, why should you have all the fun? You're right, we do need to smoke him out, and better to do it now before he's recovered from losing the Fujiwara."

"Are you sure it's wise not to confide in Jones? If I live and you die, who's going to tell the whole story?"

"Well, you make sure you stay alive, and I promise to do everything I can to stay alive too. In the meantime, the less anyone else knows about it the better. Somehow we'll both come out of it all right, I'm sure."

Tessa looked doubtful, but then smiled at him determinedly.

"Well, we'd better get cracking then, hadn't we?"

"Indeed," replied Sinclair. "I suggest we meet here in a few days to review progress. If anything urgent crops up, I'll send you an SMS."

Tessa nodded and they left Antonio's separately. Now she needed to explain her impending absence to David and Lee.

It proved remarkably straightforward with Lee. He immediately saw through her story.

"Look," he said, "at least credit me with some intelligence. You are obviously undertaking a clandestine action. The mere fact you are not willing to tell me the details makes me suspicious of its legality. I can see you have made up your mind; but you are a respected Peacekeeper now. Act outside the Treaty and you are committing a crime for which the consequences are dire. Remember what you have been taught and make sure you know the difference between right and wrong. Above all, please come back in one piece – and without a guilty conscience."

Tessa nodded. It worried her that Lee's remarks had focused so precisely on what continued to trouble her. Was assassinating Chalmers justified?

Convincing David she wanted to go away alone for a couple of weeks proved to be far more problematic. She told him she wanted to visit a friend, and was quite taken aback by how distraught he became. He said he didn't care where she intended to go, he wanted to come too. However, she knew he had some business commitments in Europe, so she implied that she had timed her trip to coincide with his. Eventually he acquiesced on condition they spent as much time as possible together before she left, to which Tessa readily agreed. Nevertheless, it disturbed her that he had been so upset. She even mentioned it to Sinclair, who passed it off as the lover of a beautiful woman being worried by the thought of being without her for a while. This sounded far too glib for Tessa's liking, but she let it go.

The days passed quickly. Sinclair and Tessa met occasionally to update each other, and Lee complied with her desire to train even more aggressively than usual.

Ten days after they had first discussed the project it was time for her to leave. Tessa had already said her farewells to David and Lee, and was packed and waiting when she heard the taxi pull up outside her house.

She intended to take only a small suitcase with her, a strong nylon bag which converted into a frame rucksack. She closed the security shutters, set the house alarm, went out and locked the door.

"Good evening," she said, climbing into the taxi. "It's good of you to drive me."

"Not a problem," replied Sinclair. "Besides, this way no one will be able to trace your journey. By the way, I'd like you to take this with you."

He passed a most unusual-looking knife through the partition. It was a fairly conventional sleek shape, a nice weight and beautifully balanced; but it was the colour which was strange. The entire knife, including its hilt and scabbard, were matt grey.

"This is weird," said Tessa, studying it. "It's very nice. But I don't think even a cute English academic will be able to get this onto an aeroplane."

"Ah, well, like the bag, it's rather special. It's made from sintered ceramics and has no magnetic or X-ray signature. It's incredibly strong, and sharp, and flies perfectly. The UK has the world lead in making these and that is the latest, fully functional, prototype. It's only by chance I managed to lay my hands on it. Admittedly it's not as valuable as your Kimi Amakuni sword, but you'd probably be surprised if you knew how much it is worth. It might come in handy and it will fit into one of the pockets by the rucksack frame. It would be good if you could let me have it back sometime, since I'll be implicated straightaway if it's captured."

"Isn't it a bit risky, giving it to me?"

"Not as risky as your going."

"Well, it's a lovely knife," she said, admiring it. "Thank you."

"You're welcome," he replied, and the Special Forces taxi moved off.

They both sat deep in thought for most of the journey to Heathrow. But as they drove up the ramp to the Departures Area, Sinclair broke the silence.

"Here we are. I think we're as prepared as we can be. So, it's down to you and your plan now. There's just one more thing. Try and stay away from General Soe Gyi. He's nasty, and no fool; don't underestimate him."

"OK. Hopefully I won't meet him, anyway."

He turned round as she pretended to pay.

"And for heaven's sake, be careful. I know it's my fault you're going, but please don't make me feel even more guilty by not coming back with that beguiling smile of yours…"

On the plane, Tessa tried to get as much rest as she could. But her sleep proved again to be superficial and uneasy. She remained uncomfortable about what she was doing and concerned by David's having been so upset about her going away.

CHAPTER 11

At Bangkok's Suvarnabhumi airport, a limousine was waiting to take Tessa to the Oriental Hotel. She enjoyed staying there; its subdued opulence and attention to detail always delighted, as did the warm welcome she received. On this occasion the manager, Mr Georges, greeted her personally.

That evening, she went to the Verandah restaurant for dinner. Ice, the impeccably groomed supervisor of the terrace restaurants, greeted her enthusiastically and showed her to her favourite table. While eating she re-checked her plan. Although nervous, she didn't feel what she was attempting was impossible, just very difficult. As the night drew in, she sipped iced water and watched dinner-boats cruising the Chao Phraya river.

Tessa started the next day with an early work-out across the river in the hotel's fitness centre. Then she had breakfast, bade farewell to Ice and checked out. It was already hot, and getting hotter. She took a tuk tuk to a shopping mall in Sukhumvit Road and walked into some seedy backstreets. Eventually she found the dingy hotel she wanted, the one without security cameras.

Using her fluent German, she checked in as though having recently arrived from Frankfurt and wanting to sleep. She used an assumed name and a false passport Sinclair had supplied. She paid in advance for one night and went upstairs. In her room, she transformed her bag into a rucksack and reorganised its contents. She had several passports, all stored in separate secret compartments. In another was the knife Sinclair had given her. Otherwise, she only had some clothes, her camera, two books and several bottles of hair dye. She drew the curtains and, half an hour later, had black hair again.

"Hmm. Looks alarmingly familiar," she muttered. "Now for coloured contacts and the fake tan."

Finally Tessa was satisfied she had transformed herself into Dr Anna Wood, an academic from Lincoln College, Oxford, studying ancient Far Eastern architecture. She wanted people to believe she had arrived from Cambodia, as shown within another of her passports. She ruffled the bed to make it look as though it had been slept in, and quietly crept downstairs. Unseen, wearing the prescribed dark blue Oxford University tee-shirt and sunglasses, she left the hotel and took a taxi to Suvarnabhumi Airport. Armed with the ticket stubs from bogus flights to Siem Reap and various other receipts from the area, she checked onto the Rangoon flight, and bought a bottle of single malt whisky for her contact.

The plane departed punctually, arriving ninety minutes later at Rangoon's Mingladon Airport. She ambled across the tarmac to the Junta's extravagant new terminal building, and, once through immigration, walked out of the Arrivals Hall into the bright sunlight. It was late afternoon, incredibly hot and oppressively humid. Her challenge now was to find her contact. The seething mass of drivers closed in, noisily vying for her custom. Suddenly someone spoke quietly from behind.

"Miss Oxford, please let me drive you. I need money to buy books for my children."

Tessa turned and studied the clean-cut man who had addressed her. He seemed to be an archetypal Burmese man. Not tall but with a friendly face and clear brown eyes which glinted in the sunlight. Slim and fit, he was dressed in a light blue short-sleeved cotton shirt and a blue-and-red-checked *longyi*.

"Have you a reliable car with air conditioning?" she asked cautiously. "I want to go to Pagan."

"Yes, Miss. I take many tourists to Pagan."

"OK. You can drive me to my hotel in town now, and we'll agree a rate for the rest if I like what I see."

He led her to a battered old Toyota.

"The Panorama Hotel, please," she said loudly while getting in.

"Which of the temples in Pagan would you like to visit first, Miss?" asked her driver, when they were safely away from the airport. "Ananda, Thatbyinnu or Shwezigon?"

"Dhammayangyi," she replied.

"But have you been to Kyaiktiyo?"

"Twice!" she replied.

"Honestly, whose idea was that code?" he laughed. "I was sure I'd get it wrong."

"Sorry, my fault. I was showing off."

"Well, welcome to Burma," replied the man. "My name is Htet. I don't know what you hope to accomplish here, but I will do everything I can to ensure you are successful."

"*Mingalabah, Htet. Kyay zu tin bar de.*"

"You speak Burmese?" He grinned in surprise, displaying a fine set of white teeth in the mirror.

"Only a little, I'm afraid. But I can get by in a restaurant. Anyway, for now, my name is Dr Anna Wood. I am posing as an Oxford academic studying ancient Far Eastern architecture. I've come from Cambodia and propose to spend two nights in Rangoon before heading north. Tomorrow I suggest we follow the tourist circuit: Schwedagon, National Museum, Scott Market, Sule Pagoda, etc. Early the day after I would like to leave for Kalaw, although I suggest you still say we're going to Pagan. I know it's a long way, but do you think you can get there in a day?"

"Hmm, it's two hundred and fifty miles, but it should be possible if we don't hit any problems. Getting to Thazi will be fairly straightforward as the main north-south road is quite good now, albeit at the expense of many press-ganged villagers' lives. But from Thazi the going will be slow. I suggest we leave at four thirty in the morning, and see how far we get?"

Tessa nodded and settled back in her seat. As they drove into Rangoon she shook her head in disapproval as they passed the smart offices of companies which had ignored international pressure not to trade in Burma. Once in the city, she found herself grimacing at the increasingly dilapidated state of the buildings. Htet noticed.

"What did you expect? The Junta doesn't spend any money on its people's welfare, and even less on where they live. As soon as the capital moved to Naypyidaw, the leafy colonial splendour of Rangoon started to decay… You don't look like the sort of person I would normally expect to be active here?"

She smiled.

"Well, I doubt what you're doing is normal either… Anyway, here's a little something for you."

Tessa slid the bottle of whisky under a newspaper on the front passenger seat. Such gifts were always welcome given the widespread poverty inflicted by the military Junta.

"Thank you, that's kind," said Htet. "I'm getting a knife for you, but is there anything else you need?"

"No, I don't think so, and I won't need you again tonight. Let's start at eight tomorrow morning."

It was dusk by the time she had checked in. She was delighted to have been allocated a room with wonderful views of the floodlit Schwedagon pagoda on the hill not far away.

The following day, she and Htet mingled with the few tourists who were there. Tessa wanted the Junta's spies to see her visiting the sights and Htet played his part well. He recounted numerous historical facts to which she listened studiously. By the end of the day they were getting on well together and had established an excellent working rapport.

"Thank you, Htet," said Tessa as they returned to the hotel. "I think we've done what we needed to do today. I'll be ready and waiting at four thirty tomorrow. Don't bother to come in, just stop outside and I'll join you."

"OK. I'll be in a different car. It will be a grey Subaru four-wheel-drive saloon. It's better equipped for a long trip."

The following morning, Htet had barely stopped in front of the hotel when she got in the back. He nodded and they set off. After two hours of travelling in silence, Tessa felt they were far enough from Rangoon to relax.

"How about stopping for breakfast?"

"Good idea. I know somewhere which is not overrun by Junta spies. By the way, the knife is in the bag underneath the driver's seat."

She inspected the Chinese weapon. It was good, by Burmese standards, but she doubted it would fly well.

"Sorry," said Htet. "I know it's not ideal, but it's the best I could get."

At 7 a.m. the car turned off the main road. They went up a long rough track between tall sugar-cane plants, eventually stopping in front of a small guest house. They received a rapturous welcome; clearly Htet was held in high regard here. They enjoyed a hearty breakfast, but were soon on the main road again, with Tessa sitting in front with

Htet this time. She had bought several bottles of water at the guest house and an hour later asked him to stop at a busy market.

There she brought a bucket and a selection of dried fruit while Htet bought his favourite snack: roast locusts. Tessa stared aghast at the pile of enormous blackened insects nestling in some newspaper.

"Try one," he offered. "They're like prawns."

"Hmm. Maybe next time."

He roared with laughter and waxed lyrical about the locusts' nutritional value as he loudly crunched his way through them.

It was a wonderfully sunny day and Tessa revelled in the views: fertile green paddy fields, bustling villages and impressive gold-topped stupas and pagodas. Occasionally they would stop for a rest at a particularly interesting place and Htet would show her round. The two of them had become friends and chatted idly as they continued northwards.

Late-morning, she asked him to stop somewhere secluded and after another thirty minutes they drove into a forest of cultivated castor oil trees. Htet parked, wondering what she was going to do.

"Have a rest," she said. "I'll be about twenty minutes."

Tessa grabbed the bucket, her rucksack and several bottles of water and disappeared into the trees. In just over fifteen minutes she had transformed herself again. Now she had red hair, freckled skin and green eyes. Then she replaced her black *I love Myanmar* tee-shirt with an orange one displaying pictures of carvings from Banteay Srei in Cambodia.

Htet laughed when she returned.

"I'm Dr Celia Drummond now," she said, smiling, "an academic from London studying Far Eastern ancient religious buildings. We're stopping in Kalaw for a few days so I can catch up on my writing. Here's my passport. It already has a visa, but it needs updating with the entry stamp and signature."

Htet nodded. They'd already discussed this, so he'd come prepared. He returned her passport five minutes later.

Eventually they arrived at Thazi, a characterless town. Its only claim to fame was that it lay at the juncture of the north-south and east-west roads and railways dissecting Burma. But given the paucity of cars and trains, this didn't mean much.

"We're making good time," observed Htet. "But apart from being asked to research a couple of people…"

"Yes, it is time you knew more. It's a long story, and the key protagonist for us is a man called Bill Chalmers…"

Htet listened to Tessa intently.

"Hmm," he said finally. "Unfortunately, Chalmers is very friendly with General Soe Gyi. So, if you need any additional motivation for this, you should know that both Chalmers and Soe Gyi have a habit of indulging themselves with young children, usually girls, but not always. They take whoever they want and the parents have no recourse. Some of the kids have been hurt quite badly."

"Really?" she exclaimed in disgust.

"I'm afraid so. I was quite surprised myself. We soon found out about Chalmers, but no one in the Rangoon office knew General Soe Gyi was similarly inclined. Why else do you think Chalmers keeps changing location? If he stayed in one place any longer than he does, the locals would arrange an accident, regardless of who his friends are."

Tessa sat back.

"Even so, I think such things are better addressed in a Court of Law. No matter what he's done…"

"Or is doing?" interjected Htet.

"Maybe, but I still don't feel comfortable with being judge, jury and executioner all rolled into one. Especially in a country which hasn't signed…"

She stopped abruptly, regretting she'd said so much. Htet smiled.

"Not signed? Well, I can guess what you mean. Though I don't think we've had one of your kind here before… I can arrange for you to talk with some parents, if that would help?"

"No, that won't be necessary," sighed Tessa. "I believe you."

"You're the boss. Now, I have prepared three exit routes. The first is via Tachileik to the east. It's two hundred miles past Taunggyi, which is forty miles from Kalaw. The roads are poor but pass through bandit country where I have many friends. I have already arranged our safe passage, and the army won't dare follow. Alternatively, we could go south to one of the crossings near Nanaklwe. It's a tiny, little known village and there are several unrecognised border crossings there.

That would be a bit closer, but might still take longer as we'd have to traverse areas which are much more active militarily. The third option would necessitate a long and difficult cross-country trek. We would go south into Karen territory and on to Myawaddy. It would take many days."

"Hmm, my preference would be Tachileik. I've been to Mae Sai on the other side, once."

"OK. And, just so you know, the choke on this car is automatic. So be careful with the choke knob. If you pull it out, it will slowly retract. When it's fully home, about twenty seconds later, the car will explode. If you pull it out and push it straight back … well, you can guess what happens."

"How nice," mused Tessa. "Let's hope we don't run into cold weather."

"Well, I presume you won't want to be taken alive?"

"Probably not a good idea."

Slowly the car picked its way up the winding picturesque roads to Kalaw. Htet drove well though the surface was far from good and the light was fading fast.

It was early-evening when they reached the junction at the brow of the ridge which marked the entrance to Kalaw. Htet had arranged accommodation for them in different guest houses on Nat Sein Road. They decided to separate for the evening. Tessa would settle into her room and walk into Kalaw for dinner, while Htet would find out the latest information on Chalmers. They arranged to meet again after breakfast in a Burmese tea house near the market.

Tessa liked her family-run guest house. Although somewhat dilapidated, it was spotlessly clean. Its two storeys were arranged in a U-shape around a small courtyard at the front. Big wooden lattice doors slid together to block access from the street. On the ground floor were the family rooms and a large open storage area with some chickens in it. Upstairs were three guest bedrooms – only hers of which was occupied, a communal bathroom and an open verandah which doubled as the dining area.

After she had unpacked and washed, she sat on the candlelit verandah with the two children of the house, a boy of seven and a girl of nine. They laughed as she practised her rusty Burmese. She could understand a lot, but speaking required considerable mental effort.

Eventually, she decided to refresh her memories of the town, and set off to explore and to find dinner.

Not surprisingly for a hill station, the small picturesque town of Kalaw was set on a mountainside, giving it a wonderful climate. It was a typical evening; cool with a gentle breeze. Tessa enjoyed her walk and soon found a street cafe which served excellent local cuisine.

The following morning, breakfast at the guest house comprised curried eggs, rice noodles and fruit. Afterwards, Tessa walked down to the market which proved colourful, bustling and noisy. The stalls stood on hard-trodden soil and were mostly open, though some had been covered with makeshift roofs of blue plastic sheets secured to bamboo poles. For sale were numerous vibrantly-coloured flowers together with various fruits and vegetables, all of which had been freshly harvested. There were also meat stalls and a few selling river fish, including small turtles and frogs struggling in bags of tight-fitting netting. In another section the stalls sold cheap Chinese goods, from cooking utensils to shampoo. Some offered Chinese medicines, together with a selection of date-expired Western pharmaceuticals. Savoury and sweet snacks were available everywhere and people seemed determined to smile and practise their English on her. Between a stand selling *longyi* and another where broken umbrellas and flip-flops were being mended, Tessa found a woman offering hand-woven Shan scarves. She bought one and then went to the Queen Victoria tea house, picking her way between the glistening red betel nut splashes on the ground. She sat down in a quiet alcove. Htet soon joined her at the adjoining table. Separately, they both ordered tea while he had a chapati too.

"Are you sure we won't cause any problems for our guest houses?" asked Tessa in concern, without looking at him.

"Oh, yes, don't worry. There are many sympathisers in Burma, and a lot more here since the arrival of our friends. It's all taken care of. And if you need to leave anything there, it will never be found. Thanks for thinking of it."

Tessa shrugged, screwing her face up as she sipped her strong bitter tea. She resigned herself to adding some condensed milk to mask the taste. Htet chuckled as she inspected the contents of the cracked milk jug. She fished out the dead insects before pouring some of the thick glutinous liquid into her cup.

"Our man hides away in the Kalaw Hotel for most of the day," Htet continued. "He seems to have taken the place over. I checked again on their hobbies, I'm afraid what I said is still true. They have caused much distress here. Anyway, he eats dinner in town nearly every evening and his friend frequently joins him. But there aren't many good restaurants in Kalaw, so it should be fairly easy to track him down. I suggest we split up tonight and each watch a few until we find them. I'll take the restaurants on the west side if you take those on the east. We can meet in the middle near the Kathmandu K2"

"I've eaten there. It's the best one, isn't it?"

"Yes, if you like curry. They ate there yesterday, so will probably choose somewhere else tonight."

"OK," acknowledged Tessa. "But I'm attracting too much attention, I'm not sure we should stay here more than a couple of days. We need to find him quickly and plan from there. What time does he eat?"

"About seven thirty."

"Well, you'd better prepare the car. You never know; it might all go down tonight."

Htet nodded, finished his food and left.

Tessa stayed in the tea house until lunchtime reading one of her books. Then she went back to the market to eat and spent most of the afternoon walking around. For a while she practised throwing the knife Htet had given her, but she couldn't aim with any accuracy as it wouldn't fly well. However, she didn't want to use the one Sinclair had given her without being sure she could retrieve it. She eventually returned to her guest house and washed, ready to walk back into town. When she came down, she found Htet waiting.

"Chalmers is eating early, at the Phyu Thant Shein."

"Hmm, that was easy. I'll eat there too. Hopefully he'll be on his own."

When they reached the restaurant, they found two army jeeps parked outside.

"The first belongs to Chalmers," said Htet, as they stood round a corner some distance away, "the other is probably Soe Gyi's."

"Great! Two introductions for the price of one. Are we all set?"

"I think so. Do you need anything from your room?"

"No. I always carry everything with me," replied Tessa, studying the setting of the restaurant. "I'll see you later then."

She strode nonchalantly across the road, stopping outside the restaurant to read the sun-bleached menu, as though deciding whether to eat there. Htet watched her go in.

The restaurant had a lot of tables, so the few people dining were widely dispersed. The furniture had seen better days, as had the threadbare tablecloths and the sullen flickering lights. The decor was Chinese with a strong Shan influence, like the menu. She recognised Bill Chalmers sitting at a corner table with a Burmese military man, presumably General Soe Gyi.

The waitress invited Tessa to sit wherever she wanted. She chose a table in a large empty area in full view of Soe Gyi and Chalmers, whom she sensed had already noticed her. She ordered some tea and, after having put on some studious-looking, but totally unnecessary glasses, picked up the menu.

"Food's OK 'ere," shouted Chalmers, in his strong cockney accent.

Tessa turned, as though trying to identify from where the words had come; then she looked at him over the top of her glasses and smiled.

"Oh, good, I'm starving," she replied, speaking with a Scottish accent. But quickly returned her attention to the menu; she didn't want to appear overly enthusiastic.

She ate a pleasant, if chewy, meal while pretending to read her book; but most of the time she was surreptitiously studying Chalmers and Soe Gyi. Chalmers, still with his crew cut, now appeared unhealthy, bordering on the obese, and decidedly unfit-looking. However, General Soe Gyi was entirely different. He looked extremely fit, strong and agile. This disparity was accentuated further by their clothes. Chalmers was dressed in a scruffy tee-shirt and shorts, while Soe Gyi wore a smart well-pressed uniform with numerous medals pinned to it. Furthermore, while Chalmers was unarmed, Soe Gyi had a pistol and a knife, and gave the impression he used both frequently. This all served to bolster her desire to corner Chalmers on his own.

As the evening progressed, both men got drunk. Tessa decided it would be prudent for her to leave, and paid her bill. However, just as she was preparing to go, Chalmers spoke to her, slurring his words.

"Dan't go, luvy. Come'n' 'ave a drink wiv us?"

"Oh, thank you, but I've been travelling a lot and desperately need an early night. Maybe some other time? I'm staying here a few days to catch up on my writing."

"You journalist?" asked Soe Gyi, in broken English.

The question was simple enough, but there was a menacing undertone in his voice. Western journalists or indeed anyone who might tell the truth about what was happening in Burma, were not welcome.

"Oh, no," she replied. "I'm a historian, studying ancient Far Eastern religious buildings. There are some fine examples in this country."

The General nodded and called for more beer.

"Fuck me," continued Chalmers, "smart tart!"

Tessa smiled.

"Good night, gentlemen."

Outside she set off in the wrong direction, doubling back later to find Htet.

"How did it go?" he asked as they drove back up the hill.

"Well, I'm definitely introduced. But trying to separate them was out of the question tonight. They're too busy getting drunk together. As I expected, Chalmers is an obnoxious lecher who seems willing to consider an adult female when he can't get a child. But Soe Gyi's completely different. He's a killer first and foremost. I'd prefer to avoid him, if possible."

Htet nodded and the car stopped in the darkness, a couple of hundred yards from Tessa's guest house.

"So, what's the plan for tomorrow?" he asked.

"Well, I'll set myself up in the tea house again. If Chalmers doesn't find me, I'll wander up the hill and try and take afternoon tea at the Kalaw Hotel…"

Late-morning, Htet discreetly joined her. Soe Gyi, who rarely stayed in town during the day, had left Kalaw early. Chalmers had also gone out, but he was expected back that evening. So, since it was a glorious day, Tessa walked into the hills to get some exercise and enjoy the views. She stopped once to watch a train puffing exhaustedly up the narrow-gauge track into Kalaw's quaint, if ramshackle, Victorian station. But, distracted as she was by the prospect of meeting Chalmers again that night, the picturesque sights were wasted on her.

CHAPTER 12

Htet met her on her way back; he looked worried.

"They might be on to us," he gasped breathlessly. "Apparently Chalmers liked you a lot last night, but Soe Gyi wanted to do some checking first. He's a perceptive bastard and probably sensed you weren't scared, which would have worried him. He's flown to Rangoon. He may be trying to establish whether your disappearance would cause a fuss. I think we should leave before he returns, which will probably be tomorrow. So you may only have tonight to get Chalmers."

"I thought it was too good to last," replied Tessa, taking a deep breath. "All right, so we need to get Chalmers alone, in a restaurant of our choosing. I think the layout of the Kathmandu K2 would work well, especially if we can herd him into the alcove."

"I know the owners. They have a young boy who ... anyway, I can make sure you are not disturbed, no matter what happens."

"All right, but how do we get him there? He's unlikely to go back to the Phyu Thant Shein, but that still leaves, what, three or four others?"

"Well, they'll just have to be closed this evening. That shouldn't be too difficult to organise," replied Htet, grinning. "Then Chalmers will be forced to go where we want him. Besides, he doubtless wants to meet you again, so he might follow you there. Let's just hope London has prepared your cover well."

"Indeed. OK. I'll set up in the Kathmandu at six thirty and wait for him. We should check out of our guest houses and prepare for a quick getaway. We'll just have to sleep rough if we need to."

Tessa had always known this operation would be difficult, but Soe Gyi hovering in the background, complicated matters considerably. She hoped he wouldn't return; any confrontation with him could have catastrophic consequences, not least for the people of Kalaw. She walked back to her guest house and paid them generously. Soon afterwards Htet arrived with the car, which looked quite different. She nodded in appreciation.

"I've adjusted it a bit," he said, proudly. "We'll need to travel quickly and the roads to the border are rough. I normally have the engine and suspension detuned to attract less attention, but now we might need its full capabilities. I haven't heard any more news, but I agree we should abort if we can't complete tonight. I have a bad feeling about this. The security systems in Burma are as decrepit as the Junta, but eventually someone will put two and two together. If they come after us in force we don't have many options. Neither of us can be taken, and neither can allow the other to be taken."

"Fun, isn't it?" observed Tessa. "General Soe Gyi is the wild card we could do without."

At 6:25 p.m. the car stopped in Aung Thaybe Road, round a corner and up the hill from the Kathmandu K2.

"The restaurant won't be busy and the alcove table will stay free, that's all arranged," said Htet. "Furthermore, the parents eating there will finish soon after Chalmers arrives … assuming he shows. The staff will leave as soon as they can."

Tessa pursed her lips and nodded.

"I'll wait here with the lights off," he continued. "If you can't do it, so be it. Let's plan to leave at nine-thirty regardless?"

"OK. Expect me at nine-twenty-nine."

"Good luck, and be careful. Chalmers is not as stupid as he looks, and Soe Gyi is very dangerous. His hands are already stained with the blood of many innocents."

Tessa glanced round to check no one was watching.

"Htet, would you mind looking the other way for a moment, please?"

She reached inside her tee-shirt and removed her bra which she rolled up and put in her rucksack. He looked at her in surprise.

"Sorry, but for once I'm trying to attract a lecher," she replied, shrugging. "See you later."

She walked down the hill and turned right towards the restaurant. Shortly afterwards, she went in and sat down opposite the secluded alcove where she wanted Chalmers to sit. Its table couldn't be seen from the street, but any diner there would have a clear view of her. She pretended to be absorbed by her book as she re-familiarised herself with the layout of the restaurant. The white walls usually reflected the bright lights, but tonight, most of them were off.

At 8 p.m. a jeep stopped outside and Chalmers swaggered in, immediately spotting Tessa. He had already been drinking, but was on his own. He settled down at the table in the alcove, apparently pleased to find it vacant.

"Yer 'ere!" he shrieked. "Ain't I the lucky wun?"

Tessa, who had pretended not to have seen him, looked up and carefully removed her thick-framed glasses.

"Oh, hello," she said, "fancy meeting you here. It looked like a nice place, so I thought I'd give it a whirl."

"Best curry in Kalaw, an' the beer's good an' all. Me name's Chalmers, Bill Chalmers, why dan't yer come o'er 'ere and sit wiv me? I'm bett'r than a borin' book, ain't I?"

He spoke loudly, slurring his words.

"Actually, the book's not boring at all, but I've done enough today and I'm hungry. I'm Celia Drummond, by the way."

Tessa returned everything she had spread around her to the rucksack and went to join him, leaving the bag undone so she could reach the knife easily. She sat on his right and after a while, let Chalmers order food for them both. He also got some beer for himself, but she drank water.

As the evening progressed the other customers left. By 8:45 they were alone. The waitress came out shortly afterwards to bring Bill another two bottles of beer. She apologised for having to leave for a few minutes and disappeared into the back of the restaurant. Chalmers had talked continuously and appeared delighted to find himself tête-à-tête with the new visitor in town.

"Yer know, we don't often 'ave a prime bit of stuff like you out 'ere. 'Ow about comin' back to my place t'night?"

"Wow! You don't beat about the bush, do you?" replied Tessa, still using her Scottish accent. "I'll bet you have a shower that works too. The offer's tempting, but I'd better not."

As she tensed herself to act, someone outside started playing loud, thumping music.

Chalmers smiled and calmly placed a revolver on the table.

"'Let's stop pissin' about shall we, Tessa? 'Ow long's it been … fifteen monfs? Took me a while, yer 'air's bloody gud, but it is you,

114

ain't it? You was wiv those Special Forces fuckers 'oo nicked me an' Beauchamp. S'ppose I should a recognis'd you before, but it don't matter. Beauchamp'll be fuckin' over the moon!"

He clearly felt very sure of himself, convinced he was in control of the situation.

Tessa tried to look confused although in truth her mind was racing. It seemed that there weren't many options open to her now, but at least the whole place was deserted.

"Soe Gyi'll be back soon," continued Chalmers, no longer slurring his words. "'E'll be interested ter learn I've rumbled yer wivout his help. 'Ave I just been lucky or did some fucker send yer 'ere? Who cares, Soe Gyi gets his kicks outta interrogatin' folk. Does it well too. 'E'll enjoy havin' yer to 'imself. After I 'av, o' course."

Chalmers took a long swig of beer, banging his glass down on the table afterwards and making the gun bounce. He looked at Tessa and laughed.

"Funny ol' world, ain't it? I got your friend, and now I got yer."

Tessa looked at him and smiled, determined to try and bluff her way out.

"I'm really sorry, Bill, but I've absolutely no idea what you're talking about." She spoke quietly and calmly. "If you, or your friend, want to see my papers, you're more than welcome. You can ask me anything you like about Far Eastern stone buildings, and not just here but in Cambodia too. Surely you don't think there are lots of people wandering around Burma who know about that sort of stuff?"

Chalmers roared with laughter and drank some more beer.

"Yer a fuckin' cool 'n, I'll giv' yer that."

"Actually I'm roasting. It's far too hot in here for me," she replied, tugging at the neck of her tee-shirt. "Look, if what you're really saying is that the only way I can get out of Kalaw in one piece is to come back to your place, well, that does put a different perspective on things. But if I agree, you've got to use protection. And I want a visitor's licence to the ruby mines at Mogok. That's the deal."

By now Tessa exuded an air of relaxed confidence, and clearly Chalmers was beginning to have doubts. She saw it in his eyes and knew she needed to capitalise on the moment.

"To convince you I'm a good investment, let me give you a taster of what's on offer."

She stood up seductively, prompting him to sit back so he could admire the view. He didn't pick up his gun. She smiled, and leant over the table towards him. Tessa watched as his gaze moved down towards the gaping low-cut neckline of her tee-shirt. She reached out and put her left hand on his shoulder and moved forward as though about to kiss him.

For a moment she felt as though she was back at Matsumoto Castle, standing in front of a dummy with a large pile of broken eggs beside her. But then she quickly pushed Chalmers back to improve the angle as her right fist crashed into his chest, close to his heart. The blow propelled him back further and his head hit the wall behind with a bump as his lungs emptied. Stunned, the only sound he made was a pathetic wheezing as he desperately inhaled. From the erratic pulsations in his neck, she knew his heart was pounding furiously. As soon as he stopped breathing in, she punched him again, just below his Adam's apple. The blow made a horrible crunching sound and his eyes bulged outwards. Twisting his chair round slightly, she punched him a third time, forcing his diaphragm abruptly upwards into his chest cavity. It was too much for him and his heart stopped. She stared into his shocked eyes.

"Say goodbye to Penny," she said quietly, "before you burn in hell."

His whole body quivered and he died. Justice had finally caught up with the man responsible for her friend's murder. But the process had been very disturbing for Tessa. It had been bad enough practising on a dummy in Matsumoto Castle, but doing it to a real person was much worse. Being so close to his face, looking into his eyes as she hit him, had been something she would not easily forget.

She snapped back to reality. Nobody appeared to have seen or heard anything. So she let go of his chair, took a deep breath, turned and grabbed her rucksack. Then she heard something behind her and a strong experienced arm reached around her neck and clamped it tightly. She was quickly pulled backwards off balance and the hold tightened. She couldn't breathe and knew it wouldn't be long before she passed out. Then a hand reached up inside her tee-shirt and grasped her right breast, painfully hard.

"You poison him?" hissed General Soe Gyi. She could feel his breath, hot and moist, against her ear, and smell his cologne mixed with the garlic he had recently eaten. Then he moved his head round so he could stick his tongue in her ear. Tessa was revolted and couldn't help writhing in his grip. His response was to tighten his hold and she heard the bones in her neck creak in protest, and still she couldn't breathe.

"Oh, not like that? You will soon; you even tell me who sent you. In fact, there won't be anything you won't do for me. I want to do this with Bill, but fool lets you slip something in his drink. Well, I not so stupid."

Tessa was in agony, and furious with herself for being on the verge of capture. She was desperately short of air and her breast felt as though it was being wrenched off. However, her mind remained clear. He seemed to be on his own, so she didn't want to make any noise that might attract someone else's attention. She relaxed, feigning surrender.

Soe Gyi released his grip slightly and air rushed into her lungs. She made a loud noise as though inhaling painfully, but didn't try to move.

"Give me bag," he rasped. "You not play tricks on me."

She held out her hand and moved the rucksack as far away as she thought he might accept from someone seriously disorientated. But as he stretched out for it, she dropped the bag. Grunting, he dragged her towards it, slightly slackening his grip. That was all she needed.

Despite his arm still being round her neck, she managed to spin round. Suddenly their faces were only inches apart. General Soe Gyi found a woman glaring at him with eyes filled with calm, calculating, defiant rage. Then he felt a massive pressure in his chest, as though someone had hit him with a sledgehammer. He had never experienced anything like it and heard several of his ribs cracking under the impact. He had been winded many times, but never anything like this. He felt his heart pulsating heavily and unnaturally; his vision blurred and he wanted to cry out, but only groaned pathetically.

As his hold on her fell away, Tessa gripped his shoulder with her left hand and brutally shoved him back. His head made a loud *thump* as it banged into the wall, cracking the brittle plaster. For the first time in his life he was defenceless and afraid.

They both heard him stop inhaling and for a moment he wondered whether he might still have a chance to call for help. But then he felt the impact of another punch in his neck. It made a dreadful *scrunching* sound and was the most painful blow anyone had ever inflicted on him. Stars filled his eyes. A moment later he felt another impact low in his chest. It seemed as though his lungs were being pushed up into his mouth. A bright flash filled his eyes. Terrified, he realised that the irregular beating of his heart had stopped. He couldn't move and stared wide-eyed at Tessa.

"Go and be judged for your crimes against the people of Burma," he heard her say, and then his vision faded.

As his body crumpled, Tessa dragged him over to her chair and sat him down facing Chalmers. Both men were staring wide-eyed with shocked expressions on their dead faces.

"No qualms about that bastard," she muttered. "Poison indeed!"

She stood up shakily and steadied herself against the wall. Slowly her senses returned, as did the gravity of her situation. He had hurt her. Her neck was extremely painful, her right breast throbbed and she still had difficulty breathing. She began to worry she might not make it back to the car.

Trembling, she drank some water. Swallowing proved to be extremely difficult, but it did help. Breathing deeply, she took out her Shan scarf and wetted the middle before carefully wrapping it round her neck. Then she used a paper serviette to wipe her fingerprints off everything she had touched. Finally, she tipped some beer into her glass and generally tried to make it look as though Soe Gyi had eaten rather than her. But her strength was fast running out. She picked up her rucksack and, trying to look as relaxed as possible, walked out into the darkness.

A few yards up on the other side of the street a brightly lit general store continued to play loud music.

Suddenly four soldiers, barely in their teens, appeared from an alleyway and barred her way. Tessa made as if to walk past them.

"All foreigners must stop," commanded the sergeant, brandishing an old Chinese copy of an AK47 assault rifle, with the safety catch off.

"*Mahouq pa,*" retorted Tessa, refusing indignantly in Burmese. "I've come from the restaurant with General Soe Gyi and Bill Chalmers. I'm going to my hotel now and then we'll possibly all go back to the

Kalaw Hotel."

"OK. I take you to your place."

"Not necessary. But I will tell the General how well you followed his orders. He will be very pleased with you."

Unsure what to do, but keen to be seen as in charge, the sergeant gestured her to continue.

"*Kyay zu tin bar de*," said Tessa.

Her path cleared and she walked to the end of the road. As she turned left, she could hear the soldiers talking, but knew no one was following. She continued up the hill, quickening her pace. She reached the car at 9:34 p.m. and slumped into the passenger seat.

"Drive!" she croaked. "Tachileik."

Htet stared at her, shocked by her dishevelled appearance.

"Just go!"

He started the car and set off, without lights.

CHAPTER 13

In agony, Tessa attempted to stay still as Htet picked his way through the back streets of Kalaw to the dirt road which led over the hills to Taunggyi.

"Hold tight," he said, "it's going to get rough."

Forty minutes later he slowed down.

"Are you all right?" he asked, clearly concerned by her grimacing.

"Just about," she said, hoarsely.

"Did you get him?"

"Yes," whispered Tessa. "But he'd worked out who I was. Then, as I was leaving, Soe Gyi grabbed me from behind and tried to crush my neck. But he made a mistake, and I got away."

"Is he after us?" quizzed Htet worriedly.

"No, he's dead too," she murmured apologetically. "I had no choice."

Htet thumped the steering wheel and whooped with joy.

"Now I'm really impressed! You've just rid the world of two very evil men. I didn't tell you earlier, but Soe Gyi personally killed many of my family."

"I'm sorry... Can we take a break near a stream, please?"

Htet nodded and, ten minutes later, the car stopped. Tessa got out unsteadily, removed her scarf and submerged it in the cool flowing water. She bathed her neck and, not bothering to warn Htet, took off her tee-shirt and rubbed the cold wet scarf over her breast. Then she made a paste from some of Matsumoto's healing mixtures and smeared it on all her bruises, before eating some other herbs. After putting her bra and tee-shirt back on, she soaked the scarf again and wrapped it back round her neck.

Htet had been busily tapping a message into an encrypted communicator.

"I've told Rangoon that Chalmers and Soe Gyi are dead. What shall I say to our friend in London?"

"Er... Two down *stop* target and general alas in way *stop* exiting *stop.*"

Tessa got back in the car and flopped into her seat.

"You look terrible," observed Htet.

"I feel far worse," she groaned, coughing as gently as she could.

"Try and get some rest," he replied. "You've done your part; now I must do mine. The army is usually slow to react, but we must move quickly. Hopefully we'll be a long way away before they come after us."

She nodded, wedged her head in position with a cushion and closed her eyes, soon slipping into unconsciousness.

When she came round, the car was bouncing around as Htet negotiated the dirt road at remarkable speed.

"We're near Taunggyi," he muttered, seeing her eyes open. "How are you?"

"Awful."

He pulled on to the metalled main road and a while later drove slowly through the town. But once clear of it, he stopped to empty several jerry cans of petrol into the tank. Tessa took the opportunity to bathe her neck again. As he drove on, she drifted in and out of consciousness. She woke at dawn.

"Good morning," said Htet.

"If you say so," she replied stiffly.

"You look better."

"Hmm, I used some very powerful medicines. Where are we?"

She sat up and tried to make herself more comfortable.

"About forty minutes from Kengtung I stopped to speak with the bandits, but there were no problems."

"Really?"

He smiled.

"I didn't want to disturb you. My cousin was there, so it didn't take long. If you agree, I'll just push on. The road is not so bad now and I'd like to get as far as we can before they set up road-blocks."

"Go for it. But you've been driving a long time."

"I'm fine," continued Htet. "As soon as we're through Kengtung, we'll cut up into the hills for the last part of the journey. There are too many army checkpoints on the main road for us. It will be rougher but a lot quieter and I have friends there." Tessa shrugged. "By mid-morning, every soldier in Burma will be looking for you, and probably

121

this car too. The airwaves have already been buzzing about detaining a Caucasian woman with red hair."

"Then maybe we should stop and I'll change my hair colour."

"No time," said Htet, driving like one possessed. "There's some face paint and freshly ground *thanaka* for your cheeks in the glove compartment. Use them and cover your hair with this headscarf. You can change the colour later. Just try and make your face look Burmese for now."

Tessa did her best, using the mirror in her sun visor as the car lurched from side to side.

"Looks good," observed Htet, grinning.

Kengtung was a medium-sized town, relatively affluent by Burmese standards following years of smuggling and black-market trading. Fortunately this had produced a predisposition towards ignoring the unfamiliar, so their dirty grey saloon car attracted no attention whatsoever. Htet drove sedately past the lake, around which the old British colonial town had been built, and veered right by the Independence Monument. They were soon heading south out of the town towards Tachileik.

An hour later, Htet suddenly slowed. He turned off the main road and the car struggled up a steep dirt track. After fifty yards, he stopped behind some trees.

"So far, so good," he said, stretching. "There's a stream over there if you want to do your hair. I'll cover our tracks from the main road."

Tessa nodded and undid the scarf around her neck to inspect the damage. The flesh there looked very raw with a number of dark bruises.

"No wonder it hurts," she muttered.

She got out and found the bucket. Twenty minutes later her hair was black again and her freckles were gone. She had also changed back into her dark blue Oxford University tee-shirt. Again she wrapped her wetted scarf around her neck.

They continued up the hill more cautiously so as not to create a dust cloud.

"We've made good progress, but the time has come to make a decision. Do we go to the main Tachileik border post or somewhere less official?"

Tessa looked at him with a sly smile.

"Well, if I was an angry Military Junta trying to catch an assassin, I would expect them to head for somewhere quiet. So maybe we should go for the main crossing."

"That's what I'd do," replied Htet. "They'll be better prepared than usual, but Tachileik is still fairly primitive. I'll find out what's happening there when we stop for breakfast."

Two hours later they rounded a corner, went over the brow of a hill and stopped near a substantial wooden house. It had a dried grass roof and diagonally criss-crossed slithers of bamboo woven into panels for the walls. A column of grey smoke rose welcomingly from the chimney.

As Htet got out of the car, several people came out of the hut, smiling. However, when Tessa got out, she was studied with a mixture of awe and caution. She put her hands together, bowed and said, "*Mingalabah*".

Everyone smiled and a little girl wriggled out from the middle of the group. She put her hands together and bowed, and then came over. Tessa smiled and knelt down.

"*Mingalabah*, little one."

The girl shrieked with delight and threw her arms round Tessa's neck. As excruciating pain shot through her, Tessa visibly swooned, prompting Htet to come to her rescue. But she recovered, and, after adjusting the child's grip, lifted her up. The little girl grinned and eased Tessa's scarf away from her neck to look at the bruises.

"Ouch," she said.

"Oh, yes," replied Tessa, solemnly.

Then the girl gently kissed her neck.

"Ahh. Now it feels better," said Tessa.

Htet laughed.

"Dr Wood, welcome to my hill station. You have met my daughter, Nyunt, these are her grandparents, on my wife's side."

With the ice duly broken, they all went inside. However, on the way in, Tessa noticed carefully concealed sheets of bullet-proof Kevlar in the walls. The flimsy-looking house had in fact been equipped to withstand a determined attack.

It was very cosy inside, and an excellent meal had already been prepared. Sitting on the floor, they ate well. Nyunt refused to leave Tessa's side throughout and, when they'd finished eating, she nudged even closer. Tessa responded by lifting her on to her lap.

"As you probably realised," said Htet, laughing and gesturing towards the empty food dishes, "we were expected. My cousin told them. He's also had Tachileik checked and it looks OK. So far, the military response has been surprisingly muted. It was expected Soe Gyi's death would result in immediate reprisals, but nothing has happened. Perhaps people on both sides wanted him removed. Nevertheless, his supporters will still want revenge. It won't be easy."

"I'm sure it won't," replied Tessa. "However, the sooner we're at Tachileik, the less time they'll have had to prepare. Furthermore, the longer we stay here, the more we risk endangering your family."

"In that case," replied Htet, "I suggest we get moving; maybe we can still get you over today. The border is open from six in the morning for twelve hours. The best time will be just before the evening rush of people with day passes returning home."

Carrying Nyunt, they all went out. Tessa laughed on seeing the car, now completely hidden under a camouflage of leafy branches.

"That's where we're going," said Htet, pointing south to the forbiddingly high, tree covered hills. "When we get close, we'll swap cars. If all goes well, I'll return later for this one."

"Let's do it."

Tessa turned to her hosts.

"*Kyay zu tin bar de*," she said, bowing politely.

They bowed back and smiled at her. Then she looked at Nyunt and kissed her on the forehead.

"*Thwa dau me*, little one," she said. "I have to go now. But may you grow up strong and healthy to enjoy a free Burma."

Nyunt smiled and carefully gave her a hug. Tessa put her down reluctantly and got in the car with Htet.

The narrow track soon deteriorated from bad to appalling, but Htet seemed totally relaxed. Not a word was spoken as he pushed on relentlessly. At 4 p.m. they crossed a wide exposed ridge and entered a dense wood. He stopped the car and they both lowered their windows to listen. All was quiet.

"This seems a bit too easy," remarked Tessa.

"Maybe luck is with us. We'll find out soon enough."

Leaving the car, they scrambled down a steep path; stopping on a small crag where they had an excellent view of the Burmese side of the Tachileik border post.

"The pagoda on the hill over there is in Thailand," said Htet, pointing to a white octagonal tower with a Thai-style roof.

"That doesn't look so far," replied Tessa wistfully.

Htet smiled and studied the activity on the border crossing.

"It still looks OK, but it's difficult to be sure," he observed pensively. "The alternative now would be to backtrack round Tachileik and go north along the Rauk river. That would take at least a day, possibly two if the going gets complicated. Then you'd have to swim across the river at night, near where it flows into the Mekong."

"I'd prefer to avoid water if I can. Let's try here. Nice driving by the way."

"You're welcome," he replied, grinning. "So, at the bottom of the hill, there's another car waiting for us. It's very old and probably won't be able to travel far, but it has one redeeming feature. It's packed full of explosives."

"You do like your exploding cars, don't you?"

"Yes, but I've never had to set one off, so far."

"Let's hope we don't ruin your record. Bombs hurt innocent people."

"True. But once we have the other car, we'll signal a truck of ours to drive towards Kengtung. It will block anyone following us to the border. The crossing is the bridge, but as you see, it's a long way down to the Mae Sai river."

Tessa studied the crossing. The road came round the hill beneath them, broadening out near the check-point to form two parking areas, one on either side. The left rank of parking spaces finished near a large cream-rendered concrete building. This seemed to be the main immigration and customs office. People were visiting it before crossing the bridge. The parking spaces on the right ended by a smaller building, slightly closer to the crossing; a Burmese Military flag was fluttering listlessly outside. A short distance away stood a rickety blue arch; constructed from second-hand scaffolding, it spanned the entrance to the bridge. Across the top was a large sign with Burma written on it in English and Burmese, and a yellow outline of the country. Underneath, barring access to the bridge, was a manual counterbalanced barrier. A couple of armed guards stood nearby, smoking.

"There are big metal gates on the Thai side of the bridge," continued Htet. "Any trouble and the authorities close them straight away. The gates are high, solid and on rollers. There are not many things which move quickly in Southeast Asia, but I'm afraid those gates do. They're about five foot high. Once on the bridge, it's forward to Thailand or..."

Tessa had never been fond of jumping, but anything was preferable to braving the water.

"Oh, great."

"They might stay open," said Htet encouragingly. "But the guards here know that one bullet is enough to get them closed. If all goes well, you'll only see the inside of the larger office. They'll process your papers, and then you can cross the bridge. The building with the flag is where the Major in charge hangs out. There's a small ante-room, but basically the whole hut is his office. That's where the problem cases are taken. The crossing's camera systems are all controlled from there too. I'll park the car as close as possible to his office, just in case."

"OK. Let's wait until there are fewer bystanders."

"No need," said Htet. "As soon as we give the signal, they'll be replaced by our own people, and they know what to do if it gets difficult."

"In that case, Htet, I just need to thank you for all your help. Hopefully, we'll both get out of this alive and enjoy another cup of tea in Kalaw one day. But if not, I would never have got this far if it weren't for you."

"We make a good team. And, regardless of whether we live or die, I personally am delighted that you have been successful where others were not."

"You mean someone else has tried to eliminate Chalmers?" she asked.

"Not Chalmers, Soe Gyi. Didn't our friend in London tell you?"

"No, funnily enough he didn't! Anyway, I'll leave my books and the knife you gave me. They're all yours if you manage to get back. Also, here's my torch. It's a good one, with a bright blue neon light." Then she took off her belt and undid the zip on the inside. "And here's two thousand dollars, it might come in handy. Use it for Nyunt. I'll give you a couple of hundred of it down there as though I'm paying you off."

Htet smiled.

"Thank you. She liked you too. She doesn't normally take to strangers. Soe Gyi killed her mother; so you can understand why I am not grieving over his passing."

Tessa didn't know what to say to that.

"I'm so sorry," she said finally. "But Nyunt is delightful, you should be very proud. Whatever happens to me, you make sure you get back to her. And Htet, if either of you ever need my help, I will do what I can."

"Thank you, I'll remember that. I know you mean it."

They shook hands and started walking down the forested hill. After a while, through a gap in the trees, Tessa got a good view of the bridge leading to the Thai border. It was flat and straight, but much longer than she'd have preferred. Eventually they found Htet's men with the booby-trapped car. He took the keys, together with a small green box which looked as though it contained betel-nut mixture.

"Remote control," said Htet, nodding to his colleagues. "You just need to press the red nut on the top."

Tessa smiled and got into the car as a large truck set off towards Kengtung. Htet drove down a steep embankment and turned right on to the main road...

Fifteen minutes later they arrived at the check-point. Htet parked his car in a space next to the Major's hut, which one of his men had just vacated. They got out and Tessa put on her rucksack. She made a big show of paying and thanking him as they walked over to the main office. She went in while he waited outside.

Barely two minutes later, she came out with a soldier on either side; the one on her left was carrying her rucksack. She motioned with her eyes for Htet to leave. But he didn't; he joined the group, protesting she was simply a nice British tourist who shouldn't be treated this way. As a result, all four of them passed through the ante-room and entered the Major's peppermint-green painted office.

"What on earth is this all about?" exclaimed Tessa, glaring at the Major sitting behind the large mahogany desk. He seemed slightly overweight, which confirmed for Tessa that the higher the Burmese military rank, the more corrupt and better fed they were.

The Major looked at her with an expression of intense disdain.

"You tell me," he replied. "I've been ordered to hold any red-haired Caucasian women attempting to leave the country."

"My hair's black, not red!" protested Tessa.

"Yes, but you are Caucasian, so you'll do." One of the soldiers handed Tessa's passport to the Major and told him that Htet had been her driver. Another soldier came in and stood with his back to the door. The Major looked at Htet.

"Shut up and sit over there, if you're determined to be involved."

Htet put his hands together, bowed, and sat down obsequiously to the right of the door. Near him was a shelf with all the surveillance equipment. Standing in front of the Major's desk, Tessa had a soldier on either side of her. The Major paged through her passport.

"You arrived in Rangoon by plane, so why leave from Tachileik?" he asked.

"I spent some time in Pagan, then I went to Kakku. From there it seemed more sensible to come here, rather than go back to Rangoon."

"Have you pictures?"

"Of course, lots," replied Tessa, pleased she had copied some of her older photographs on to a memory card before she left London. "Would you like to see them?"

"Later," replied the Major dismissively. "Did you go to Kalaw?"

"We spent a night on Inle Lake. But that's not the same, is it?" She looked back at Htet, as if for confirmation. He nodded in agreement, fiddling with the betel-nut tin. Meanwhile, she had taken the opportunity to check the soldier behind her. The Major took out a cigarette and lit it. On his desk was a heavy round glass ashtray, stacked high with cigarette ends.

"Oh, dear, your ashtray is full," said Tessa, leaning over the desk and picking it up. "Let me empty it for you."

She immediately turned it over, depositing the contents on top of his desk. The Major looked up at her incensed. But he didn't have time to say anything. Using the ashtray as a bludgeon, Tessa hit him hard on the forehead. There was an abrupt *crack* and he crumpled towards the desk. But she wasn't watching. She had already spun round to her right so she could hit the soldier there, also on the forehead. *Crack!* The soldier in front of the door went for his gun, but Htet grabbed his hand. Tessa continued turning and hit the other soldier on the back of his head. With another *crack*, he started collapsing, still holding her rucksack. Then Tessa threw the ashtray like a discus at the third soldier. It hit him on the head. As he fell, the ashtray bounced back. She caught it, cleaned her fingerprints off with her tee-shirt, and returned it to the Major's desk. Htet muffled the sound of the soldiers falling by laughing loudly as though sharing in a joke. Then he retrieved his betel-nut tin and looked at Tessa.

"You move very quickly, don't you?"

"Well, let's hope my speed isn't further tested today, but it's definitely time I left Burma. Can you fix my passport?"

"Of course," said Htet, quickly picking up the correct stamp and finding a letter signed by the Major to help him forge the signature. Tessa meanwhile removed the cassettes from the security video recorders.

"OK," she said. "Let's go. With a bit of luck, if we can dispose of these, they won't have any pictures of us."

"Let me take them," said Htet. "I'll put them in the car for safe keeping."

"Ah, yes, that should do the trick," replied Tessa, chuckling. "Now, if I turn to face you and nod, it means I'm planting two stun grenades. They have three- and five-second fuses."

"You never mentioned those before."

"Well, we were going to share the services of your car, weren't we?"

"This should be interesting," mused Htet.

They went outside, laughing jovially and appearing to say a cheery goodbye to the occupants of the hut. Htet closed the door and he and Tessa shook hands again as though saying their final farewells. Then, as she walked towards the rickety blue arch, he went back to his car to unload the cassettes.

Tessa stopped at the barrier. The two soldiers checked her passport, waving her through as soon as they saw the Major's signature. She started walking across the bridge, as quickly as she felt was advisable without attracting attention.

However, she hadn't gone far before shouting broke out behind her.

She turned to see that one of the soldiers from the barrier had gone to the hut, and raised the alarm. She found Htet, and for a moment their eyes met. She nodded and spun round, pressing two buttons at the base of her rucksack frame. As she sprinted towards the Thai border, she heard the metallic clunk of the first grenade hitting the ground behind her. A moment later there was a deafening blast as Htet detonated the car bomb. Tessa carried on running. Shortly afterwards she heard the second grenade land. She was halfway over the bridge when a gun-shot rang out from behind her. As it clanged into the gates a long way ahead, she started to weave.

Tessa focused on the gates. To her dismay she realised they were already moving, and remarkably quickly too. They would be closed well before she reached them. As debris started to fall, more shots sent plumes of dust up around her. Then with an incredibly loud bang, the first of her stun grenades exploded and the shooting stopped. With her ears ringing, she continued sprinting for the gates. As they clanked shut, the second grenade went off. They were designed to disorientate rather than cause material damage, and seemed to be having the desired effect.

The gates were certainly not an easy jump. Tessa decided the only way she could get over would be with a Fosbury Flop. But five foot was about her limit on a good day, and these gates looked higher. Sporadic shooting began again, but by now she was rapidly closing on the gates. From somewhere she found an extra burst of speed and ran the last few yards in an arc. As she heard clangs of more bullets hitting the gates, she jumped for her life and rolled on to her back.

A moment later she was positively ecstatic as her head cleared the gates. She quickly flicked up her legs to get them over too. But then her rucksack clipped the barbed wire on top and she abruptly spun over the gate, falling vertically down on the Thai side. She landed heavily, rolling and slithering down a short stony ramp, eventually coming to a halt in a cloud of dust. She gathered her senses, muttering expletives in rebuke for her rough landing, stood up and dusted herself off.

She was standing near a small wooden sentry box from which a Thai military officer was studying her. He seemed to be totally unmoved by her unconventional arrival. She put her hands together and bowed.

"Welcome to Thailand," acknowledged the man, nodding. "Passport, please."

Tessa smiled, and reached into her rucksack and gave her passport to the official. He glanced at the column of acrid black smoke rising from the Burmese side of the border.

"And what do you intend to do in Thailand?"

"Have a holiday," she replied. "Shall I complete an Immigration form?"

He nodded.

"And where will you stay?"

"The Oriental, Bangkok."

"Enjoy your vacation, *Dr Wood*," he said, emphasising her name and gesturing behind her.

She followed his gaze and saw a sun-tanned man leaning against a grey Range Rover. About six foot tall, he looked to be in his early-forties, and had short dark frizzy hair. She thought he had a military air about him. He smiled at her.

Tessa looked away and walked back to the border gate to find a place from which she could safely peer around it. The bridge was intact, albeit with a couple of large dust-free patches where her grenades had exploded. But the Burmese border post had been badly damaged by Htet's exploding car. It was absolute pandemonium, but as far as she could make out there were no dead bodies, which pleased her greatly. She could even see the Major, sitting up nursing his forehead some distance from the ruins of his hut. She only hoped Htet had got away. Then, as she scanned the hillside where she knew he would be climbing back to his car, she saw two distinctive blue flashes from the torch she had given him. She smiled and put her hands together, bowing her head in the classic Burmese style to wish him a respectful goodbye. A single blue flash answered her. She turned and walked back towards the Range Rover.

CHAPTER 14

"Good afternoon. Quite an entry," the driver greeted her. "Dr Wood, I presume?"

Tessa studied him suspiciously. Sinclair had warned her about the trustworthiness of some of the Special Forces at the British Embassy in Bangkok and hadn't said she'd be met.

"Who are you?" she asked coolly.

"My name's Curtis, here's my ID. I paid the border guard to tell me when you arrived; unnecessarily as it happens. Anyway, Kincaid sent me, he's Head of UKSF in Thailand, and my boss. Apparently someone in London wanted you met. We also have people at Mae Hong Song and Mae Sot. But I've got your diplomatic bag. I'm to take you to the embassy... You are Dr Wood, aren't you?"

Tessa returned his card.

"Yes. Diplomatic bag?"

"Indeed," replied Curtis, opening the SUV and taking out a black metal briefcase. "No one here knows what's inside. It's completely secure, X-ray proof and everything. I presume you know the code to open it? Otherwise, best not to try, it's probably booby-trapped."

She smiled and took the briefcase.

"Let's go and find some tea."

Curtis nodded and went as if to open the door for her.

"Don't worry, I'm fine," said Tessa with a smile. "But thanks anyway."

She preferred to keep him where she wanted him for the time being.

They drove into Mae Sai, eventually stopping by a Burmese tea house. Curtis had suggested stopping earlier, but they'd carried on until Tessa found one she liked the look of. They sat down at a small table outside; tea and snacks were quickly placed in front of them.

"Any idea what these are?" asked Curtis surveying the plate of brown triangles.

"Oh, they're very good. I think they're called *Be-Mok* – deep-fried rice-flour pastries filled with strands of coconut and honey."

He tried one and nodded approvingly. Tessa put the briefcase on the table and carefully entered the code Sinclair had given her. It flipped open and she found a handwritten note on top.

Welcome back, and well done! Here are some clean clothes, water, snacks, and a secure communicator. Please use it to call me as soon as you can, any time, 24/7 – it will open a direct line to me. Anything else will go via the Bangkok and London offices. As I said, don't trust <u>anyone</u>. As soon as we speak, I'll finalise the plans for your safe return to London.

Sinclair

P.S. Believe it or not, this is almond-flavoured rice paper. Enjoy!

She chuckled and ate the note. It proved surprisingly tasty. Curtis sat opposite her, not making any attempt to see what she was doing. She switched on the communicator, dialled and waited. She was surprised by how pleased she was to hear Sinclair's familiar voice.

"Hello," he greeted her warmly, "it's good to hear from you! You really are something, aren't you? Are you all right?"

"Pretty much," she replied, beaming. "I'm having to wear a scarf round my neck to hide some nasty bruises, but I'll live. I'm afraid there's not much left of the Tachileik border post."

"I know. I've just seen some satellite pictures. Not to worry, it needed decorating anyway. I'm just pleased you're out in one piece."

"Amen!" continued Tessa. "Your contact was brilliant. He got away too."

"Excellent. Now, who's met you?"

"A man called Curtis," she replied, looking across the table and smiling.

"Excellent, I think he's OK. Has he said where he's taking you?"

"Straight to the embassy."

"Is he driving a grey Range Rover?"

"Yep."

"Good. It's armoured, although I doubt you'll need that," replied Sinclair. "Give him the impression you're playing along, but I think we can do better than the embassy."

"Fine. We'll be on the road for about twelve hours."

"I know ... hold on a second." She could hear papers being rustling in the background. "Tell Curtis you want to go via Chiang Rai and Phitsanulok. And try and get some sleep. I'll wake you in a couple of hours. All right?"

"Sounds good to me."

Tessa and Curtis finished their tea and set off. She dozed as he settled in for the long night drive. Eventually her phone rang.

"Hi. Everything OK?"

"Yes, we're making good progress."

"So I see from the car's GPS. In about twenty minutes, just north of Phitsanulok, you'll find a Siamovnt hotel on your left. A room's booked there for Dr Wood. You can have a shower, change and get something to eat. After that, I want you to take control of the vehicle. If Curtis is worried, I'll talk to him. If it goes really badly, I'm afraid you'll just have to leave him. Curtis is probably fine but I don't want to take any risks, and I don't want you going to the embassy. I want to get you out of Thailand as quickly and as quietly as I can. We don't want to give the Thais an opportunity to hand you back to Burma. After Phitsanulok, I want you to head instead for Ayutthaya. OK?"

"Perfectly," said Tessa, smiling at Curtis and wondering whether she had just jumped out of the frying pan into the fire.

"Good. The vehicle you're travelling in is equipped with two GPS transponders and a single communications system. I'm going to tell you how to disable the lot. The transponders are separate units, which should be located behind the dashboard on the driver's side and under the floor in the boot. If you can't find them, you'll have to persuade Curtis to. Once you've got them, put them in a waste bin or something. Hopefully, everyone will think you've stopped for the night. The communications are all handled through the unit in the centre of the dashboard. If you undo the knurled thumb screws on either side and pull it out, you'll be able to unplug all the cables. Finally, Curtis should have a spare set of keys. I suggest when you stop for dinner, you get them and his mobile phone. Oh, and if your hair isn't black, make it black, please. Still OK?"

"Absolutely."

As soon as Tessa saw the hotel she told Curtis to stop. At first he hesitated, but she insisted a room had been booked for her and that she wanted to get cleaned up. They both went in and Curtis waited patiently, cat-napping in the foyer. Meanwhile Tessa enjoyed a wonderfully refreshing hot shower and delighted in being able to change into some clean clothes.

She came down and Curtis stood up to greet her.

"Quite a transformation," he said. "I understand why you wanted to stop."

She smiled and led the way into the dining room. They ordered a vast amount of food and were about halfway through the meal when she turned to him.

"Oh, I'm sorry, I've left something in the car. May I borrow the keys, please?"

After confirming she didn't mind going on her own, he passed her his keys and returned his attention to dinner. Tessa went to the car and unlocked it. There were several lights in the car park and she had no difficulty following Sinclair's instructions. She unplugged the communications unit and looked for the transponders. But she could only find the one in the back. She put that in the glove-box and returned to dinner. As they were finishing, the volume on the communal television was increased.

General Soe Gyi, second-in-command of the Burmese Military Government has been assassinated in Kalaw. The unidentified female assassin also killed a British holidaymaker called Bill Chalmers. The assassin escaped to Thailand, destroying the Burmese border post at Tachileik...

Curtis looked at her with raised eyebrows.

"Fancy that," remarked Tessa. "Shall we go?"

He paid, only asking for his keys as they neared the car.

"Actually, Curtis, I'm afraid there's been a slight change of plan," said Tessa. "First, I would like you to tell me how many GPS transponders there are in this vehicle?"

He looked at her dumbfounded.

"Er … one."

"Bad answer. You'd better put four in my hand very quickly or we'll really have a problem."

"What! But I'm on your side. Why are you doing this?"

"I have my orders, and one of them is to instruct you to do precisely as I ask, and absolutely nothing else. Now, how would you like to play this?"

For a moment, Curtis considered taking her on, but wisely decided against it.

"I'll do as you ask," he said resignedly. "But there are only two transponders."

"Get them for me, please," ordered Tessa, "and give me your mobile phones and other keys."

He unenthusiastically passed her everything, and started rummaging in the car.

"That's strange," he said, after a while. "One of them's missing, but here's the other."

"Thank you," said Tessa, taking it from him, retrieving the first, and hiding both in a nearby waste bin.

She removed the remote battery from the key, and gave it back.

"OK," she continued, "let's go. You've still got a long drive in front of you. We're going via Ayutthaya now."

"Please get someone to square this up with Kincaid or I'll be for the high jump," said Curtis as he started the engine.

"No problem, I'll set that in motion now," she replied, and called Sinclair who promised to have a word with Kincaid after she had left Thailand. He told her the next stage was in hand and that he'd contact her again in a few hours...

The Range Rover was near Ayutthaya when Tessa's phone next rang.

"Good morning," said Sinclair. "It's all set, but don't say anything to Curtis until the last moment. The less he knows the better."

"OK."

"You should reach Don Muang airport about nine a.m., and I don't mean Suvarnabhumi. Have Curtis drop you at the VIP Centre. It's on the left off the approach road, before the terminal buildings. Now, before you get out, I'd like you to incapacitate Curtis so he doesn't contact the embassy for a while. It'll be better for him if he's out cold. Try not to hurt the poor chap too much, though. In the VIP Centre, a Japanese woman will meet you. She'll take you to a private room where you can change into a kimono. You do know how to wear one,

136

don't you?"

"Of course," replied Tessa, amused by the complexity of his plan.

"Good, well, keep the secure communicator, your own and Dr Wood's passports, but give everything else to the Japanese woman in the diplomatic case. She'll secure it and get it back to me. She'll also get Dr Wood on the ten a.m. flight to Tokyo. From there you will be catching the next flight to London. OK?"

"Oh yes, that sounds perfectly straightforward," replied Tessa sarcastically.

"Some people are never satisfied," said Sinclair laughing. "Good luck!"

As they neared Don Muang, Tessa turned to Curtis.

"Go in here, please. I want you to drop me at the VIP Centre."

"No way! Kincaid'll kill me," replied Curtis, clearly worried.

"No he won't. And if he even tries, I'll have a word with him myself. I'm sorry if this is difficult for you, but it's what you've got to do. Now, turn off."

A couple of minutes later the car stopped outside the VIP Centre, and Curtis switched the engine off.

"Thank you, Curtis. You've done very well. I promise London will clear all this with Kincaid."

He looked very uncomfortable.

"Now, I've got to go… Heavens, who's that?" she exclaimed, gesturing in front of the car. As Curtis looked round, she punched him hard on the jaw. She guided his unconscious body gently against the seat back, muttering, "Sorry Curtis," and tightened his seat belt to keep him upright. Then she got out and walked through the double doors into the VIP Centre.

"*Konichiwa*," said a smartly dressed Japanese woman, bowing. "Please come this way, we don't have much time."

Thirty minutes later, Tessa was dressed in a fine red silk kimono with a pinned hairpiece and white sandals. She had hidden her communicator behind her *obi* and taped Sinclair's knife to her right calf. It took quite a while to hide the bruises on her neck, but she eventually managed with several coatings of white Geisha face paint. Then she joined a group of three similarly dressed women. It turned out they were part of a famous Japanese pop-star's Geisha entourage.

Tessa found the situation quite comical, but followed in silence.

Once the plane had taken off, she was desperate to sleep, but had to settle for cat-napping as her Geisha colleagues were intent on nattering excitedly. The abrupt bump of the plane landing at Narita woke her. On reaching Immigration, she bowed and handed her passport to the clerk. He looked at it and nodded to a uniformed police officer standing nearby. The woman approached and took Tessa's passport.

"Dr Wood, please follow me," she ordered tersely.

Sinclair hadn't said anything about how she would be met, so she simply bowed and followed the woman in silence. Eventually they entered a large, brightly lit, sparsely furnished room. Her escort reversed out, bowed, and closed the door from the outside. In the office, seated behind a large table, was Chief Inspector Maeda flanked by two policemen. Hachiro stood opposite him in his full Samurai armour with both his swords. He smiled as Tessa sidled in, but noticed she had torn her kimono at the bottom. The atmosphere in the room felt cold and tense. Tessa turned to Maeda and bowed, but said nothing. He addressed her angrily.

"Nariko…" Tessa's eyes widened at his overt use of her Peacekeeper name, "…this is an official enquiry, and I must remind you that I am one of your Guardians. I have been led to believe that you have brought the name of Peacekeeper into disrepute. Is this true?"

"*Konichiwa*, Maeda-san. I thought you knew me better than to suggest such a thing. If you wish to find out what I have been doing, then I suggest you call our mutual friend in London," replied Tessa pithily.

"Do not be evasive. I have neither the time nor the patience. I listen to the news just like everyone else. However, I am obliged to interpret what I hear, in light of my official responsibilities."

Maeda paused and took a sip of the green tea in front of him. Meanwhile Tessa was starting to get angry, she didn't need this. She also sensed Hachiro felt uncomfortable. He started to say something, but Maeda raised his hand to stop him.

"News is circulating that a female Peacekeeper assassinated two people in a country which has not signed the Treaty. One was a high-ranking government official in…"

Tessa had had enough, and interrupted him.

"Maeda-san. When you say *government* are you by chance referring to the corrupt and oppressive Military Junta in Burma, the one notorious for its human rights abuses? If the elected party is not governing, how can someone be accused of assassinating a government official?"

Maeda banged his fist down on the table so vehemently his cup fell over, spilling the tea.

"Don't play games with me! As an independent Peacekeeper, it is not for you to express opinions as to the political correctness of any country's ruling organisation. I am also led to believe that the Burmese border post at Tachileik was almost completely destroyed by someone matching your description."

For a moment there was silence.

"Well, if it was only *almost completely destroyed*, Maeda-san, you can't seriously believe it was me, can you?"

Hachiro started laughing.

"Hachiro-san," yelled Maeda, "do I have to remind you of the gravity of this matter?"

Maeda pushed a picture across the table towards Tessa.

"This was taken by one of the surveillance cameras. It looks like you."

Tessa studied the poor-quality print. The woman shown did bear a passing resemblance to her, but that was all.

"I accept there is a similarity," she replied, "but in all honesty, it isn't me. Not only do I not possess a tee-shirt as garish as that, but my nose is nicer. That one's bigger and flatter."

Hachiro took the picture and examined it himself. Then he looked at her nose.

"She is right, Maeda-san. Her nose is much nicer."

Tessa couldn't resist smiling. The Inspector looked exasperated.

"Nariko, I have had enough of your frivolity! This will need to be investigated before you can be permitted to leave Japan. If your involvement is proven beyond reasonable doubt, your Peacekeeper licence will be revoked. Now, please, answer my next two questions completely and honestly. First, were you involved in the death of Bill Chalmers?"

Tessa looked Maeda straight in the eyes.

"Yes, Maeda-san," she admitted quietly, "I killed him."

He sighed.

"Did you also kill General Soe Gyi?"

"Yes. I killed him too."

"You must have known you had no Peacekeeper immunity for actions in Burma?"

"My Mission to stop the Calver Cats both justified and necessitated the elimination of Bill Chalmers. Unfortunately, General Soe Gyi attacked me and I had no alternative but to defend myself with deadly force."

"Did Sinclair ask you to do these things?"

Tessa looked at him in stunned amazement; now he had mentioned her UK Guardian by name.

"I have said all I am going to say."

"In that case, you leave me no choice."

Hachiro tensed up.

"Nariko, you have admitted breaching your Peacekeeper rights by killing two people within a country which has not signed the International Peacekeeper Treaty. There is only one penalty for such a heinous crime. You will be detained in Japan pending a formal hearing, after which you will be returned to Burma. I alone cannot rescind your Peacekeeper licence, but you should be prepared for this to happen in due course."

Tessa looked shocked, as did Hachiro.

"Maeda-san," he objected, "you cannot be serious? You know what Nariko…"

"Hachiro-san," continued Maeda, "please do not interfere. This is nothing to do with you. You are only here to escort Nariko to secure quarters."

Hachiro grunted in disgust and turned to Tessa.

"Nariko-san," he whispered, "do you swear you have done nothing dishonourable?"

"I assure you, I have only done my duty," replied Tessa, still watching Maeda, "and certainly nothing worse than we once did together. But do not risk your reputation to help me maintain mine."

Hachiro smiled and looked back at Maeda.

"If she says she's done nothing wrong, I believe her," he said. "Her word should be good enough for you too, Maeda-san."

Hachiro flexed his huge frame and in so doing moved his short sword into a position where she could easily draw it.

This prompted a whirl of activity. One of the policemen behind Maeda drew a stun gun, while the other went for his truncheon. In response, Tessa kicked back with her right foot. This catapulted Sinclair's knife up through the tear in the kimono and into her outstretched hand. She caught it by the point and threw it. The blade knocked the Taser out of the policeman's hand, cutting him as it did. The knife then pinned the stun gun to the concrete wall behind Maeda, effortlessly sinking in for several inches. Everyone looked on in surprise. Then Tessa reached down and drew Hachiro's short sword. As the second policeman hesitated, Hachiro stood motionless with a satisfied expression on his face.

"Stop it! All of you!" shouted Maeda. "Nariko, return the sword… Please."

"Maeda-san," she replied quietly. "You have spent the last few minutes quoting the rules at me. However, you made it clear my Peacekeeper licence is not revoked. That man of yours attacked me. His life is mine if I choose to take it."

Maeda turned to the policeman who was nursing his bleeding hand.

"You fool!" he shouted. "I told you both not to do anything unless I ordered it. She is right, her licence *is* valid and you *did* attack her! She has every right to kill you. Get out! Both of you. Leave me alone to try and convince Nariko not to claim your life. Because of your incompetence, I am obliged to deal with a very difficult situation. Go to the First Aid Centre. Now!"

The policemen left the room and Tessa re-sheathed Hachiro's sword. When the door had closed, Maeda looked at Tessa and smiled.

"Nice sword that," she said to Hachiro, grinning.

"Not as nice as your swords," he replied, confused by the way the atmosphere had changed. "What on earth are you doing travelling without them?"

"That is a long story, isn't it, Maeda-san?"

"Indeed, but it will have to wait for another time. For how long have you known?"

"I knew for sure when you mentioned Sinclair by name," she said.

"You would never normally have done that, so I presume this charade was all part of his plan?"

"Yes, he asked me to make it happen this way. I chose those two because I believe they are on the Calver Cats' payroll. The names Sinclair and Nariko will be reported as having been responsible for the elimination of Chalmers and Soe Gyi. It is a brave, if foolhardy strategy. But still no one knows what Nariko looks like, thanks to your Geisha disguise."

"Would somebody tell me what's going on?" interrupted Hachiro.

"I'm sorry, Hachiro-san," replied Maeda. "But you don't really think I suspected Nariko of doing something bad, do you? Dangerous, yes; but bad, never. I'll fill you in on the details later. Now, we must move quickly, as I still want to get her on the London flight."

Maeda stood up and walked over to where Tessa's knife had stuck in the wall. With some difficulty, he pulled it out and slid the Taser gun off. He looked at the knife, smiled and tossed it back to her. She scooped it out of the air and nonchalantly lifted up her right leg to return the weapon to its scabbard.

"Thank you for not hurting the constable too seriously, he could be useful later," continued Maeda. "I hate to think how much that knife cost, it's beautiful. I bet Sinclair wants it back."

"He did say something to that effect," replied Tessa, looking at the hole it had left in the wall. "But I have to admit, I'm growing rather fond of it."

"Absolutely right," interjected Hachiro, "to lose a knife is the least he deserves. Mind you, I did wonder about that tear in your kimono. So did you use the knife to kill Chalmers and Soe Gyi?"

"No," said Tessa. "I used a little-known technique called Harmonic Induced Cardiac Arrest. It's a bit tricky but very effective."

Hachiro shrieked with admiration.

"Amazing! I thought that was just a legend. Nariko-san, is there no limit to your skills?"

"Unfortunately, Hachiro-san, we both know our skills are strictly finite," she replied soberly. "All we can hope is that we die of natural causes before they are tested beyond their limits."

"Sorry, no more time," interrupted Maeda, "people will get suspicious. Now, Hachiro-san, I want you to collect the decoy for

Nariko from the room behind that door over there. She's already wearing the same kimono but you'll need to put a matching tear at the bottom. Escort her to Gate 42 and make sure she gets on the San Francisco flight … here's her paperwork. Be convincing. Anyone watching is to believe Nariko is going to America.

"Nariko-san, through the other door you will find a suitcase with everything you need to change back to normal. There's also a ticket and boarding pass for your flight. Whatever you do, don't take more than thirty minutes. Once you're ready, put everything you don't need in the suitcase and spin the combination lock. Then let yourself out through the other door in that room. You will find yourself already past Immigration. Go straight to Gate 12 and get on the JAL flight to London. It will be better if you just go on your own. Let me have your passports please, I will authorise your departure. If you are asked, simply say you have been visiting Tokyo for four days on business. OK?"

"Yes. Thank you, Maeda-san."

"No, again it is we who should thank you, although I must admit, this action was somewhat unorthodox. But we have no time for that now. Go and start preparing yourself. Hachiro-san, I will pretend to work here until you return. Then we will go back to Tokyo together."

Hachiro smiled at Tessa.

"One day we will have time, Hachiro-san. But for now, it is goodbye," she said.

"So be it. But when we do have time, perhaps you could wear a kimono again?"

She laughed and they bowed to each other. Then she went into the other room and started rummaging through the suitcase. As she was sorting out what she needed to return her hair to its natural blonde, Maeda came in with her passport.

"Good luck," he said. "I don't think you will have any more trouble getting home. Sinclair will meet you at Heathrow. *Sayonara*, Nariko-san."

They bowed to each other and the door clicked shut.

CHAPTER 15

Blonde again and dressed in a smart suit with a toning neck scarf, Tessa walked out into the bustling airport corridor. She felt elated as she merged inconspicuously into the crowd. She went to the departure gate and was soon settling into a First Class seat, whispering her thanks to Sinclair for providing her with a bed. Once they were airborne, the Japanese steward came over to her.

"Dr Pennington, you look as though you've had an exhausting trip," he ventured, in English.

"Yes, it has been rather hectic," she replied, in Japanese, "but very successful. However, I'm almost as hungry as I am tired. How quickly could you prepare me a plate of mixed sashimi, a large bowl of rice, a small jug of hot sake and a pot of green tea?"

"Ten minutes. I'll see to it myself," said the man, bowing and reversing away.

She had soon eaten and, for the first time in a long while, Tessa relaxed and fell fast asleep.

When the plane landed in London, Sinclair met her at the top of the jet-way.

"Good morning," he said cheerily, "how do you feel?"

"A bit tired, but very pleased to be back in the UK. It's always nice in the Far East, but maybe just a little too hot for me this time."

He smiled and they set off, barely pausing for the formalities at passport control. They were soon in the Special Forces taxi heading for London.

"How's your neck?" he asked.

"Sore," replied Tessa, unfurling the scarf.

"Ouch!" exclaimed Sinclair, peering in the mirror.

"That's what Nyunt said."

"Hah! Can she speak English now? Fantastic," replied Sinclair; continuing when he noticed Tessa's raised eyebrows. "I'll tell you how I met her later. Anyway, we'll stop off at the hospital first. I think the experts should check you over. Any other battle scares?"

"Er, yes," she replied with a coy smile. "I don't think it's too serious, but it's not in a place I can show you."

"Oh, right, I see. Sort of. We'll get that looked at too."

Sinclair made a telephone call.

"I'm afraid I'll still need a full report," he continued. "Any chance you could do it today?"

"Yes, I suppose so. If I've got to write one, then I might as well get it out of the way quickly. I presume it's not going to be circulated?"

"Heavens, no! But one day the truth will come out, so better to be prepared."

When they arrived at Kensington and Chelsea Hospital, Sinclair took Tessa to the secure top floor. A Dr Perkins examined her and X-rays were taken of her neck. Eventually, he decided she was not suffering from anything which a little time and rest wouldn't cure. She accepted the offer of a rigid neck collar since it removed some of the strain and concealed the bruising. She thought this would be especially helpful when she met David. She agreed with Sinclair that she would say she'd been involved in a minor automobile accident in America…

That evening, Sinclair visited her at home. He sat on one sofa, sipping green tea and paging through her report. She sat scrunched up on the other sofa in a long warm dressing gown, clutching her mug of tea in both hands. Every now and again, he would raise his eyebrows. After he had finished reading, he looked up and smiled.

"That's one hell of a report and one hell of an action. It had quite an effect on you, didn't it?"

"Yes. It wasn't pleasant watching them die like that."

"No, I'm sure it wasn't. So what did you say to him?"

"Who?"

"Chalmers. I suspect it's part of the emotional release, but in situations like that, one tends to say something."

"I told him to say goodbye to Penny, before he burnt in hell."

Sinclair smiled.

"Welcome to our select if sober club. I must confess, you succeeded where I failed. Some time ago, I tried to get Soe Gyi myself. Htet helped me, which is how I knew he would be good and how I met

Nyunt. It's also why I met Matsumoto. I stayed two weeks with him and tried to learn what you describe in vague terms as HICA. He did his best to teach me, and I did my best to learn, but I wasn't ready when I left for Burma. I got to Soe Gyi and hit him, but even the first punch wasn't right. Anyway, I picked up a bullet and this limp in reward for my failure. It was only because of Htet that I got out alive. He sends his regards, by the way. He gave you a glowing report too. I also cleared things with Kincaid and even had a quick word with Curtis. He says you've got one hell of a right jab. But he's fine.

"Anyway, the really good news is that the removal of Bill Chalmers seems to have made an even bigger dent in the senior management of the Calver Cats than we expected. The criminal airways are ablaze with rumours. Also, Soe Gyi's death appears to have unsettled the Burmese Military Junta. They complained to China, who simply said it was nothing to do with them."

He drank some tea, and continued.

"As you no doubt gathered from your meeting with Maeda, my name has been sent loud and clear to the Calver Cats as the instigator of their recent losses. I am hoping it will make them come after me, again. We'll be waiting this time, and maybe we can end it there and then. But the name Nariko has been sent equally loudly. You continuing to use the name Yoshino will probably buy you a little more time, but it won't be long before Beauchamp realises that you, Yoshino and Nariko, are all the same person. However, now it's Beauchamp, Ryuu Fujiwara and this Japanese woman against you, me and Jones. Even-stevens!"

Tessa smiled, and he left ten minutes later. Only then did she permit herself to make the call she'd been putting off until after her report had been cleared. David was almost speechless with joy to hear from her, and they arranged to meet as soon as he returned from a business trip to Switzerland.

In Cambodia, Beauchamp had just answered the phone.

"So, what's the latest?"

"Not good," replied Ryuu. "Bill and Soe Gyi are definitely dead; a very professional job. A couple of our guys in Tokyo found out that Sinclair orchestrated it out of London, but Nariko was the assassin.

We cornered her in Narita, but she got away. We really need to stop that bitch. Don't you think we should focus on her instead?"

"No, I bloody well do not!" interrupted Beauchamp angrily. "Leiko's planned this well, and we're too far advanced to stop now. Anyway, if we're lucky we might get her too as I'm beginning to suspect our contact is playing for time. Just sort things as best you can, and come back here."

Tessa happily returned to focussing on her life with David. Frequent applications of Matsumoto's healing mosses helped her neck heal and she soon stopped wearing the collar. However, as preparations for the general election gathered momentum, so did the media frenzy concerning restraining Peacekeepers. It had become a major campaign issue...

One day, while Sinclair was working late, Timothy Lamper, Manager of UK Overt Security, burst into his office.

"We've got him," he exclaimed, clearly delighted to be delivering the news personally.

"Lamper," said Sinclair dismissively, not even bothering to look up, "what are you talking about?"

Everyone knew he had an extremely low opinion of Lamper. Sinclair had wanted to sack him after Beauchamp and Bill Chalmers had escaped from his custody en route to the Old Bailey. But Lamper's political contacts had protected him.

"Beauchamp Caille, I think we can get at him," continued Lamper, breathless with excitement.

Sinclair raised his head and studied the man standing in front of his desk. He saw a short, overweight, unhealthy-looking person, with a ruddy round face which was nearly always dotted with beads of perspiration. The remnants of his black hair were greased and combed over his head in an unconvincing attempt to hide his advancing baldness. He seemed the perfect example of a man failing dismally to appear dapper and in control. His ill-fitting garish designer suit didn't help. Within milliseconds Sinclair had confirmed that of all the people in the world who disgusted him, this man effortlessly maintained premier position. As though unenthusiastically conducting an orchestra, he gestured for Lamper to elaborate.

"We've intercepted a coded message from the Calver Cats. It seems they're running so short of senior people, Beauchamp himself will have to come to London to oversee the handover of a shipment of drugs."

"When?" asked Sinclair, rarely inclined to believe anything Lamper said.

"Saturday."

"OK, so we've got a few days. We'll discuss it tomorrow with Jones. My office, nine a.m. Bring everything, Lamper. Coded message, decoded message, how you got hold of it, the lot. I'll decide then what we're going to do."

"Oh … shall I tell Jones?" replied Lamper, deflated.

"No. Just make sure you leave nothing out, nothing whatsoever."

"Right. Well, good night then, sir."

The following morning Sinclair, Jones and Lamper discussed in great detail the intelligence which had been intercepted. Lamper left them just before lunch.

"So, what do you really think?" asked Sinclair when he'd gone.

"Well, at first sight it seems credible," replied Jones thoughtfully, looking again through Lamper's papers. "But I'm struggling to understand why Beauchamp would be so stupid as to allow a single message with all that information to be intercepted and so easily decoded. Normally such things are sent in at least two tranches and in complex codes. This could just be a thinly veiled attempt to get at you."

"I agree. I think it's all been too easy."

"It could also be a trap for Nariko," continued Jones, "or Yoshino; or all of us."

"Actually, I think that's what it really is," replied Sinclair. "Beauchamp's probably banking on us all going and hoping he'll be able to pick off at least one of his top targets, maybe more."

"The location sounds straightforward, until you remember how many gang members they lost there last year. Maybe we should just let Flood and his people handle it? He's perfectly capable."

"Yes, he is, but we can't selectively avoid events we think are too risky. They all are. We've got to go. As for Nariko, she'd never forgive us if we didn't take her."

"There is that," mused Jones. "We don't want to burn our boats with her again. It was difficult enough getting things back on an even keel after Kawasaki-ku."

"True," acknowledged Sinclair. "So, how about if we bring her along as Yoshino? We'd need to lend her a car, since it's rumoured Nariko drives a Bugatti."

"Yes, that would work," mused Jones. "She'd still be a target as Yoshino, but they won't realise they'd actually be confronting Nariko, and I'm sure she'd welcome an opportunity to face off Beauchamp. Mind you, Maeda says there are rumours circulating in Japan that the Fujiwara were killed by an Amakuni sword. So maybe she shouldn't take her Kimi sword. That should further reduce the likelihood of her being recognised as Nariko."

"Oh, she certainly won't like that. Anyway, let's run it by her and see what she says," said Sinclair, picking up his *cbc*…

Later that day the three of them met in his office. After some refreshments had arrived, Jones turned to Tessa.

"I trust you've recovered from the accident in the States?"

She smiled.

"Yes, thanks. Can't say I miss the neck collar. So, what's all this about?"

"Well," he continued, "we've got some news which we thought would interest you. First, believe it or not, someone has bumped off Bill Chalmers. He was in Burma and whoever it was got a leading chap from the Military Junta too, a General Soe Gyi. One hell of a brazen action, but no one seems to know who did it."

"Really?" she said, straight-faced.

"Yes. Fortunately it's only the Burmese who are publicly upset, and I don't suppose you'll lose any sleep over Calmers having met with a violent end. Anyway it now transpires that both he and Soe Gyi were linchpins of the Calver Cats' Southeast Asian operations. Their deaths, together with your *removal* of two of the Fujiwara, have left the Calver Cats bereft of senior people. So, Beauchamp is coming to London personally to oversee the handover of a shipment of drugs. We're still working on substantiating the source. But the deal is ostensibly going down on Saturday night, at the same industrial estate to the east of London as before."

Tessa's brow furrowed.

"How did you learn all this?"

"Lamper."

Tessa burst into laughter, making Sinclair smile too.

"Come on, guys," remonstrated Jones. "Just because we don't think much of him doesn't mean we should dismiss everything he brings to the table."

"It doesn't sound like a bad place to start," retorted Tessa. "Do you believe him?"

"Not entirely. But I don't think we can afford to ignore this. We just need to tread carefully."

"Very carefully," interjected Sinclair. "Beauchamp has lost another two key people; he's probably desperate to even the score."

"So, you'd like Nariko to come and keep an eye on you?" she asked with a playful glint in her eyes.

"No," interjected Sinclair. "We think it's too dangerous for Nariko. We could just be setting up another prime target for Beauchamp. But we thought Yoshino might like to come along, for the experience! Then, if an opportunity does present itself to get at Beauchamp, Nariko will be there to capitalise on it."

"Hmm. But Yoshino's only a beginner. Without a license she isn't allowed to carry a sword in the open."

"She'll have a Restricted Carrying Licence by Saturday. Potter is preparing the paperwork. That will mean Yoshino can bring a sword and draw it with permission from the action's commanding officer."

"You?"

Sinclair nodded.

"It still smells like a trap to me."

"I think so too. But I also think Beauchamp himself will come to spring it. We've just got to make sure we take the initiative."

"Fine, count me in."

"Don't be too hasty," continued Sinclair. "We thought you'd say that. But the devil is in the detail. First, we don't think you should go in the Bugatti. It's rumoured that Nariko drives one of those, and there aren't exactly many around. But we can easily get you an alternative armoured car. However, there are also rumours circulating that Nariko used an Amakuni sword to kill the Fujiwara. So we don't think you should take your best swords with you."

"Oh, hold on. I could live with not taking the Bugatti, but going without my proper swords! That would be asking for trouble."

"It is a risk, but Potter has some quite reasonable ones. You can take your pick."

"I'm not sure," said Tessa unenthusiastically.

"I understand. But we believe it's the best way. It will protect Nariko's identity, and you won't need to be involved at all unless Beauchamp shows. Flood, who you'll remember from your Proficiency Test, is handling the assault. He's highly competent and will be well supported. We'll all stay back from the main force, with our own support. However, it's your decision. We might just be going on a wild goose chase."

"Or walking into the mouth of a tiger. The more I think about it, the less I like it, especially Beauchamp using the same place as before." Tessa considered the options. "Hmm. I suppose you're right. We've all got to go, just in case…"

On Friday afternoon, she visited Potter in the Special Forces building. He was the smart, military-looking man, well on the way to being bald. He had adjudicated during her Samurai Proficiency Tests. Since then, mutual distrust had evolved into a relationship where they liked and respected each other. He gave Tessa the keys to an armoured Audi TT, and she chose the best sword he had. It was tolerably good, but nowhere near as good as her own swords. Furthermore, she would have to carry it in her prototype shoulder harness, as the others were specifically designed for her Amakuni and Amafuji swords.

"I sincerely hope I don't have to use this," she mumbled, studying the sword one more time.

"So do we all," acknowledged Potter. "But at least Yoshino has a licence now… Oh, and, er, Yoshino. Please be careful with the car, it's brand new."

"I'll try not to get any blood on it," she replied. "But I make no guarantees for the sword."

That evening, Tessa explained to David that she wanted to meet a friend of hers who had arrived unexpectedly from overseas. Somewhat disappointed, he cancelled their dinner reservation and planned to stay at home.

Late Saturday afternoon, she dressed for battle and unenthusiastically put her borrowed sword in her old single-sword case. She would only be allowed to wear it when she reached Rippleside Industrial Estate. Then she put on the tracker watch which Potter had given her a long time ago. Although only a prototype, she always wore it, even though she had rarely bothered to switch on its tracking mechanism. It seemed like her one concession to normality. She was to meet Sinclair and Jones at midnight on East Smithfield, half a mile from Tower Bridge.

She put on a long black leather coat to hide her combat clothes and her sword case, and walked to where she had parked the loan Audi TT. It was a nice car, but nevertheless reminded her she was going into action without all her usual equipment.

Just before midnight, she stopped behind a dark blue-grey BMW. Sinclair got out and climbed into her car.

"Heavens, couldn't Potter find you anything bigger?" he said, after finally managing to squeeze his not inconsiderable frame into the passenger seat.

"Apparently not," she replied with a smile.

"Right, well, here's a plan of the estate in case you don't remember it. This is where all the fun and games are due to go down. Flood will lead the offensive himself. You do remember him, don't you?" Tessa nodded. "Potter will arrive first in the Mobile Control Centre; it's an innocuous-looking container truck. He'll park here." He pointed on Tessa's map. "Jones and I will park nearby and stand here, close to the truck. You should park and stand here ... well out of the way behind us, but still with a good view of the action. Our backup is here, so they can get to us quickly if we need them. Here's your headset. OK?"

"Not really. So, what do you want me to do apart from stand around, feeling useless?"

"Well, keep out of the line of fire, and stay on the lookout for anything suspicious. We'll all be a long way from the drugs bust, but you and I are prime targets and Jones is in the frame. However, since Beauchamp had no guarantee that you would come, we must assume he's really after me and Nariko. We all have headsets, so we'll be in constant communication."

"Don't you think it would be better if I stood with you? One for all and all for one?"

"I don't think so. If I'm targeted, then it's better if you're not next to me. We don't want to make it too easy for him. If you stand where I suggested, you can watch our backs, and still be able to join us quickly if necessary."

"OK. But I've got a bad feeling about this."

"Me too."

"So, which of us gets to castrate Lamper if he's screwed up again?"

He looked at her and smiled wryly.

"Whoever gets to him first, assuming we're both still alive."

"That's not funny. We've been through too much together not to be in at the end."

"Indeed. Let's just hope we can control whatever goes down tonight. Follow us, and switch into full stealth mode when we do."

As they neared Rippleside Industrial Estate, Tessa saw their car blur and become a vague indistinct outline. She followed suit with hers.

CHAPTER 16

Just before 1 a.m., the two cars cruised unseen and unheard into the estate. They took up their respective positions. When Tessa saw the dark, now derelict, Rippleside Industrial Park, it brought back memories of her bloody baptism some twelve months earlier, increasing her sense of foreboding. The only noise was the familiar *whoosh-whoosh* of the wind turbines near the main road; which only served to make her even more uneasy. In the distance, she could see the warehouses which were about to be stormed. Moments later, there were a number of flashes and loud bangs from stun grenades, and Special Forces people swarmed into the buildings.

Standing beside her car, Tessa had a clear view of Sinclair and Jones in front of her. To their left, stood the large black truck from which Potter was handling all the communications and imaging equipment. She looked round to check for anything untoward. It appeared quiet, but despite the protection afforded by her car, she felt uncomfortable having her back to so many warehouses.

When she next looked at Sinclair and Jones she had to blink to check that her eyes weren't deceiving her. On their backs shone the tell-tale red dots from laser sights. She was just about to say something when her *cbc* vibrated. A shiver went down her spine as she put the phone to her ear.

"Hello, *Yoshino*," sneered a familiar voice. "Do anything foolish and your friends die. Place your headset on the ground and listen to me."

For a moment she couldn't decide what to do. But then she eased her headset off and carefully put it down. She turned slightly to ensure the camera on the truck could see her mouthing her words.

"Hello, Beauchamp. How nice to hear from you," she said sarcastically.

"Bullshit," her brother replied. "I thought we should have a chat. But I wanted to make sure I had your undivided attention first. Now, if you want your friends to live, then you need to do precisely as I say.

No nonsense, no funny games. Nod if you agree."

"First, promise me you won't hurt them. Then I'll do what you want."

"Typical. I'll take that as a yes. Get into your car and drive back to London. Leave your *cbc* on the ground by the car so they can't track you. Stop and switch out of stealth mode when you reach the A13. You'll be given a walkie-talkie, which will communicate only with me. Do it now and I'll give your friends a reprieve."

"I'm not coming unless you promise you won't hurt them."

"Well, if you're not in your car in five seconds I guarantee I will. Five, four…" Beauchamp was clearly enjoying the situation.

Tessa sighed and put her *cbc* next to the headset. She got into her car and drove silently away. When she last glimpsed Sinclair and Jones, they were engaged in earnest conversation, still with red dots on their backs.

While driving, she quickly removed her tracker watch and hid it inside her suit. She didn't want it to be seen when she received her walkie-talkie. As instructed, she stopped near the A13, and a particularly distasteful-looking man came over to her car. Tessa lowered the window.

"Any bugs?" he asked.

She cringed involuntarily at his foul smelling breath.

"No," she replied, no longer so sure. "I'm only here as a spectator."

He peered inside the car and held up a scanner. Then he grunted, peeled some tape off a small black box and pressed it onto the car roof. Tessa heard it sizzling as it set in position. He raised the scanner again, nodded and handed her a walkie-talkie.

"OK. Drive to Tower Bridge. Don't stop, you'll be told what to do."

She put the walkie-talkie on the passenger seat, closed the window and set off. Then she retrieved her watch and pressed the light-on knob, three times in quick succession, checking the second hand had started moving in one-second intervals. Satisfied the tracker had been activated, she put it back on. She hoped Potter would remember he had given it to her. Unusually, it frequency-hopped, so he might find it while Beauchamp probably wouldn't.

Hearing Tessa had collected the walkie-talkie, Beauchamp smiled and turned round.

"Leiko, your guys can shoot now. Maybe we'll get three out of four tonight, after all."

Meanwhile, Sinclair and Jones had just agreed they couldn't see the action properly now. So Sinclair moved to his left, while Jones went to the right. They immediately saw the red lights appear on the ground in front of them and heard a couple of dull *thuds* as plumes of dust rose from where the dots had been. Jones dived down and rolled away, while Sinclair sprinted behind the truck. A moment later the red dots were gone. After creeping along behind a low wall, Jones rejoined his boss.

"That was close," he said, peering cautiously towards where the shots had come from.

"Very," replied Sinclair. "Why didn't Yoshino warn us?"

They both looked back to where they had last seen Tessa.

"Oh, no!" exclaimed Sinclair. "Bloody Lamper … it *was* a trap! Beauchamp used us as bait to get her; we were the icing on the cake."

He yelled into his communicator.

"Potter! Where's Yoshino?"

"She's standing behind you… Oh, she's gone."

"We know that, and she wouldn't have left without good reason. Tell Flood to mop up here as quickly as he can, this is just a diversion. Wind back the cameras until we can see Yoshino leave."

A minute later the three of them were studying a television monitor. Suddenly they saw Tessa take out her *cbc*. Shortly afterwards she put her headset down. Then she had a brief conversation before leaving her phone and going back to her car.

"What do you think she said?" asked Sinclair.

"Hmm," said Potter, zooming in and playing it again. "I reckon it's *Hello, Beauchamp*, and she said it looking into the camera."

"I agree," said Sinclair. "Get this to the interpretation guys and see if they can make out the rest of what she says."

"OK."

"So, where's she gone? Has the car a tracking device?"

"Of course," replied Potter. "Damn! The signal's being jammed."

"Dear God, we've let her down," groaned Sinclair. "Scramble the 'copters, she can't have gone far."

Potter rattled off some orders and the previously calm atmosphere within the Control Centre quickly assumed a frenzied buzz.

"Come on, Jones, we might as well go to the edge of the estate and be ready to move as soon as someone finds her."

A couple of minutes later they stopped near the entrance to the industrial estate. Sinclair was fuming. The car-phone rang.

"I have something," exclaimed Potter. "When she got her OCL, I gave her a prototype tracking watch. It's rather unusual, and the clever thing's activated it. She's on the A13 heading back into London."

Immediately, Jones was thrown back in his seat as Sinclair put his foot down, hard. The BMW screeched onto the main road as he drove flat out after Tessa.

"Thanks, Potter," muttered Jones, "we're on our way."

"So I hear," he replied. "OK, she's approaching the Tower and turned left..."

When Tessa turned onto the approach to Tower Bridge, she found what looked like a police roadblock. But it wasn't long before she realised the men were members of the Calver Cats dressed as police officers. She stopped in front of a row of bollards and several pretend constables looked at her, laughed and cleared her way.

"Go on!" barked Beauchamp impatiently. "We don't have all night. Park by the first abutment and walk to the North Tower, on the right of the road. Go through the blue door and down the steps."

Tessa nudged the car forward and parked. She got out, put her sword on and, with the walkie-talkie in her hand, locked the car, armed its security systems and started walking. Thinking she had heard something, she stopped and held the walkie-talkie up to her ear.

"What did you say?"

"Duck!"

Tessa saw a bright flash from the southern side of the bridge and threw herself to the ground. A missile whistled past and a loud explosion erupted from behind; fragments of hot metal started landing around her. She looked over her shoulder.

"Oh dear. Sorry about the car, Potter," she muttered. "Let's hope the sword fares better.

"Was that really necessary, Beauchamp?" she continued indignantly into the walkie-talkie. "It was brand new!"

"Necessary? No! But it was damned good fun. Now, get on with it. The door's open. I'll meet you at the bottom of the stairs in the tunnel under the river."

Tessa climbed the stone steps to the door and went in. As she started down the cast-iron staircase, the door slammed shut. Then she heard it being locked and a shutter being closed over it…

"Explosion on the north side of Tower Bridge," reported Potter.

"Damn!" rasped Sinclair, as somehow he coaxed more speed from the car. "He doesn't need to hide any more. Blue lights, Gareth, get everyone there as quickly as possible…"

Tessa walked down the stairs as slowly as she dared. If she hadn't been so preoccupied, she would have liked to study the hydraulic engines which moved the north bascule of the bridge up and down. But eventually, the stone walls became markedly colder, and she knew she was below water level. At the bottom, she turned and entered a long brightly lit tunnel; a subterranean walkway with shiny white tiles on the walls, reminiscent of a Victorian public lavatory. Essentially horseshoe-shaped, it was not a particularly large tunnel, just wide enough for three tall people to walk abreast. Presumably it allowed engineers direct access to the base of the South Tower and the bridge's original engine room. Along the ceiling were some sputtering incandescent lights, not all of which were working. At both ends were thick iron doors which closed vertically. Her brother stood at the opposite end of the tunnel, grinning. He moved past the door and signalled she should do the same. He appeared to be on his own. She walked forward and stopped about six feet into the tunnel.

Suddenly she remembered some wise words of Matsumoto's.

"…discretion is the better part of valour; survive to win another day."

For the first time in years Tessa realised she was scared. This had all happened according to Beauchamp's plan. She had no backup, was without her own weapons, and didn't have an escape route. For all she knew, Sinclair and Jones were already dead. She might still be able to get away, but only if she left now. She had to decide quickly and the voice inside her head started screaming, *Run, you fool!*

"You took your time," said Beauchamp, smirking.

"Sorry, but it's really interesting here," Tessa replied calmly. "Anyway, how does it feel to be back in England?"

"Oh, these days I'm too busy having fun to notice what country I'm in. For example, when did you last blow up a car?"

Tessa shrugged.

"Well, it's nice to see you again," she continued, "but why did you bring me here?"

"So you can die too," he replied.

She started to get angry.

"You bastard! Have you...?"

The doors at both ends of the tunnel started moving down, making a loud grating noise.

"Good Lord," exclaimed Beauchamp sarcastically. "If we stay here, we'll both be trapped!"

Tessa was about to give in to the voice inside her head when she saw a flash of reflected light from the other end of the tunnel. From behind Beauchamp an arrow shot out of the darkness towards her. However, its trajectory was high and she knew it wouldn't hit her, though she doubted it had been aimed in error. She reached up to draw her sword so she could use it to deflect the arrow in flight. But her unfamiliar sword, in a harness not built for it, conspired to turn her usually lightning-fast draw into a laughably slow and sticky affair. Horrified by her own tardiness, she started reversing towards the door. Then the arrow struck an unlit ceiling light above her. It shattered, releasing a cloud of acrid fumes which completely engulfed her. The effects were immediate, and totally debilitating. She started choking, barely able to breathe. She collapsed to her knees with her eyes stinging and running with tears. Through the fumes she could just make out a Japanese woman carrying a composite bow, joining Beauchamp. They were both laughing at her.

"Good shot, darling. Now, the *coup de grâce* if you will!" said Beauchamp.

Tessa tried desperately to marshal her senses.

"Why?" she yelled plaintively.

But he didn't reply. Instead she heard the *twang* of another arrow being shot at her. Normally, she would have been able to catch it, but not now. She simply hoped she could prevent it from hitting a vital organ. She swept her hand round. It contacted the shaft and at the last moment altered the arrow's course. Instead of striking her just below the heart, the barbed tip made a deep gash in her left side. As it cut, Tessa knew it had been poisoned. She grasped her side, and rolled over in agony as the toxins coursed through her veins.

"Beauchamp, please!" she yelled in desperation.

"Sorry, *freak*, got to go. But don't worry, it'll all be over soon. The shaped charges above the tunnel will ensure the Thames puts a speedy end to your pathetic existence. Enjoy the bath. Goodbye and good riddance!"

Through glazed eyes, Tessa watched him turn and duck under the closing door at the far end of the tunnel.

Racked with pain, her eyes still streaming, Tessa summoned all her strength. She glanced back towards the door at her end of the tunnel. It closed with a loud metallic *clang*. She struggled to think.

"Shaped charges," she repeated slowly. "Jets of molten copper … bloody hell!"

She needed to get off the floor. Trembling from the exertion, she forced herself up. She re-sheathed her sword and looked for something to hold on to. There were some copper pipes clipped to the wall above her and, at her second attempt, she managed to grab one of them. Gasping to fill her lungs with fresh air, she hoisted her feet up and closed her eyes, clamping her arms over her ears. She didn't have long to wait.

There was an incredibly loud *bang* and a brilliant streak of light shot through the roof of the tunnel not far away. Moments later, streams of orange liquid darted across the tunnel floor burning anything in their path. Then another *bang* announced a second shaped charge. More molten metal spread across the floor. As the searing brightness faded, smoke and flames rose from the tarmac surface. But then water started flooding in and the smoke changed to steam as the temperature began to fall.

Tessa let go of the pipe and dropped on to all fours. The water was already a foot deep and she quickly splashed some on to her face. Her brain was working frustratingly slowly and her ears were ringing, but at least the pain was easing. She hadn't ingested much of the poison, but, together with the gas, it was enough to disorientate her. She staggered to her feet.

"Not good," she muttered. "But *don't panic* ... yet. Think."

She waded uncertainly to the door and tried moving it. It wouldn't budge. She knew it would be impossible to get out through the holes in the roof, so she would either have to find a pocket of air and tough it out or lever the door up...

When Sinclair and Jones arrived the traffic build-up was enormous. People were panicking and their BMW had difficulty approaching the bridge, even with its siren and blue lights.

Eventually, they stopped in front of the row of bollards, just in time to see the roadway bascules finish going up. They walked to the abutment and inspected the smouldering remains of the Audi TT.

"She wasn't in it," observed Sinclair tersely, continuing towards the bridge. "Beauchamp wouldn't have brought her all this way to kill her in a car."

"Potter," barked Sinclair. "Where did she go?"

"North Tower, right of the road, then I lost her signal. Is there a door?"

"Yes."

He went up the stairs and tried to move the shutter. Then he noticed a padlock.

Jones was looking over the side of the bridge when the two shaped charges ignited. Both created huge plumes of water; then mini-whirlpools appeared as water started spiralling downwards.

"There must be a tunnel joining the towers," yelled Jones. "She'll be down there."

Sinclair drew his pistol and fired at the padlock. It shattered and he raised the shutter. He fired again, and again, at the door lock. It grudgingly swung open. The sound of rushing water could be heard far below...

By now, Tessa had concluded that the tunnel sloped down from both ends. This meant any trapped air would exhaust past the door mechanisms; there would be no residual air pocket anywhere. She had to try and force the door up, but she didn't have much time; the cold water was already past her waist. She looked at the two copper pipes she'd held on to. They ran along the full length of the tunnel.

"Pressurised water pipes," she muttered, shivering, forcing herself to think logically. "Engine room's on the south side. One pipe for the bascule, maybe the other does the door. If the door is counterbalanced, like the bascules, all I need to do is to take the pressure off the closing mechanism. Just cut the pipes. Easy!"

She took out her sword and hit the top pipe. Her Kimi sword would have severed it with one stroke, but this blade simply left a groove.

"Oh, no," she moaned, hitting the pipe again and again.

Suddenly it fractured and water spurted out, but nothing else happened. She wasn't convinced she'd holed the right pipe so she started hacking at the other. The water had almost reached her armpits by now. Then the blade broke.

"Oh … dear!" she shouted, almost laughing at her own predicament. "Good one, Beauchamp. The water's a thoughtful touch!"

Using the remaining twelve inches of the sword, she feverishly hacked at the second pipe. Finally, it gave way and, as more water spurted out, the door behind her groaned. She waded back to it, took a deep breath, and knelt down. The door had opened an inch and she could feel a current of water under it. The stairwell would continue filling until level with the river. She would need to swim up a long way before she reached air. Holding the blade upright for rigidity, she forced it under the door and with all her strength tried to prise it up. To her immense surprise and joy, it moved a few inches; and stayed up when she let go. Lungs close to bursting, she went back up, took a deep breath and dived down again.

After two more dives, the gap under the door was more than six inches. However, given the shortness of her lever, the only way to force it further open would be from directly beneath it.

She returned to the surface to find the water had nearly reached the tunnel roof. This might be the last breath she would ever take; she'd have to make it count.

She plunged down, lay on her back and forced her arm under the door. She started squeezing under it, pushing the door up as she went. It was hard work, but she was soon halfway through. Then the door juddered and moved abruptly down. She heard several of her ribs crack as the door crushed her chest, forcing valuable air out of her lungs. Worst of all, she was stuck, she couldn't move in either direction. With resigned acceptance, she watched the air bubbles drift away. Soon, the temptation to breathe became unbearable. A buzzing noise grew louder and louder in her head and coloured shapes danced in front of her eyes. More of Matsumoto's teachings came back to her haunt her final moments.

"...do not be over confident ... no one is invincible. A Samurai rarely appreciates the gravity of a mistake until it is about to kill them."

So be it, she thought. Live by violence, die by violence. Serves me right…

Far above, Sinclair and Jones were running down the stairs. They stopped at the water's edge. Sinclair started stripping off.

"You're mad," shouted Jones. "We've no lights, and you don't know how far down she is. You'll never find her."

"I've got to try," yelled Sinclair. "She would."

He waded down the stairs as quickly as he could, diving as soon as he knew which way to go. The water was dark, murky and freezing cold, but he soon reached the bottom of the staircase. He found Tessa, motionless under the large iron door. He grabbed her arm and pulled. Without any air left inside her body, she came out easily. Her eyes were wide open and her white face glowed eerily. With one arm round her, he started back up.

He gasped loudly as he broke surface. Jones grabbed Tessa's body and dragged her on to a landing. He laid her flat as Sinclair joined him.

"She's not breathing," exclaimed Jones, slapping her face.

Sinclair knelt down, pinched her nose, moved her head back and breathed forcibly into her mouth. Then he half-pushed and half-punched her chest, hard, five times. Then he started all over again. Jones watched as Sinclair worked like one possessed to revive her.

Suddenly Tessa coughed, and spluttered some water out. Sinclair rolled her on to her side.

"Welcome back," he said softly.

Tessa concentrated on breathing and slowly her senses started to return.

"Ugh!" she groaned. "Anything to stop you hitting me."

Sinclair smiled.

"Just stay still, and breathe."

"Good idea," she gasped. "That was close. Thank you."

"Well, you saved my life at Rippleside a year ago, so now I only owe you for tonight and the other thing. What happened?"

She took a couple of deep breaths, but didn't move.

"Beauchamp was down there with some Japanese woman ... didn't see her clearly. Then I was gassed, shot with a poisoned arrow, blown up, crushed and drowned. But apart from that it's been fun. Oh, and I got Potter's car blown up and broke his stupid sword too."

Sinclair laughed.

"So, just another banal day at the office. Get an ambulance Jones, she'll be fine."

Sinclair helped her up and together they slowly climbed the stairs to street level. They moved away from the tower and Tessa sat on the curb, about halfway towards the abutment.

"Stay here, take it easy for a minute. Jones, any sign of Beauchamp?"

"Nope," he said, shaking his head. "I've got some people going to lower the south bascule. I've no idea why this one's come down."

Sinclair nodded as an ambulance stopped short of the smouldering wreckage of the Audi TT.

"Come on," he said to Tessa. "Your carriage awaits."

Jones and Sinclair hoisted her up, and, supporting her between them, moved towards the fast-approaching stretcher. Tessa's feet were barely working and she struggled to stay upright. As she was laid on the stretcher, a doctor started fussing over her. Before she knew it a drip had been inserted into her arm. Sinclair and Jones laughed as they watched her objecting.

Suddenly they were alerted by the noise of a powerful aero-engine starting up and a helicopter rose from behind the South Tower. Then there was a *bang*, and a streak of light shot down from inside the cabin towards Sinclair and Jones's BMW. It exploded in flames, and fragments of hot metal rained down on everyone. Several policemen were injured.

Tessa glanced back at Sinclair and Jones as they looked over her towards the remains of their car. Through the smoke, she saw two pencil-beams of red light shining from inside the helicopter. One targeted Sinclair, the other Jones.

"Move!" she yelled, jumping up and wrenching the drip from her arm as she lunged forward. Moments later, her left hand struck Sinclair in the chest, while her right hit Jones. Both men were forced violently backwards and to the side. But Tessa could see that while the red beam on Jones had lost its target, the one on Sinclair followed him. Above the din of the helicopter engine there were two cracks as rifles fired. One bullet missed Jones by a hair's breadth, sending up a plume of dust from the road. But with a horrible dull *thwack*, the second bullet hit Sinclair in the back. He groaned as he collapsed.

Tessa landed face down next to him, stunned by the impact. She gathered her senses and looked up to see the helicopter banking away. She yelled angrily after it.

"Fuck you, Beauchamp!"

As if in response, there was an ear-shattering *whoomph*. Tessa instinctively rolled on top of Sinclair to protect him. As she moved, she saw the stone walls of the North Tower ballooning outwards as though being inflated. The masonry cracked into myriad pieces, momentarily suspended in the air. But then, in unison, they all fell, and she flinched as pieces of rubble glanced off her.

As the dust cleared, Tessa lifted herself off Sinclair and knelt by his side. She looked at his wound, it was very nasty. He smiled up at her; they both knew he didn't have long to live. She pulled out a wad of bandages and spread some herbs and moss on it. Then she placed it over the wound to help ease the pain and stem the blood. He spoke to her in a weak voice.

"Finally got you on top of me, and there was nothing I could do!"

"Next time."

"I wish… You look terrible."

"You don't look so good yourself," she replied, forcing a smile.

"They'll be hell to pay," he whispered. "But, Nariko-san, promise me you'll bring justice, not vengeance, to Beauchamp? But while you're at it, get even with whoever did this to me."

"I swear," she said as a tear ran down her cheek.

"Don't grieve," he remonstrated. "This was bound to happen sooner or later."

"It's not exactly been a good night, has it?" she said, wiping the tear away.

"Definitely my worst ever. Have a good life; it's been a pleasure and an honour. Oh, and lighten up bit, eat more chocolate cake or something. I need to talk to Jones."

She shook her head, knelt down and kissed him on the forehead.

"*Sayonara*, Isamu-san. Go in peace."

Sinclair smiled.

"You remembered the name Matsumoto gave me? That's nice. *Sayonara*, Nariko-san."

"Jones," yelled Tessa, only to find he was standing next to her looking pale and drawn.

Tessa stood up. No longer energised by Sinclair's plight, she staggered as the pain flooded back to her. The doctor just managed to catch her when she collapsed. A moment later, she was back on the stretcher, drifting into unconsciousness. But she woke as they rolled it towards the ambulance.

"Not yet," she whispered, "I can't leave yet."

She forced herself up and saw Jones kneeling beside Sinclair who was talking urgently, but increasingly faintly. Occasionally Jones nodded. Then Sinclair fell silent and his body went limp. She watched Jones sigh and reach over to press down his boss's eyelids. Tears welled up in Tessa's eyes. Jones came over to the her.

"He's gone."

"I know," she said. "Please, phone Lee at SKS. Tell him what's happened and ask him to meet me at the hospital. And tell the doctors they're not allowed to do anything to me until I've spoken with Lee."

"OK. Just lie back, there's nothing more you can do here."

Tessa was distraught. Sinclair had been her rock, her tacit adviser as she navigated through these strange uncharted waters. Without his encouragement and support, she wasn't even sure she would be able to continue as a Peacekeeper. And besides that, she had always felt they had so much in common, both knowledge and experience, never discussed. Now, her vindictive brother had seen to it that they'd never even have the chance. Tessa lay back on the stretcher and wept...

CHAPTER 17

Tessa woke up in Kensington and Chelsea Hospital. Dr Perkins and a nurse were fussing over her. She was uncomfortably short of breath.

"Hello again," said Perkins. "You passed out. Anyway, you have a partially collapsed lung and some cracked ribs. I need your permission to operate."

"Cut me open? No way," exclaimed Tessa, wincing in pain as she tried to move. "I'd be out of commission for months. There must be another way?" She watched a nurse preparing a syringe. "No anaesthetics or..."

"It's only anti-tetanus," Perkins assured her.

Jones and Lee came in, and, standing well away from her, Perkins described her condition, occasionally pointing to some X-rays. Tessa felt irritated to be excluded, but eventually Lee came over to her.

"I bet that hurts."

"Oh, yes," she gasped, clutching her left side in pain. "But there must be an alternative to letting them cut me open. Phone Matsumoto, ask him what I should do. I need to be active again, quickly."

Lee nodded, spoke briefly to Jones and Perkins, and left. Then, to the doctor's surprise Tessa insisted the bandages were removed from her arrow wound. It was a nasty cut, but clean. She had her waist bag brought over and pushed a selection of herbs and mosses into the wound. Then she watched critically in a mirror as the nurse stitched it closed.

Perkins talked in animated and frustrated tones to Jones throughout, but he simply shrugged his shoulders. Shortly afterwards, Lee came back with a wry smile on his face.

"Matsumoto sends his regards, and says he too will grieve for Isamu. However, he hopes neither clumsiness nor over-confidence led you into this situation, and recommends you get him a camellia."

"What! A camellia sprig?" Tessa interrupted, eyes widening in horror.

Lee nodded.

"Oh, boy."

Tessa swallowed and painfully took as deep a breath as she could manage. Then she sat up, with considerable difficulty, and inspected the bandaging around her ribs. She looked at Perkins. In anticipation, he offered her the board with the consent form on it, but she smiled and shook her head.

"I'm checking out."

"What?" he exclaimed. "Don't be ridiculous, you're in no state to go anywhere."

"I'll be all right, I think. I'll sign whatever release forms you need; but I am going to leave. Jones, what's the time?"

"Four thirty in the morning."

"Excellent, the park's open." She looked at Lee. "Would you come with me, please?"

"Of course," he replied. "I could do with some exercise; besides, you will need help with part of your treatment."

Chaos ensued as Tessa dressed and Perkins pleaded with her to stay. But she was adamant, and was soon sitting in the back of a car as Jones drove her and Lee to South Kensington. Every bump was excruciating, but if she complained, Jones simply told her she had been mad to leave hospital. He dropped them off at her house and returned to his office.

Standing in her lounge, Tessa shook her head despondently, and stared at Lee.

"I was dead and Sinclair brought me back. Now he's dead in my place."

"He won't be holding you responsible and I'm sure he was pleased to have helped you. He knew he couldn't finish this, but wanted you to go on. So, you must focus on the future, not the past... Are you going like that?"

"No," she said. "I'll have to do this properly."

She went to her sword safe, opened it, and put on both swords.

"I always wore my swords at Matsumoto Castle, so I will now."

Lee nodded and soon they were jogging side by side up Queensgate.

Tessa struggled to keep up despite Lee's only moving at a snail's pace. Every step was agony to her. Her ribs ached terribly, and, with only a fraction of her lungs filling with air, she had difficulty breathing. At Manson Place, she stopped and clung to the bollard on the corner, close to fainting.

"Don't worry," she gasped, "I'm still alive. I'm sure it wouldn't hurt this much if I weren't."

In silence they continued up Queensgate, stopping frequently. Despite every sinew in her body begging her to stop, Tessa forced herself on. In the park, she staggered uncertainly up the incline to the floodlit Albert Memorial and they turned left into the path leading to the Physical Energy Statue. As they reached the Flower Walk, she stopped, groaned and grabbed the railings to support herself. She bent over and retched violently, again and again. Every time she convulsed, she wanted to cry out from pain; tears were streaming down her face and her heart was racing. Lee stood nearby, watching in silence. It seemed like an age, but finally she stopped retching. She stood up, panting, wiped her mouth and looked at him.

"Trust me, that was even more painful than it was disgusting," she moaned. Her face was ashen, shiny with perspiration and twisted with pain. "Shall we?"

"In a moment," he said, approaching her.

"Do you trust me?"

She nodded, wondering what was about to happen.

"Put your hands on my shoulders and hold on hard."

He smiled, pulled down the zip to her tunic and felt for a space between her ribs. Then, before she could react, he thrust a shiny metallic tube deep into her chest. But as she groaned and clenched her fingers, her chest heaved and she could hear air hissing from the tube. Her pain started to ease.

Lee pulled out the tube and stood back. Tessa moaned and sank to her knees. But when she breathed in, she found her lungs had cleared. Her ribs still hurt, but she felt much better. She got to her feet, gathered her strength and set off again, quickly overtaking Lee. Panting, with her hands on her hips, she waited for him to catch her up.

"Matsumoto's very good, isn't he?" she croaked.

"Oh yes, the best. He said it would either kill you or cure you. If the latter, he told me to say, *Strike one*."

Tessa smiled.

"Definitely. I think I'll be all right now. You can go back, if you like. I have another hour to do."

"Very well. I shall wait in your house."

She nodded, turned round and painfully plodded on towards the Serpentine.

When she did eventually return home, she found Lee sleeping on one of her sofas. She quietly put her swords away, grabbed the bandages the hospital had given her and went upstairs for a long shower. Feeling somewhat refreshed, she re-dressed her wounds, and went downstairs to make some tea for herself and Lee.

"How do you feel?" he asked as she came back to the lounge.

"As well as can be expected. I'll need some time to recover, but otherwise, physically, I think I'm doing pretty well. But no matter how you look at it, last night was a disaster. I've lost a friend and close ally, and I can hardly hide this from David. I wonder what the media will make of it all. Beauchamp will be delighted."

Lee sat up and gratefully sipped his tea.

"Going into battle is always dangerous. It would be unrealistic to expect only the bad people to be hurt."

"I know. It's just that Sinclair was … special," she said falteringly, her eyes watering.

Lee looked at her sympathetically.

"He was. But be thankful you did not die also. You are no doubt exhausted, get some sleep. The world will seem a better place once you have rested. I must go, the students will be arriving at SKS soon."

They said their farewells and Tessa switched on the television to watch the news.

Reports were remarkably circumspect concerning the events of the previous night. They simply said there had been two major confrontations between the Calver Cats and the Special Forces during which Tower Bridge had been damaged and a number of people injured, some fatally.

Shortly afterwards her phone rang.

"Morning, Tessa," said David cheerily. She could hear his television in the background. "How did your evening go?"

"Not so well."

"I'm sorry. You must tell me all about it over lunch. Have you seen the news? It seems the good guys and the bad guys were at it hammer and tong last night. Apparently several people are dead and Tower Bridge was blown up."

"Yes. David, there's something I need to tell you. Could you come over here, please?"

"What, now? We're meeting later."

"I'm not going to be able to make that. I'm … I'm a bit damaged."

He paused.

"You're hurt? How?"

"I'm OK. But, yes, I am hurt. Come over when you can and I'll tell you what happened."

"I'll be there in ten minutes," he said, putting the phone down.

When the doorbell rang, Tessa opened the door carefully so no one could see how she looked. David came in and turned round to face her as she closed the door.

"Good lord!" he exclaimed. "What on earth happened to you? You look dreadful."

"I know," she said. "Have you time for coffee?"

"I have now. Sit down, I'll make it for myself. Would you like some green tea?"

She nodded and gratefully went back to the sofa. A couple of minutes later David returned with mugs of steaming black coffee and green tea. He sat next to her and they both sipped their drinks.

"All that stuff you heard on the news really did happen, and more. I was there. You remember Sinclair, the Special Forces man who helped expose Beauchamp at the Guildhall? He'd heard that I'd taken up the sword and suggested I attend last night as a spectator. He thought it would be good experience as they were hoping to spring a trap for Beauchamp. He even got me permission to take a weapon, but I was under strict orders to stay well back and out of harm's way. As I was standing there, minding my own business, Beauchamp phoned me. He said he'd kill Sinclair if I didn't do as he said. So, I followed his instructions and ended up in a tunnel under Tower Bridge. Beauchamp was the one who really sprung a trap. Anyway, he tried to drown me, and would have succeeded if Sinclair hadn't rescued me. But as Beauchamp escaped in a helicopter, Sinclair was shot. He all but died in my arms. I ended up in hospital with cracked ribs, and cuts and bruises all over."

"I can see that. How were you injured?"

"Well, my ribs were cracked while I was squeezing under a heavy door to get out of the tunnel. The blasted thing closed on me. Sinclair dragged me out, but then he was shot. To cover his getaway, Beauchamp blew the stone cladding off Tower Bridge. I was peppered with masonry, trying to protect Sinclair. I went to hospital for X-rays and so on, and they told me to take it easy for a while."

"Oh, Tessa, you fool. You could have been killed."

"I know. What started out as a harmless training exercise turned into a near death experience for me, and Sinclair did die."

"Why didn't you tell me you were doing this?" continued David pointedly.

"I didn't want to worry you, and Sinclair ordered me not to mention it to anyone. I thought it would be like going to the cinema, but somehow Beauchamp knew I was there and, well … I'm sorry David, really I am. I wish I'd never gone. I was the catalyst that sparked off the whole catastrophe."

David's expression softened.

"Who knows? Good always triumphs in the end, but fate has a habit of throwing in nasty surprises along the way."

He put his arm round her and pulled her to him. Tessa burst into tears. Never before had she felt so vulnerable, and yet so protected.

"I watched Sinclair die," she sobbed, "it was awful. He was such a good man. He didn't deserve to die, not like that. Why does Beauchamp do these things? I wish he'd killed me instead."

"Don't be silly. Your death wouldn't be enough, he wants more than that. Much more. Oh dear, what a mess. I'm amazed the news was so restrained. Sinclair was well known and highly respected. I'm surprised his death hasn't been reported yet."

Through her tears, Tessa wondered how David knew that Sinclair was highly respected.

"You just wait," she moaned, "Tower Bridge's North Tower looks really weird without any stone on it."

This roused David's curiosity.

"Really?"

"Yes, the Victorian cast-iron structure is all exposed now. I don't know whether it's damaged, but it will take ages to put the cladding back."

David thought for a moment.

"Hmm, I'd have thought it would be rather interesting for people to see how it was built. It'll certainly increase its tourist value for a while. Perhaps you should visit the House of Commons next?"

Tessa chuckled painfully.

"That's better," he said encouragingly.

"I want to go to the funeral."

"We'll both go," agreed David quickly. "We can say we knew him from the Guildhall operation."

Tessa looked up at him and smiled.

"Thank you."

"You're welcome," David replied, kissing her on the forehead.

"Now, I don't suppose you slept last night, so you go and get some rest. I've got to go and see someone, but I'll come back as soon as I can. Forget lunch out; have something here, and I'll bring food back with me for tonight. You just concentrate on getting rid of all those bruises. But promise me one thing? You won't do anything like that again without giving me the opportunity to dissuade you first."

"I promise," she replied, crossing her fingers behind her back.

"Good, now go to bed. I'll be back as soon as I can."

Tessa went to bed and slept for most of the day. At 5 p.m. she showered and stiffly negotiated her way into a tracksuit. David returned and cooked dinner.

She remained distraught over Sinclair's death and began to worry about what might be reported in the news. None of her past experiences with the media had been good. Even the best of news appeared false when reported and, in this instance, even the truth seemed far from palatable.

The following morning, as she and David were having breakfast together, her worst fears were confirmed. The television report started with library pictures of Tower Bridge in all its pristine glory. Then it showed the intact South Tower and panned over to the heap of masonry at the base of the North Tower with its exposed ironwork.

Tessa swallowed.

"Yes, well, it certainly does look different," observed David. "But not too bad, just different."

A TV presenter stood gesturing towards the bridge.

"...this is what happens when inexperienced Peacekeeper trainees are permitted to attend Special Forces operations. Not only has the UK lost one of its greatest tourist attractions, but also several of its most experienced Special Forces team. The political fallout is unimaginable. According to one unofficial source, Major General Sinclair was one of those who died. After a distinguished military career in the Far East, he became Head of UK Special Forces, leading an international initiative against the Calver Cats. At present we are not permitted to divulge the name of the Peacekeeper trainee implicated in these events. However, it seems this disastrous outcome was largely due to her incompetence. Yes, we do know it was a woman and apparently her name may be released soon too. As a trainee, it is not clear that she is protected by the controversial anonymity laws. It is also being rumoured that Major General Sinclair died while rescuing her..."

Tessa looked wide-eyed at David.

"Ah," he said. "Look, you must appreciate this is a veritable gift to the media. They're hardly going to worry about making sure you come out smelling of roses."

"Oh!" groaned Tessa, head in hands. "If only Beauchamp had got me instead."

"Stop saying that," said David, raising his voice. "You should never wish for death, it might just come. No, if your conscience is clear, you will come out of this in good order. Nobody believes anything the media says. It's almost always the politicians manipulating the truth to suit themselves. I bet a bunch of them stayed up all night trying to work out how they could make maximum mileage out of this. Don't forget, there's an election in a few weeks."

"I don't wish for death really. I just wish someone would stop Beauchamp."

"I know," he continued, pensively. "You should lay low for a while. There'll be media scouts searching for people who might have been involved. They must know whoever was there got hurt. I'll get Andrew to come back after he's dropped me off. He can go shopping for you.

Meanwhile, I'll find out about Sinclair's funeral and get a couple of places reserved for us. I presume you still want to go?"

"Yes, of course."

"OK. Well, with me handling the invitations and you just being there as my partner, it should deflect attention... Don't worry, it will all blow over in a few days."

Tessa looked at him doubtfully.

"It will... The election will monopolise the headlines soon enough."

After he left, Tessa picked up her *cbc* and called Jones, securely.

"Hello," he answered. "How do you feel?"

"Much better, but I ache all over and I'm covered in bruises. But that's not why I called. Have you seen the news?"

"Yes, it's difficult to believe we were at the same event, isn't it?"

"Very. But they said the trainee might be named."

"I know, but I don't think they'll be allowed to."

"When is Sinclair's funeral?"

"A week on Tuesday. It's going to be a big affair at St. Paul's Cathedral. Look, I've seen you want to attend, but it's not a good idea. The media will be out in droves, and they'll be on the look-out."

"Yes, but I've got to go. I owe it to him. Hopefully, people will just see me as David's partner."

"It's risky. Don't forget, a lot of people witnessed the confrontation between you and Beauchamp at the Guildhall, and everyone knows he's after you. It won't take a genius to connect the two things."

"But I can't not go," she said, half pleading.

Jones reluctantly acquiesced.

"Fine. Then we'll just have to accept that it's an enormous risk. I'll try and get you some places well away from the reporters. Look, sorry, but I'm going to have to go. I'm taking over from Sinclair, Potter will be my right-hand man. I've got Sinclair's private files too."

"His private files?" she asked, pointedly.

"Yes. I've even read some of them, like your Burma report. Don't worry. I'd have done the same in his position, and I take my hat off to you for seeing it through. Anyway, I really must go. By the way, I'm Nariko's UK Guardian now too."

The phone clicked as the call ended.

"My commiserations," she muttered.

175

Tessa spent the next few days recovering; eating healthily, not exerting herself too much and frequently applying Matsumoto's medicinal herbs and mosses. She even started running again. But only when it was quiet, either at the dead of night or very early in the morning, and even then heavily disguised and without her swords.

On the day of Sinclair's funeral, David came to collect her in the Rolls. Both of them were dressed in black. Tessa's neighbour Helen had bought her a large hat with a thick veil to cover her face since despite her best efforts, some of her bruises refused to be concealed.

"Are you sure we should be doing this?" said David, as they neared St Paul's Cathedral. "The place will be swarming and the media will be watching like hawks."

"I know," replied Tessa dejectedly. "Now I understand how Sydney Carton felt in *A Tale of Two Cities*. But I couldn't face myself if I backed out."

"Well, I have to admit, I'd quite like to go. Sinclair was a good man and his being shot in the back with a rifle like that just was not right."

Tessa nodded, thinking to herself again that David seemed to know far more about Sinclair and his death than she would have expected. She'd been under the impression they'd only met once. Her deliberations were abruptly interrupted as the Rolls stopped outside the main entrance. Tessa looked in horror at the crowds of photographers.

"Oh, my!" she said adjusting her veil.

David looked at her and smiled.

"Don't worry. We'll get through this together."

A steward opened David's door and he walked round the car to open Tessa's. As she got out, he offered his arm. She looped hers through it and they started walking, serenaded by the clicks and flashes from numerous cameras.

While David looked sombre, calm and in control, Tessa's heart was in her mouth. She was petrified someone would connect her with Sinclair and started inwardly trembling. Inside the abbey, two bagpipers played a mournful dirge.

The service started a few minutes later and her eyes immediately filled with tears. The next hour was purgatory for her. Jones gave a stunning eulogy, which made her feel very proud. But eventually they had to walk the media gauntlet again.

David pressed the bleeper for Andrew to bring the car. Back in the open, they could see his Rolls queuing up behind several other limousines. They were some ten feet from the curb when they had to stop and wait for the people in front of them to pull away.

A voice suddenly shouted out above the others.

"Lord Kensington, how do you feel about Sinclair's death?"

David looked at the reporter with an expression of polite, but complete, contempt.

"*Major General* Sinclair was a good, brave and righteous man. He died doing his duty, to protect the likes of you and me. I have only respect for him."

"Dr Pennington … it is you, isn't it? What do you think?"

Tessa felt like replying with a torrent of abuse, but knew that would be foolish. She took a deep breath.

"By all accounts, Major General Sinclair was brutally murdered by nothing more than a cowardly fugitive from justice. He didn't deserve to die, and he doesn't deserve to have people like you making commercial mileage from his death."

Another reporter chipped in, a woman this time.

"So, what do you think should happen to this female trainee Peacekeeper?"

"That's not for me to say," retorted Tessa pointedly. "It should be left to those who know what really happened. People who don't know all the facts, aren't qualified to publish their opinions."

"That's why I thought it would be interesting to ask you," replied the woman quickly. "Anyway, Beauchamp Caille has sworn to kill you. Have you considered taking up the sword?"

"I hear many people have been tempted to do so," Tessa replied, wishing the Rolls was closer.

"Does that include you?"

"Please," she retorted, exasperated, "we're here to show our respects to a fine man who gave his life for us. Why can't you just leave everyone to reflect on that sad fact?"

"Will you show us your face, Dr Pennington?"

Suddenly angry, David rounded on the reporter.

"Don't be impertinent! This is not a photo opportunity. We will not be commenting further."

With that he yanked Tessa forward, forcing her to clench her teeth to prevent herself from crying out with the pain he had unwittingly caused her. They walked quickly round the barriers and got into the Rolls. Only when they were travelling back along the embankment did Tessa break the silence.

"A bit pointed that, wasn't it?"

"No more than I'd have expected. You were the only one there to have a go at and they obviously thought it worth a punt. Your answers were safe enough. But she was out of order, asking you to lift your veil."

"I fear it's going to get worse before it gets better."

"So be it. I think you were right, we had to attend. It would have been wrong to have been too scared to show our respect. We'll just have to tough it out…"

As time passed, Tessa healed well. However, media investigations concerning the Peacekeeper trainee continued doggedly. This prompted Tessa to prepare for a hasty departure from London, should it become necessary. She packed a small suitcase and put it in the Bugatti and, when Lee visited, she asked him to fill the car's tank in readiness. She also stopped locking her swords in the safe; instead she always kept them ready in their carrying case.

Eventually, David had to go to Orkney for a week. Tessa considered going with him, but decided it would be safer to stay put.

She looked at her watch; David had just left Inverness on the last leg of his flight to Kirkwall. She switched on the television to watch the news while finishing her sashimi dinner. She wanted to find out what was happening in Burma. Apparently, General Soe Gyi's death had sparked considerable unrest and a UNWP Under-secretary had been sent to Naypyidaw to investigate a possible return to democracy. Suddenly the programme was interrupted.

"Breaking news. We have just received a statement from the Calver Cats concerning the trainee Peacekeeper whose incompetence resulted in the damage to Tower Bridge and the death of Major General Sinclair. Apparently, she is called Yoshino. If this is confirmed, it won't be long before we know Yoshino's true identity. We're going over now to the

178

Queen Elizabeth Centre where we're hoping to talk to Timothy Lamper, Special Forces Manager of UK Overt Security..."

"That's creative, Beauchamp," observed Tessa, stopping eating and gritting her teeth in anticipation.

The picture changed to one of a reporter holding a microphone towards Lamper. He looked just as she remembered, short, overweight, inappropriately dressed and perspiring.

"Mr Lamper, we have just heard from the Calver Cats that the trainee Peacekeeper involved in the Tower Bridge debacle is called Yoshino. Is this true?'

Lamper looked bemused. Then a smile crept across his face. Tessa's eyes widened and she leaned forward in trepidation.

"Well, it's not for me to confirm her identity."

"You repugnant little bastard!" yelled Tessa.

"Thank you, Mr Lamper. So, do you think this Yoshino should have her sword licence rescinded?"

"Such decisions are not within my department's jurisdiction. Sorry, no more, I must go."

Tessa switched off the television and took a deep breath. Things would probably deteriorate quickly now...

She had just finished clearing up when her *cbc* rang; it was an encrypted call from Jones.

"Yoshino's cover is blown. Lamper is on his way. You have less than ten minutes. He must not find you at home."

"*Pennysview*," she rasped, and switched off the phone.

In three strides she reached the house alarm control panel. She entered the code to close all the external shutters, except over the garage door and heard the whirring of the motors as she bounded upstairs. She switched off her computer network, threw a few more items into a rucksack and rushed downstairs. She grabbed her sword case and went through the kitchen into the garage, arming the house alarm on her way. She put her rucksack and sword case in the passenger seat, got in herself and opened the garage door. Then she started the engine, selected partial stealth mode and, with the car looking and sounding like an Audi TT, reversed out of the garage. She pressed the remote control to shut the garage door and security shutter, waiting for ten nerve-racking seconds to confirm they had both closed. She then drove as quickly as she dared down the mews. As she passed under the white arch, she saw blue flashing lights approaching from Onslow Square. She turned into Cranley Place, towards Old Brompton Road.

"Well, Lamper," she murmured, "if you're any good at your job, the road'll be blocked."

She smiled as she turned into the main road. Everything looked perfectly normal and the traffic lights were green. With a burst of power, she was away...

A minute later several police cars were parked in Tessa's mews. Lamper got out and looked at her house.

"Oh, that's not good," he said, raising his radio to his mouth.

"Sir, it's Lamper. I'm outside her house... I don't think she's home."

"What gives you that impression?"

"Well, the place is shut up like Fort Knox. There are what appear to be armoured shutters over all the doors and windows, and apparently there's even one over the rear patio too."

"Bloody hell, Lamper! I told you to be quick. Why on earth did you have to appear on television!"

"Er... I could always have the guys break in, but it'd be messy."

"No, I doubt there's any point. We'll have to try something else."

"What?"

"Lamper, I don't know yet! I wasn't expecting to have to make a new plan for you quite so soon! Come back here while I think."

"Right, sir. On my way."

Jones put down the phone and smiled.

Meanwhile, Tessa had been following the quietest route out of London. It was dark by the time she reached Northolt and the A40, so she switched the car into full stealth mode and started accelerating. The engine noise disappeared and the car's infra-red cameras burst into life. She had a crystal-clear view in front and behind on the windscreen's head-up displays. She felt perfectly comfortable driving her Bugatti like this, but it did mean others couldn't see her car so she had to take extra care to avoid getting into a situation where someone might run into her. On the M40, she reached 140 m.p.h. and soon passed Oxford, Birmingham and then, as the night wore on, Preston and Lancaster. By the time she reached Edinburgh, the roads were deserted. She was confident of making the first ferry to Orkney, so she stopped near Aviemore to buy some fruit and more petrol. As she drove on, she prayed only Sinclair, Jones and David knew about *Pennysview*. David would have arrived at Burrody Castle a long time ago and would have tried to call her, but she'd switched her phone off to ensure it couldn't be tracked. The car's phone was secure and untraceable, but if she used it to call him, his line might be tapped. She considered phoning Jones and asking him to contact David but decided that would be too risky. She sighed and continued northwards.

Alone on the moors in pitch darkness, she stopped to eat and stretch her legs. She hid her sword case in its special compartment and generally organised things inside the car a little better. Satisfied and refreshed, she pushed on.

When she reached the harbour at Scrabster the *St Ola* had already started loading, but since the ship was going to be almost empty, she left the car in partial stealth mode. She bought a ferry ticket with cash at the quayside and, ten minutes later, was safely on board.

She whiled away the crossing huddled in a corner of the lounge with a mug of steaming hot black tea, planning her stay at *Pennysview*. Clearly she would have to use her moped to get around since the Bugatti was likely to attract attention, but that would mean she couldn't carry her swords.

As the ship docked in Stromness, she wondered whether there would be a reception committee. But she saw nothing suspicious. An hour later, she drove up the steep track to *Pennysview*. Heaving a sigh of relief, she parked the Bugatti in the garage and took out everything she needed. Then she watched the car move down to the underground level. She unlocked the cottage and raised the shutters; she hadn't done it remotely because she wanted to make sure no one else was there first. She hid her sword case upstairs, and made herself a cup of green tea. Although she had some food in the freezer, she would need more. She considered phoning Jones, but decided he would call her if he needed to.

Mid-morning, Tessa went to Burrody Castle on her moped. David was flabbergasted to see her. But she immediately felt better for being with him, even though she knew there was little he could do to protect her now.

"I was worried about you," he said as they embraced. "There was some rather unpleasant stuff on the television last night. Yoshino has been named as the trainee at Tower Bridge, so I thought you might want to talk."

"I did," she said smiling. "That's why I'm here. After all, out of sight, out of mind!"

"Quite. Well, it's a wonderful surprise, and I'm delighted. Look, I've got a busy afternoon ahead, but how about if we meet for dinner tonight? Shall I come over to your place?"

"Yes, why don't we go to St Margaret's Hope?" suggested Tessa. "No one will bat an eyelid seeing us together there."

"Super. I'll pick you up at six… By the way," he said, putting his arms round her and pulling her close, "I should have everything wound up by the end of today, so I'll be completely free tomorrow."

"Hmm, that sounds promising," she replied, kissing him for a long time…

He watched as she left the castle on her moped. As she disappeared from view he picked up his mobile phone, selected a number and pressed the call button.

"Ryuu? It's me, she's here. I told you she'd come… Yes, I'm sure it was a good idea not to have scouts about. She would have seen them… What car is she driving? I've no idea; Beauchamp blew up her TT. She probably flew here; she's riding her moped now. Anyway, we should be able to complete the transaction the day after tomorrow but I need to speak to Beauchamp first, personally. Yes, tomorrow morning would be fine. Ask him to ring me. No, that's non-negotiable. It's got to be him. I want to clarify our deal, one on one."

He finished the call, flopped down in an armchair and sighed. With his face twisted in anguish, he put his head in his hands and groaned.

David was in high spirits when he arrived at *Pennysview*. He had completed his business and made no secret of wanting to celebrate. They went to St. Margaret's Hope in his car, and ate well. Afterwards, they stood on the quayside admiring the moon's reflection on the ripples of Water Sound. It was a crisp clear night and the sky was filled with stars. Suddenly the silence was interrupted by the sound of dance music.

"What on earth is that?" asked Tessa.

"No idea. Shall we find out?"

Arm in arm, they walked up School Road to the recently refurbished Cromarty Hall. There, much to their surprise, they found a Rhumba dance session in progress. The teacher announced the last dance, and Tessa turned to David.

"Do you Rhumba?"

"Of course, my love. May I have the pleasure?"

"Yes, but let's dance first."

They were each delighted to find the other could dance an excellent sensuous slow Rhumba. As the music finished, David held her close. Tessa couldn't stop her eyes watering and tears started rolling down her cheeks.

"What's the matter, Princess?" he whispered.

"I'm fed up with the world, and where my life's going. But at this moment in time I'm so happy, I don't want it to end. I just want you to hold me like this, for ever."

He smiled and wiped away her tears.

"No matter what happens, I will always be holding you next to my heart… even when we're not together." He looked into her eyes and kissed her on the forehead. "Let's go home."

CHAPTER 18

In *Pennysview* the following morning, David went downstairs to make hot drinks. Tessa heard him talking on the phone. When he hadn't returned after twenty minutes, she decided to investigate and slipped on a skimpy negligee. She found him in the lounge, sitting in an armchair with a strangely pained expression on his face. He stood up when he saw her.

"What's the matter?" she asked.

"I've been trying to work out how best to handle this."

A cold shiver ran down Tessa's spine.

"Handle what?"

He reached into the pocket of her dressing gown and pulled out a pistol.

"Look, this is not what it seems but I know I only stand a chance of controlling you if you're unarmed and a good distance in front of me. So, just stay where you are, and let me explain. Do you have any concealed weapons?"

Tessa was dumbfounded. Sinclair had suspected the UK Special Forces had a mole, but to be betrayed by David was inconceivable to her. For a moment she thought she might be sick.

"Tessa! Have you any weapons?"

She slid the straps of her negligee off. It fell down, leaving her naked.

"As you see, no weapons. What would you like me to do for you now?"

"I'm sorry, but it's a long story and I'm not sure how much time we have. Things are moving more quickly than I'd intended. But, that," he continued, waving his gun at her, "is definitely not necessary. Please put your gown back on."

Tessa didn't move.

"I suppose this is why Beauchamp was never caught?" she hissed. "Have you just been using me all this time? How could I have been so naïve as to think we had something special?"

"Don't be silly, it's not like that at all. We do have something. A lot actually, maybe more than you realise. But we're out of time. The Calver Cats will be here soon."

"How could you?" she screamed, a single tear rolling down her cheek.

"No, please, listen! Don't worry, you won't get hurt, it's all arranged," he replied earnestly.

"Won't get hurt? Do you really believe Beauchamp wants to see me any other way than dead? Do you think you'll be of any use to him once he's got me? Get real! We're both as good as dead. Did last night mean nothing to you? Was it just another opportunity for you and Beauchamp to have some cheap laughs at my expense?"

"No! For goodness' sake, Tessa," he implored, visibly upset. "You don't understand. Please, let me explain."

His mobile phone rang and he glanced down, prompting Tessa to start bounding silently upstairs. When he saw who was phoning, he punched the air. She heard the beginning of their conversation.

"Hello, Beauchamp…"

In the bedroom, she punched some numbers into the alarm system and the security shutters started closing over the doors and windows. More numbers followed, and an encrypted *Urgent Assistance Required* message went to Jones. Furious, she flung open the wardrobe and grabbed her sword case. Not bothering to unlock it, and still naked, she started back down the stairs. She leapt on to the half-landing and used the newel post to spin her round towards the remaining stairs. David was standing in the hallway now with his mobile phone pressed to his ear.

"…you're welcome," he said, and ended the call. He smiled and returned the phone to his pocket. Only then did he become aware of Tessa, completely airborne, heading for him.

Holding the sword case by its straps, she launched it at David. It struck him in the chest and threw him against the wall. By the time he had bounced back, she had landed and swung the case round again. It swept his legs from under him and he performed a neat pirouette, landing on his back. She calmly stood the sword case on the floor and knelt on his wrist. She prised the pistol from his hand and raised her clenched fist over his chest.

He looked up at her and smiled.

"You're even more beautiful when you're angry."

She looked back at him in surprise.

"There's no magazine in this gun."

"Of course not, one of us might have got hurt. I was trying to explain…"

There were several *clunks* as the security shutters locked down. Tessa noticed some light coming from under the front door. It had been a windy night and presumably a pebble was preventing the shutter from closing.

"For goodness' sake," she exclaimed, "what's going on?"

"We're springing a trap for Beauchamp. It all started the day you decided to go back to Japan. Sinclair called me … we'd known each other since childhood; the Sinclairs are an old Orkney family. Anyway, he told me you had to go but didn't want to, and I told him I'd been diagnosed with terminal cancer and had, at best, a year to live. After you left, I checked into a Swiss clinic hoping, it would at least improve my quality of life for whatever time I had after you came back. That's where I got this scar which you correctly noted is not over my appendix.

"When I came back, Sinclair and I hatched a plan and I contacted Beauchamp, but he would never talk to me direct. I slowly worked my way through his network and eventually managed to agree a deal. Sinclair felt sure he could spring a trap and still rescue both of us. But it isn't important for me to be saved, only you. So, a few days ago, I suggested to Gareth Jones that the information about Yoshino be leaked. I was sure it would force you here. Then I demanded to speak with Beauchamp to confirm our deal. When I got up this morning, I still didn't have his satellite phone number. But he just called me, Tessa. You can find out where he is now! He only called because he's convinced we'll soon be dead and the phone destroyed. You see, he's double-crossing me. His people aren't coming tomorrow as we'd agreed, they're coming now. So you've got to make sure you get away with my phone. That's it really."

Tessa lowered her fist.

"So, where's Jones?"

"Well, I was about to phone him when someone floored me …

embarrassingly easily for an ex-SAS man too. Anyway, that's why I've put my family's Orkney holdings in trust for the Orcadians. I thought if the plan worked, Sinclair would get Beauchamp, and you'd be free to get on with the life you deserve. But it was always going to be without me."

"Why didn't you tell me?" moaned Tessa, finally remembering to take her knee off his wrist.

"We weren't sure it would come off."

Suddenly there was an explosion as a shell hit the lounge window, bowing the shutter inward and shattering the laminated glass. Tessa looked up at the surveillance displays under the stairs and saw a substantial truck with stabilisers down and a large gun on the back.

"Wow! They're not messing about," she exclaimed. "They've got a cannon!"

"Ah, but he doesn't know how strong this cottage is. It will take a lot to get through three feet of Orkney stone." David chuckled, "and I told him the land surrounding it was mined!"

Tessa laughed.

"Sinclair told me a lot about you," he confessed. "I'm so proud of you, Tessa. What's more, Beauchamp still thinks you're Yoshino. He has no idea you're Nariko too." He pulled the magazine for the pistol and his mobile telephone out of his pocket, and looked up at her. "Anyway, I really don't feel up to a fight just now. I think you'd better take it from here."

"Not without you," she said fiercely.

More shells started battering the house. The front wall seemed to buckle momentarily inwards with every impact, throwing small clouds of dust and plaster into the air.

She was just about to help David up when a loud *bang* announced the arrival of something different. The hall filled with dust and she saw a neat semi-circular hole had been punched near the bottom of the front door. David twitched momentarily, and the shutter finished closing with a noisy rattle and a clunk. It seemed the shot had moved the pebble.

"Oh, dear," she muttered, trying to work out how they could both escape. "This is getting serious."

She looked back at David and saw a pool of blood spreading from his side. As the armour-piercing dart had perforated the door it had disintegrated and a fragment ricocheted into him. He hadn't made any noise and bore a relaxed, accepting smile on his face. She knelt down beside him and stroked his forehead.

"Don't worry," he said weakly, "I wanted to go quickly anyway. But in answer to your earlier question, I think last night was probably the best night we've ever had together. I told you it would be a good way to go."

Tears started streaming down her face.

"David," she sobbed, "I only did this to be with you. I can't go on without you!"

"Of course you can, Princess. You must, someone's got to stop Beauchamp. Please don't cry, I can't bear to see you sad. Just don't let me die in vain... *Pennysview*, like me, is part of your past. You need to move on, so give it to the Burrody Castle Trust. I've already bought another beautiful place for you. My solicitor will send you all the papers. Enjoy it, Tessa, and think of me when you're there. Try to remember me fondly … I can't tell you how much I have enjoyed our time together. It has been wonderful, beyond my wildest dreams. I never thought there would be another life for me after Anne died, but you showed me the way."

"David," she wailed, "please, don't leave me."

"Hey, I'm dying a happy man. To have loved completely and utterly once in one's life is wonderful. To have done it twice is truly remarkable. But now it's time for me to be with Anne again."

There were more shell impacts and the air swirled thick with dust and the smell of spent explosive.

Tessa bent down and kissed him, stroking his hair.

"Say hello to her from me, and thank her for letting me borrow you."

As she raised herself, he smiled and stopped breathing.

Tessa shook her head in disbelief and gently closed his eyes. The cottage shuddered under the impact of more shells. Strong as it was, this was too much. She wasn't sure she could stand much more either. For nearly a minute, she was almost paralysed, unable to do anything but wish David would open his eyes again.

"Get a grip, girl," she ordered herself sharply. "Or die." For a moment she wondered which was preferable. "Don't be selfish," she continued, "if you die, so do the dreams and aspirations of many Peacekeepers."

She bent down and kissed David on the lips one last time. Then she stood up and looked round; for a moment the shell impacts had stopped.

"Beauchamp!" she yelled out at the top of her voice. "Damn you!"

She wanted to cry, she felt alone, angry and cheated. But then more shells arrived and thumped into the walls. *Pennysview* shuddered violently as if trying to shock Tessa her out of her misery. She took a deep breath and snapped back to reality.

She wiped her fingerprints off the magazine, slid it into the pistol and took the safety catch off. She chambered a bullet, pressed the gun into David's still-warm hand several times and let it fall by his side. She picked up his phone and rushed back upstairs. The bedroom was already strewn with debris. She grabbed her *cbc* and quickly put David's SIM card in it. As the data from his card copied into her *cbc's* memory, she put on a black tracksuit and trainers. A shell hit the shutter on one of the bedroom windows. The laminated glass shattered and fell in a large sheet on the floor. But she was oblivious to the wanton destruction around her, nonchalantly tying her shoe laces while the phone finished copying. She replaced David's SIM card, carefully removing her fingerprints, and then returned her own SIM card to the *cbc*. She switched it off so it wouldn't transmit a signal, slipped it into her rucksack, and went downstairs. There, she wiped her fingerprints off David's phone, and slid it back into his pocket.

Another armour-piercing dart hit punched a new hole through the front door shutter. It zoomed over Tessa and buried itself in the wall with a metallic *twang*. She smiled at David one last time, blew him a kiss, and grabbed her sword case. In the kitchen she put a couple of apples and a bottle of water in her rucksack. Then she pulled out the washing machine from under the work-surface to reveal a large drain inspection cover.

When *Pennysview* had been built, a substantial storm-drain had been needed to handle the water from the hill behind. However, although a twenty-five centimetre diameter pipe had been specified, the builder had purchased twenty-five inches by mistake and installed it without amending the plans. Tessa had only found out by accident, but now was very grateful to have an otherwise unknown two-foot diameter pipe running underground away from the cottage. It followed the access track down the hill, passed under the coast road at the bottom, and went on to Scapa Flow. With a bit of luck she should be able to slither down and come out through one of the larger manhole covers, or at the outlet near the water's edge. She only hoped she could get both herself and her sword case into the pipe. She slid the heavy cast iron cover under the neighbouring cupboard and peered into the dark, damp and unwelcoming, black hole.

"Well, dear," she muttered, "your life is going down the drain, so you might as well follow it."

She lowered her sword case until a gentle splosh announced it had landed in the chamber below. Then she climbed into the hole with her rucksack. She hauled the washing machine back into position and found she could still just reach the inspection cover to slide it back too. For a moment she wondered whether her Bugatti would be safe in the garage under David's Rolls. But the cold water she trod in quickly refocused her priorities.

"A torch would have been good," she grumbled, groping round.

She soon found that although the drain was large for its purpose, it was still quite small for what she had in mind. But she finally managed to manoeuvre her sword case into the pipe, and, with a strap from the rucksack looped round one of her ankles, she squeezed in and turned on to her back. She started wriggling down, pushing the sword case with her head. With *Pennysview* close to collapse, she wanted to get well away from the building. Fortunately the residual mud that had accumulated in the base of the pipe muffled the sounds of her movements. She used some to darken her face too so she wouldn't be seen as she slid under the drain grilles.

Soon, she could see light streaming in from the first drain opening. She was determined to get past it before anyone came to inspect the ruins. No doubt they would want to locate the bodies. Shortly after clearing the grille, a massive rumbling crash announced *Pennysview* had finally conceded. A gust of dusty air swept down the pipe. Then she heard someone yell "*Clear!*", and a truck drove up the track. As she approached the second grille, she heard voices above her.

"Beauchamp? Hi. I think they must be dead," said a man with a Japanese accent. "They were definitely in the cottage when we attacked, and no one has come out… We've found his body, but not hers. Yes, I've got his gun and phone though… Because I heard her yell '*Beauchamp! Damn you!*'; she sounded fucking angry, but I've no idea where her body is… Well, you should see the mess. The place was built like a fortress, the walls were four foot thick, but it's just a giant heap of stone now; she could be anywhere under it. We'll carry on looking for as long as we can but we're going to have to leave soon. A couple of jets have been scrambled from Lossiemouth. …Yes, yes, we'll look for as long as we can. No, there's no other way out; we've got the plans. Yes, we've checked the cesspit, and the storm drains aren't big enough… Well, there's only the Rolls and her moped in the garage... I really think you can strike them both off your list…"

Tessa continued down the pipe. It proved claustrophobic, cold, slow, exhausting and nerve-racking. On one occasion she found herself looking through a drain grille at some of the Calver Cats, but they didn't see her. She wondered whether anyone would drop a hand grenade into the drain just to be on the safe side.

She was about a quarter of the way down to the coast road when she heard the thunderous roar of planes approaching. Shortly afterwards there was a lot of agitated shouting followed by the truck driving away at high speed. It seemed the Calver Cats had left. She wondered how long it would be before Jones arrived and when she could switch her phone on without risk of detection. The jets swooped over the cottage several times, but then went away. At last there was silence.

Relieved to be alone, she manoeuvred the rucksack up and drank some water. Then she ate an apple and transferred the phone into her pocket. Suddenly a rat scampered down the pipe, hesitating as it reached her. Its fur had been singed and it had lost most of its tail. They looked at each other in the light from a drain grille.

"So, you're having a bad hair day too, are you? Well, here's an apple core to make you feel better," whispered Tessa, offering it up. The rat scuttled over her, grabbed the apple core, and disappeared.

As dusk approached, she heard a car stop and people walking up the track. Through a grille she could just make out the burly figure of the local constable. But Tessa didn't make any noise; she just wished he'd been wearing his kilt. Then some helicopters arrived, presumably landing near *Pennysview*. She could hear voices, but not what was being said. She had no idea whether they were friends of foes, so she decided to push on towards the road.

When it was quiet again, she took out her phone, switched it on and dialled #*[ALT] and Jones's number. After a short delay, he answered.

"Hello?"

"Jones, are you coming?" she asked, tired and exasperated.

He paused, sensing the tension in her voice.

"Are you all right?"

"Just tell me when you'll be here, will you?"

"We're in a helicopter about twenty minutes from *Pennysview*. You're not still in the cottage, are you?"

"No, I'm safe and not far away."

"Do you have your swords?"

"Of course I have my bloody swords," she replied hotly.

"You know Lord Kensington is dead?"

"Yes. I was with him when he died."

"I'm very sorry, Tessa," said Jones. "Did he tell you about the plan?"

"Yes, he told me. Will you just come and get me, please!"

"OK. I'll phone when we're over the cottage."

Tessa ended the call and a wave of remorse and despondency engulfed her. She started to sob uncontrollably. It suddenly dawned on her how close Beauchamp had come to eliminating her small band of close friends. In this deadly contest, he had all but won. For the next ten minutes, tears streamed down her face as she cried for the people who had died. She wondered how different her life could have been if they had not, and realised how much she already missed David.

Shortly after she'd stopped crying, her phone vibrated, announcing an incoming call.

"Tessa?"

"Yes, who were you expecting?" she replied sharply.

"Hmm. We're almost there. Lots of our people are at the cottage already, but I'd like to get you out unnoticed if I can. Where can we pick you up?"

"Land in the middle of the coast road at the bottom of the track. Straddle the manhole cover, but don't block it."

"Ah, that's clever. Right, we'll land and switch off all the lights. Get straight in from the cottage side. I'll be back as soon as I can."

"OK."

Tessa ended the call, wiped away some straggling tears and slithered on towards the road. She heard the helicopter land above her and waited for Jones to start walking up to *Pennysview*. Then she pushed the heavy manhole cover open and clambered out, sliding it shut after her.

Jones spent twenty minutes inspecting the wreckage of the cottage. She watched him in silence from the helicopter. The pilot didn't say anything; he simply handed her a blanket, some sandwiches and a flask of coffee.

When Jones returned he could hardly believe his eyes. Tessa was a shivering bedraggled mess, her face and hair black with mud. Her rucksack was on the seat beside her and the strap of her sword case was wrapped tightly round her wrist.

"Let's go," he said to the pilot. Then he glanced sympathetically at Tessa. "But circle the cottage a few times first."

As the helicopter took off, she looked down at the floodlit heap of stones which had been *Pennysview*.

"Jones, tell them to be careful with the garage," she said. "My Bugatti is on the lower level, under whatever remains of David's Rolls. Have them contact John Brown at PE Cars in Stanhope Gate. He'll take care of it."

He nodded and issued some orders into his radio.

Some men carried a stretcher into the rubble. It came out again with a body on it.

"That's Lord Kensington," said Jones quietly.

Tessa nodded as tears again trickled down her cheeks.

Then another stretcher went in. It emerged carrying the body of a blonde-haired woman.

Tessa's heart jolted. It was strange seeing a corpse that should have been hers.

"Who's that?" she asked.

"Well, the Calver Cats will be watching and we wouldn't want to disappoint them. That poor girl died in hospital earlier today and hasn't any relatives. We borrowed her body. She's got a wig on to make her look more like you. She's not been harmed in any way, and we'll ensure she gets a decent burial."

"Maybe Tessa did die down there anyway. Only Nariko's left now, and she has work to do."

Jones tapped the pilot on the shoulder.

"OK. Northolt, please, as quick as you can."

Tessa continued to shiver as the helicopter sped south. She wasn't cold any more; it was because David, the first man she had ever loved, was gone forever. He had given her so much, and all she had wanted was to give herself to him, completely. All her hopes and dreams for the future were gone. She felt frozen to her soul.

Suddenly, Jones broke the silence.

"This is a fast machine, we'll be in London in an hour. The other two will follow, one body in each."

Tessa nodded.

"What am I going to have to do to end this?" she asked.

"I don't know," he replied, shaking his head. "I wish I did. I wish I could say something that would make it all better for you, but I can't. I suppose we'll both just have to carry on doing our duty."

Tessa sighed and looked out of the window. They were already over Edinburgh and she had a wonderful view of the floodlit castle below.

"Has anyone decapitated Lamper yet?" she asked.

Jones, who had been dozing off, opened his eyes.

"No. But, I'm working on it. He's a slippery customer though."

"Keep him well away from me."

Jones looked at her. All he saw was an angry, exhausted woman he wanted to comfort, but couldn't.

"Obviously you can't go back to your house," he continued. "Somewhere safe is being prepared."

Tessa shrugged carelessly.

When they landed, she stood on the tarmac, wanting to wait for David's body.

"I'm sorry, we can't stay," urged Jones gently. "It'll be at least another hour, and there's nothing you can do here tonight."

He gestured towards the waiting limousine. As they drove across the Thames, Tessa took out her *cbc* and started flicking through the numbers. She stopped at Beauchamp's, memorised it, and gave her *cbc* to Jones.

"All the numbers from David's phone are in the memory. There are several Calver Cats numbers, including Beauchamp's satellite phone, the last number to call him."

"Thanks," he said. "I'll return it tomorrow."

Eventually, the car drove into a secure underground car park beneath a block of luxury flats. Jones led her to a comfortable well-equipped suite on the seventh floor.

"I think it would be best if you don't go out. Have a look round. Hopefully most of the things you'll need for now are already here. There are some clothes in the cupboard which should fit. I'll call round tomorrow morning to check everything is all right, probably about nine-thirty."

Tessa nodded.

"Will you be all right on your own?"

"I'll see you tomorrow."

Jones nodded and left, putting the keys to the flat on the table by the door. Tessa was desperate to be on her own, while regretting dreadfully that she was. She looked round for a moment, then sat on the wooden floor hunched up against the sofa. The silence soon proved too much for her. Overcome with grief, she wept tears of pent-up emotion.

"I can't go on," she wailed, "I can't do this…"

She finally stopped crying long enough to find the bathroom and have a much needed hot shower. Then she clambered into bed and fell fast asleep.

CHAPTER 19

Tessa woke early. She lay in bed analysing how she felt; lonely, grief-stricken, broken-hearted. But despite everything, her mind was clear. She was focused and determined. Nariko would have to finish what Beauchamp had started. Only then could whatever remained of Tessa construct a new life for herself. Only then could her deep wounds start to heal. She knew her feeling of loss would never go away completely; indeed, she didn't want it to. She didn't want to forget any of them: Penny, Sinclair, and especially David. All of them would always have a place in her heart. But now she needed to concentrate on doing whatever was necessary to honour the oaths she'd sworn. She looked at her sword case and sighed.

"OK, Beauchamp, we'll play by your rules now. See how you like it."

Full of new resolve, she got up, wrapped a towel round herself and went exploring. The sitting room was gloriously large with full-length windows facing the river. She opened the shutters and sunlight flooded in through the heavy net curtains. There was a dining alcove at the end of the lounge, with a kitchen area opening on to it. She also found another en-suite bedroom, and, to her immense surprise and satisfaction, a well-equipped fitness studio. In the kitchen, she found several packs of sushi, fresh fruit, natural yoghurts and even some green tea bags.

"Not bad," she muttered appreciatively.

She decided to have a work-out before eating. She finished at 8 a.m. and had a long hot shower. Dressed in jeans, a tee-shirt and some trainers, she enjoyed an excellent breakfast. She had just cleared up when Jones arrived.

"Good morning, how do you feel?" he asked sympathetically, surprised to see her so composed.

"Numb, but fit. I'll no doubt get used to the new status quo eventually; assuming I live long enough. Anyway, although this is a very nice place, I hope I'm not going to be cooped up here too long?"

"No, you're not. But you're right, it is a pleasant flat. We use it for people who are a security risk one way or another. Mind you the last occupant was a famous Japanese pop-star *with a Geisha entourage* to whom we owed a favour... Anyway, you'll be pleased to hear your Bugatti escaped unscathed. Apparently the lifting mechanism's jammed, so it's stuck on the lower level. But they'll get it up eventually and ship it to Stanhope Gate. John Brown said he'd check it over."

He passed her a newspaper and Tessa read the lead article:

Orcadians grieve: Lord Kensington of Graemeshall and Dr Tessa Pennington shared an untimely death in Orkney yesterday. They were last seen publicly together attending the funeral of Major General Sinclair at St Paul's Cathedral. The two were believed to be very close. They died following several unexplained explosions at the cottage where they were staying...'

"Do you think Beauchamp'll buy it?"

"He might. He'll certainly want to believe it, as will his people. All that remained of *Pennysview* was a very large pile of heavy stones. We know they found Lord Kensington's body; his phone and pistol were gone. But the jets were there very quickly and apparently the Cats weren't using any heat-sensitive scanning equipment, so they couldn't have been sure you weren't under the rubble. Let's just hope we've bought ourselves enough time to get to Cambodia and give Beauchamp a little surprise."

"Cambodia?"

"Yes, near a town called Siem Reap, to be precise. It's about two hundred miles north of Phnom Penh."

"I know. I've been there, many times."

"There too?"

"Absolutely, Burma's not the only place I've been in Southeast Asia. Beauchamp couldn't have chosen better. When do we leave?"

"Two days," replied Jones, grinning. "First, we need to make sure we're going to maximise our hard won advantage."

"OK. Let's get on with it."

"I am. We'll have to tread carefully as Cambodia only recently signed the Peacekeeper Treaty. They're not used to Peacekeepers being active in their country, and the Calver Cats are well established there. So, amongst other things, we're taking our own transport. Here's the plan so far…"

They spent the next hour deep in discussion. Jones had expected simply to tell Tessa what he intended. However, he soon understood what Sinclair had said to him once; if anyone could plan an action, she could.

"I'd better be off," said Jones eventually. "Here's your *cbc* back. If you need anything … food, clothes, whatever, call this number. It's Gwen Johnson's, she's Potter's assistant. I think you've met her. Smart woman, similar build to you with short auburn hair?"

"Yes, I remember her, thanks. Do you think you could get Lee to come over? I'd like to have a practice session with him. Can you ask him to bring some good knives, and one of Kono's special boxes? He'll know what I mean. Oh, and a sword-cleaning kit, please?"

"No problem, I'll get Johnson to bring him. He'll be delighted to know you're all right."

Jones called Gwen straightaway.

"OK. She's going to collect him. Now, just for the record, hardly anyone knows you're still alive, and especially not Lamper. So don't forget to maintain both your Yoshino and Nariko identities. Be sure to use the right name to the right people."

Tessa nodded.

"You know, Jones, I hardly dare befriend anyone these days. They always end up dead, while I don't seem to do anything except reap mayhem and destruction. I never thought the sword would lead me to hurt so many people. Violence offends me and yet it follows me wherever I go. Is there no way out?"

He smiled.

"I frequently ask myself the same. These days, when I get up, I wonder whether I'll live to see the day out. It's no coincidence Sinclair never married. Neither have I, or Potter. The odds are against me making it to retirement. And if I did, there's always the risk that a villain I locked up will be lurking in an alley bent on settling an old score. Is it the same for you, now? Possibly. Once one starts in this business, it's almost impossible to stop. However, one thing I do know. Until Beauchamp has been stopped, none of us will be able to relax."

"I agree with that, but I hope you're wrong about the rest. You presumably chose to do what you're doing. I didn't, I just got caught up in it. Anyway, maybe we should just concentrate on getting to Cambodia and ending this."

Without telling Tessa, Jones waited for Lee in the underground car park. He was worried that she might not be ready for further action and wanted Lee's opinion.

"Is she hurt?" asked Lee.

"Physically, no. Emotionally, yes, gravely. Given what's happened she's too quiet, like a bomb with a burning fuse."

"In that case, I'd hate to be Beauchamp when she catches up with him," replied Lee. "Grieving or not, Nariko is a natural. The finest swordfighter I've ever met. If she is in a situation where she needs to perform as a Peacekeeper, she will do so. And professionally, not emotionally."

"Hmm, I hope you're right. I'd hate to lose her, and this is going to be even more complicated than she thinks."

"Really? Well, I don't think you have any cause for concern. We all want her to come back, Jones… Is she wearing her swords?"

"No, I didn't even see them."

"Excellent," said Lee enthusiastically. "In that case, I might stand a chance." He unpacked his own sword and slid it into his belt, smiled, bowed and left.

For a moment Jones wondered what he meant but soon decided it was better if he didn't know. He simply hoped whatever happened upstairs wouldn't cause too much damage.

The next day followed much the same pattern. But in the evening a man arrived with Gwen Johnson to make up the second bedroom; neither of them seemed to know why the room was being prepared. However, Johnson did confirm preparations were complete for a departure late the next day.

So, in the morning, Tessa trained early with Lee. Once he'd left, she dyed her hair black and applied some instant tan to help change her appearance. She'd just finished when Jones arrived with Potter. He smiled at Tessa's new look, while Potter was aghast.

"Wow," he said, "I'd heard that stuff was good, but that's amazing."

"Well, I prefer being blonde, although it's hard to believe they have more fun. So, when do we leave?"

"Nineteen forty-five," replied Jones. "Flood left yesterday with most of the gear, including your wooden box. He'll meet us in Bangkok."

They discussed logistics until just before lunch. Tessa offered them some sushi, apologising for not having anything else, but neither Jones nor Potter wanted any. As they were packing their papers, Jones's mobile phone rang. He said little apart from "OK" several times, but ended with, "Fine, now is good." When he'd finished he met Tessa's eyes.

"There's just one more thing," he said. "I don't think you should carry your swords to Thailand. From Bangkok to Siem Reap should be fine, but on the aeroplane from London is a different matter. You travelling as an OCL Peacekeeper would be too risky, even with black hair. It'll draw far less attention if you go as a civilian."

"Jones," replied Tessa, dismayed, "I accept it's an issue, but surely you understand it's more than my life's worth not to have my swords with me. Remember what happened last time I didn't have them? Couldn't I take them in a diplomatic bag or something?"

"Quite possibly, but I think I've come up with a better solution."

At that point the doorbell rang.

"Potter," said Jones, "get that will you?"

"OK," continued Tessa, "so what is this solution of yours?"

Jones paused, waiting for Potter to open the door. As someone came in, a broad smile spread across Tessa's face.

"Now that is very good, Jones. I'd recognise those footsteps anywhere."

She stood up and turned round.

"*Konichiwa*, Hachiro-san," she said. "I thought you didn't like working outside Japan? How on earth did Jones manage to persuade you to come here?"

"*Konichiwa*, Nariko-san," replied Hachiro as they bowed to each other. "As I understand it, Jones spoke to Maeda-san, and he suggested it might be *convenient* for me to come and help you this time. So, here I am. And, from what I've heard, it sounds as though we might be quite busy."

As Tessa and Hachiro continued to speak in Japanese, Jones and Potter looked at each other. They'd heard about Hachiro from Maeda, but neither of them had expected him to be quite so large. Although dressed casually, it didn't take much to imagine how terrifying he'd be in full Samurai armour.

"Jones," said Tessa in English, "you're right. This is the one person whom I would trust to carry my swords. We'll just need to cover my OCL number."

With a smile, Jones threw her some black adhesive tape.

"Good, well, that's settled then," he said, clearly pleased. "Potter and I will go back to the office and leave you two to catch up."

"Oh, I'll need my leather suit," added Tessa. "It's in my house, I'm afraid."

"Actually, something better's being made," replied Potter. "It's a Kevlar suit, highly practical and resistant to small-calibre bullets. But only *resistant*, not impervious. It wasn't ready this morning, but I'll have a fitter come over with Johnson later."

"Sounds interesting. Could you ask the fitter to bring some additional material please? I'll need to have some pockets added to it."

"Pockets?" queried Potter, curious to know what for. But Tessa just nodded.

"Also, I'll need some gloves, some boots and a full-face balaclava."

"Gloves and boots are already in hand, but we'll need to get the headgear. Not a problem though."

"OK. All set?" asked Jones, looking round. "Right, we'll collect you at nineteen-thirty."

Tessa and Hachiro spent the next few hours talking. They were both pleased to see each other, and she was delighted not to be on her own. She hoped the trip would lead to a final confrontation between her and Beauchamp. However, since she doubted he would ever surrender, knowing Hachiro was there to back her up would be invaluable.

Early that afternoon Tessa's new suit arrived. She rather liked it; light and strong, and like her leather suit, in the traditional Ninja dark bluish-purple night-time camouflage colour. The matching gloves and boots were also good. Once she had tried everything on, the suit was duly taken away for some additional pockets to be added. During the remainder of the afternoon Tessa and Hachiro continued to talk and cleaned their swords. Her new suit was returned and, after a hearty meal, they showered, packed and prepared to leave.

At 7:29 p.m. there was a knock on the door and Jones came in.

"Ready?"

Tessa and Hachiro nodded. Jones's phone rang.

"We're on our way down."

Hachiro looked at Tessa, smiled and then carefully picked up her double sword case and slid it with his into a large golf bag. Then he left, followed closely by Tessa and Jones. In the underground car park they found a minibus waiting with Potter holding the sliding door open. Gwen Johnson would drive.

At Heathrow, Hachiro was ushered into the VIP lounge with great pomp and circumstance. Tessa and Jones followed a discreet distance behind. Their plan seemed to be working perfectly; all eyes were on Hachiro and his apparent escort, Potter. On the plane, they split up to avoid drawing attention to themselves. Potter was travelling in Business Class, while Tessa and Jones were in a pair of centre seats in First Class. Hachiro had the window seat across the aisle from Tessa. The golf bag with the sword cases went in the locker above him.

At Bangkok's Suvarnabhumi airport, they quickly passed through immigration and were soon being greeted by the enormous smiling figure of Flood who was even larger than Hachiro. He guided them to a private underground car park where, in a dark corner, they found two smart-looking Range Rovers.

"Right, sir," said Flood, turning to Jones. "Yours is the green long-wheelbase one. It looks normal enough now, but it's already carrying a lot of extras and has been prepared for the upgrade." He looked at Potter. "Yours, sir, is the grey one with the four-wheel trailer. It's a low specification PE vehicle with all the tools and other equipment needed to finish the green one. Here are the customs clearance papers; they shouldn't arouse any curiosity. Suffice to say you need both vehicles to upgrade the one, and you should allow at least a long hard day for the work. Be warned, neither vehicle handles quite how you'd expect. Although they both have powerful engines, they weigh nearly five tons. Anyway, they're fully tanked and ready to go, and there are secret sword safes in both."

"Well done, Flood," said Jones, as Tessa retrieved her swords. "Potter, we'll start straight away. I suggest you and Hachiro follow us in an hour or so. Have an early dinner or something. Use secure comms throughout. Anyone got any questions?"

There was silence.

Jones and Tessa left shortly afterwards. Neither of them said much, both wondering what lay in store for them. A few hours later, they reached the Cambodian border. No awkward questions were asked, and the formalities were completed quickly. As far as the border guards were concerned, they were simply a newly married couple visiting Angkor Wat. As they drove into Poipet, Jones announced he wanted to stop for a break and something to eat.

"Not here," objected Tessa. "Hardly anyone stops here unless they want to gamble or buy sex. I know a good restaurant in the next town. It's only an hour away."

Grudgingly Jones drove on.

At Sisophon, Tessa had him turn right at the junction on the edge of town and a hundred yards later they turned into the car park of the Banteay Top Restaurant.

"Dinner time," she announced gaily.

However, by the time she joined him in front of the range-rover, he was looking decidedly unenthusiastic. To him, the large open-air dining hall with its vast array of tables and tatty plastic cloths didn't seem in the slightest appealing. A conclusion not helped by the half-hearted glow from a haphazard string of flickering light bulbs.

Tessa burst into laughter.

"OK, OK," said Jones. "So I'm not used to, er, this sort of place. But don't forget, we're meant to be married."

"Honestly!" she retorted, grinning. "Are you scared to eat, or just trying to take advantage?"

"Aren't both allowed?"

"Probably neither."

She looped her arm through his and led him past the main dining hall to a small straw-roofed private area containing three tables.

"It's quieter here," she said, sitting down.

"Are you sure the food's OK?" he asked, surveying the convoy of ants marching across the table.

"Absolutely. Now, I'm going to the loo, which is in that white building over there. I'll organise some mosquito coils on the way."

Fifteen minutes later, Jones was happily tucking into his meal and drinking piping hot black tea.

"How come you know this place?" he asked between mouthfuls.

"Oh, I used to travel to Cambodia and Burma a lot to get away from work. Out here, no one could reach me by telephone or fax. It meant I could relax and indulge my passion for ancient stone buildings."

"Ancient stone buildings?" repeated Jones.

"Yep. Even that part of my Burma report is true," she replied, grinning.

They finished their dinner and Tessa directed him back to the main road.

"By the way," he said after a while. "There's something I need to tell you."

"Really?" observed Tessa suspiciously. "Something you wanted to leave until after you'd eaten?"

"Suffice to say, I'm not terribly proud of this. But we've still got to do it. For a while now an international initiative has been brewing to offer Beauchamp a soft landing. Sinclair fought against it, but after he was killed, well, it went through. So, whether we like it or not, we're tasked with offering it to him. The final text for an amnesty offer will be forwarded tomorrow."

Tessa looked at him dumbfounded.

"You don't seriously believe he'll accept it, do you?"

"I don't have an opinion either way. Why, are you determined to go after him with your sword?"

"No, definitely not. At Tower Bridge, I promised Sinclair to bring justice, not vengeance, to Beauchamp; so that's what I'll try to do. But offering him an amnesty will be a complete waste of time. It will probably do far more harm than good."

Jones looked troubled. After a while, she sighed.

"All right. I still think it's madness, but if that's what the collective wisdom wants, then so be it. I'm willing to give it a whirl on the basis that it might reduce the number of people who get hurt."

"Good, thanks… But while we're at it, did you make any other deathbed promises to Sinclair?"

"Yes. I said I'd get whoever shot him."

"*Get* sounds a bit ominous. Suppose it was Beauchamp?"

"I don't think it was. Whoever fired that shot had faster reactions than my brother. I think Beauchamp was aiming at you and missed. But if it was him, I'll try and bring him in for trial and let someone else spill his blood."

"Fair enough. I know it won't be easy, but I'm pleased you're willing to give the amnesty a go. Of course, we need Beauchamp to agree to a meeting first, but I doubt he'll refuse if you ask. I think I should present the offer to him though..."

As they neared Siem Reap, Tessa telephoned ahead. They were going to stay with Khon, a long-standing friend of hers. He used to guide her round the archaeological ruins when she first visited. Over the years they had become friends, and now she knew many of the sites almost as well as he did; some even better.

Ten minutes later they entered the courtyard in front of Khon's three-storey house. Large wooden gates were quickly closed behind them. Khon was a small chubby man with a friendly suntanned face. He greeted them euphorically.

"Khon!" said Tessa with glee. "It's been a while."

"Too long," he replied. "But it's good to see you here again. I've had Chhaya take the children away for a few days, but she asked me to send you her love. And theirs!"

"Thank you. I'm sure it's better if they don't risk getting caught up in all of this, but I would have liked to see them again. Hopefully next time. This is Gareth Jones, a friend of mine. We've just spoken to the other car. It will be here shortly..."

Ten minutes later, Potter arrived. After more introductions, both Range Rovers were driven into a large shed cum-workshop behind Khon's house. Soon afterwards, the house was quiet as everyone slept.

CHAPTER 20

The following morning, Tessa started exercising at 5 a.m., having already changed her hair colour back to blonde. The others were less accustomed to dealing with jetlag and didn't rise until 7 a.m., after Khon had left for work. She cooked breakfast, while Potter set up the speaker-phone in the lounge at the top of Khon's house, where Tessa slept. After breakfast he started work on the Range Rovers while Tessa, Jones and Hachiro discussed how to open communications with Beauchamp.

"So, it's agreed then," said Jones eventually, exasperated. "You do the talking and get a private meeting, in a public place, between you, me and him. And I'll present the amnesty, OK?"

"As I said, I'll try," replied Tessa, equally exasperated. "But he won't want to meet you, and I just don't believe an amnesty will interest him."

"I understand. But the amnesty is bona fide, and on generous terms. What's more, we need to be able to demonstrate we made him consider it seriously. I'd have thought he'd at least be curious. Let's see what happens." Jones tinkered with the telephone. "Right, the call will be bouncing around so he won't be able to trace it."

The speaker-phone resembled a large grey mottled three-pronged starfish dumped unceremoniously in the centre of the round table. Jones pressed some buttons; lights flashed and the phone clicked and beeped a few times. The three of them watched it expectantly, as though it was about to move. It started ringing.

"Hello?"

"Good morning, Beauchamp," said Tessa in as friendly a tone as she could muster, "how are you today?"

"Who's this?" asked the voice. "How did you get this number?"

"Don't you recognise me, Beauchamp? It's your sister."

There was a disbelieving silence at the other end of the line.

"Oh, bloody hell! You again. I thought you died in Orkney?"

206

"I'm afraid your guys messed up, just like you did in London."

"Oh, really? I was under the impression that we had noteworthy successes at both venues," he replied with a satisfied lilt to his voice. "Anyway, what do you want?"

"Well, as you said in London, we need to have a chat. You, me, and a friend of mine, face to face, quietly and calmly. We have a serious proposition to put to you which we think you'll find interesting."

She was trying as hard as she could not to betray her feelings of intense anger and distrust. Impressed so far, Jones nodded encouragingly.

"What a pain in the arse, you are! Some things never change. You don't expect me to come to London for this chat, do you?"

"No, we'll come to you," she replied, convinced the advantage had swung in her favour since he clearly didn't know they were in Siem Reap.

Beauchamp could be heard talking in muffled tones to someone else.

"Is this call being traced?" he asked.

"No. We already know where you are and our signal is satellite-hopping, so don't bother trying to trace us."

"Sounds like you're using Special Forces gear? I thought you were in disgrace."

"Oh, I still have some friends..."

"Wonders never cease!" interjected Beauchamp.

"Ha-ha! Look, I'm serious. We just want to meet on neutral ground, for half an hour or so. No tricks, no traps, no violence. That would be all right, wouldn't it?"

"Hmm, you appear to have me at a disadvantage. How about levelling the playing field and telling me where you are?"

"Far enough away to be well out of reach, but close enough to be able to attend a meeting," she replied. "How about in Siem Reap?"

There was a pause with some more muffled conversation in the background.

"All right, we can meet," replied Beauchamp. "I'll give you thirty minutes at five-fifteen tomorrow morning, but only if you come on your own. Nobody else and no bugs. Do you think you can find Angkor Wat?"

She smiled, knowing he was trying to annoy her since he was well aware she'd been there many times. Meanwhile, Jones had started gesticulating wildly to signify he wanted to attend.

"Yes, I think so," continued Tessa. "How about meeting at the northern corner of the northern washing pool, within the main enclosure? That's the bottom left-hand corner of the left-hand pool as you walk up the causeway. Do you know where I mean?"

She couldn't resist demonstrating her intimate knowledge of the temple.

"Yes, that's fine."

"Good. But please, may I bring my friend? He really wants to talk to you, it's important."

"No, just you. Will you be armed?"

"Yes, I'll be carrying blades," continued Tessa. Jones started shaking his head and Hachiro shifted uneasily in his chair. She shrugged her shoulders.

"Hmm, all right," replied Beauchamp, after another pause, "but no knives. I won't be armed, so I'll bring a colleague with swords, to even things up."

"OK," said Tessa. "But since you'll be two, can't I bring my friend with me, unarmed?"

"No, no, no! How many times have I got to fucking tell you?"

By now Jones was so agitated he reached towards the telephone's mute button. However, Tessa quickly clamped her hand over his, pinning it to the table. He glared at her.

"Right, we've got that," she continued. "But just to make it absolutely clear, I only want to talk. I have a serious proposal for you, and I want to present it as such under a flag of truce. OK?"

"Yes, yes," retorted Beauchamp with a bored lilt to his voice.

Meanwhile, Jones was struggling to nudge his spade-like hand towards the phone. Tessa's vice-like grip tightened and his face started going red as she began to hurt him. He ran his other hand across his neck, ordering her to terminate the call.

"One last thing, Beauchamp," continued Tessa. "How about if you use the eastern entrance while I use the western causeway?"

"Oh, good grief! Yes, that's agreed too. Is there anything else or can I get on with my life now?" he retorted, irritated as always by her attention to detail. A facet of her character which Tessa had often used against him.

She smiled, pleased with the result of her negotiations.

"I think that's the lot, Beauchamp. I'll see you tomorrow at five-fifteen then."

A loud click indicated he had terminated the call and Tessa released Jones hand. He pressed a button on the speaker phone.

"For goodness' sake!" he exploded, massaging his wrist. "We agreed you, me and him, in a public place! Not you alone with him and a friend, in the back of beyond, with two of you armed."

"Well, you heard what he said. You wouldn't want me to go on my own unarmed, would you? We've gone the extra mile and now he's interested. I think that went well."

"You know what I mean. We should discuss variations before accepting them."

"Jones, we've been discussing all morning. And don't forget what it says in the Peacekeeper Manual. *'In order to bring a Mission to a successful conclusion, Peacekeepers are permitted to vary Mission tactics if only they are compromised.'*"

"Honestly, you're … incorrigible!"

Hachiro looked puzzled.

"Don't worry, Hachiro-san. He's angry with me but didn't want to swear," explained Tessa.

"I see," said Hachiro. "Have you and Beauchamp always hated each other?"

"Oh, definitely not, although I'm not sure we've ever respected each other. But now, given the terrible things he's done, it's difficult to see how anyone on our side could ever like him that much."

Hachiro nodded, while Jones continued to fume.

"I think we should call it off," he said, abruptly. "You'll both be on a knife edge, metaphorically speaking – I hope. And I'm not comfortable with some of the undercurrents here. A huge international effort has been expended on pulling this amnesty together. It deserves to be offered openly and amicably, and I'm not sure that's likely at tomorrow's meeting."

"Yes, it will, I promise. Anyway, I doubt he'd answer the phone again. It's done, just leave it. I promise I'll give it my best shot. You'll just have to brief me on what to say. How long is the document?"

Jones suddenly looked sheepish and went quiet. Tessa laughed.

"You haven't got it yet, have you?"

"No, but I'm assured it will have arrived by tomorrow. They've sent a preliminary summary which we can use for the time being."

"Right," she continued, grinning. "If Beauchamp says he's interested, we can take it from there. If not, I'll just come back and we can plan the next step."

An awkward silence followed which Hachiro eventually broke.

"You are taking a big risk going on your own. I should come with you. He only needs one well-placed sniper with a rifle to kill you."

Tessa thought about it for a moment.

"No, I don't think we should go back on what's been agreed, especially if we want him to take the amnesty offer seriously. I gave my word. He gave his. I think we should give him the benefit of the doubt. But I'll take a transponder, and press the *Urgent Assistance Required* button if I run into any trouble. Don't worry, I'll be back for breakfast."

Hachiro shrugged his shoulders. Jones, still angry and decidedly suspicious of Tessa's motives, grudgingly nodded his head.

"So, you know Angkor Wat?"

"Yes, very well. But we'll need to empty the temple grounds. It's usually pretty busy at dawn and we don't want a bunch of photo-happy tourists getting in the way. Perhaps you could pull a few strings with the Cambodian government? Also, there are a few other details which ought to be thought through…"

They spent most of the morning planning and preparing. Jones phoned various Cambodian officials and briefed Tessa on the contents of the amnesty. Eventually, Khon returned for lunch and confirmed his cousins would be willing to be involved. Potter appeared only briefly to eat, determined to continue upgrading the long-wheelbase Range Rover into something he doggedly refused to discuss. So, feeling relaxed, and pleased to have the afternoon free, she and Hachiro practised, meditated and cleaned their swords.

In the evening Khon brought with him a rented moped for Tessa together with his two cousins, Pheakdei and Sopheap. They were going to act as decoys to make sure no one followed her back to

Khon's house.

Pheakdei and Sopheap proved to be extremely enthusiastic participants. They were both about twenty, fit and healthy, with bright brown eyes and rather scruffy long black hair. They had enrolled at the Cambodian Peacekeeper training school in Phnom Penh and had been travelling down and back on the bus to attend classes. However, their progress had been slow since they couldn't afford swords.

Tessa explained her plan and eventually they left, tasked with buying three rucksacks.

CHAPTER 21

At 3:00 a.m., dressed in her Kevlar suit, Tessa crept down to the kitchen. From his mattress, Hachiro watched her making some green tea and followed her as she returned to the lounge. He poured two cups for them as she wound black tape over the Amakuni and Amafuji emblems on her sword sheaths. Jones joined them.

"Here's your *UAR* transponder," he said. "You know how it works, don't you?"

"Yes, of course," she replied, "don't fuss. Has the amnesty arrived yet?"

Jones sighed and shook his head.

"Sorry," he complained with a wry smile. "A plethora of politicians probably pontificated purposefully, positioned the pen, but proceeded to procrastinate so pervasively that no particular position prevailed."

Tessa cocked her head to one side.

"Well, personally, I perceive politicians as pompous with preconceived prejudices and a predisposition to prevarication.

"Hah! I can do this," interjected Hachiro. "If the pair of you pedants persist in pursuing this particular play on pronunciation, perhaps I should go for a pee."

Tessa and Jones looked at each other, and everyone laughed.

"Congratulations, Hachiro-san," acknowledged Tessa. "That was very good. Seriously though, not having the full amnesty document means we might well need another meeting. After all, Beauchamp was a lawyer once."

Jones nodded, frustrated.

"They assure me it'll be here by this afternoon." He continued with a slight tremor in his voice, "Look, for goodness' sake, be careful."

Tessa looked at him and smiled, surprised by the hint of emotion in his gruff voice.

"I will," she said, momentarily laying her hand on his as he reached for his cup.

Hachiro raised his eyebrows.

"I'd better be off," she said, standing, "see you later."

"Why no knives?" queried Hachiro.

"Beauchamp saw me throw one in London before he killed Crick. I think he's nervous."

"But doesn't he know you're even more dangerous with a sword?"

"Not yet," she replied, chuckling at Jones's exasperated expression.

Downstairs, she wrapped a scarf round her neck, taking care to obscure her sword hilts, and put on a matt black crash-helmet. Then she nonchalantly climbed on her moped, pressed the starter and checked her watch. Then she winked at Jones and bowed to Hachiro. He bowed back, pulled the gate open and she rode out.

"All we can do now is wait," observed Jones dejectedly. Hachiro nodded, and went back to his mattress. Potter joined Jones.

"She's gone then?"

Jones nodded.

"I don't like it."

"I gathered that," replied Potter. "You didn't seriously expect her to do just as you wanted, did you?"

"No, I suppose not. But this is throwing caution to the wind."

"Ah," said Potter, smiling. "She did seem to get over the deaths of Sinclair and Lord Kensington rather quickly. This has probably got something to do with that, not to mention Crick and Penny Reid."

"I agree," acknowledged Jones. "She's still hurting and furious, and that anger is being channelled into ruining Beauchamp and destroying the Calver Cats, irrespective of the risk to her own life."

He sighed and turned to Potter again.

"You look knackered. I'll cook you some breakfast."

"Thanks. I'll need your help again later. The turret's even heavier than the bogey!"

Tessa rode through the empty backstreets of Siem Reap. At the appointed junction, Pheakdei and Sopheap pulled in behind, dressed like her. At the agreed separation point, she headed off towards the West Baray while they took different routes to Angkor, to confuse anyone who might be watching.

As she'd expected, her journey round the ancient reservoir proved far from easy, especially in the dark. The rough narrow track was deeply rutted and strewn with rocks. But she'd allowed ample time. At last, looming high in front of her, Tessa saw the majestic silhouette of the west gate to Angkor Thom. She knew that once through this, the going would be easier. She reached the Bayon and turned right to Angkor Wat. It looked as though she was completely alone, and all she could hear was the chugging of her moped. She continued along the road through the forest towards the south gate. Then the moon came out and she saw King Jayavarman VII's enigmatic smile from the four-sided carvings above the massive stone archway. He had built the city of Angkor Thom nearly nine hundred years earlier.

Tessa crossed the bridge over the moat, and, as she neared Angkor Wat, started looking for a place to hide her moped. Finding a narrow path leading into the forest to her right, she stopped the engine and wheeled her moped into the trees. Safely off the beaten track, she parked, looked round and listened for anything untoward; there was nothing. She checked her swords and put on her balaclava. Then she walked quietly out of the forest towards the west entrance to Angkor Wat.

Quietly she climbed the stone steps and set off across the long causeway over the moat. Occasionally, she had to avoid the prostrate body of someone sleeping, but those who were partially awake noticed only the passing of a shadow and a slight breeze. She wondered whether Beauchamp had forgotten how well she knew this part of the world. If so, it could work to her advantage. Most of all, she hoped this uniquely beautiful religious building would not be defiled by yet more bloodshed. It had seen more than enough during Cambodia's troubled history.

Stepping down from the causeway, Tessa turned left towards the northernmost of the three entrance towers in the perimeter gallery. She went up the stairs and walked round the imposing Buddhist statue, serenaded by bats screeching high overhead in the underside of the corbelled roof. She continued down the steep stone stairs into the large grassed enclosure. For a moment she paused; still she could neither see, nor hear, anything suspicious. This was how she'd hoped it would be; empty, peaceful, and awe-inspiringly beautiful. She smiled, admiring the familiar distant outline of the five central towers to Angkor Wat. She was sure only those who had visited this place could appreciate its scale and grandeur.

Not wanting to use the more popular exposed central causeway, she set out on the path leading diagonally off to her left, passing the north library. It seemed all the priests were still asleep in their nearby huts; hopefully none would accidentally interrupt the meeting. Some police officers were arriving later to prevent tourists from entering, but the monks who were already there couldn't be moved.

Thirty minutes after leaving the perimeter gallery, Tessa finally reached the embankment leading down to the northern, female, washing pool. She could see the reflection of the moon in the water, while far to her right lay the central causeway. On the other side was the male washing pool, long since drained.

She had planned to arrive early, partly for strategic reasons but also for her own enjoyment. She loved this place and had dreamed of bringing David here one day to witness the dawn, but that was not to be. Nevertheless, as usual, the imposing moonlit form of the Angkor Wat temple mountain looked sublime and comforting to her.

She expected Beauchamp to come from the northern side, so walked along the northern edge of the pool. Finding a gentle undulation in the grassy bank, she sat down close to the water's edge. After a while she took a deep breath and lay back. Attracted by her body heat, mosquitoes buzzed around her, but couldn't find any exposed skin. With a relaxed smile Tessa stared up at the sky. All she could see were stars twinkling against the deep blue background and, occasionally, a passing satellite. She sighed in disbelief as she considered the twists and turns her life had taken during the last few years. She was proud of almost everything she had achieved, but her sword-wielding skills continued to impress and depress her in equal measure. Lost in reminiscing, she closed her eyes, allowing her thoughts to merge with the surroundings…

Twenty minutes later her dreamy cogitations were interrupted by the sound of two people approaching; one male, one female. She smiled, took a deep breath and lay absolutely still. She knew it was both risky and childish to play a trick on Beauchamp, but wondered whether they would notice her. She opened her eyes slightly to ensure she could not be taken by surprise.

The two people strode down the stone stairs behind her and passed only a few feet away. Tessa quietly stood up, removed her balaclava and went after them.

"So where the hell is the pillock then?" said Beauchamp. "Are you sure this is the right place?"

"Of course I am," replied the woman in a strong Japanese accent. "Let me lead ... just in case."

Tessa closed in silently from behind.

"Hello, Beauchamp," she said suddenly. "Thanks for coming."

He spun round, surprised to hear a voice from so close by. They studied each other suspiciously, barely six feet apart. He was wearing knee-length khaki shorts and an un-tucked short-sleeved shirt with a leather bag over his shoulder. Tessa took this in a flash, and then considered how easily she could end it – but she couldn't betray her oath to Sinclair. Meanwhile, her brother's companion, who had walked several paces ahead, now found Beauchamp between herself and Tessa. She was completely unable to defend him, which clearly annoyed her intensely. However, she looked ready for action, dressed all in black; tee-shirt, jeans and trainers. She quickly moved up alongside him.

"Hmm, well, I suppose you're welcome," replied Beauchamp backing away in response to a gentle pull on his arm from his companion. "I hope there's a good reason for me getting up so early?"

"Oh, definitely, but we can get to that in a moment. Beautiful isn't it?"

"What? Your suit? Yes, you must get one of those, darling," he replied, nodding to his companion.

Tessa smiled. This was definitely the same brother she'd always known.

"Not me, Beauchamp, Angkor Wat! You always were a bit of a philistine where such things were concerned. Especially if you thought it would wind me up."

Beauchamp glanced at the majestic building beyond the pool.

"Oh, it's all right, I suppose."

"Right... So, how are you keeping? You've a few more wrinkles. Is being on the run taking its toll?"

"Hah, you wish! I'm enjoying myself. My empire has grown considerably since you interfered in London. It was that minor inconvenience which goaded me into doing what I really enjoy, albeit more successfully and on a much grander scale than I would ever have imagined. So, thank you for that. At least you've done one useful thing for me during your pathetic existence."

Tessa smiled.

"Aren't you going to introduce me to your bodyguard?"

"Oh, yes, this is Leiko. Actually, you've met. At Tower Bridge, remember?"

"Vaguely," muttered Tessa with distaste.

"As you know," he continued, "she's very good with a bow, but even better with a sword. She's not bad with a rifle either. I presume you remember that bit?"

"Did she shoot Sinclair?"

"Yep. I'm embarrassed to admit I missed the other bugger. But hers was a nice clean shot, wasn't it?" Arrogant and uncaring, he beamed with pride.

Although stung by this reminder of her friend's death, Tessa couldn't believe how pleased she felt to find herself within reach of Sinclair's assassin. She looked Leiko up and down. She had the archetypal sinewy Japanese build; not tall, but very fit. Her long black hair had been gathered in a single plait at the back. Like Tessa she wore two swords slung over her shoulders, but hers were conventional ninja short swords.

"Beauchamp, using a gun is never *nice and clean*," replied Tessa. "And as for shooting someone in the back with a laser sight, that's just cowardly. So, Leiko, it would seem we have some unfinished business."

"Any time you want to die, bitch," replied the other woman angrily.

"Her English is very cultured isn't it, Beauchamp?" observed Tessa.

"I'll cut you in ribbons and watch the life drain from your weeping eyes," she hissed, glaring at Tessa.

"Hmm, how nice."

"Works for me," mused Beauchamp. "But I warn you, don't mess with her. She really is very good with a sword."

"Is she good in bed too? Or do you still satisfy your urges elsewhere?"

"What!" screamed Leiko.

"Oh, please, grow up, you two," intervened Beauchamp. "Let's just try and keep our collective cool, shall we? My understanding is that we're here to have a friendly chat, not a verbal sparring match."

Tessa smiled sweetly at Leiko, who stared back defiantly.

"You're right," agreed Tessa, "let's get down to business. I've been asked by the signatories to the International Peacekeeper Treaty to extend to you a formal offer of amnesty. It's intended to let you down gently, before things turn nasty. I'm led to believe the Calver Cats have suffered several major setbacks over the past months: South America, Japan and Burma were all cited. So, before you go down with your gang, people thought they would offer you an alternative, to save unnecessary bloodshed. Let me give you a summary of the deal…"

For twenty minutes, she recounted verbatim what Jones had told her to say.

"…with good behaviour, you'd be back with Caprice and the kids in no time at all. You're the lawyer, so I understand you'll want to study the text yourself. But if you're interested, I can get the document to you later today. Apparently it's a really good offer in the circumstances. What do you think?"

Beauchamp walked down to the water's edge, thinking. He picked up a stone, and threw it in. They all watched the ripples spreading out round the lilies.

"You don't expect me to decide now, do you?"

"My expectations are unimportant as far as this is concerned," replied Tessa. "All you have to do is say you're seriously interested and tell me how you'd like to have the papers delivered. Personally, I wouldn't have thought it could do any harm to go through the document. After all, it's the only way you're likely to be able to get out of this alive."

Beauchamp laughed confidently.

"Really? Well, I've an amnesty for *you* to consider. If you go home now and stop irritating me, I won't have you killed."

It was Tessa's turn to laugh, equally confidently.

"I'm touched. I didn't think you had it in you to be so generous. But you already know my answer, don't you?"

Grinning at each other, they were like peas in a pod. Each as intransigent as the other, they were well matched. Unfortunately, though, they had very different views as to what was right and what was wrong.

"Actually," replied Beauchamp, "I'd have been very disappointed if you'd accepted. It would spoil the fun, wouldn't it?"

"Beauchamp, this is *not* fun. Lots of people are dying. It's got to stop. And you will be stopped."

"Bold words from the freaky wimp to whom I'm regrettably related. But I have many people to keep me safe, here and elsewhere; it seems it is you who are losing all your support. Are you sure it's fair to expose any remaining friends you might have left to my wrath?"

"What you're doing is just not right," retorted Tessa, "and you certainly shouldn't be involving my friends. However, you could even things up a bit by letting me take this coward back to face justice for the murder of Major General Sinclair."

Beauchamp had to put his arm out to hold Leiko back.

"There's no chance of that, as you well know," he sneered. "Furthermore, Leiko would have to be part of any deal I accepted."

"I'm surprised. You deserted your parents and me, and Caprice and your children. What's so special about Leiko … or don't you want to say in front of her?"

A fleeting expression of annoyance flashed across Beauchamp's face.

"I see your tongue hasn't lost any of its sharpness. However, I've made more than ample provision for Caprice and the kids, and she's definitely not lonely. Meanwhile, I'm enjoying the excellent support and companionship I receive from Leiko. She is indeed good at many things. Superlatively good, in fact. But since you're so keen to take the conversation in that direction, there is a question I've been burning to ask. Er, did it hurt? You know…?"

Leiko roared with laughter. Tessa forced a smile.

"Touché! But disappointingly reminiscent of gutter-press sensationalism. However, since you asked, no, it didn't. It was simply part of the treatment needed to correct a birth defect."

"Fascinating. Well, I'm sure there are lots of arousing stories you could tell us about your antics with that toff Kensington," he said, turning to Leiko and winking.

Tessa felt her hackles rising. She'd dealt a number of insults so it was only fair she should take some. However, anything involving David was deeply hurtful to her, as it was meant to be. But it did give her an idea.

"Why is it you want me dead?"

"Oh, I was bored, and you were and remain an embarrassment, and that volte-face of yours was one step too far. So I decided the time had come for me to lance the boil that had irritated me for so long. Unfortunately, it didn't quite go according to plan, but everything else has worked out fine."

"Beauchamp, apart from being naive, these pubescent prejudices of yours are completely outdated. I thought maybe what you did to me in the bath, and before, still bothered you? If it does, you should just try apologising. Or are you worried you might be partly responsible for..."

"Don't be ridiculous," he interrupted uneasily, looking rattled.

With furrowed eyebrows, Leiko looked at him closely.

"My, she is perceptive," mocked Tessa.

"You know, you always were a nasty piece of work," said Beauchamp vehemently. "I bet there are lots of people who'd like to see you dead."

"Only your friends, Beauchamp, and they really don't count… Anyway, I know old habits die hard, but we're getting distracted again, aren't we? We're both having fun, but let's get back to the serious stuff. What about this amnesty? I understand you want Leiko included and will relay that back to the relevant authorities. But otherwise, I suspect this is the only time you'll be offered a choice between life and death."

"And that's precisely what I'm giving you too, kiddo. We're locked in a deadly game of poker here, but I only need to get lucky once to win, while you've always got to be lucky to avoid losing. And, sooner or later, your luck will run out."

"Perhaps, but back to the amnesty. You first."

Beauchamp thought for a moment, and then smiled at Leiko.

"I will think about it. I'll give you my answer tonight at the Beng Mealea temple complex, it's about forty miles east of here. Come alone at ten and bring the full text of the offer with you."

"Beng Mealea. All right. So, I can go back and say you're willing to consider the amnesty, but Leiko must be included?"

Beauchamp nodded.

"I presume you'll grant me safe passage tonight, even if neither of us is interested in the other's amnesty?"

"Oh, quite possibly. Beng Mealea, ten p.m., alone. Use the south entrance."

"OK. But first, I'm going to watch the sun come up over Angkor Wat. It really is sensational and it's unusual to get the place to ourselves like this. Why don't you stay too?"

"Oh, if we must," he drawled.

Slowly, a semi-circle of pinkish orange sunlight started to rise behind the temple's five towers. It formed an incandescent flame of warming brightness, engulfing the temple and casting a magnificent reflection on the pool in front of them. The deep turquoise sky became a patchwork of thin streaky orange clouds. Then a point of white light appeared and a single brilliant sunbeam illuminated the temple enclosure. Tessa couldn't resist smiling; she thought it was wonderful. Beauchamp, however, seemed only vaguely interested, and Leiko even less so.

With much of the sun now visible and the mosquitoes gone, the sounds of the monks in their nearby huts grew louder.

"Can we go now?" asked Beauchamp impatiently.

"Yes. I'll take the main causeway to the right. I suggest you take it too, but to the left, and then go round the temple to the right. There's more shade that way."

Beauchamp nodded and the three of them set off past the pool. When they reached the stone stairs up to the causeway, Beauchamp went up, but Leiko and Tessa stopped at the bottom.

"After you," indicated Tessa.

"You must be joking," replied Leiko. "I'm not turning my back on you, even if you are only a pathetic Caucasian bitch."

"I'm not the one who kills from behind. How about if we both go up together, you on the left, me on the right?"

Leiko nodded and they climbed the stairs watching each other closely. Beauchamp waited at the top, clearly finding the process hilarious.

Once on the causeway, Tessa and he looked at each other, both apparently unsure what to say.

"Hmm, well, see you this evening then," said Tessa, reversing towards the main entrance. They set off in the opposite direction. After a while Tessa shouted back.

"By the way, Leiko, I understand Japanese names have meanings.

I know Yoshino is *good and respectful*, but what does Leiko mean?"

The Japanese woman stopped abruptly and spun round.

"You fucking bitch! Are you trying to make fun of me?"

Tessa stopped and turned round too.

"Why would I do that? Have I said something wrong, Beauchamp?"

He looked at Leiko.

"Does your name mean something?" he asked.

"Forget it," she muttered, "let's go."

"Oh, come on," persisted Tessa, already knowing the answer. "Don't be shy, share it with us. We're all friends for now, aren't we?"

Beauchamp looked expectant.

"Arrogant," mumbled Leiko.

Tessa burst into laughter, and even Beauchamp couldn't resist smiling.

"Honestly, you two, that's enough," he said, seeing Leiko was close to exploding. "Let's all go our separate ways and get some breakfast. We'll see you tonight."

Tessa shrugged, turned and walked away. However, she listened to the conversation behind her with a satisfied expression on her face.

"Come on, Beauchamp," implored Leiko, "let me finish the dyke now."

"Er. Well, I did promise I wouldn't…"

"Yes, but you didn't say I wouldn't, did you?"

"That's true. But I think in all fairness you'd have to ask first. If the two of you want to do something – that's your affair."

Leiko glared after Tessa's retreating figure.

"Hey, bitch!" she yelled. "Are you just going to run away, or have you the guts to finish it here and now? Just you and me?"

Tessa looked round, as though expecting to see someone else.

"Were you talking to me? Beauchamp, I thought we had an agreement, no violence during the meeting?"

"Yes, and I'm not going to initiate anything. And I fully accept that you haven't either. So, honour has been satisfied in that respect. However, our meeting is over, and this is entirely Leiko's idea. She appears to have developed a marked disliking for you. It used to take longer, but there we are. So, she has challenged you. However, if you don't fancy your chances, we'll just put it down to you being a coward.

But, as I said, she is very good with swords. I could well understand you not wanting to fight her. Just say the word and…"

"Let's do it, bitch!" interrupted Leiko, drawing her swords and starting down the causeway towards Tessa.

"Ah," continued Beauchamp with an amused smile, "I suppose that's agreed then."

Tessa checked round. She had plenty of room on the twenty-foot wide causeway. And although there was a low stone balustrade to her left, there was nothing to her right. If necessary, she could easily jump down on to the grass below. Meanwhile, Leiko was approaching fast with the sun almost directly behind her. Tessa took a deep breath, closed her eyes and relaxed. As she waited, she timed Leiko's steps and gently flexed her muscles in anticipation. Leiko was delighted to see the sun had forced Tessa to shut her eyes and raised both her swords in anticipation of the attack. But then Tessa opened her eyes, and, as Leiko blinked, drew her swords. The speed of the draw shocked Leiko, but she was already committed.

Tessa now stood with both her swords crossed and pointing downwards in front of her. She held Bryani's heavier sword in her left hand, just in front of her Kimi sword. She twisted the blades to create reflections of the sun on the balustrade behind her assailant.

Screaming at the top of her voice, Leiko began her attack. Tessa repositioned her swords to reflect the sunlight directly into her assailant's eyes, simultaneously broadening her stance and twisting her body to the left. Then she bent her left knee, to lower her torso slightly, and moved Bryani's sword upwards with a strong, fast anti-clockwise swing. Meanwhile, she moved her Kimi sword out to her left and swung it upwards with a strong clockwise motion.

For the most crucial of moments, Leiko had been blinded by the reflected sun. She didn't see the attacking blades; she simply heard the proud, confident ringing of Tessa's Kimi sword and the *cl-clang* announcing the determined arrival of Bryani's sword as it noisily brushed aside both her weapons. Leiko realised she had seriously underestimated Tessa. Then she felt a searing pain near her appendix which rapidly spread through her body. As Tessa continued the sweep of her Kimi sword, she unwound the twist in her body to add speed, ferocity and power to her stroke. The result was a deep wound extending diagonally upwards across Leiko's torso. Finally, Tessa pulled back. Leiko took a few more steps and stopped. They both knew the duel was over.

Not understanding what had happened during the incredibly fast exchange, Beauchamp sat grinning on the balustrade.

"Well, I have to admit, it's good sport watching you two having a go at each other," he said. "But will this take long? I'm hungry."

Tessa flicked the blood off her Kimi sword and re-sheathed both her weapons.

"Beauchamp, if you had anything going with this woman, you'd better come and say goodbye. But be quick, she hasn't long. Otherwise, go and get your breakfast. Either way, I'll see you later."

Leiko moaned and sank to her knees, dropping her swords noisily on the causeway. Her strength was fast draining away.

Tessa turned and started walking, pausing as she passed her opponent.

"Silly girl!" she said. "That was for Sinclair."

As Leiko watched Tessa go, she wondered where Beauchamp was. She really wanted him to be with her now.

Tessa stopped and turned round. Her brother hadn't moved. To her surprise, he actually looked sad.

"You really did like her, didn't you?" she shouted. "Well, you've only yourself to blame."

Beauchamp was indeed extremely upset, and annoyed. But he'd never been good at expressing his feelings, especially to his sibling. So, just as before, he elected to say nothing. He took a deep breath, stood up and walked away. He couldn't bear to see the wilting body of his girlfriend, surrounded now by a widening pool of blood. She had been the last of a long string of liaisons he'd had since leaving Caprice. But Leiko had been different; she was special, very special. Until that moment, he wouldn't have believed it possible for his hatred of his sibling to intensify further. But now he realised she had actually managed to provoke new extremes within him.

"Fuck you!" he yelled after her.

"What … again?" retorted Tessa defiantly.

For a moment their eyes met. Tessa was shocked to see nothing but enmity in her brother's gaze. She shook her head; something made her want to try again. Just one last time. Her parents would have wanted that.

"Beauchamp, I'm sorry. I know we have our differences, but this is bigger than both of us. Surely enough of our friends and loved ones have died? You can stop it now if you want, and I promise I'll do everything I can to help."

"I'll see you tonight, on your own," he shouted, continuing to walk away. "You'll get my answer then."

Tessa watched him go. Then she glanced back at Leiko, sighed and walked back to her; she'd always been convinced no one really wanted to die alone. She knelt down and took the woman's weight.

"I'm sorry, Leiko," she said in Japanese.

"Don't be," replied Leiko weakly. "One of us had to die. Is he coming?"

"No. He's never been any good at this sort of thing."

"The bastard," she sighed, and winced with pain. "He'll kill you tonight. He's not interested in your offer. He's retiring but wants to get you first." She groaned and Tessa tightened her grip. "There are more than sixty fighters. Please, take my swords, I don't want them to…"

"I promise," said Tessa, "and I'll make sure you get a proper Buddhist funeral too."

"Thank you," whispered Leiko. "No trainee could have done this to me. And your sword…"

"Amakuni."

"Hmm. You're Nariko aren't you? I suspected, but you were so slow in London."

"Borrowed sword. It stuck."

"Be careful. Bryani's husband is hunting her killer…"

"Well, I didn't kill her…," started Tessa, but Leiko had died.

Tessa laid her body down and gently closed her eyes. Then she removed the warrior's sword sheaths and slid the swords into them. Taking a deep breath, she stood up, took out her *cbc*, and dialled a number in Japan.

"*Konichiwa*, Maeda-san. It's Nariko… Oh, I'm fine, thanks. I hope you are too…? Good. Look, I'm sorry to disturb you, but I wonder if you could do me a favour? Is there still a Japanese restoration team at the Bayon in Cambodia…? Excellent. Could you ask Professor Koide

225

to come to Angkor Wat straightaway with a stretcher and a couple of strong men? There's a dead Japanese woman on the main causeway... She's called Leiko. Yes, she was his planner amongst other things... One-on-one combat. Yes, well, she was the one who shot Sinclair, and she challenged me. I promised her a decent funeral. I'll pay... Thank you... How's it going? Well, I'm not sure really. I explained the amnesty to him and he said he wanted to think about it. We're going to meet again tonight... Yes. Thank you again, Maeda-san."

Carrying Leiko's swords under her arm, Tessa started walking along the causeway towards the central entrance tower. It was a gorgeous morning, but now she was battling with her emotions. For the first time ever, she felt pleased after having killed someone. She was sure she shouldn't, but the unmistakable bounce in her step betrayed her elation. She wondered whether this was a bad sign. However, in one stroke, she had dispatched Sinclair's assassin and deprived Beauchamp of another key advisor. She chuckled. Jones would be furious.

Nevertheless, it depressed her to think that a non-violent ending to the saga between her and her brother now appeared even less likely than before. Beauchamp wouldn't stop, which meant she couldn't. Furthermore, if she won, she'd be destined to live out her days in darkness since any light in her life had been extinguished when David died. Such a beautiful place, such a beautiful start to the day, and already blood had been spilt. Was this all she could hope for in the future?

CHAPTER 22

Tessa returned to reality when she reached the end of the causeway over the moat. Several policemen were holding back a large crowd of tourists. She stopped at the top of the stairs and an uneasy hush fell as everyone stared at her.

"Good morning," she said pleasantly. "I'm sorry for the inconvenience, but there was some Peacekeeper activity here this morning. Angkor Wat will have to remain closed for at least another hour."

She repeated her announcement in Japanese and German.

As she finished, a hybrid SUV arrived and a distinguished-looking Japanese man got out. He exchanged glances with Tessa, and they both bowed. Then he and his two colleagues, who were carrying a stretcher, went up the stairs and hurried across the causeway. The crowd parted before Tessa without a word.

As she reached the road, Pheakdei arrived. She sat on the back of his moped and directed him to where in the forest she had parked hers. He passed her a black tracksuit, like his, and while she put it on, he assembled a matching rucksack for her from the parts he'd brought with him. The frame projected from the top, looking remarkably like a pair of sword hilts. Tessa managed to slip Leiko's swords between the rucksack frame and the canvas bag, and wrapped a scarf round them. Then they wrapped scarves round their necks, put on crash helmets, and set off. Sopheap, similarly dressed, joined them shortly afterwards. They rode north from Angkor Wat three abreast, continually changing position. When they reached the Bayon, they went round twice before leaving by different exits. Tessa suspected these precautions weren't really necessary, but didn't want to take any risks.

While she followed a tortuous route back, she used the time not only to ensure she wasn't being followed, but also to think. Eventually, she arrived back at Khon's house. Jones had been pacing round nervously for nearly an hour. He was positively euphoric when he heard the moped pull up outside. He rushed downstairs, but Hachiro had already opened the door.

"Thank you, Hachiro-san," said Tessa in Japanese, "is breakfast ready?"

He smiled and cocked his head sideways, twitching his nose.

"I'm afraid so."

"Are you all right?"

"Perfectly," replied Tessa, showing him Leiko's swords. "I didn't start it, honestly."

"Of course not. Was it a hard fight?"

"No, just a single exchange. I'm neither hurt nor exhausted! But I suspect we'll be busy tonight."

"Japanese is banned," said Jones, irritably. "What happened?"

"Hello, Jones, it's a long story," she replied, handing Leiko's swords to Hachiro. "Let me wash and change, then I'll tell you…"

They reconvened in the upstairs lounge where Tessa took several gulps of her tea.

"Right," said Jones, suspiciously, "I presume those swords mean there was trouble? So, is he interested in the amnesty, or dead?"

"Oh, he's definitely not dead," she replied, pausing to drink some more tea. "I would say the meeting went well. It was a bit *tense*, but I said everything you told me to, and Beauchamp listened and said he would think about it. He wants to meet me alone again tonight, and told me to bring all the paperwork so he can have a look at it. That's not too bad, is it?"

"Possibly. But you haven't told us why you have those swords?"

"Well, that all happened after the meeting had finished and we were leaving. Beauchamp's bodyguard was a Japanese woman called Leiko."

"His girlfriend?"

"Amongst other things, yes. Anyway, she challenged me. I queried the truce with Beauchamp and he agreed I had not initiated anything. However, he also said that since the meeting was over, it was up to me how I responded to Leiko's challenge. But before I could say anything, she attacked. Honestly Jones, that's really how it happened. So, the swords belong to her. Well, belonged."

"I don't believe it!" he exclaimed. "You go to have a quiet chat with

228

your brother, and after he's agreed to consider the amnesty, you kill his girlfriend?"

Tessa shrugged her shoulders, trying not to laugh.

"I wouldn't have put it quite like that. She was begging for a fight, and I gave her one; albeit a very short one. I had no choice but to defend myself."

He looked exasperated.

"You have a very strange way of negotiating. What sort of a family are you two from?"

"Probably no more dysfunctional than anyone else's, and Beauchamp did confirm it was Leiko who shot Sinclair."

For a moment, Jones was slightly appeased, but then his brow furrowed again. Meanwhile Hachiro's smile had progressed to the point where he exploded into laughter.

"This is no laughing matter," admonished Jones.

"Perhaps not, but it is our great good fortune. The Calver Cats have lost an accomplished strategist and an excellent fighter. Leiko had quite a reputation, and her being eliminated at her own request is, well, convenient. However, I suggest we leave discussing dysfunctional families for another time. We all have some skeletons in our cupboards. Nariko-san, tell us everything from when you left."

Tessa smiled at Hachiro and nodded.

"…So, where is this Beng Mealea place then?" asked Jones eventually.

"It's in the jungle, about sixty-five kilometres northeast of here. It's pretty isolated. I suspect we'll need help from Pheakdei and Sopheap again, and from Khon."

"You know it'll be a trap, don't you?" continued Jones.

"Well, we can't be sure of that, but I accept it would be foolish to go unprepared. Suffice to say, I have a plan."

"How come I'm not surprised?" muttered Jones. "Anyway, let me have your report first so the Cambodian authorities know what happened.

It was after lunch when they met to discuss Tessa's plan in detail. Khon had returned, as had Pheakdei and Sopheap. Potter appeared briefly to eat, but on hearing the vehicle was needed that night, insisted on going back to finish the upgrade.

"OK," said Jones after they had all settled down. "Khon, you're the expert, tell us about the place."

"Ah!" Khon smiled widely. "Beng Mealea, the impressive prototype for Angkor Wat. You should ask Nariko. The first time I went was when she took me. She knows Beng Mealea much better than I do!"

A broad grin spread across Tessa's face.

"Is this some kind of a joke?" asked Jones.

"No, I know the place like the back of my hand," she said with satisfaction, "even better than Angkor Wat."

Jones shook his head in disbelief.

"You mean, Beauchamp has chosen a place for his base which you know better than the local expert?"

"My brother never did pay much attention to what I did out here. But I can understand why he chose the place. It's big, and easy to secure, and with the UK restoration team away for the rainy season, it'll be quiet too. But in arranging to meet there, he has made a big mistake."

Hachiro banged his fists on the table with glee.

"The plan is very simple really," continued Tessa, smiling. "Let's assume Beauchamp does want to consider the amnesty. That means I need to comply with his wishes and go alone with all the papers. That's your department, Jones. However, we also need to be prepared for him to spring a trap.

"Now, Beng Mealea, like Angkor Wat, is a large site nearly a kilometre square. Two years ago when the British started renovating it, the first thing they did was to secure the grounds by re-establishing the moat and putting razor wire in it. It's impossible to cross the moat unless one uses one of the bridges. There were four, one at each point of the compass, but only two are still there. The south entrance is the main access and it's big enough to take heavy vehicles. The east entrance is little more than a narrow stone walkway. Beauchamp is probably assuming these physical barriers will trap me inside, together with anyone who comes with me. But that works both ways. They won't be able to get out either.

"Khon, can you get us a couple of bales of barbed wire?" He nodded. "Good. Now, Pheakdei and Sopheap. You say you can use swords but don't have any? Well, I have some for you now. They are good ones, and their short length should suit you. But before I let you borrow them, you will have to convince Hachiro you can use them safely. If he thinks you're up to it, I want you to block and hold the east exit. Simply unroll the barbed wire across the bridge and send back anyone who tries to escape from inside the temple. Don't engage them, just force them back.

"Hachiro-san, I'd like you to wait outside the temple, out of sight. If I give a signal that a trap has been sprung, I'd like you to take and hold the south access. Anyone have any questions so far?"

There was a silence as everyone digested what she had said.

"Mistress tactician," said Jones after a while, "what signal? And how do you get out, assuming you survive long enough to try?"

"Ah, well … I'll think of something for a signal. Hachiro will know. He can be kitted out with comms gear and tell you. I'll fight my way out. As for surviving, that's an interesting point but I don't think Beauchamp will want to settle for anything quick, not after seeing Leiko die this morning. So I doubt he'll use guns unless he's desperate, and I'll be ready."

Hachiro looked doubtful.

"Nariko-san," he said in Japanese, "there might be many, it could be quite a struggle."

"Yes, Leiko said there would be sixty. If Beauchamp refuses the amnesty, it will be all out-war. If it comes to a battle, we won't be taking any prisoners, except him."

Hachiro nodded.

"But we both know, anything over twenty is very difficult, even for us."

"Yes, with swords. But there are other ways…"

"Will you two stop talking Japanese!" interrupted Jones. "It's not fair on the rest of us. What were you saying?"

"Sorry, just some details," replied Tessa, "nothing of consequence. Anyway, if Potter hasn't finished the vehicle by the time we need to leave, Khon will have to provide the wheels. Either way, I want to be dropped about a mile away. I'll walk the last bit alone."

"Oh come on, this is sheer lunacy!" remonstrated Jones. "There could be a vast force there. What happens if you get killed straight away?"

"Then I suggest you retract the amnesty."

"Be serious!"

"I was. We've got to give Beauchamp the opportunity your prudent politician pals require of us. You know what they say: it's better to talk to your enemies because then they'll find it more difficult to kill you. So I'm going to talk to him. You never know, he might just want to accept the amnesty. Leiko's death could make it even more attractive. I'll be fine and Hachiro can come and give me a hand later." Hachiro raised his eyebrows at this. "Besides, I don't think Beauchamp really wants to kill me. It's the thrill of the chase that keeps him going."

"Quite possibly," interjected Jones, "but he might only discover that after you're dead."

Tessa smiled.

"So, Hachiro-san," she continued, "please could you see what Pheakdei and Sopheap can do with Leiko's swords? I don't want to involve them if there's a risk they'll get hurt. Not to mention the fact that they'll be breaking the law by wielding swords in public without licences. Jones, could you get hold of some recent satellite images of Beng Mealea? It would be nice to know if there are any unexpected surprises waiting for us. Also, I'll need that wooden box from Potter… Has anyone got anything else they'd like to say? If not, I'm going to get some rest and check that I haven't missed anything."

Although Jones looked distinctly unhappy, nobody said anything.

The afternoon passed quickly. Potter continued working on the vehicles, while Jones sorted out the amnesty papers. Alone in the upstairs lounge, Tessa slept. The wooden box stayed unopened on the table. Late-afternoon, Hachiro came to find her.

"How are they?" she asked.

"Enthusiastic and not without talent, but totally inexperienced. I think they'll be all right, but I suggest we show them what they could be up against. A quick demonstration might put their knowledge in perspective and stop them from starting something they cannot finish."

"Sounds fun."

He looked inquisitively at the wooden box.

"What's inside?"

"Later," she replied. "Let's see to the others first."

Hachiro nodded and led the way to the large cool basement which they'd been using for the noisy training session. Jones joined them.

"OK, you two," announced Hachiro. "Before we enlist you…," a comment which prompted broad grins to cross the faces of Pheakdei and Sopheap, "…you should understand what you will be facing tonight. Nariko and I will give you a brief demonstration. Single-handed and blindfolded."

Jones and the others gasped, and Hachiro winked at Tessa.

"Oh, for goodness' sake," pleaded Jones, "do you have to?"

Hachiro handed Tessa a scarf to tie over her eyes. Once he had blindfolded himself, she went out of the cellar and tied her own. But with her outside, Hachiro took his blindfold off. He smiled and put a finger to his mouth to indicate the three watchers shouldn't say anything.

"Here I come," announced Tessa, walking slowly back into the cellar, holding her Kimi sword in her right hand.

Hachiro drew his sword and started moving round behind her. She smiled, spun round, and an unbelievably fast exchange of ferocious sword strokes followed.

"Hachiro-san," said Tessa, "you're cheating."

He didn't reply, instead he attacked again and there was another fast exchange.

"Yield!" she shouted suddenly.

She had pushed his sword out to her right and drawn Bryani's sword with her left hand. It hovered within striking distance of Hachiro's neck. He bellowed with laughter.

"Now who's cheating?" he said, taking a step back and returning his sword to its sheath.

Laughing, Tessa re-sheathed both her swords and took off her blindfold.

"Good grief, you two," gasped Jones, "you're mad. You could have…"

"No, we each knew where the other was and neither of us would dream of causing an injury."

"So, you two," continued Hachiro. "Now do you see what I mean? You are not to come into sword contact with anyone. If you do, you'll probably be killed. Just make sure you look competent and relaxed, and use your swords to scare and send people back. Understood?"

Still shocked by what they had just seen, they nodded meekly.

Soon afterwards, Khon returned with the barbed wire and their dinner. They all convened in the upstairs lounge to eat. Potter, clearly exhausted, joined them eventually announcing with considerable pride that he had nearly finished upgrading the Range Rover.

"Well done," acknowledged Tessa. "It will take us about two hours to get to Beng Mealea, and what with me walking the last mile or so, I think we should leave about seven-thirty."

"Oh," interjected Potter deflated, "it won't be ready by then, but eight-thirty at the latest."

"No problem," continued Tessa. "You just crack on and we'll all squeeze in with Khon. Jones, I suggest you join the party as soon as you can.

"Khon, you can drop me and Hachiro off and then go round to the east entrance, hopefully without being seen. We have two sets of secure comms equipment so you can have one and Hachiro can take the other. Jones and Potter can both monitor what's going on from their vehicles. Jones, any luck with the satellite images?"

"Yes actually," he replied, surprised he had been able to get anything. "These were taken two days ago." He put some A4 sheets on the table. "The resolution is not brilliant, but it doesn't look as though there's anything untoward there."

The sheets were passed round.

"I got some notes from the interpretation guys, but there's nothing we don't already know. As you said, the temple is surrounded by a square moat. The only viable entrances are to the south and east. The restoration team hasn't touched the central enclosure yet, so there are lots of large stone blocks strewn around. It's not clear what these shadows are here, to the north, but they may be some heavy equipment which has been covered."

"Hmm, well, it all looks fine," said Tessa pensively. "Have the amnesty papers arrived?"

"Yes, and Potter has donated his portable document-safe for you to carry them in," continued Jones, holding up a black padded holder. "There's a ring on the side, here. Pull it and in two seconds the whole thing self-destructs, sending out a radio pulse to confirm initiation. But throw it away as soon as you've pulled the ring. It's an extremely hot process. If Beauchamp isn't interested in the amnesty, we want to know all the paperwork has been converted to ashes. It's a one-time offer and we don't want it lying around for others to find."

Tessa nodded.

"So, if you get the radio pulse you'll sort of know how things are going. But I'll still try and give you a signal if all hell's breaking loose. Is anything at all unclear to anyone?"

Silence.

"In which case, I think we're almost done. There is just one more thing I would like to say. Hachiro and I are both Peacekeepers. This is what we do, and it's normal for Jones and Potter too. But I don't want the rest of you to risk losing life or limb. The basic rule of survival applies. If in doubt, run away, as fast as you can. OK?"

Khon smiled while Pheakdei and Sopheap nodded respectfully.

"Good. Well I suggest we all make our final preparations then. It's six-thirty now. Let's meet downstairs at seven-twenty, ready to go."

Once Tessa had been left alone, she carefully put the wooden box back on the table and unlocked it.

Inside were six items. Two grey doughnut-shaped discs, each about four and a half inches across and half an inch thick. There were also two smaller black cylinders the same size as the holes in the centre of the doughnuts, and two phials of blue liquid. The doughnuts comprised thousands of fine sharpened filaments, carefully assembled into a rigid mass. With care bordering on reverence, Tessa lifted one of the doughnuts and inspected it for cracks. Then she took out one of the phials, opened it, and carefully spread the liquid along the outer edge of the filaments. As she did so, it was drawn up between the filaments, adding a bluish hue to their deadly grey doughnut. She slowly rotated the doughnut to ensure the liquid had been evenly distributed, eventually returning the empty phial to the box.

Only the volatile central charge still needed to be inserted. This would explode the doughnut into its individual filaments and propel them in all directions. She picked up one of the smaller black cylinders and slid it inside the doughnut. It locked into position with a dull *click*. She returned the now completed shuriken to the box and repeated the process with the second. Then she changed back into her combat suit. She had just finished when Hachiro arrived.

"Nariko-san, it is time."

He came in and immediately went to the open box.

"Exploding poison shuriken?"

She nodded.

"Hachiro-san, we are almost certainly walking into a trap. We must be prepared for all eventualities. Tonight will not be easy. How are the others?"

"OK, I think," he said, studying the contents of the wooden box with awe. "Pheakdei and Sopheap were sufficiently scared by our demonstration not to try anything stupid, and Khon is determined to stay out of sight. Jones and Potter ... well they're Jones and Potter. Nariko, these are beautifully made."

She smiled.

"In case I don't get the chance to say it later, thank you for coming. I'm not sure I'd have been able to do this without knowing I have you guarding my back."

"You're welcome. After all, I need to return that favour you did me at Kawasaki-Ku. But don't forget, I won't be guarding your back. At least not until I can fight my way in to you, and I won't be able to do that until I'm sure there is no risk of anyone escaping."

"I know. Just keep that exit blocked. No one leaves or enters. We need to send a very clear message tonight, not only to the Calver Cats but to anyone else who might have similar aspirations."

Hachiro nodded and watched as she carefully picked up the shuriken, checked them again, and slid them into her suit's special pockets.

Downstairs, the atmosphere was sombre. Tessa nodded approvingly when she saw that Pheakdei and Sopheap had combed and greased their hair back and were wearing similar dark jeans, trainers and tee-shirts. She handed the, now locked, wooden box to Potter.

"No questions, please. Just ensure this is incinerated in London."

He raised his eyebrows, but didn't say anything.

"Nariko, a word, please," said Jones, gesturing her to one side.

"I'm not going to tell you I think this plan is bordering on suicidal because I presume you already know that. However, the thought crossed my mind that Beauchamp may try to have his cake and eat it, kill you and still accept the amnesty. So, I've managed to get a clause inserted which invalidates the offer if you've been attacked. You might care to mention that to him should the situation merit it."

"That's clever. Good thinking."

"Also, Potter has managed to build a bug into the document-safe. It's a frequency-hopping one-way device, very difficult to detect, but he and I will be able to listen to what's being said from our vehicles. The others won't hear. If you pull the ring, the bug will be destroyed too."

"Checking up on me?" she asked with a smile.

"No, you gave your word, and that's good enough for me. But this way, none of our politician friends will be able to say we didn't give it our best shot." Tessa nodded. "One more thing. You remember I'm your UK Guardian?"

"Yes."

"Well, I like that aspect of my job. So, don't go doing anything silly to deprive me of it just because…"

She smiled.

"Don't worry, I won't."

He handed her the document wallet and they rejoined the others.

"So," said Tessa, smiling at the small group. "Is everyone ready? Any final questions? No…? Then let's go."

"Good luck all of you," added Jones. "I'll be starting out for Beng Mealea in about forty minutes."

Khon headed towards Beng Mealea past Banteay Srei. Although further, this way was quieter and took them straight to where Tessa wanted to be dropped off. Their journey proved quick and uneventful, if bumpy and somewhat cramped. The pick-up stopped just short of the northernmost tip of the moat.

"Thank you, Khon," said Tessa, readying herself.

Hachiro looked at her.

"This time you are leading," he said with a smile, "so I think it is my job to check that it is safe."

A couple of minutes later there were two gentle taps on the side of the pick-up.

"Right, you three," said Tessa. "Be good, be safe, and whatever happens, do not be brave. I want to see all of you afterwards, upright and without any holes."

With that she opened the door and lightly stepped out. They watched as Khon turned the pick-up and started backtracking towards the east gate.

Tessa and Hachiro stood for a while in the middle of the road, looking round and listening. It was a clear dark night, cool by Cambodian standards. The sky was full of stars and the moon threw a dull glow in front of them. Apart for the buzzing of insects, there was no noise.

"This way," said Tessa.

Hachiro nodded and they set off at a relaxed pace.

"You know this will be much more difficult than Kawasaki-ku?" he said.

"Yes, but it will either end tonight when he accepts the amnesty or it will mark the beginning of a new phase. Possibly also an end if I can bring him in."

Tessa stopped by a large clump of bushes.

"Those look large enough to hide you," she observed. "The western side of the moat is about a hundred yards in that direction." She pointed to her left. "But to get to the south entrance, you'll need to continue up the road and turn left at the T-junction. Then follow the moat until you come to an eight-foot-tall, seven-headed stone Naga on your left. It'll take you about ten minutes."

Hachiro bowed and quietly slipped into the bushes.

Tessa took a deep breath and started walking, checking her swords and knives. When she came to the T-junction, she turned left along the southern side of the moat. Even in the dim moonlight she could see coils of razor wire glistening above the water's surface. A while later, she came to a wide track leading off to her left; the south entrance to the Beng Mealea temple complex marked by the lone stone Naga; its companion had long since disappeared. She barely paused as she passed it; impressive though it was, she had seen it many times before.

Across the causeway, just before the outer perimeter wall, she found her way barred by a pair of substantial steel-mesh gates. They were closed, but not locked. A group of people were joking noisily behind them. She approached unnoticed.

"Tell Beauchamp his sister is here," she announced abruptly.

They stopped talking and stared at her. Then one of them spoke into a walkie-talkie and laughed, displaying a mouth with only a few yellow teeth left in it. He gestured to a colleague and, with a loud creaking, one of the gates was pulled open.

"Follow her," said the man, nodding towards a sinewy, strong-looking woman with black hair tied back in a long plait. Tessa noticed she carried an extremely good sword, bearing a Toledo marking. The woman started down the causeway towards the temple's central enclosure.

CHAPTER 23

While walking, Tessa marvelled at what the British restoration team had achieved. On both sides, the land had been cleared of trees and levelled. On the left were huts, cranes and diggers, while on the right were neat rows of large carved-stone blocks, labelled ready for reassembly. Most of the missing stone balustrades along the causeway had already been replaced with beautiful, locally made replicas. Without a doubt, the temple grounds were beginning to reassume their original splendour.

At the end of the causeway, Tessa expected to turn right to the raised wooden platform which led straight into the temple. But they went left instead and started skirting the central enclosure towards the west entrance. By the time they reached the dilapidated raised western causeway, a group of Calver Cats had congregated to meet them. Some jeered but quickly fell silent when Tessa returned their gaze. She cut an unusual figure, clad in her Kevlar combat suit with two swords slung over her shoulders. Her steely blue-grey eyes glinted with determination in the moonlight. To them she appeared both exotic and intimidating. She and her guide continued round the north-western corner of the main enclosure, where Tessa could just make out a rebuilt tower looking immaculate with its intricate carvings of beautiful *devatas*.

As they approached the north entrance, Tessa was both surprised and irritated to see a Jet Ranger helicopter being uncovered. She chided herself for not predicting that Beauchamp would be able to escape by air and wondered how many helicopters he had here. Tessa's guide noticed her pause, and sneered to goad her on. They went round the remains of the northern causeway to a path leading back towards the central enclosure. Here they climbed up over the perimeter wall and clambered down on to the grass below. To her left, Tessa could just make out the north library. It had always been in good condition but now, in the dim moonlight, it looked more proud than ever to be standing as its original Khmer designers had intended.

Tessa's guide led on over an enormous pile of big boulders surrounding the entrance arch to the next enclosure. Tessa knew they were backtracking, presumably in an attempt to disorientate her amongst the maze of walls and galleries. As they continued, now skirting the centre of the temple, a steadily increasing number of Calver Cats gathered to watch. Eventually, they passed along the narrow ledge of an interior vaulted gallery; it was strewn with difficult-to-see vines and banyan tree roots. But finally they crossed a gallery roof and climbed back down on to grass. They rounded a corner and approached the south library. Beauchamp, together with a large Japanese man, stood on the raised stone access causeway with their backs to the dilapidated building. A small diesel generator chugged in the background powering a paltry array of flickering lights.

"Evening, Beauchamp," said Tessa, "thanks for the workout. Couldn't you have taken refuge somewhere more convenient?"

"Hello, freak... I rather like it here, although the decor's not to my taste."

"I think it's lovely. Anyway, I've brought the amnesty papers," she continued, raising the document wallet. "Are you going to come down, or shall I come up?"

"Neither. I've decided I'm not interested."

"Oh. Er, that's a shame. Care to tell me why not? I understand it's already a generous offer, but if there's something else you need adding to tip the balance?"

"Unfortunately, I don't think they'd be willing to include your head. So I'm going to take it anyway. Then I might ask for an amnesty."

"Hmm. Well, I'm disappointed, Beauchamp. Are you sure?"

"Of course I'm bloody sure!" he growled. "Do you think I'm going to change my mind just because you've come to ask?"

"Possibly. By the way, the amnesty is automatically rescinded if I'm attacked by the way."

"We'll see. And no big deal anyway. I'm going to retire soon. I just want to watch you die first, and then deliver the merchandise I have out back!"

"So, I take it you don't intend to give me safe passage like you promised?"

"I didn't promise anything, I simply said I would *quite possibly* give you safe passage. I have since decided that it's *not quite possible.*"

"Beauchamp," said Tessa, "this is a good offer and there will be no others. Please accept it, and don't start something you won't be able to finish."

He burst into laughter.

"You upstart runt. Are you threatening me?"

As Jones neared Beng Mealea, he was listening intently to the conversation.

"Ask the stupid bastard again," he muttered. "Just one more time."

"...Yes, Beauchamp," continued Tessa authoritatively. "For once in my life, I am, although it's more of a warning than a threat. But don't get me wrong, it's nothing personal. This is all about what you've turned into. For the last time, please accept the amnesty. Otherwise you'll be condemning all these people..."

"Hah! Excuse me!" interrupted Beauchamp. "I don't wish to appear pedantic, but aren't you forgetting something? The Calver Cats have continued to grow despite the best efforts of the Special Forces..."

Jones parked about a mile from the temple complex.

"Well done, Tessa, text book job. Now pull the ring, and good luck!"

"...what's more," continued Beauchamp, "I have a lot of loyal battle-hardened people here, and you are just one puny individual. You may be able to take out a few, my freaky sibling, but not all of them."

"Oh, Beauchamp," sighed Tessa. "Don't count your chickens. You still have to get to your *helicopter.*"

She held out the document wallet and histrionically pulled the ring, tossing them both aside. Everyone watched as the wallet hit the ground and, with a loud *whoomph*, exploded in a cloud of bright white flames and acrid smoke. Soon only a pile of smouldering ashes remained.

Beauchamp clapped as the Japanese man beside him whispered in his ear.

"She's armed to the teeth, but it's not possible to draw a long sword quickly over one's shoulder."

Beauchamp looked at Ryuu and smiled...

Jones sighed as he saw a message displayed on one of his computer screens.

"Information! Document safe self-destruct activation," recited an emotionless woman's voice.

He pressed a button on the communications console.

"This is Control; this is Control to all units. Code red, time to tango. Repeat. Code red, time to tango. Happy hunting! Control out.

"Hmm, helicopter," he muttered. "Just my luck."

He scrambled back to the missile magazine and started the loading procedure, talking to himself as he followed the instructions displayed on another of the computer screens…

Near the east entrance, Khon nodded to Pheakdei and Sopheap and they started rolling the bales of barbed wire towards the footbridge. On the other side of the temple, Hachiro stood up, took a deep breath and started flexing his muscles to warm them…

"Beauchamp, please don't do this," pleaded Tessa. "You've always been good at bringing out the worst in me, and if you do it now, you won't like what you see. The rules will change. Please!"

"Oh, for goodness' sake, shut up," he snapped. "Just do as you're told for once, and die."

"I suspect Tessa might," she replied sadly, counting her opponents, "but *I* don't intend to."

"I've no time for your riddles," he replied, and nodded his head.

A man behind Tessa stepped forward and drew his sword. She spun round, drawing both of hers with lightning speed. Before the man could even consider striking, she swept her weapons down. Each severed one of his arms at the shoulder and he let out a blood-curdling scream. For a moment Tessa let him cry out. Then she swung her Kimi sword again. There was brief *ping* and his head jumped from his shoulders. It fell to the ground with a dull *thump*, followed a moment later by the rest of his body. In complete silence, Tessa nonchalantly flicked the blood off her swords and returned them to their sheaths.

Hachiro heard the scream and chuckled.

"All too easy," he muttered, and started walking down the road.

"Nasty," said Beauchamp with a smile, turning to Ryuu Fujiwara. "Got that one wrong, didn't you? This won't take long, will it?"

"I don't think so, but she did that unnecessarily noisily. It might have been a signal," he replied, slightly uneasy. "That was incredibly fast and she must be good to have downed Leiko. But if you're sure she's only a beginner, then she is vastly outnumbered."

Someone approached him from behind and whispered in his ear.

"Hmm. We've just intercepted a message," continued Ryuu. "*It said 'Control to all units. Happy hunting.'*"

"They're bluffing. She obviously didn't come on her own, but we know there isn't a substantial force in Cambodia. Tell the perimeter guards to keep their eyes peeled and let's just get on with this. I'll leave the mechanics to you. I want to savour the spectacle."

Ryuu smiled and looked questioningly at Tessa.

"Beauchamp, I am not a freak. I've simply faced my demons, and conquered them," she called. "Now prepare to witness your worst nightmare." She glanced round imperiously and addressed the assembled throng. "If you want to live, leave now. You haven't much time. If you stay, you will die."

Then, slowly and purposefully, she drew her Kimi sword. Previously quiet, it now rang out, loud and confident. Then she drew Bryani's sword, which also started ringing with its low defiant throb. Tessa stood holding both weapons out in front of her; calm, relaxed and ready. The crowd of fighters went quiet.

"What's the matter?" asked Beauchamp.

"It's the swords," replied Ryuu, puzzled and suspicious. "They're ringing, which means they've been tuned to her. That's extremely rare, and it's unheard of for someone to have two. Our guys are scared, and they can see she isn't."

"Whatever, just tell them to get on with it," replied Beauchamp impatiently.

Ryuu raised his hand and started to draw it across his neck to indicate the attack should begin. But before he'd finished, Tessa turned and started zigzagging forwards with an eerie waddling movement. Lurching to the left and the right, she whirled her swords, viciously slashing the chest of a Calver Cat with every step. In two seconds, she had taken five paces, and downed five men. Then she leapt up on to

244

a large boulder and started attacking another shocked group of the Cats. She was determined to maximise her initial advantage. Before the gang had realised what was happening, nine of their number were down. But the remainder soon recovered from the unexpectedly rapid and violent start to the conflict, and converged on her.

"Wow," said Beauchamp, taken aback by the first few gruesome seconds.

"That was very impressive," acknowledged Ryuu. "She doesn't seem to give any indication of her attacks. Fighters generally give subtle clues of what they're about to do when their muscles start to move. But she's not giving out any signals at all. No wonder Leiko didn't realise she'd met her match. Anyway, I'd like to have those swords later. Although this might take a little longer than I'd thought."

"Hmm. Fine. But don't say *she*," snapped Beauchamp. "It's just a vile freak, and a very annoying one at that."

Ryuu shrugged his shoulders and smiled.

"Sexy freak all the same."

Hachiro walked past the Naga at the south entrance and continued towards the gates. There were six Calver Cats there, all distracted by the cacophony erupting from within the temple complex.

He reached the gates and kicked one hard. It swung open noisily and he strode through. In a moment he was fighting furiously. But soon the six Cats were down and he calmly pushed the gate closed. Then he continued a short distance up the causeway until satisfied he had a good defensible position. He stopped and waited. It took less than a minute for some Calver Cats to come running towards him. They wanted to escape but found their way barred.

At the east entrance, Pheakdei and Sopheap had just finished unrolling the bales of barbed wire. Satisfied that the narrow bridge had been comprehensively blocked, they drew their swords and waited.

In front of the library Tessa was fighting with a speed and ferocity the likes of which no one there had ever seen before. Beauchamp was amazed and Ryuu watched with a mixture of awe and growing concern.

Always changing locations, to avoid being surrounded, Tessa soon left bodies strewn everywhere. Sometimes she would be fighting on the grass, sometimes on boulders. Occasionally she would run along the gallery roofs, throw a knife and then jump down to engage the people least expecting her. Her swords were always whirling, and slew anyone who came within reach. With an impressive mix of gymnastics, acrobatics and merciless brutality, she evaded every trap.

After a while, Beauchamp looked at Ryuu. For the first time that evening he wasn't smiling.

"Our guys are going to get her, aren't they?"

"I think so, though she is doing unbelievably well. But we've still got a lot of people left and she must be tiring. She's got to defend herself, and kill our guys one by one. That takes a lot of energy, especially at the speed she's moving."

As the battle progressed Tessa fought on at an unrelenting pace. Wherever she passed, she left a trail of prostrate bleeding bodies. But eventually the remaining throng managed to hem her in, and force her back towards one of the gallery walls.

"Ah," said Ryuu, encouraged and relieved. "This could be decisive. She's run out of places to go."

Beauchamp looked on expectantly.

There was a brief pause in the struggle. Tessa stood on a boulder with her back some six feet away from the high side wall of a corbelled gallery. She was panting and beads of perspiration were running down her face. The Calver Cats surrounding her were convinced they were about to close in for the kill.

Tessa took several deep breaths, looked at Beauchamp and smiled. For a moment their eyes met, and he smiled back. Then she quickly returned her swords to their sheaths and, with a neat backwards somersault, disappeared from view.

"I don't believe it!" exclaimed Ryuu. "How the hell did she know about that?"

"Where the fuck's she gone?" asked Beauchamp, sensing things had not gone according to plan.

"Well, there's an access into the gallery down there. I think she's managed to jump right into it," replied Ryuu, frustrated. "But it's low down, behind the boulders, and very difficult to see. Either she knew it was there, or she's just been very lucky. Anyway the good news is that the only other way out is a hell of a squeeze. Our guys will have to go in after her, but she is trapped."

As they watched, a substantial proportion of the remaining Calver Cats rushed into the roofed gallery after Tessa. Ryuu's mobile phone rang and his brow furrowed. Then a bright flash and a loud *bang* echoed round the temple. Between the gallery's stone window balusters, Beauchamp and Ryuu saw what looked like myriad fireflies darting around.

"And what in hell's name was that?" asked Beauchamp.

Ryuu turned to him with a worried expression.

"Beauchamp, I think we should get away from here as quickly as we can."

"Bollocks to that!" he retorted. "I'm not leaving until it's dead."

"If we don't leave now, we might be the ones to die. You set a trap for her, but she's springing one on us!"

"Bullshit," snapped Beauchamp. "Tell me what that flash was."

"It's called an exploding poison shuriken. It's a modern version of an ancient Ninja weapon. It's made of lots of poison darts, compressed together to form a disc with an explosive charge in the centre. It ignites on impact and blasts the darts all over the place. Each dart is soaked with fast-acting poison; get scratched by one and you're dead in seconds. The darts are made from compressed rice paper. After a few hours, they lose their rigidity and dissolve as the poison degrades. By morning it will be perfectly safe down there. It's a very sophisticated, highly effective weapon. But they're incredibly difficult to handle, let alone throw. People have died just learning to use them. You've unleashed something very dangerous, Beauchamp."

"Don't be stupid, you're letting the freak get to you. It's like that," he muttered dismissively. "So how many of our people did she get."

"At least the dozen plus she managed to tempt into the gallery behind her," replied Ryuu.

"Well, she can't fight for ever. Bring in some reinforcements."

"I can't. She obviously came prepared. The south entrance is blocked by a very large Peacekeeper. It sounds like Hachiro, but I can't think what he'd be doing here. Not leaving Japan was part of the deal he did. Anyway, the east entrance has been blocked with a load of barbed wire and a couple of guys with swords are making sure nobody shifts it. I think we should tell the trucks to leave and get the 'copters out while we can. We'll have to get her elsewhere."

"I am not running from *that!*" raged Beauchamp.

"Beauchamp," pleaded Ryuu, "she said the rules were changing. Presumably she meant it's no longer about them targeting our top guys and us targeting theirs. She's going for all-out annihilation, and she might just do it. We should leave while she's still distracted."

Suddenly Tessa clambered out from between the remaining stone balusters of a window further down the gallery. She glanced up at Ryuu, and winked at him. But then the remaining Calver Cats spotted her and attacked.

"What is it with her?" screamed Beauchamp. "Bring me a gun. If you want a job done properly, you've just got to do it yourself."

"I don't like this. We should leave while we still can," replied Ryuu earnestly. "We've already lost Leiko and a lot of other good people."

"Get me a gun, I said, a rifle. How many have we got here?"

"Most are in the helicopters but I kept one back, just in case."

He barked an order at one of the Calver Cats behind him. The man scurried away, reappearing shortly afterwards with a formidable hunting rifle with a laser sight. He handed it to Ryuu, who checked it.

However, between bouts of fighting, Tessa had been watching the two of them from across the enclosure. As soon as the rifle appeared, she knew she'd have to act quickly. She was an easy target while preoccupied with fighting the Calver Cats.

Muttering "Sorry Sinclair" she leapt on to a large boulder, surprising a lone Calver Cat. Before he could react, she aimed carefully and thrust her Kimi sword into his chest. In agony he sank to his knees beside her, but didn't fall. With him acting as a gruesome temporary sword stand, Tessa quickly threw the second poison shuriken. It whined eerily as it sped towards the library.

"Move!" yelled Ryuu, dropping the gun. He dived at Beauchamp and together they rolled clumsily off the raised causeway. Moments later, the shuriken hit the Library wall behind where they had been standing. There was another bright flash and loud *bang* as it exploded. The platform on which the rifle now lay was enveloped in a cloud of pinpoints of burning light. As a hail of darts struck the Calver Cats nearby, they collapsed to the ground as if in slow motion.

Beauchamp and Ryuu landed heavily on the ground four feet below the causeway. Around them were a number of glowing darts.

"Beauchamp!" gasped Ryuu. "Don't move. You've got some on your jacket. I'll help you."

As Beauchamp swore profusely, Ryuu managed carefully to remove the jacket.

"We've got to go now," he implored. "That was too close for comfort. Our guys are as good as dead. She's no learner, Beauchamp. She's a Peacekeeper and some. We've got to get ourselves and the merchandise away."

Beauchamp was seething; Ryuu had never seen him so angry.

"That fucking *bitch* just tried to kill me! I want her dead!"

"I know, but it's not going to happen here. Look, she's still got to get out of Cambodia and that won't be easy. There aren't any commercial flights tonight, and we know they don't have their own plane. She'll have to go by road, probably to Bangkok. We can still get her if we send the trucks ahead and set up roadblocks. Meanwhile we can take the 'copters to Pakse. But there's something else..."

"Now what?" said Beauchamp, rubbing his bruises.

"They've got some sort of armoured SUV out there. Our guys tried to take it out, and lost a motorised cannon. It sounds as though it's one of those Special Forces vehicles we heard about. I don't know how it got here without us knowing, but it seems it has. Anyway it will be equipped with surface-to-air missiles."

"Oh, bloody hell! But they're single-shot weapons, aren't they?"

"Assuming the vehicle is the same spec we heard about, it will take a while to reload."

"OK. So, if we send the Jet Ranger out first…"

"It will be shot down, and we might get away in the Chinook?" interjected Ryuu.

"Yes. If we're lucky, both machines will make it. And if we're not, we're dead."

Ryuu shrugged.

"Bugger, bugger, bugger!" complained Beauchamp. "Let's go!"

Tessa had lost sight of her brother and Ryuu when they rolled off the causeway. But she saw them both get up before they once again disappeared from view. Shortly afterwards she heard a powerful aero-engine starting up…

Meanwhile Jones was wondering why the constant barrage of small-arms fire impacting his vehicle had stopped. Then he heard the disembodied female voice make another announcement.

"Information! Helicopter start-up detected, one point one miles southeast."

"Oh, great," complained Jones. "I wish I'd had some time to practise in this thing. Come to think of it, why am I manning a two person vehicle all on my own?"

"Information! Helicopter lift-off."

"All right!" he exclaimed, scrambling back into the gunnery position.

A moment later, a tube launcher unfurled from the top turret. The guidance system display had concentric blue distance circles on it and a pair of yellow crosshairs. Using the joystick, Jones manoeuvred the crosshairs onto the white helicopter symbol and pulled the trigger. The symbol turned orange.

"Target selected," said the woman's voice, and Jones quickly pulled the trigger again. The symbol turned red.

"Missile lock successful," responded the voice calmly.

Jones pressed the button on the top of the joystick and the vehicle swayed as the missile set off. Seconds later, everyone heard the helicopter explode.

"Target destroyed."

Jones congratulated himself, retracted the missile launcher and scrambled back to the driver's seat. Then the woman spoke again.

"Information! Helicopter start-up detected, one point two miles east-southeast."

"Blast!" exclaimed Jones.

He scrambled to the back of the vehicle, unpacked another missile and started the reloading procedure. Occasionally, swearing, he would peer into the screen to check the instructions.

Ryuu looked at Beauchamp. They were sitting in the double-engined transport helicopter, listening to its engines accelerate…

The heavily laden Chinook rose painfully slowly, only gradually gaining altitude. At last it moved off sluggishly towards Laos.

"Information! Helicopter lift-off," continued the woman's voice.

Shortly afterwards, with bruised knuckles, Jones dived into the seat behind the missile guidance system. It displayed the white image of the disappearing Chinook. Jones hastily moved the joystick to bring the crosshairs to bear.

"Target selected," said the woman's voice.

"Lock on, please," muttered Jones irritably as he pressed the trigger again.

"Chaff dispersed. Missile lock compromised," responded the woman, *"Target out of range in five seconds."*

"Damn it!" grumbled Jones, as he switched the system to manual targeting.

He pressed the fire button, but nothing happened. Instead a menu of options appeared in the targeting screen.

"Oh, bloody hell!" he screamed as he read the options. "Auto-destruct at closest estimated proximity. That'll do. Go!"

He pressed the firing button and again the vehicle rocked as the missile launched. He heaved a sigh of relief and peered hopefully at the screen.

The pilot of the Chinook shouted back to Beauchamp and Ryuu.

"Incoming! Brace yourselves."

Then there was a loud *bang* and their helicopter lurched violently as they heard the pings of shrapnel hitting the sides. Then Beauchamp smiled at Ryuu.

"Doddle!" he said, relaxing. "So, our trucks are en route to the Thai border? Well, I'll show her what changing the fucking rules means! Get me a map. I want to use the remaining flight time to plan a trap for that wretched sibling of mine."

Jones, Tessa and Hachiro all groaned as they realised the Chinook had got away. Tessa felt sure Beauchamp had escaped, which meant this would not be the final battle. All these dead people were simply more collateral damage; it made her want to weep. Meanwhile, the remaining Calver Cats were dispirited by their leader having deserted them. Nevertheless, Tessa carried on fighting relentlessly and soon there were only eight left standing. Then six; then four; then two; and finally one. It turned out to be the sinewy woman who had first led

Tessa into the temple complex.

As they stood on a patch of grass facing one other, each marvelled at how terrible the other looked. Both of them were dripping with perspiration and their faces were caked with dust and dirt. But there was one difference. Tessa's suit, her hair, her face and her swords were covered with blood spatter.

She raised her right arm preparing to fight and her Kimi sword rang out loudly. But then it stopped ringing, like a car stuttering as it ran out of fuel. It started again shortly afterwards, but markedly less confidently.

Uh-oh, thought Tessa suddenly remembering Matsumoto's warning. *Do not fight for too long. Your body is trained to ignore exhaustion. It will carry on at the pace you demand until it cannot continue, and then it will stop.*

Then she heard a loud *whoomph* in her head and saw a bright flash. As the brightness faded, all she could see was stars swirling in front of her.

She took a step back in an attempt to recover her composure.

Come on, she thought, nearly there. Concentrate.

At first her assailant seemed confused as to what was happening, but then she realised Tessa was in trouble and swung her sword with all her might.

Tessa still couldn't see clearly, but sensed the weapon approaching. So she used Bryani's sword as a block, in an attempt to protect her left side. But her defence was weak compared to the woman's strong stroke with her Toledo sword. A loud clang announced the contact, but then Tessa's sword was pushed back. The attacking blade cut into her side, just above her left kidney. The searing pain was just what Tessa needed to snap her back to reality. With a loud cry she brought her Kimi sword round hard and fast from the right. It struck the woman on her unprotected left side just below her armpit. Tessa twisted round as her sword continued to cut, and a moment later the fight was over.

Tessa glanced round to check no one else remained standing, and then looked down at her side. She had a nasty gash from which blood was already flowing, but it wasn't life-threatening. She had been very lucky. She sank to her knees and pressed some healing herbs and mosses into the wound, taking several deep breaths. Then her vision blurred again, for longer this time. She desperately strained to marshal her senses and went down on all fours. She was sweating profusely and panting as sheer physical exhaustion threatened to overcome her. She started to hyperventilate and desperately fought to maintain consciousness; a loud buzzing sound filled her ears.

Eventually, her vision began to clear and she became aware of her surroundings. She could hear the noise of fighting from the south entrance. Mustering her remaining energy, she took more deep breaths and stood up shakily. She looked round and was disgusted by what she saw. There were bodies everywhere, and she had killed them all. She flicked her swords clean and returned them to their sheaths.

"I'm sorry," she murmured shaking her head, "I'm so sorry."

She picked up the Toledo sword, broke it between two boulders and scattered the fragments. Satisfied it had been destroyed, she went to recover her knives and then walked slowly to the wooden causeway which led out of the temple. Eventually, she went down the final steps and turned right towards the south causeway. The cool breeze helped refresh her slightly and she began to feel a little better. But she knew this was only a temporary reprieve. She needed rest, food and water.

She found some remaining Calver Cats desperately trying to escape via the south entrance. They were so focused on clearing Hachiro out of the way, they didn't hear Tessa approaching. She announced her presence by drawing her swords. The tell-tale ringing caused a pause in the fighting.

"*Konichiwa*, Nariko-san," greeted Hachiro cheerily. "Have you come to help an old man?"

"Well, I don't think you're old, and I doubt you need my assistance. But I do think it's time we went home."

With that the fighting commenced again. Hachiro's opponents were down soonest so he watched Tessa's technique. He could see she was exhausted. However, she continued to inflict fatal wounds with sublime precision, always planning her next attack before her last had been completed. Soon it went quiet.

"Hah!" boomed Hachiro. "We make a team to be proud of."

"Well, I'm not sure this is anything to be proud of here," replied Tessa gesturing at the bodies, "and there are many, many more inside. Most were not even capable of fighting us, and yet they still died trying. It's so stupid, so wasteful. How many more people will be missing loved ones now?"

Hachiro shrugged and re-sheathed his sword; Tessa followed suit.

"Yes, I know. But someone has to do it. Tonight it was us. Maybe we shouldn't be proud of it, but we certainly don't have any reason to be ashamed. We've both lost people who were dear to us. These fools had their chance."

"Well, I suppose we'll find out on our own judgement day. Are you OK?"

"A few cuts and bruises, but nothing Nature won't fix in a few days. How about you?"

"Nothing major; one cut will need more than a few days to heal, but I'll live. I think Beauchamp got away in the second helicopter, so I doubt it's over yet. But at least there are a lot fewer Calver Cats, and we've sent a very clear message."

"I'm sure you'll catch up with him. Where are your wounds?"

"Oh, the only one of consequence is here."

Hachiro looked at it critically.

"Oh, quite a cut. It looks clean, but you're bleeding a lot."

"I know. Don't tell Jones, he'll only worry. Can you sew it up for me? I have a needle and thread. And tell him to come and fetch us; I've had enough of this place."

He nodded, and tapped his comms headpiece.

"Jones, it's all over. We're both fine. How about some transport."

"On my way!" he replied.

By the light of the moon, Hachiro carefully stitched her wound. As he did so, he couldn't help looking at Bryani's sheathed sword, still with its logo obscured. He adjusted the long sharp needle in his hand, glancing at Tessa's throbbing carotid artery. She looked round.

"Thanks," she said, studying his handiwork. "Nice job."

Suddenly a deep throaty gurgling noise approached and the causeway was brightly illuminated by the armoured vehicle's lights.

CHAPTER 24

By the time Tessa and Hachiro reached the Naga, Jones was standing in front of the Range Rover, grinning proudly.

"Quite something isn't it?" he said. "The latest and greatest available to the Special Forces. The UK's only allowed two."

"It certainly looks impressive," said Tessa admiringly. "No wonder it took Potter so long to *upgrade* it."

In fact, the vehicle barely resembled a Range Rover any longer. There was a tracked bogey between the two standard axles, and front and rear swivelling gun muzzles, plus an ominous turret on top. The vehicle's sides, including all the glass, were clad with reactive armour. Although none of the plates had exploded off, nearly all were pockmarked from the impact of various munitions.

"The bogey goes up and down automatically as needed," continued Jones enthusiastically, "so it has all-terrain capability. It's meant to be operated by two people, but one can just about manage it."

"Boys with toys. Shame the UK wasn't willing to stump up for the fast missile reload option," observed Tessa, chuckling.

"That's not fair," rebuked Jones wistfully. "It's supposed to take two minutes and I managed it in much less, and I'd only done it once before. Anyway, I'm pleased to see you're both all right. What's it like in there?"

"Dreadful," replied Tessa sadly.

"Well, the airwaves have been buzzing," continued Jones. "It seems we've caused quite a rumpus. Potter has been talking with a number of senior officials and the consensus is that you and I should leave Cambodia as soon as we can. He left for Bangkok a while ago."

"But someone will have to prepare the report, and there are a couple of areas inside which won't be safe for another few hours."

Jones looked puzzled.

"Don't worry, Hachiro knows what I mean."

"Well, it's your call, Hachiro, but Maeda did suggest you might be willing to stay and tie up the loose ends?"

He shrugged.

"I don't mind. Where did you throw them, Nariko-san?"

"Inside the central gallery and on the causeway leading to the south library."

"Fine, I will take care of it," he said. "You two can go now, if you like."

"I want to make sure the others are all right first," said Tessa.

"Oh, they're fine," interjected Jones. "I spoke to Khon a while ago. He's coming here."

As he finished speaking, they heard Khon's pick-up approaching. After greetings and congratulations had been exchanged, Pheakdei and Sopheap described what had happened.

"Well done, both of you," said Tessa warmly, "but you'd better give me those swords back now."

Crest-fallen, they untied the weapons and passed them back to her.

"Now," she said, grinning, "I am willing to forward these for you to the Phnom Penh training school. But only if you promise to obey all the sword-licensing laws, and continue training to be Peacekeepers. If you don't get your RCL's within a year, I shall be back to collect them. Understood?"

They nodded and thanked her profusely. Then she turned to Khon.

"Jones and I must leave now, and I think you should take Pheakdei and Sopheap away too. Hachiro has very kindly agreed to handle the clean-up. Khon, I can't thank you enough for your help. It made this evening's success possible."

They said their farewells and Khon, Pheakdei and Sopheap left.

With the three of them alone again, Jones looked at Tessa.

"Are you sure you're all right?" he asked.

"Pretty much," she replied, "exhausted, but OK."

"You look a bit … pale," he said, glancing at Hachiro for his opinion. "Anyway, let's be off. Potter's going to wait for us at the border, so we've got a five hour drive in front of us."

Tessa turned to Hachiro and they bowed to each other. As Jones walked round to the driver's side, Tessa went to the passenger door.

"Nariko-san," said Hachiro, holding the door open for her. "You never did say where you got that Amafuji sword."

She looked at him in surprise. It was not the done thing for one Peacekeeper to ask another how they obtained their weapons.

"Why on earth do you ask, Hachiro-san?"

"I just wondered, I…"

"Sorry, guys," interrupted Jones impatiently, "no time for idle chit-chat. We've got to go!"

Tessa smiled at Hachiro.

"I'll tell you next time. Until then, *domo arigato gozaimas. Sayonara*, Hachiro-san."

"*Sayonara*, Nariko-san. Do you agree my debt has been cleared?"

"Of course it has," acknowledged Tessa as she eased herself into the passenger seat. "Thank you."

He nodded, and closed the door. Deep in thought, he watched the Range Rover drive off towards the nearby T-junction.

"Don't turn right, Jones, go straight on," ordered Tessa.

"But isn't it right to Siem Reap?"

"Yes, but straight on is faster, even though it's further. It's a toll road, but there won't be anyone manning the booths at this time of night."

As Jones drove, he spoke to the disembodied female voice concerning their revised route. Meanwhile, Tessa admired the comprehensive computer and camera head-up displays. They were soon speeding towards the NH6 highway at Dam Dek, which would take them northwest, back through Siem Reap and on to the Thai border.

Ten minutes later, Tessa broke the silence.

"Jones, have you got any food?"

"There are some bananas and stuff in the box behind me."

"Perfect," said Tessa. She didn't want to say anything, but she felt terrible. However, she knew water and calories would help her recover. Jones glanced round and noticed her wince as she twisted to reach the food box.

"Are you sure you're all right?"

"Yes, I'm just really tired and hungry."

She ate a bar of chocolate and several bananas, and then drank a large bottle of water.

"Phew! That's better," she exclaimed. "I think I'll rest now. You'll have to wake me, if I'm needed for something."

She took a deep breath and closed her eyes.

Shocked, Jones watched Tessa's head loll back against the headrest. He stopped and checked her pulse. It seemed fine, a strong slow rhythm, and her breathing appeared normal. It looked as though she had simply fallen into a deep sleep.

"Well, so much for stimulating conversation to help keep me awake," he muttered. He tightened her seat harness, adjusted her headrest, and set off again...

Four hours later, Tessa became aware of him gently shaking her awake. The Range Rover had stopped by the side of the road.

"Tessa," he said, "I'm sorry, but I think you need to be conscious for this."

Wearily, she eased open her eyes. He looked worried.

"Hi," she said weakly.

"You look dreadful."

"Thank you, it's nice to see you too. Anyway, I take it you didn't wake me up to tell me how awful I look. Where are we?"

"Just outside Sisophon."

"Great! Do you want to buy me breakfast?"

"Yes, but not here," he replied, relieved to hear her joking. "The next few miles could be tricky. Potter has been doing some talent spotting for us. It seems some Calver Cats trucks left Beng Mealea before the conflict was over. They've set up roadblocks between Sisophon and the border."

Tessa pulled herself up and blinked as she focused her eyes on the head-up displays.

"Those are really cool... Are the roadblocks those two flashing red crosses?"

He nodded.

"Well, we can go round the first one. Didn't your lady-friend tell you?"

"Essylt."

"I beg your pardon?"

"I had to pass the time somehow and found the naming function, so she's Essylt now."

"Well, of course she is. I don't think I'm going to ask why."

"Good. Anyway, Essylt seems better versed in the etiquette of aggression than she is in Cambodian cartography."

"Actually, it would have been asking a lot for her to know the roads I have in mind. It'll be rough going, but shouldn't be a problem in this. I don't think we can avoid the second roadblock, though, unless we go a long way north. Do you want to do that?"

"Not really, Potter is across the border from Poipet with a trailer and cover for this thing. But we don't know what weapons the reception committee will have."

"Well, if we avoid the first bunch, we might be able to surprise the second?"

"That's true," mused Jones. "Let's give it a go"

"OK. In that case, go into Sisophon and turn right at the second roundabout. You can't miss it, there's a twelve-foot-high red sandstone statue on it. The road you want is sign-posted Banteay Chhmar."

Jones raised his eyebrows.

"That's what you woke me up for, wasn't it? I'll handle the countryside and Essylt can be the aggressive female for a change."

Jones smiled, checked various displays and the vehicle started to rumble forwards. Thirty minutes later, he broke the silence.

"So, how do you know about this? And don't tell me it was in pursuit of Far Eastern stone architecture."

"It is partly, but there's something else too…"

He glanced at her expectantly.

"Hold on," said Tessa, studying one of the camera displays. "Slow down… Yes, this is the one. Turn left here, it'll get very bumpy."

They lurched down an embankment and the road immediately changed from bad to little more than a very rough, narrow dirt track. The Range Rover slowed and they heard the bogey move down.

"While I was training those last nine months," continued Tessa, "I visited a number of different places to experience other climates and terrains. I don't know why I've suddenly remembered it, as I can't remember much else. That's part of my teacher's technique; the student doesn't remember what it is they've learnt until they need it. But presumably the jaunt to Beng Mealea has somehow jogged my memory. Anyway, I now have memories of training there, and also at Banteay Chhmar. It's another large temple about an hour further on from where we just turned off. It has some wonderful bas-reliefs."

"Can you remember anywhere else you trained?" asked Jones.

Tessa frowned, thinking hard. Then suddenly she smiled.

"Yes, Bhutan! I spent some time at King Jigme Wangchuck's winter palace near Trongsa. Bhutan's incredibly beautiful, but you've got to be able to handle some almost unpronounceable names, very hot chili peppers and high mountains!"

"Right," said Jones. "That'll teach me!"

Tessa smiled and closed her eyes.

"Hey, no nodding off, I haven't finished with you yet."

"What else do you want me to do? Just carry straight on for about forty-five minutes, turn right when you hit the main road, barge through the road block and sprint for the border."

"I'll try, but if necessary I'd like you to fire the missile, please," replied Jones. "It will shift anything they put across the road. I reloaded it at Beng Mealea. It's the last one we've got so it needs to count."

She looked at him.

"I can't do that."

"Why not?"

"Well, for a start, I'm only licensed to use swords and knives, etc, not missiles. Secondly, I've never approved of that sort of weapon. I think if one side uses them, it's easier for the other to justify using them too."

"You are joking, aren't you?"

"Nope."

"After what went down at Beng Mealea, you won't pull the trigger to help us escape?"

"No, but I have faith in you, Jones," she continued. "Besides, I bet Essylt can fire the thing while you're driving."

"What happens if we're stopped and have to get out?"

"Ah, that's different. Assuming I can stay awake."

"Oh, great!"

He slowed down and, while continuing to drive, started pressing buttons and talking to Essylt. Eventually a set of yellow cross hairs appeared on the main head-up display. Tessa smiled and settled back into her seat. Slowly the flashing red crosses designating the roadblocks moved closer; then they passed north of one and it moved out behind them. The other still lay ahead, between them and the border.

Eventually, the Range Rover slithered down into a stream, scrambled up a steep bank and back on to the main road. They turned right and the bogey moved up as Jones put his foot down.

Five minutes later they'd reached the roadblock. It comprised a number of trucks, one of which had been parked directly across the road. Tessa glanced at Jones, concentrating hard as guns started firing at them. She heard the pings and bangs of shells hitting the armour. Jones responded by firing back; guns on the front of the vehicle sprayed the roadblock from left to right as he weaved the vehicle so he could point them without taking his hands off the steering wheel. Then he straightened the wheel, had a brief conversation with Essylt, and pressed a button on the dashboard. The vehicle rocked as the missile was launched. Moments later the truck barring the road exploded and flew into the air, scattering the Calver Cats in the blast. It landed in flames in a paddy field some distance away. Jones accelerated and barged through the remainder of the roadblock.

In the rear head-up display, Tessa saw the bright flash of a large weapon being fired at them. A moment later, there was a loud *bang* from the back and they were thrust forward. Then there was another flash, and moments later, another loud *bang*. Again their vehicle lurched violently, but Jones continued regardless. They could see the lights of the Thai border in the distance and the shell impacts stopped.

"Good job," said Tessa. "The pair of you handled that nicely."

"Thank you. It's amazing what destruction one can reap when one has to."

"Indeed," she acknowledged dryly.

As they neared the border crossing, Jones contacted Potter and all the barriers were raised in advance of their arrival. Apparently the Cambodians were more than happy to forego the formalities of stamping passports. He drove straight through and brought the vehicle to a halt on the Thai side. He parked behind the grey Range Rover which towed a substantial trailer. Potter and another man were leaning against it, smiling.

As Tessa got out she was surprised to find it was nearly dawn. The sky had already turned orange in the east. Jones joined her.

"Good morning," said Potter cheerily. "Nice quiet run?"

Jones laughed, prompting Potter to wander round their vehicle.

"I don't know, look what you've done to my handiwork. Small-arms fire, maybe a rocket propelled grenade here, and a couple of shaped charges recently." He glanced towards the red glow in the distance. "So it did its job well then?"

Jones nodded.

"Good grief!" exclaimed Potter, looking at Tessa. "You're covered in blood!"

Everyone stared at her combat-suit. There was blood caked all over it, as well as her face and hair.

"Ugh! How disgusting!" acknowledged Tessa. "I suppose the good news is, not much of it's mine. Hello, Curtis, nice to see you again."

"Hello indeed," he replied. "I won't come too close, if you don't mind. This time, I'd like to stay out of reach of that right jab of yours."

Tessa laughed, while Potter looked surprised to learn that they knew each other.

"It's a long story," she said, winking at Jones. "It really is good to see you, Curtis, but, why are you here?"

"Oh, Kincaid heard you were active in Cambodia. He asked me to handle the paperwork and escort you back to the embassy. That is all right isn't it?" he said histrionically taking a step back.

"Oh, yes, fine. But is there somewhere I could get cleaned up first?"

"Sure. There's a Siamovnt Hotel about ten miles up the road. We can take a room there for a while, if you like?"

"Excellent idea," interjected Jones. "I could do with a shower too, and some breakfast. Let's get our vehicle on the trailer and cover it up, and then you can lead the way, Curtis."

Two hours later they all felt refreshed after a hearty breakfast. Tessa and Jones shared a room, and, as he dozed, she took a long shower. She changed into some clean clothes and, much to Jones's surprise, put her swords back on. As they were finishing their breakfast, Tessa, who had clearly been deep in thought, suddenly turned to Curtis.

"I'm sorry, but would you mind leaving us alone for five minutes, please? I need to have a private chat with these two about what went down at Beng Mealea."

He smiled.

"No problem at all. I'll go and pay the bill."

As soon as he'd left, Tessa addressed the others.

"Look, I don't want to get into all the details, but I passed through here a while ago and Sinclair indicated he didn't trust all the UK staff in Bangkok. He did say he thought Curtis was probably OK, but even so, I think we should tread carefully. So, I am not willing to go to the embassy, and I don't think either of you should either. What Beauchamp organised at the border will only have been a taster. What do we need to do to ensure the special vehicle gets home?"

Potter looked shocked, but Jones nodded to him to go along with Tessa.

"Hmm. Fair enough," replied Potter, shrugging. "The Range Rover's easy. Flood left the secure container at Suvarnabhumi; all we need to do is to seal the vehicle in it. If you're really worried, then I suppose we could get ourselves on a flight as well. But Cambodia has requested we remain in Thailand for a day or two in case they decide they want to talk to us."

"OK. We wouldn't want to antagonise them so soon after they've signed the Peacekeeper Treaty. Let's get the Range Rover shipped and go to the Oriental Hotel for as long as we need to. I've been before, we'll be well looked after, and the security's excellent."

"I'm afraid our publicly funded expenses won't run to that," said Jones. "We're obliged to go to the embassy unless there's a good reason why we shouldn't. But we can take you there, if you like."

"I think it would be very unwise of us to split up. Beauchamp looked really angry, and that was before he lost a helicopter. You two will just have to be my guests. I want you there to keep an eye on me. That'll be all right, won't it?"

Jones raised his eyebrows, nodded and shrugged his shoulders.

"I suppose so," he said. "We'd better tell Curtis."

"No, let's not tell him," continued Tessa. "He can help us get the Range Rover shipped, and then we'll follow him into Bangkok. We can easily lose him in the traffic, and go to the Oriental instead. You can phone Kincaid from the hotel and blame it on my being exhausted and determined."

"Well, that last bit sounds plausible enough," mused Jones, laughing.

Ten minutes later they were back in their cars. Curtis led in his

Range Rover. Potter, Jones and Tessa followed, towing the trailer with the converted Range Rover on it, now covered by a large tarpaulin. They reached Suvarnabhumi in the late-morning and Potter organised the loading and sealing of the vehicle into its high security container, ready for shipment back to the UK.

Afterwards, they followed Curtis into Bangkok. But in the horrendous traffic, it proved extremely easy for the two vehicles to become separated. Twenty minutes later Potter drove up the ramp leading to the courtyard in front of the Oriental Hotel, prompting Tessa to slip her swords back into her sword case.

While Potter insisted on parking the vehicle himself, Tessa and Jones walked towards the entrance doors. The central two were pulled open by a Thai man and woman as they approached.

"*Sawadee Ka*. Welcome back, doctor," said the Thai woman to Tessa.

By the time she had reached reception, now carrying a garland of fragrant jasmine flowers, the desk clerk had already phoned the manager. Moments later a tall Englishman approached.

"Good afternoon, Dr Pennington, how nice to see you again," he said.

"Hello, Mr Georges. It's good to be back. I'm sorry we haven't made a reservation, but can you find us some rooms, please? There are three of us."

"We're quite full actually, but let me see," he replied with a smile.

Georges went behind the desk and watched as the clerk flicked through various screens on his computer.

"Hmm, there's nothing in the Authors' Wing, but we do have two rooms. Would it be possible for two of you to share?"

Tessa looked at Jones just in time to see him smile.

"Cheeky! How about you and Potter?"

"Of course," he said, chuckling.

With the booking made, one of the clerks escorted Jones and Tessa to the lifts. But as they were going up, she suddenly staggered and grabbed Jones's arm.

"Are you all right?" he asked taking her weight.

"Sort of," she whispered weakly, supporting herself on him and her sword case. "I think my body has decided it's going to go to sleep again, regardless. Sorry."

As soon as they were in the room, Tessa headed straight for the bed. She laid her sword case on one side of it and pulled the covers aside on the other. Jones and the Thai clerk watched dumbfounded as she flicked off her shoes and climbed into the bed. Without a word, she pulled the covers up, wrapped one of the straps of her sword case tightly round her wrist, sighed and fell fast asleep.

"Oh, well, I think we'll just leave her to rest," said Jones quietly to the woman. "I'll keep one of her room keys, you can leave the other on the bedside cabinet. Now, where's the second room?"

Jones checked later, but Tessa was still fast asleep.

CHAPTER 25

The following morning, Jones let himself into Tessa's room. The bed had already been made and on it was an envelope addressed to him, with a note inside.

Good morning, Gareth. Thank you for keeping an eye on me. I'm looking forward to you both joining me for what I think is the best breakfast buffet in Bangkok! Come to the Verandah Restaurant. 'Ice', the maître d', will be looking out for you.

He rejoined Potter.

"She's invited us to breakfast."

"Oh, that's nice. She's all right then?"

"So it would seem," replied Jones, shrugging.

They went downstairs to the Verandah Restaurant at the back of the hotel. A young Thai man, smartly dressed in a dark suit, approached them.

"Good morning, gentlemen. The doctor is expecting you. Please follow me."

Ice led them towards the riverside. It was a glorious sunny morning, pleasantly hot but not humid. A gentle breeze rustled the leaves of the nearby trees. Only the occasional roar of a longboat speeding by with its un-silenced engine disturbed the sophisticated atmosphere. Potter let out a cry of amazement as they approached Tessa's table.

"Great heavens!" he exclaimed. "Are you sure this is the same woman we came with?"

"I think so. The contents of the golf bag look familiar," replied Jones, laughing.

Tessa looked up and smiled.

"Morning, boys. You've brushed up nicely."

"So have you," observed Jones.

Tessa was sitting at a table by the river beneath a large green umbrella. Her hair had been neatly styled and she was dressed in an expensive white and green Italian designer dress with matching hat, shoes and sunglasses. She looked stunning. Only her sword case, discreetly hidden in a large golf bag, gave any indication of her Peacekeeper status. She gestured towards two chairs.

As Jones and Potter sat down, their orders for coffee were taken and Ice insisted on exchanging her green tea for a fresh pot.

"It's very nice here, isn't it?" said Jones.

"I love it," replied Tessa. "It's not the newest hotel, but I still think it's the best. I've been coming here for years and I've known Ice for ages, he's great. Now, why don't you go and get yourselves something to eat? I've been round a couple of times already, but I think I might just go and get some more fruit juice."

Jones and Potter wandered over to the various buffet bars, eventually returning with a mountain of food.

"So," asked Jones between mouthfuls, "what have you been up to this morning, apart from buying expensive clothes?"

"Well, I got up at five and went to the Health Spa for a workout," she replied, pointing across the river. "Then I came back, showered, persuaded some shops to open and started a pleasantly slow breakfast. How about you?"

"Oh, grunted and groaned a lot while getting up, showered and staggered down here. That was quite enough after yesterday's dinner."

"Suffice to say," added Potter, acknowledging Jones's wistful glance, "we discovered they have an *extensive* menu."

"Fancy that!" replied Tessa, laughing. "Anyway, while not wishing to curtail your enjoyment, I think the sooner we can get back to London the better. Any idea when we can leave without causing a rumpus?"

"We should work through Kincaid for that," said Jones. "I called him last night. He seemed a trifle miffed we weren't at the embassy, but I said we felt it was for the best. Anyway, I told him we wanted to leave today if possible, and asked him to check whether that would be all right with the Cambodians. I'll call him again later..."

Breakfast turned out to be a relaxed, pleasantly drawn out affair. They were all well fed and in good spirits when Ice brought a tall, well-dressed, fit-looking man to their table.

"Good morning. I'm Colonel Kincaid."

Tessa studied him carefully, but didn't respond. Jones, however, stood up and shook hands, quickly followed by Potter.

"Morning, Kincaid, I'm Jones."

"Good morning, sir."

"This is Potter," he continued, "and may I introduce Yoshino?"

"Oh, yes, hello," replied Kincaid, casting a vaguely irritated glance in Tessa's direction.

"Good morning," she replied, "nice to meet you. Ice, may we have a chair for our guest, please, and maybe some refreshment?"

Kincaid nodded and sat down. They exchanged pleasantries until they were again on their own.

"OK. I've been in touch with the Cambodian government," said Kincaid, glancing round uneasily. "They said it's not necessary for you to remain in Thailand any longer as they're happy with the clean-up and the incident report. So I would recommend you leave now, before the media catch up with you here. I have brought a car to take you to the airport and Curtis can organise the transport of your other vehicle."

"I presume the sealed crate has gone?" asked Potter.

"Oh, yes," replied Kincaid. "That left yesterday evening."

"Fine," said Jones, shrugging. "In which case, I'll need a few minutes to gather my wares."

"What plane are we catching?" asked Tessa.

Kincaid smiled.

"It's a Quantas flight. It stops off once a week in Bangkok en route to London. I have a First Class seat for you, and two Business Class tickets."

He handed the three tickets to Jones who checked them. Tessa smiled, and signalled to Ice that they were leaving. Then the three of them went upstairs while Kincaid waited in the foyer.

Half an hour later, Tessa paid the hotel bill and they started to leave. Talking in subdued tones, Jones and Kincaid led the way into the secluded courtyard car park. Potter and Tessa, with her sword case over her shoulder in its golf bag, followed some distance behind. As the double doors were held open for them, Jones and Kincaid momentarily disappeared from view as they walked round the large flowerbed, behind some columns. When Tessa next saw them, the two of them were fighting.

"Trap!" yelled Jones. "Go back!"

Tessa yanked Potter into the shadows and shrugged the golf bag off her shoulder. She flipped the lid of her sword case open and drew Bryani's Amafuji sword. Still carrying the case, she moved quickly forward and her hat flew off. By the time she reached the struggling men, Kincaid had drawn a gun but Jones had grabbed his hand. Suddenly two shots were fired; both hit the ceiling, showering them in plaster. Then Tessa swung her sword down and Jones found himself holding only a hand clasping a gun. Kincaid groaned and staggered back, blood gushing from his severed arm.

Tessa looked round at the waiting cars. A black Jaguar, with a Union Jack sticker on it, was parked slightly down the ramp. A uniformed man was standing watching by the open driver's door. He reached into the car and produced a machine pistol. Almost immediately bullets started hitting the walls around them. Tessa whirled her sword round and launched it at him. As more bullets smacked into a nearby column, her sword struck the man in the chest. So powerful was her throw that most of the blade passed though him, breaking the car window behind. As the man crumpled, the sword lodged in the door and cut upwards through his chest, stopping only when his body landed on the ground.

Meanwhile another man got out of the passenger side of the car brandishing a similar weapon. Tessa reached into her sword case and drew the knife Sinclair had given her. As the man raised his gun, Tessa threw the knife. It was another powerful throw. The knife hit him in the centre of the forehead, sinking in up to the hilt. As he collapsed backwards, he fired a burst of shots harmlessly into the air.

Then there was silence. The brief calm which Tessa knew would be the precursor to screams of terror from the many innocent bystanders. She looked round to check no one else had been hurt…

"Well done," said Potter, catching up and returning her hat.

"Oh, no!" she moaned.

"Are you hurt?" he asked.

"No, I've got some blood on my dress," she replied, deeply irritated. "Are you OK, Jones?"

"Yes, thanks. It looks as though Sinclair was right."

"Indeed."

Apprehensively, she studied the buildings opposite trying to decide whether she dared step out of the shadows to recover her weapons.

Potter smiled.

"Why don't I get one of the security guys to go and get them?"

"Oh, thanks. I don't think any of us should go out in the open just now."

She turned and shouted towards the head doorman.

"We need two buckets of ice, two clean polythene bags and two clean sheets. Now!"

The man snapped out of his shock, bowed and scurried away. Kincaid slumped to the ground clutching his bleeding arm.

"How long have you been working for the Calver Cats?" she demanded.

"Ever since that bastard, Beauchamp Caille, threatened to kill my family if I didn't," he moaned.

"Why didn't you tell someone?"

"I wish it were that easy. I couldn't risk it."

The buckets of ice and sheets arrived and Tessa started tearing one sheet into wide strips.

"Well, look where it's got you now," she rebuked, bandaging his arm. She retrieved his severed hand, wrapped it in a strip of sheet, and put it in the polythene bags. Then she put that in a bucket of ice and tipped some more over it.

"So, where is Beauchamp," asked Jones, "and where's he taking the shipment?"

"Don't know," continued Kincaid weakly, "he doesn't speak to me often. He phoned me from Pakse last night and told me to do this, but he'll have left by now... A while ago, he did mention something about a big European deal he had coming up and said he'd be going to oversee it. But I don't know where."

Jones was just about to ask something else when Kincaid passed out. Potter came back and handed Tessa the sword, but held on to the knife.

"Unusual knife this," he said quizzically. "Unique, in fact. Sinclair signed it out just before Bill Chalmers and General Soe Gyi were killed in Burma. There was a hell of a stink when nobody could find it."

Tessa looked at him; she was worried he might want to keep it.

"Hmm. It's really good. I've grown rather fond of it."

"I'm not surprised," replied Potter, laughing. "Well, Sinclair clearly entrusted it to a safe pair of hands, so let's just leave it there, shall we?"

Tessa smiled as he passed it back to her.

"Thank you."

"But while we're on a roll, a couple of tubular stun grenades went missing at about the same time. I don't suppose you happen to know whether they're ever likely to resurface, do you?"

Tessa grinned sheepishly.

"They're gone, permanently."

"Oh, right, good to know."

"Could you see Kincaid gets to a decent surgeon?" she continued. "It should be possible to sew his hand back on. Also, could you take care of the formalities concerning all of this, please? I got us into the Oriental, so I'd better come up with a safe way for us to get out. I'll be at the Verandah."

"Sure. I'll talk to the Thai authorities. But with so many witnesses, it should be pretty straightforward."

Tessa walked back into the foyer carrying her sword case and nearly bumped into the manager.

"Ah, Mr Georges, sorry about the mess."

"On the contrary, I'm pleased to see you're not hurt," he replied. "I sincerely apologise that this could have been allowed to happen here."

"Oh, don't worry, this is not your or your staff's fault at all. The security here is the best in Bangkok. It was an embassy car with full diplomatic clearance. Anyway, my dress has got some blood on it. May I leave it at the desk, please? Perhaps you could have it cleaned and forwarded to me in London?"

"Of course," said Georges, waving to one of his colleagues.

Tessa found her tracksuit, changed in the ladies room and returned to the Verandah.

"Back so soon?" asked Ice.

"Seems I can't keep away. But I think I'll stay under the shadow of the trees now."

He took her to a secluded table.

"Green tea please, Ice."

"Of course. Anything else?"

Tessa shook her head and smiled. He nodded and left.

Jones joined her a little while later and sat down opposite. As she followed the progress of the longboats on the river, Jones watched her. The sun reflected off the marble floor, illuminating her face with a warm glow while a light breeze gently wafted her blonde hair. He finally admitted to himself, unprofessional or not, he found her extremely attractive.

"I'm sorry about the dress," he said cautiously. "But are you OK?"

Tessa smiled.

"I suppose so. But that dress says it all, doesn't it? One moment I have a nice new frock, and the next it's splattered with blood and two more people are dead. Not to mention however many it was at Beng Mealea."

"Forty-two."

"What?"

"The number of bodies attributed to you at Beng Mealea. Hachiro claimed the nineteen at the south entrance, and, since no other Peacekeepers were involved, we attributed the rest to you. Even though many of them didn't have sword wounds."

She sighed, but wondered why Hachiro would claim all the kills at the south entrance. Proud or not, she had dispatched several of them.

"How awful. Doesn't it just go to show that if one deals out violence, sooner or later it gets dealt back? What have I turned into?"

"You haven't turned into anything bad, if that's what you mean; just different from your previous, dare I say it, idealistic expectations. You've only done what you had to do. One often has to push the pendulum to extremes in order to bring it back to the norm. However, as far as you and Beauchamp are concerned, it's probably all or nothing now. This brazen, if clumsy, attempt on our lives marks a considerable escalation. Even if he is about to transact his last deal, I don't think he'll rest until he gets you, or dies trying. Suffice to say, I will do everything in my power to make sure it is you who walks away!"

"Hmm. After I destroyed the amnesty papers, I said if he tried to harm me the rules would change."

"And now sixty-three of his people are dead."

"Yes, and it's all my fault," sighed Tessa. "I told Hachiro that if we had to fight our way out, we wouldn't be taking prisoners."

"Well, I think Beauchamp's got that message."

"Wouldn't bet on it. Same genes," she added with a wry smile.

"I really would never have guessed. Remember, he started it, and he's the one who's broken the law."

"So," she continued, "you don't think there's any other way out for me? I've got to be in at the end, to make sure it really finishes?"

"You already know the answer to that. Sorry, but not all stories have happy endings."

"I've always worried it would lead to this. Oh, good grief, what a mess."

An awkward silence followed until Ice came over to their table.

"May I bring you anything, sir?"

"Yes, I'll have an espresso, please. In fact, make that two. My colleague will be joining us in a minute."

As Tessa continued gazing at the river, Potter joined them. After a look from Jones, he sat down in silence. Their coffees arrived... Eventually, Tessa was ready to make her next move.

"Potter, do you still have that bag of stuff I put in your Range Rover in Siem Reap?"

He nodded.

"Great, we're going to need it. I think I have a plan. See you later."

She got up and went in search of Ice.

"It's weird this, isn't it?" remarked Potter.

"What?" asked Jones, signalling for the coffee cups to be refilled.

"Well, only being required to clear the paths the Peacekeepers choose. We used to be the ones blazing the trails, but now … well, just look at her."

"Well, don't forget we're out of our jurisdiction here. But, yes, I know what you mean. It is *different*, and it's changed her too, but I think this system is showing every sign of working. A few more years and I suspect things will be a lot better. However, for now, everyone is watching how the Calver Cats' resurgence is faring; and Lamper still doesn't have a clue who's orchestrating it in the UK."

"Well, don't hold your breath waiting for any change there," muttered Potter.

It was thirty minutes before Tessa returned.

"You know, it'd be quite nice if you would tell us boys what you're planning," said Jones pointedly.

"Ah, yes, sorry," replied Tessa, laughing. "My mum always used to say I'd slip into CEO mode when really busy. No offence, it's just another of my numerous character defects."

Jones shrugged, winking at Potter. "We can live with it…"

Ice came to their table, looking somewhat flustered.

"Dr, I can only get twenty-six pairs. Will that be sufficient?"

"That's perfect. Well done. You'll get them all kitted out?"

"Yes, and they'll be ready to leave from the Ballroom at four-thirty, to clash with the rush hour. Here are yours," he said, handing Tessa two white polythene bags.

"Excellent. And thank you for organising it all."

"It is my pleasure to be of assistance," he replied, bowing and instructing some waiters to serve their lunch.

As they finished eating, Ice returned, handed Tessa a message, and hurried away again. She looked at the note and smiled.

"We're in business!" she said, grinning. "The final piece of the jigsaw just fell into place. Now, let me tell you what I've done." They huddled together over the table. "The plan is that Jones and I escape in the midst of a host of look-alike pairs of decoys. We'll merge with them in the Ballroom and all leave in different directions. Jones, here's a key to the new room I've taken. Give me forty minutes and then come up. Potter, I hope you don't mind, but I thought you could stay and see whether you can squeeze anything else out of Kincaid. Here's the key to a room for you to use. I'll fill you in on the rest of the details later, but I need to get moving now."

"Are you sure this will work?" asked Potter. "And how are you going to get out of Thailand?"

"That's what the note was about," replied Tessa proudly. "By the time we get to the airport, a private plane will be waiting for us."

Jones shrugged. Tessa smiled, quickly drank some water, grabbed the bags Ice had left and the one Potter had brought from the Range Rover, and went up to her room.

She started by dying her hair black again. Then she put on a black tee-shirt, black jeans and black sneakers.

Jones joined her.

"Right," said Tessa, "here's your stuff. We'll do your hair and tan in the bathroom. Strip, please … only the top half."

Jones nodded and proceeded to undo his shirt while Tessa sat down, keen to savour the view. By the time Potter arrived, they were both identically dressed.

"Looks good," he admitted, but still doubtful the plan would work.

"Glad you like it. Wait until you see the hats," she replied. "Can you bring our stuff back to London, please?"

"Sure. By the way, Kincaid's having his hand sewn back. They reckon it'll take, although he'll never recover its full use."

Tessa nodded and looked at her new garish glitzy white watch.

"It's twenty-past, we should go."

When they arrived in the Ballroom, they were absolutely flabbergasted. Ice was standing on a small podium frantically trying to organise a seething mass of people all dressed completely in black, like Tessa and Jones. They were in mixed pairs, with all the women carrying golf cases, stuffed and weighted to look just like Tessa's. Also, black baseball hats were being distributed with a yellow logo reading *'Remember Beng Mealea!'*.

"Very good," acknowledged Potter, laughing as he struggled to make himself heard above the racket.

"Ice," said Tessa. "This is fantastic. Great job! Do they know they're not to take any risks? We don't want anyone getting hurt."

"Oh, yes. They're just pleased to be earning some easy money and being allowed to keep the clothes."

"So, are the boats and taxis ready?" continued Tessa.

"Yes, all waiting."

"Brilliant, you really have done well. Thank you."

"Thank you!" he replied, beaming with pride. "I have written out twenty seven numbered cards, as you asked, and have the coloured cards too."

"Perfect," she said, checking the time. "We'll have number seventeen and a blue card please, but otherwise I think we're ready to start?"

She looked at Jones and Potter questioningly; both of them nodded.

"OK. Give each pair a number and a colour card, and then every two minutes announce the number of the next pair to go. Tell them the green cardholders leave on foot, yellow by taxi and blue by boat. Oh, and just to be on the safe side, pairs one, two, three and four should all leave together."

Ice passed Tessa card number seventeen and a blue card, and distributed all the others. Then, after a brief announcement, he histrionically wrote '1, 2, 3, 4' on the white board nearby. To the sound of much cheering and applause the first pairs left the Ballroom.

Eventually number seventeen was called and Tessa and Jones walked out. They made their way through the foyer and the Authors' Lounge to the hotel jetty. There they were greeted by a scene of absolute pandemonium as numerous longboats milled around, jostling for position. Everyone seemed to be shouting and the hotel porters were struggling to keep control. A backlog of people trying to board boats had built up and Tessa and Jones simply merged into it. No one paid any attention to them, they were just one of many couples dressed precisely the same.

Slowly the queue of look-alikes moved forward as longboats sped away. Some boats went upstream, some down, while others just zoomed across the river and disappeared from view. Jones had no idea where he was going, he simply followed Tessa. Finally they reached the front of the queue and boarded a longboat. Then they sped off across the river into a *klong*. Despite the narrowness of the canal, the boat accelerated, twisting and turning at breakneck speed. Eventually it erupted back out on to the Chao Phraya river some distance downstream. The longboat continued across, turned upstream, slowed and moored at a pier under a bridge.

Tessa stood up and got out, carrying her golf bag. Jones followed.

"That was fun, wasn't it?" she said, grinning.

"If you say so," he replied, brushing some water off. "To think people pay good money for that."

"I just did," she laughed, and led him up some stairs to the street. A moment later they were riding up the escalator to the Saphan Taksin Skytrain station.

"So, we're going to the airport now?" he whispered.

"Yes, Don Muang not Suvarnabhumi," she replied, giving him a ticket. "But we'll catch a taxi for the last bit."

They reached the platform and almost immediately caught a train.

They changed at Siam, eventually getting off at Phra Khanong and going down to street level. Tessa went to a vendor and bought some different tee-shirts and they surreptitiously changed, discarding their hats. Then they hailed a taxi and were soon speeding down the toll road towards the airport.

"Neat," acknowledged Jones quietly. "I don't think Beauchamp will have been expecting anything like this."

"I hope not. Several pairs are heading to Suvarnabhumi where we're booked on the late flights. But a few are going to wander round Don Muang too. Ultimately, they're all over the place."

As the taxi drove up the ramp to Bangkok's now superseded international airport, Tessa leant forward.

"Stop at the VIP Centre, please."

The taxi driver nodded and pulled up outside the main doors. She paid and they went in. They were quickly ushered into a private lounge where Inspector Maeda stood up to greet them.

"*Konichiwa*, Maeda-san" said Tessa, bowing. "There was no need for you to come personally, but it is always good to see you. Thank you again for taking care of these arrangements and at Angkor Wat."

"Nariko-san, it was a pleasure. We all want to see this Mission drawn to a successful conclusion. Jones-san, it is nearly four years since we last met. Far too long."

With Jones and Maeda talking like old friends, they walked over to a smart Japanese executive jet. Ten minutes later they were airborne en route to Tokyo from where they would fly to Heathrow…

In central Bangkok, Ryuu had just telephoned Beauchamp.

"I think we've lost her," he reported, fearing the reaction. "She's using decoys, lots of them, all over the place… Beauchamp, there are far too many to shoot them all! …We'll carry on watching, but it's impossible to know which of them, if any, is her… They're all dressed completely in black and baseball hats with a bloody irritating logo! She obviously had them made especially… What does it say? Well…"

Beauchamp exploded with rage in a torrent of expletives, so vehement that Ryuu moved the phone away from his ear.

"…All right," said Beauchamp eventually. "Stay in Bangkok as long as you need to, then join me in Đà Nẵng. I need to think."

CHAPTER 26

When Tessa and Jones arrived back in London, the election had taken place and the media focus had moved away from Peacekeepers, Yoshino in particular. As a result, Tessa was able to return home. She knew the Calver Cats represented an ever-present risk, but, although willing to take precautions, she refused to let them control her life.

She collected her mail, taking a deep breath when she found a letter addressed to her in David's handwriting. At home, needing to prepare herself emotionally first, she put the envelope to one side and gave her swords a comprehensive clean. Then she did all sorts of other chores until finally having to admit to herself she could procrastinate no longer. She settled down on the sofa with a cup of green tea and opened the letter. Then, unable to stop her hands from trembling, she started to read it.

My darling Tessa,

Please don't mourn for me, or feel sorry for yourself. Although my life turned out to be shorter than I would have preferred, I really can't complain. Twice, I loved completely; with all my heart, my body and my soul. Few are so fortunate!

You will have received this letter some time after my death since first my passing will have had to be confirmed by my solicitor. Hopefully I will already have told you what I have done, but just in case, here it is again.

Throughout the centuries the Orkney lairds amassed a substantial landholding in the islands. But, alas, it seems I was to be the last of this long line. After discovering I had terminal cancer, I struggled to decide what to do with the long-term stewardship of the estate. I seriously considered bequeathing it to you but worried it might be a bit of a poisoned chalice. So, instead, I decided to put everything in trust for the Orcadians.

As you know, the landholding is contiguous except for Pennysview.

However, while you were away, an opportunity arose to resolve this slight inconsistency. I couldn't ask whether you approved or not, so I decided to proceed anyway and leave the rest to you.

I know you love Orkney and would always want to have a haven of peace and tranquillity here. So I purchased some land for you elsewhere within the islands. Well, it's a complete island actually, Papa Edinsay! It's not terribly big, but large enough to have a small farming community, a school and a dilapidated Victorian moated manor house with a delightful, if overgrown, walled garden.

It's all in desperate need of attention, but I thought that might rather appeal to you? It is beautiful, and the house and grounds have considerable potential. The title deeds are enclosed. I completed the purchase with cash (!) in the name of Dr Anna Wood. Sinclair suggested the name…"

She had wondered why he had given her those documents back.

…I'd been friends with him since we were children. Sinclair is a common name in Orkney and his family lived here for generations. He held you in very high regard, and, although he didn't share many details with me, I'm not surprised. Anyway, the important point is no one should be able to connect the real you with ownership of Papa Edinsay, so you should be able to enjoy it discreetly. My only regret is that I will not be able to spend some time with you there.

If you like the island, I would be most grateful if you could donate Pennysview to the Burrody Castle Trust. But Papa Edinsay is yours regardless.

Now, I have been working with Sinclair on a complex plan to trap Beauchamp. It's a deadly game, but I have nothing to lose and hopefully might be able to gain a lot for you. I'm not convinced we will be successful, but I hope so.

I'll continue later…

My dearest love, you have been away for eight months now and I am concerned I may die before you return. Strangely enough, I still look to be in pretty good shape, but inside my body is failing. Drugs keep me alive and suppress the pain that fortunately only comes in waves at present. The doctors say I have only a few months to live. That in itself is not depressing; it is the thought of our not having the chance to be together again which really upsets me. I do so yearn to hold you in my arms just one last time. But I suppose that is in the hands of a higher power...

I have spent several days struggling to find words to continue, only to fail dismally. There is so much I would like to say, but nothing which comes to mind even approaches adequacy. It seems I just don't know how to articulate my emotions and the depth of the feelings I hold for you. So, rather than settle for something which falls dreadfully short of the mark, I will simply trust in the knowledge that you already know what I want to say. Therefore, all I need to write now is, I love you, Tessa, and always will.

Thank you for everything. You were so good to me (and for me) right from the very beginning. I cannot imagine how the second phase of my life would have had any laughter, brightness or happiness in it had I not met you. It has been a pleasure and an honour to have loved and been loved by you.

Until the next world, au revoir.

David xx

Tessa broke down for a while, swamped by happy memories of their time together, which had been tainted by images of his brutal death. Her heart had been deeply touched by his letter. She vowed to visit David's family crypt in Kirkwall, as soon as she could.

But after a while she realised her tears were no longer for him; they were for herself, her life and what she had become. Her hopes of one day enjoying a comfortable, quiet existence seemed even more unlikely than ever. Penny's murder and the bequest of the Amakuni sword had started it all. But the deaths of Bryani, Crick, Chalmers, Sinclair, David and Leiko had cast the die, and Beng Mealea had sealed it. The only question now was who would survive. If she wanted to live, she would probably have to kill Beauchamp, otherwise he would just keep on coming after her. But she wasn't sure she could live with herself knowing she had been the means of her own brother's destruction. Then she began to question what she would have to live for anyway since her life would be empty without David. So, maybe there was only one equitable way out? She took a deep breath. She should use whatever time she had left wisely.

Tessa got out an atlas and found Papa Edinsay. It looked idyllic. Equidistant from Rousay and Shapinsay, it even boasted a small airstrip. She decided not to bother viewing the place; she would simply trust David's judgement. She phoned Mr Coyle, her solicitor, and asked him to organise the transfer of *Pennysview* to David's Orcadian Trust. Although first she had to explain how she had survived the total destruction of *Pennysview*, but he was soon appeased.

As the days passed, Tessa knew that, at any moment, she might require all her faculties simply to stay alive, so she maintained her focus by practising hard with Lee. She also collected her Bugatti from John Brown at Stanhope Gate and always kept it fully tanked. Although a nagging loneliness haunted her, some semblance of normality did return to her life. Meanwhile, Jones and Potter were doing everything they could to find the location for Beauchamp's final transaction.

One morning, at 4:30 a.m., Tessa went for her usual run wearing her swords. It was still pitch dark in Hyde Park, so she avoided the floodlit Albert Memorial, skirted the Physical Energy Statue, and sped on towards the Serpentine. But as she ran, her suspicions were aroused. She knew what noises to expect in the park at that time, and there were too few today.

Suddenly a dark shape appeared from behind a substantial horse chestnut tree. Instinctively, Tessa dived to the ground. Simultaneously, the staccato bang of a single shot rang out. She felt the draught of the bullet passing and knew it had only narrowly missed her. As the noise echoed round the park, Tessa completed two quick handstands and stood up almost in front of her attacker. She reached out and grabbed the hand holding the gun, pushing it up and back against the tree. At the same time she drew Bryani's sword and brought its ringing blade to the neck of her assailant.

"Drop the gun, Caprice, or I'll break your wrist … for starters."

Her sister-in-law struggled against Tessa's iron grip and doggedly refused to let go of the gun. So Tessa banged her wrist hard against the tree trunk, several times. Caprice yelped in pain, and let the gun fall.

"What are you doing here?" demanded Tessa, stepping back slightly, but staying within easy sword reach.

"What do you think, stupid?"

"Well, *wanting* to see me dead doesn't mean you have the right to try and kill me."

Caprice glared at Tessa with hatred and contempt in her eyes, but said nothing.

"Furthermore," continued Tessa, "whether you like it or not, it's a capital offence to threaten the life of a sword licensee. If I want, your life is mine to take. But if you promise never to try anything remotely like this again, I will let you go. I suggest you go back to your children."

Caprice glared, and then spat at her.

With a flick of her wrist, Tessa's sword put a deep gash in her thigh.

"Go home, Caprice. While you still can. If we meet again in similar circumstances, I guarantee I will not be so generous"

Caprice clutched her wound as tears streamed down her face and blood oozed from between her fingers.

"Bitch!"

"Thank you," laughed Tessa. "Now, leave, before I change my mind."

Caprice turned and limped off.

Tessa picked up the pistol, ejected the magazine and, together with the bullet from the breech, put it into her waist bag. Then she ran on; deep in thought. Why would Caprice come here, alone? She had presumably got the gun from Beauchamp, but he was nowhere near to egg her on, and she must have known about his relationship with Leiko...

Once home, she made herself some green tea, and sent Jones an SMS asking to meet. They convened that afternoon in Sinclair's old office; Potter was there too.

"Hello," said Jones. "What can we do for you?"

"Well," Tessa replied, "you can take care of this for me, please."

She removed Caprice's gun and its magazine from her bag and put them on his desk.

"Where on earth did they come from?" exclaimed Potter.

"Suffice to say, you'll never guess what happened to me in the woods today. Do you remember Caprice?"

"Beauchamp's wife?" replied Jones, as Potter inspected the gun.

Tessa nodded, and described her early morning encounter.

"I don't like the sound of that," said Jones, "you might have been better off killing her."

"Jones, please, she has kids to look after. My niece and nephews."

"Well, if I remember correctly they've all left home. Adam, the eldest, the one who suffers from alopecia, was admitted to a US hospital shortly before Beauchamp did his vanishing act, and we lost track of him after that. While Belinda and Carlyle have both flown the coop, announcing they intended to distance themselves from their parents. It's likely Caprice met all sorts of unsavoury characters given her proximity to the Calver Cats. Who knows what she'll be tempted to do next." He turned to Potter. "What do you think?"

"I agree with you. This is definitely too serious to ignore. Also, it does seem odd that she tried direct action. I suggest *Yoshino* submits an Incident Report and then we send someone to read Caprice the Riot Act. She needs to understand she's lucky to be alive. Simply possessing a gun can be a crime punishable by death, not to mention attempting to take the life of a Peacekeeper, notional or not."

Tessa shrugged her agreement...

A few days later, she had just started to prepare dinner for herself when the doorbell rang.

"Hello, Jones," she said, smiling and beckoning him in. "House calls now? I'm honoured."

"Well, I thought you might be interested to hear the news."

"Indeed. What's Caprice been up to now?"

"No idea, but Flood and Johnson did go and see her. Interestingly, she's quite a markswoman. She even had an old licence for the gun, although the international arms ban had invalidated it. Anyway, they tried to emphasise she was lucky to be alive, but weren't convinced she was taking much notice. However, I came tonight to tell you about something completely different."

"Really? Well, if it's not desperately urgent, I'm preparing dinner. Are you hungry?"

"Depends," he replied cautiously. "It's not raw fish, is it?"

"Yes, but like you've never tasted before. What's more you're going to have some now or I won't let you out."

"Oh, boy," moaned Jones, momentarily wondering whether he could still make it past her to the front door. "Actually I've never tried it. Quite frankly, the thought alone is enough to put me off."

"Men! You didn't want to eat at Sisophon, did you? But that turned out all right. Come into the kitchen. You can tell me the news while you watch me prepare it."

He took off his jacket and reluctantly followed her into the kitchen where he baulked at the sight of several complete fish lying on one of three large wooden cutting boards.

Tessa put on an apron and proceeded to fillet and slice the fish. Soon afterwards there were two settings of mixed sashimi on the table, together with bowls of miso soup, steamed rice, pickles and some fruit, and a large pot of green tea. Jones and Tessa had chatted throughout the preparations, about everything except his news. They sat down and Jones looked sheepishly at his plate.

"It won't bite, it's already dead," chided Tessa, laughing. "I'll tell you what, have you ever tried hot sake?"

Jones shook his head.

"In which case you've just earned a temporary reprieve."

A few minutes later she returned to the table, carrying a tray with two beautiful hand-painted blue-and-yellow Fukagawa flasks containing hot sake and two small matching porcelain cups and saucers.

She filled their sake cups.

"Now, *Kampai!*" she said, raising her cup to him and smiling. "A couple of these and, unlike me, you'd probably eat grilled locusts."

"I very much doubt it."

Jones downed the sake and a broad grin spread across his face.

"Hmm, this is nice!"

"Of course it is! What a gastronomic philistine you are! Try the fish."

Jones picked up his chopsticks and, with considerable difficulty, manoeuvred a piece of fish into his mouth.

"Wow, it's good. It just melts in your mouth!"

"Well, you can't get much fresher than this. What's more it took me ages to learn how to prepare it ... I think."

"Oh, more of that *not remembering what you've been taught* thing?"
She nodded.

"That really is weird," he said, refilling their sake cups. "Anyway, back to business. We've intercepted a coded message from the Calver Cats. It's probably been relatively quiet for you because Beauchamp

284

is focusing on finalising his transaction first. He must know we're pulling out all the stops to find him."

"Who found the message?"

"One of Lamper's people," he replied with a wry smile.

"Oh, please. Not again? Everything that man touches seems to go badly wrong."

"Hmm, I know what you mean. But it's the only lead we have."

"That's what we said last time. So what does the message say?"

"We're not sure yet, which is why I wasn't in a rush to contact you. It's hidden within a complex Vigenère code which our experts are convinced they can crack, in a day or so. But in the meantime it's gobbledegook, I'm afraid."

He spread a piece of paper on the table:

F	P	H	P	I	R	C	X	J	G	V
X	F	T	M	V	M	V	U	O	P	V
V	P	V	M	E	H	R	E	Y	T	B
K	E	A	T	Z	A	S	T	S	R	I

"Hmm. Gobbledegook indeed." Tessa confirmed.

"Potter is going to call Kincaid again to see if he knows what the key-phrase might be, or at least what language they're usually in. Otherwise the cipher chaps will just have to carry on doing their clever stuff…"

They continued talking and eating, but eventually Jones stood up.

"Right, well, I'd better be off. I have to admit, that was an excellent dinner. Thank you."

"You're welcome."

She walked him to the front door and Jones turned to look at her. He was standing just a little too close to her, and their eyes met. Tessa knew precisely what he was thinking.

"Jones," she said quietly, "it's dangerous getting close to me."

"Gareth, please. And I don't think my life expectancy is particularly high anyway."

Tessa smiled, and thought for a moment.

"I've some excellent aged Orkney malt whisky. Fancy a tot before you go … it's quite peaty?"

"Love some."

They settled back on the sofa and she showed him some pictures of temple ruins in Cambodia and Burma. Eventually he left, and Tessa went to bed, thinking…

The following evening, there was another knock at her door.

"Gareth! Heavens, hungry again?"

"Yes, actually. And I've got some news."

"Wow, a double whammy," she replied, locking the door behind him. "So, what do we do first, news or dinner?"

"Well, if this information is correct, we still have a couple of days. So, let's do dinner first…"

They went back to the kitchen and Tessa donned her apron.

It was two hours before they'd finished their meal. They sat on the sofa again and Jones had some more whisky; Tessa drank water.

"Potter did get something more from Kincaid. Of course, it might just be a red herring. Beauchamp will probably have expected us to extract it. However, when Kincaid received his final instructions from Pakse, he overheard Beauchamp saying to someone else that the key-phrase will be *The Calver Cats Big Triple*. It's not unusual to have a daft key phrase which may or may not mean anything of consequence. Anyway, we applied it to the coded message, and the result is:

M	I	D	N	I	G	H	T	S	E	V
E	N	S	E	P	T	E	M	B	E	R
C	I	R	K	E	W	W	A	H	R	B
R	M	A	L	T	A	B	L	D	G	E

"Malta!" exclaimed Tessa. "Why would Beauchamp choose Malta?"

"Oh, lots of reasons. Easy access, especially by sea, and there are several discreet airfields."

"But it's hardly central to Europe, which is presumably where all his buyers are likely to be coming from. Surely they would want him to bring the stuff closer to them? Forcing them to find ships and cross several borders just doesn't sound right to me."

"I'm not so sure. Malta is small, quiet, and not overly inconvenient, especially if some of his shipment is bound for Africa or perhaps *Irabya* in the Middle East. Also, if people know Beauchamp intends to retire, maybe not everyone is happy about it, so it would be a good place for a swift getaway."

"It still sounds odd to me."

"Well, there's something else which might make Malta attractive to him," added Jones with a glint in his eye.

"Which is?"

"Malta is a small but proud place, and although they've signed the Peacekeeper Treaty, they won't accept non-Maltese Peacekeepers. They have a couple of their own and are convinced that's enough; so Beauchamp knows you won't be in attendance. I'm going to take the 'A' Team to Malta, and Potter will stay here to keep an eye on you."

Tessa looked at him in disbelief.

"But I've got to go! I can't conceive of this ending without my being there."

"I don't think it will. This isn't Beauchamp's last transaction. You are... There's certainly nothing more I can do on your behalf with Malta. I've tried everything, including several conversations with their Head of Special Forces. But she's adamant. You will not be permitted to attend, even as an observer."

"I don't believe it!" exclaimed Tessa in frustration.

"I'm afraid that's the way it's got to be."

"Oh, I didn't mean the Maltese exclusion order. This is not the way Beauchamp would plan to do it. He'll want to get it all over and done with in one go. Maybe this is just a red herring to lure the 'A' Team away, and only when you're fully committed will his true plans become clear?"

"Potter thought that, too, but I have to go. However, as I said, he'll be staying in London, and so should you. If we do change location, you must be ready to leave immediately."

It was late-evening when Jones prepared to leave.

"Well, be careful," said Tessa, kissing him lightly on the cheek.

"I will be. You too … and stay within reach. Potter will contact you if anything unexpected happens."

CHAPTER 27

The following morning, as Tessa ran round Hyde Park, she pondered further Beauchamp's choosing Malta for his final transaction. The more she thought about it, the more convinced she became that it was a diversion. She developed an alternative scenario and went unusually early to SKS to tell Lee. As they sat drinking green tea, she explained her thinking…

"So, where do you think it will be?"

"Well, I know it's a bit simplistic, but according to Jones, the drugs and weapons markets in Europe are pretty much equidistant from Germany. Drugs go to all the European countries, while guns go predominantly to the eastern bloc countries and further south. That would make Germany a much more sensible place for the handover. Furthermore, since the border controls in mainland Europe are almost non-existent now, everything could be transported by road in a single trip. From Malta, first there would be a sea crossing and then some much longer road journeys."

"But are you sure the shipment is only bound for Europe?"

"Not entirely, but let's assume it is."

She unfurled a map of Southeast Asia.

"We know Beauchamp flew to Pakse with, say, ten tons of cargo. So, where would he go from there? It's not practical to fly the Chinook to Germany, so he'd be better off going by boat. It's slower, but much more discreet. Just another container, like the millions of others moving that way. Since he'd left Cambodia after Beng Mealea, it's unlikely he would go back there; and if he intended to go to an international seaport, then he only needed to continue over the Bolovens Plateau to Đà Nẵng. It's very large and busy and less than two hundred miles from Beng Mealea as the crow flies; nothing for a Chinook. From Đà Nẵng it would be easy to ship the stuff to Germany."

Tessa unfurled a map of Germany.

"Sounds logical," agreed Lee studying the maps. "That would suggest the cargo could come ashore at either Bremerhaven or Hamburg. Or maybe somewhere quieter but nearby."

"Precisely! Makes sense, doesn't it?"

"Yes. What does Jones think?"

"I haven't told him."

"Ah... So I suppose you're going to Germany then?"

"Yes. I'll take the Bugatti and head for Hamburg."

"Do you want me to come with you?"

"No, I just wanted you to know what I was doing and why. Apart from that, I suppose you could wish me luck!"

"Hah! You know I am always happy to do that. But these things rarely have much to do with luck. It is more likely to be a matter of skill and destiny."

She smiled.

"If I'm right and this is all about luring the 'A' Team away, Beauchamp will either drop me a clue to get me to the right place, or he won't be expecting me at all. Also, if Jones suddenly decides to rush north, I'll already be on my way ... and Hamburg isn't such a bad place to visit."

Lee smiled.

"Be careful, Nariko. You are going out on a limb ... again."

"I know. But I have to try and be close to where I think the deal is likely to go down. There are several UNWP airfields round there, so Jones will still be able to get to me, or vice versa."

"I understand. Also, I accept there is nothing I can do to stop you. But, Nariko, please believe me when I say I really do want you to come back in one piece..."

Tessa walked briskly home, finished her preparations and drove to Dover.

Several hours later, she had just turned north on to the A3 autobahn, passed Duisburg, when her car-phone beeped to alert her to a newly arrived SMS message.

She thought Jones had probably caught up with her and wanted to vent his fury. She looked to see who had sent the message, but there wasn't any sender information. She paged down to find:

A	V	G	J	D	L	C	P	V	T	M
T	J	L	B	K	K	B	Z	P	E	L
L	V	Y	V	H	P	I	X	I	A	E
E	W	W	M	T	M	Y	Q	G	E	C

"...and here we go," she mumbled.

Tessa considered her options. She couldn't decipher the message on her own; but even if she could, she'd be unwise to act on it without backup. She had no choice but to ask for assistance. Switching her car phone to encrypted communications, she called Jones.

"Hi, getting a nice tan then?"

"Oh, hello, Yoshino. Not really. What can I do for you? You sound as though you're in the car?"

"Yes, I am, and something very peculiar just happened. I've received an SMS message with no name or sender number."

"That is weird. Have you told Potter? He might be able to trace its origin."

"Er, no. I decided to call you first. You see, it's another coded message, just like the one you showed me."

Jones went quiet.

"Damn! Hold on a second, I want Potter to be in on this."

Shortly afterwards, with the three of them on the call, Tessa related what had happened and started reading the message...

"OK," interrupted Potter. "Forward it to me, please. I'll get the encryption people on to it and see if our tech team can trace the sender. I'll call you both back in a couple of minutes."

Tessa pressed some buttons on the central console. Following a grunt of acknowledgement from Potter there was a click as he left the call.

"Where are you driving to?" asked Jones suspiciously.

"Right now I'm going to a petrol station to fill the Bugatti," she replied evasively. "How long do you think Potter will need?"

"Five minutes."

"OK, I'll be done by then," said Tessa, quickly ending the call. She put her foot down and stopped at the next services. Soon back on the autobahn, she started considering where she might need to go to catch an aeroplane. Her phone rang again.

"OK, everyone on board?" asked Potter, barely pausing for a reply. "We tried decoding the message using the same key-phrase; it worked a treat. It reads:

H	O	C	H	D	A	H	L	E	R	*M*
A	*R*	*K*	*T*	E	R	K	R	A	T	H
S	*O*	*U*	*T*	*H*	E	N	T	R	Y	*E*
L	*E*	*V*	*E*	*N*	T	H	I	R	T	Y

"Bull's-eye!" exclaimed Tessa with an unmistakable air of satisfaction.

"Really? But, that's in Germany, near Düsseldorf," commented Potter. "Though it does look authentic as the Calver Cats often send their instructions in two tranches: actual date and false location with one message, and then the true location and time with another."

"Where did this one come from?" continued Tessa, pushing some buttons on the Bugatti's GPS system.

"It originated from a Cambodian mobile phone somewhere in the Far East. But that's all we know."

Suddenly the Bugatti GPS started talking.

"Bitte neue Address Angeben?"

"Hochdahler Markt. Stadt Erkrath," replied Tessa, wondering how Jones would react.

"Akzeptiert. Bitte warten."

"Yoshino, where exactly are you?" demanded Jones in alarm.

"Er, Germany."

"Potter!" he shouted.

"Vorgesehene Ankunft in ein und fünfzig Minuten," interrupted the Bugatti's navigation system. *"Nächste Ausfahrt in drei kilometre, bitte umkehren."*

Tessa responded by flooring the accelerator, prompting a powerful roar from the engine; loud enough to be heard clearly over the phone.

"Potter," shouted Jones again. "You've let her get away from you!"

"Yes, well" he stammered, "have you ever tried holding water in your hands?"

Jones muttered some expletives.

"Look," continued his second-in-command, "we don't know which location is the real one, if either of them is, and we don't know why this second message was issued now in such mysterious circumstances."

"Well, my money's on where Yoshino's going to be in fifty-one minutes," retorted Jones. "Where's yours?"

"Hmm, I see your point."

"OK. I'll leave our force here with Flood in charge, just in case, and fly to Frankfurt. Contact Oberst Müller and ask him to get his 'A' Team ready for action. We'll need 'copters, and ask him to get sniper licences too. I'll liaise with him myself when I'm underway."

Meanwhile Tessa had turned round at the autobahn exit and started accelerating south towards Düsseldorf.

"*Vorgesehene Ankunft in vier und neunzig Minuten,*" interjected her car.

"Oh, hell!" muttered Jones as he put his hand over the telephone's mouthpiece to issue some orders. Tessa and Potter waited.

"So how did you know it was going to be Germany?" asked Jones when he resumed the call.

"I didn't," replied Tessa. "But Malta just didn't sound right, so I thought about it and felt it'd be more likely for him to ship the stuff into northern Germany. I was on my way to Hamburg when the message arrived. You know the rest."

"Does that mean you've got all your gear?"

"Yes, even the communicator you gave me…"

"Excuse me, you two," interrupted Potter, "but I'd better contact Müller, unless anyone has anything else for me?"

After a moment's pause, a click announced he had hung up.

"It's going to take me several hours to get there," continued Jones.

"I know. Don't worry, I'll keep an eye on things until you arrive."

"That's what I'm worried about. This reeks of a trap."

"It does rather, doesn't it?" replied Tessa as her car's engine continued to roar in the background. "But I'd like to know who's trying to trap whom, and why?"

"What do you mean?"

"Well, why would Beauchamp hide his identity if he sent me the message? And why bother to code it and send it from a Cambodian

292

phone? Also, I used to work near Düsseldorf; I've even been to Hochdahler Markt. Beauchamp may not have paid much attention to what I was doing with my life, but for him unintentionally to choose so many places I know, seems more suspicious than fortuitous."

"True. I wonder what's really going on here?"

"I don't know. Maybe it's something to do with his retirement."

"Hmm. I'll ask Müller to get you a detailed update of the area."

"Vorgesehene Ankunft in vierzig Minuten," interjected her car.

"Look, I've got to go," rasped Jones. "I'll call you again in a few minutes."

Jones put his telephone down.

Tessa looked at the time. 6:45 p.m. After a few minutes, she smiled and dialled another number. Moments later a polite quietly-spoken male voice answered the call.

"Druckmaschinen und Service."

"Guten abend, Herr Schneider," replied Tessa in German. "I thought I told you to stop working so late?"

"Ah! Frau Doktor," came the delighted reply from her former employee. "It is wonderful to hear from you. How are you?"

They talked for a while. Then, Tessa confirmed there was no one apart from him in the offices and asked him to open the door to the private underground garage in ten minutes.

She had always got on well with Herr Schneider. She had hired him into her old company long before she'd sold it, and for many years he had proved to be both a good and loyal finance director. She trusted him to help her out one final time.

Just as she ended the call, Jones phoned again.

"Yoshino, I have Oberst Müller on the line. He's got some information about Hochdahler Markt for you."

"Guten abend, Herr Oberst."

"Guten abend, Yoshino. *Es freudt mich Sie kennen zu lernen."*

"Gleichfalls."

"I understand you know Hochdahler Markt from a while ago," he continued in English, "it has changed a lot recently. Some of the accommodation blocks were condemned and that triggered a redevelopment of the whole area. Now, all the shops and apartments are empty and the market square is fenced off. The only people left are some security guards, who may well have been bought off. I am e-mailing you a map of the area. We are putting together our team now, but we won't be able to reach Hochdahl much before midnight, and some bad weather is forecast."

"No problem, Herr Oberst. Assuming the Calver Cats turn up, I'll keep them busy until you arrive."

"Good luck, Yoshino," continued Müller. "Herr Jones, I have some organising to do. I will talk to you later."

"OK," replied Jones. "Thanks again for your help."

There was a click as Müller put down his phone. After a brief pause, Jones spoke with a marked note of concern in his voice.

"You do know you can't take them all on single-handed, don't you? If what we expect really goes down, then there will be an awful lot of people involved. We want Beauchamp alive, not you dead."

Tessa knew he was right and that she would be foolish to try to fight them all. Also, making an entrance too early could simply mean she would get killed and Beauchamp would escape before help arrived.

"Yes, I understand. I'll try and stay below the parapet, but I do want to make sure Beauchamp doesn't get away. After tonight, he'll go to ground. We may never get another chance like this."

"Not true. Even if he did escape, we'd catch up with him eventually. There is certainly no point in your risking your life in a futile attempt to delay him."

"True, but you know me, I don't do futile things. I suspect the mere fact you were decoyed to Malta will have convinced Beauchamp he's safe tonight..."

"In drei kilometre rechts einbieten, Ausfahrt Hilden nehmen," the Bugatti interjected.

"...I'm about to pull off the motorway," Tessa continued. "I'll call you when I'm in position."

"Please don't do anything reckless," pleaded Jones...

Tessa soon reached her old factory and drove down the slope into the empty garage. She could see Herr Schneider standing at the back awaiting her. She got out, smiling, and embraced him, kissing him lightly on both cheeks.

"Good to see you, how are you keeping?" she asked warmly.

"I am very well, thank you. I retire in less than a year now, so the end of these long days is in sight for me. But you look fantastic … and as for your car! Wow! Come upstairs and tell me what you've been up to."

Tessa nodded and retrieved her rucksack and the large golf bag containing her sword case.

"Thanks, I will. But I'm afraid I need some more favours. Are you sure there's no one else in the building?"

"No one, I'm sure," he said, beginning to sense this was far from a social visit.

"Excellent. First, I need to change but then I'll tell you a tale which is so fantastic, you'll have difficulty believing it. However, when you get back to your office, could you close your windows and pull the blinds down, please? I don't want anyone to know I'm here, for both our sakes."

Herr Schneider recognised her *serious* tone; he nodded and led the way upstairs.

Tessa changed in the female cloakroom and then marched into Herr Schneider's office. He was sitting studying some papers at the conference table. He looked up as she entered. His mouth fell open and his eyes widened in amazement. She was dressed in her dark bluish-purple Kevlar combat suit and already had her swords slung over her shoulders.

"Bit of a shock, isn't it?" she said. "But this is how I dress for work these days." She sat down opposite him. "I thought seeing me like this might help you accept my story. It all started after Penny's murder and my return to England…"

Tessa related as much of her unhappy saga as she felt it would be safe for him to know.

"Incredible! What else can I say?" he said finally, shaking his head. "So, you'd better tell me about these favours you need?"

Tessa smiled.

"Well, I'd like to leave my car here for a while, please. Also, I'd like you to take me to Hochdahler Markt. Drop me off in Beckhäuser Strasse, near the entrance to the car park. If we go up the hill from Sandheim, I'll be on the right side of the road to slide out into the bushes near the pedestrian tunnel. You don't need to stop, just slow down enough for me to get out. Finally, after you've dropped me off,

I'd like you to go straight home and not mention any of this to anyone. Don't even say I was here, or that my car is in the garage. I'm afraid that will mean the garage is out of bounds since the Bugatti doesn't like being approached by anyone it doesn't recognise. I'll come and collect it as soon as I can. But if for some reason I don't appear in a couple of days, no problem, just phone this number in London. It will get you through to a man called Jones, or maybe Potter. Just say I asked you to call, and that you have my car. They'll know what to do. Is that OK?"

She looked at Herr Schneider and waited. After a brief pause, he took a deep breath and smiled.

"Of course that's OK. Isn't it always?"

"Thank you," said Tessa. "I'll put my bags in the Bugatti on the way out, and arm its defence systems. And I promise we'll catch up properly later."

He looked up at her quizzically as he stuffed his lap-top into his already bulging briefcase.

"That would be nice, and I'm sure Hildegard would love to see you again, too. But I suspect there'll be those who will be trying hard tonight to ensure you are not able to keep such promises."

"Well, I promise to do my best," replied Tessa, laughing to lighten the atmosphere.

Fifteen minutes later, they were sitting in Herr Schneider's BMW travelling towards Hochdahler Markt. Tessa was not terribly comfortable since it had not been designed to seat someone wearing swords. As they neared the drop-off point, Herr Schneider switched off his car's headlights. He slowed down and rummaged under the dashboard, pretending to look for something.

"Good luck," he whispered as the car almost stopped.

Tessa nodded, and, keeping as low as she could, stepped out of the car and ducked into the bushes. The passenger door clicked shut and the BMW drove off, quickly disappearing from view.

CHAPTER 28

Crouching down, Tessa waited until her eyes and ears grew accustomed to the surroundings. Eventually, convinced she was alone, she crept through the bushes to where a pedestrian access tunnel surfaced from under the road.

All the usual entrances to the market square had been blocked with high metal fences. But she followed the line of one through the bushes and found a gap in it large enough for her to squeeze through. A couple of minutes later, she was standing in the shadows at the southwest corner of Hochdahler Markt.

She remembered this large cobbled square well; it sloped upwards slightly to the north. When she'd last visited, it had been a pleasant bustling place, filled with market stalls. Now the friendly commercial centre had been replaced with a dark, empty, neglected space, strewn with litter. The surrounding tower blocks were all derelict, with many of their lower windows broken.

Although the shops had been boarded up, she remembered that some to her left had deeply recessed entrances. Still listening for signs of activity, she walked quietly up the side of the square, looking for somewhere to hide. She found a passage leading to what had been a photographer's shop, partially filled with stacks of cardboard boxes. It was dirty, dank and unpleasantly smelly, but that would help mask her presence. Tessa cleared a space for herself, leaving two openings. One for when she wanted to get out, and another from which to watch what was happening in the square. She listened again; still there was nothing. As she had hoped, she had arrived before any advance guards whom Beauchamp might send. It was 8:15 p.m. Keeping well out of sight, she put on her headset and lightly tapped the side.

"Jones, can you talk?" she whispered.

Tessa had turned down the volume to ensure no one could hear him reply, but he sensed the situation and spoke quietly.

"Yes, where are you?"

"I'm hiding in Hochdahler Markt. At the moment there's no one here apart from me, but I'll let you know if anything interesting happens."

"OK. Just keep out of harm's way, and don't do anything brave. In fact, don't do anything without talking to me first. It's a long story, but we're all in Munich. There has been some horrendous weather and our travel plans have been delayed," he said dejectedly. "We'll be leaving shortly, but we are behind schedule."

"When do you think you'll get here?"

"Eleven-forty-five is the current ETA. But Müller is doing his best to improve on it," replied Jones, barely able to hide his annoyance.

"So be it," sighed Tessa. "Talk to you later, Yoshino out."

Jones felt sure Tessa intended to try and capture Beauchamp, with or without them; he turned abruptly to Oberst Müller.

"I've had enough of this," he exclaimed angrily. "We need to leave *now!* Otherwise we're going to be responsible for the death of a Peacekeeper! If you can't get clearance, then let me talk to them."

Meanwhile, Tessa relaxed, and prepared for what she suspected would be a long wait.

At 10:30 p.m. some trucks drove into the square. One stopped close to Tessa's hiding place and a number of crates of heavy equipment were unloaded. Then some perimeter lights were erected together with more in the centre, near a raised podium. She smiled; Hochdahler Markt was the correct location.

Then she noticed a pair of dogs being led round, presumably to check for vagrants and the likes of her. Eventually, they came towards Tessa's row of shops. She was fairly confident her alcove smelt sufficiently foul for them to be unlikely to detect her presence. However, she still moved further back into the passageway and prepared to fight her way out. The dogs stopped about eight feet away from her, sniffing the air interestedly. Through the gap in the boxes, she watched the dog handler stop to talk to a colleague. Just as a dog looked inquisitively in her direction, something ran over her foot. Tessa apologetically coaxed the unfortunate rat out from behind the boxes. The dogs went wild and killed it and, after a few choice words, the handlers dragged them away.

A few minutes later, she heard someone talking on a radio saying that the area had been secured and they were setting up the *HAD* system. As work started on the crates near her, Tessa wondered whether she should adjust her plan. She knew that *HAD*s were sophisticated listening systems conceived by the criminal fraternity to detect people and Special Forces stealth equipment by the noises they made. However, they were notoriously difficult to calibrate. All *invited* sound sources, together with normal background noise, had to be programmed into the system in order for it to be able to identify anything *uninvited*. Nevertheless, it still posed a serious threat to her remaining undiscovered. Also, Jones and Müller would be detected some distance away. She tapped the side of her headset.

"Jones," she whispered, "it's all go here. They've secured the perimeter and are installing one of those *Hypersensitive Audio Detection* systems. I'm going to have to stay quiet now until I have no choice. But if you let me know when you're a few miles off, preferably down wind, I'll try and disable the thing for you."

"Understood. For goodness' sake, be careful."

Tessa was encouraged by the sound of a helicopter engine straining in the background.

She stood stock-still and relaxed completely, slowing her heart rate to conserve energy and minimise any sound she might make. If surprised, this would be a problem, since she would need several seconds before she would be ready for action. But she had to take the risk. She drifted into a semi-trance.

Through veiled eyes framed in the gap between the boxes, Tessa watched the detection-system control centre being assembled. Under a canvas roof, a long table was erected with five large monitors standing on it. The processors were set-up underneath. The wires were connected and various buzzing and beeping sounds could be heard as the screens burst into life. A bespectacled youth started tapping keys enthusiastically. Apparently satisfied by the information being displayed, he waved away the two burly men who had been helping him. This prompted Tessa to while away several minutes trying to decide whether the bespectacled young man was a geek or a nerd. She eventually concluded she didn't know, and didn't care.

Then some more vehicles arrived; three people-carriers. A number of tough-looking thugs got out. Most of them were carrying swords and they quickly took up position around the square. Meanwhile, four men with rifles went into different tower blocks.

A few minutes later, two more SUVs arrived together with a box truck; Tessa suspected these were the first buyers. They stopped to exchange greetings with people already there and parked their vehicles at the northern end of the marketplace, with the truck reversing back towards the raised podium.

Shortly afterwards, another two SUVs and a truck arrived. More noisy greetings were exchanged as the SUVs were parked and the truck was left with its open loading bay facing the podium, like the first one. It seemed the second buyers had arrived.

Disappointingly for Tessa, everything appeared to be happening according to Beauchamp's schedule and there were already a lot of people there. It would definitely be easier if Jones arrived soon.

Then she heard the rumble of more vehicles approaching. An SUV came into view followed by a large black Mercedes limousine; then an articulated truck with a forklift truck slung at the back. The trailer was reversed up to the podium, and the SUV parked. A large man, wearing a vermilion neck scarf, got out and walked over to the Mercedes. Tessa recognised him from Beng Mealea. He spoke through the barely open window. Then Beauchamp got out, looked round with obvious satisfaction, and spoke briefly to the man beside him. They walked over to the podium and welcomed the people there. As the sound of their voices drifted over to Tessa, she suddenly realised the man from Beng Mealea was the same one she had heard at *Pennysview* when David had been killed. Being reminded of her repressed grief caused her heart rate to increase and thereby to bring her involuntarily out of her semi-trance. Whether she liked it or not, she would have to act soon or risk being discovered.

Fortunately the bespectacled *HAD* operator was totally absorbed in watching the group on the podium. So, Tessa took a slow deep breath and started flexing her muscles. Then she tapped her head-set, twice, switching it on permanently.

"Jones, everyone's here. How long will you be?"

"Twenty minutes," came the muffled response.

"Well, I'm going to have to gate crash."

"Look, I know how important this is to you, but it's important for us too. Please wait!"

"Sorry, Jones, I really can't. I'm about to be discovered."

"Tessa," he whispered, his voice trembling with emotion, "there must be too many, even for you. Please, hold back, we're nearly there."

"There's no longer anyone here by that name; just keep the pedal to the metal. Headset on continuous."

"Make this bloody thing go faster," shouted Jones frantically, "or I'll start throwing balast out!"

She smiled, took a deep breath, and squeezed out from behind the boxes. Quickly and quietly, she walked towards the *HAD* equipment. The operator was still preoccupied with the podium proceedings. However, as Tessa drew closer, she could see from the changing colours on his back that one of the displays had started flashing alarms. The bespectacled operator suddenly noticed the reflections on the ground in front of him and turned to look at the screens. His eyes widened in surprise and he looked up to find Tessa standing a few feet away. She smiled and put her finger to her lips. He realised that whatever she intended to do, she would do it regardless. He had to choose between maybe being alive at the end of it, or dying there and then. He chose life, and obligingly froze.

She glanced down at the cables and with a flick of her left arm, drew the heavier Bryani sword. With one powerful left-to-right sweep, she cut virtually all the wires. There was surprisingly little noise, but in unison all the screens flashed and went dark.

"*HAD* is down," she muttered into her headset. She returned her sword to its sheath and walked round the equipment towards the podium. The crowd of people there were clearly not expecting visitors. None had noticed the disruption of the detection system; they were too busy watching their respective bosses agreeing the deal. She could see there were now a number of briefcases open on a table there. Beauchamp and the buyers were engaged in earnest conversation, while others were inspecting the contents of the articulated lorry.

"Jones," whispered Tessa urgently. "There are four snipers on the top of various buildings around the square. It would be good if you could take them out soon."

He responded in a low whisper.

"No problem, we're ready. Ten minutes."

"Well, it's time to tango down here. Don't be late for the last dance...

"Beauchamp, hello!" she shouted out loud. "Fancy finding you here!"

A blanket of silence fell over the square. Everyone turned to stare at her, while the *HAD* operator simply shrugged. When Beauchamp saw who it was, an expression of angry exasperation crossed his face.

"What the fuck is it with you?" he retorted in disgust. "Why won't you just die?"

"You're the eldest; you should go first," she replied. "So, you weren't expecting me then?"

"No! I bloody well was not."

"Hmm. Well, in that case, one of your so-called friends tipped me off."

Beauchamp went quiet, clearly taken aback.

"Did you get that, Jones? He's surprised."

"Yes, indeed! It's something for us all to think about."

Finding her way barred, Tessa stopped still.

"I'll look into that later," replied her brother.

"Even in jail, you won't have much time to do that before ... you know." She drew her hand across her neck in an expressive gesture. "Anyway, just to show how generous I am, if you and your friend give yourselves up now, everyone else can leave. But without the merchandise."

"Oh, don't start that again!" sneered Beauchamp, gesturing to the crowd of men avidly watching them. "What are you going to do against all these guys? I admit, you surprised us at Beng Mealea, but these people are tougher, better armed and better trained. And I don't see any cavalry galloping to your rescue. Presumably they're all in Malta? You're the one who should give up."

"You know I can't do that, and my friends will be here soon enough," continued Tessa. "Although I'm fed up with the monotony of killing your cronies, I am going to see this through, because it's going to end tonight."

"I know," announced Beauchamp, confidently. "I'll get richer and retire, and you will die."

"We'll see."

"Keep stalling," whispered Jones.

"She's bluffing," whispered Ryuu Fujiwara to Beauchamp. "We'd know by now if she had back up. She probably disabled the detector to confuse us, and we still have our look-outs. These guys are good, much better than the ones in Cambodia."

"Come on, Beauchamp, give up," Tessa shouted. "No one else need get hurt."

"*Yoshino*, for once in your regrettably prolonged life, get real," he replied, laughing.

Tessa smiled. He had just given her an idea.

"I keep telling you not to count your chickens," she continued. "Let me enlighten you as to my track record against the Calver Cats. I killed your people in London, then Bill Chalmers in Burma, Leiko at Angkor Wat together with lots more at Beng Mealea. Oh, and there was that little shindig in Kawasaki-ku too. I got a couple of your mates there, didn't I? *Yoshino* is just a red herring, which you obligingly swallowed hook, line and sinker. My real Peacekeeper name is Nariko."

A nervous whisper spread through the crowd.

"Yes, that's right," she yelled. "Nariko is who you are up against, and the Special Forces *will* be here soon. Leave now if you want to live! If you don't get in my way, I won't harm you. I only want him."

Beauchamp started clapping slowly.

"OK, *freak*! So you're still full of surprises. Big deal! But that only makes me more determined to make sure you die tonight, something which is clearly long overdue."

"That bitch killed my father and my brother," hissed Ryuu. "I'll take care of her myself."

Beauchamp nodded and the big man stepped down from the podium. Tessa watched while also keeping an eye on the snipers. For the time being at least she did not present them with a clear shot.

"It seems my friend Ryuu would like to say *hello*," continued Beauchamp. "Well, actually, I think he intends to dismember you in front of all these spectators. I trust that's OK? Shall I give the thumbs down now?"

"I'd hold off if I were you. And, check your history, I think you mean thumbs up, actually."

"Hah!" bellowed Ryuu, striding towards her. "So it was you at Kawasaki-ku with that double-crossing bastard Hachiro?"

"Er, yes, that's right," she replied, momentarily puzzled. "I remember the place well. It stank of rats and needed cleaning, so we washed it with the blood of the Calver Cats. Shame you weren't there. My goodness, I suppose they were all your family and friends? What a shame. But it was a perfect night for exterminating vermin, and one can't find more disgusting vermin than the Fujiwara."

She watched with satisfaction as Ryuu's face reddened with rage.

"Don't let her wind you up," interjected Beauchamp. "It's all she's good for."

Grunting, the Japanese man stopped some ten feet in front of Tessa. He looked large, fit and strong. He was wearing an unusually long Samurai sword, she noticed, with a five-foot blade. It looked old, and it didn't surprise Tessa to see a worn Amafuji emblem on it. However, this seemed a strange choice of weapon as it would be quite ungainly in close one-on-one combat; although, it would give him considerable reach.

"I am Ryuu Fujiwara, head of the Fujiwara clan. We have a score to settle with you."

"I didn't think there were enough Fujiwara left to call it a clan any more. As I understand it, just one more to go and the line is finished for ever."

It was clear from his expression that she had trampled on some tender nerves.

"You really are a cold-hearted bitch, aren't you?"

"That's a trifle rich coming from you. The Fujiwara have a long-held reputation for being cold-hearted. People like you always get what they deserve in the end."

Ryuu pursed his lips and breathed in. Then he looked away from her to signify he didn't intend to attack immediately and slowly but purposefully, drew his sword. He held it out in front of him, but left it pointing downwards.

This didn't surprise Tessa, since otherwise she would have had a distinct advantage in speed of draw. However, she could see that although the sword had been good once, there were now numerous chips along its cutting edge, and the blade had a number of deep scratches. She wondered whether all this damage had compromised its integrity.

"Family sword?" she queried.

Proudly, Ryuu nodded.

"Thought so. Your father mentioned you had it. I think that was just before I chopped his head off."

He breathed out noisily, shaking his head.

"It was christened near Kanazawa and has not been defeated in a hundred and fifty years. It is only right that this sword should avenge the murders of my father and brother."

Tessa took a step back and drew her Kimi sword. It immediately started ringing; loud confident and cold. Adopting a two-handed grip, she pointed it towards his neck. He raised his sword, they bowed and closed on each other.

Then their swords *clanged* together. A moment later they exchanged strong blows; then again, forcing the crowd to shuffle quickly away.

The duel continued for several minutes, with neither fighter being able to deliver a winning stroke. Although his long sword was ungainly, Ryuu was very strong and wielded it with considerable skill. He was continuously attacking, but Tessa was content simply to defend herself while playing for time. She knew it would be a strain for him to sustain the pace of his attacks with such a heavy weapon. Repeatedly blocking him, she saw he was beginning to grow impatient. Also, from the stilted ringing that came from his sword when she hit it with hers, Tessa knew it had at least one serious metallurgical fault and noticed a particularly jagged chip in the blade.

Suddenly, determined to end the fight, Ryuu mustered all his energy to deliver a powerful stroke from his right. He intended to use brute force to smash Tessa's sword out of the way and push through her defence. He turned away from her and swung his sword back, twisting his body to add momentum to his swing. Then he unwound and his long sword swept menacingly towards her. She sensed an opportunity, albeit a dangerous one. Making no effort to avoid his blade, Tessa twisted her body to the right. As he roared with delight, expecting victory, she flicked her sword over and, with all her strength, swept it round to meet his. She was aiming at the large chip in his blade. Only at the last moment did he realise what she was trying to do.

Their swords met with an incredibly loud *clang* and sparks flew from the point of impact. The sound echoed round the market square, but was immediately followed by a brief *chink* as the old Amafuji blade shattered. Ryuu was stunned; he had never heard of an Amafuji sword being broken before. Furthermore, he was defenceless and well within Tessa's reach. Then he felt an intense searing pain in his right kidney, but barely had time cry out. So strong and sustained was her cut that the sword eventually reappeared from the other side of his torso.

Tessa stood up straight, bowed and took a step back.

"Good effort, but that was for David … and all the Matsumoto."

Ryuu keeled over backwards with the two halves of his body lolling awkwardly apart as his corpse hit the ground. She took a deep breath, flicked the blood off her sword, and re-sheathed it.

"Ryuu Fujiwara is down," reported Tessa into her communicator.

She checked the snipers' view remained obscured and turned back to Beauchamp.

"I warned you, and now another one's gone. It seems you're running out of gullible people to do your dirty work for you."

"You really are irritating!" he retorted. "But there again, you always were."

"Give up, Beauchamp. You can't win."

"Depends how you define winning, doesn't it? As far as I'm concerned, winning is all about protecting the interests of everyone here, except you."

He reached into one of the open briefcases and held up two large wads of notes.

"This is for the person who brings me that *freak's* head!" he shouted.

Nobody moved. Tessa grinned.

"Thank you, Beauchamp. I'll come and collect it myself."

But as she started forward, a man drew his sword and strode confidently towards her. She let him get close enough to start his attack before she even drew a sword. But then, with lightning speed, she drew both her weapons. She used the Kimi sword to hit his away and Bryani's to slash him across his neck. He collapsed, dead. She flicked her swords clean and re-sheathed them.

"I only want Beauchamp; the rest of you can go. Anyone who takes me on will die. Leave now. The Special Forces are nearly here."

For a moment they hesitated. Then Beauchamp reached back into the case and added another two wads of notes to the reward. That spurred two of them on, and with a collective roar they drew their swords and converged on her.

"She's ours!" they yelled, breaking out from the crowd.

But Tessa was in no mood to mess around. She didn't want to lose sight of Beauchamp and felt making a clear statement now might dissuade others from becoming involved. She drew both her swords. Immediately they started ringing, but she simply used her Kimi sword to fatally slash one man across his chest and launched her Bryani sword at the other. Its blade passed through the heart of the man, killing him instantly. However, before his body had even started falling, Tessa had walked up to him and yanked her weapon out. She flicked both blades clean, re-sheathed them, and winked at Beauchamp. He was still on the podium holding the money.

"This is your final warning. If you want to live get out of my way," yelled Tessa in German at the crowd.

Unnerved, they cleared out of her way, and still the snipers could not get a clear shot.

"And I thought you were men!" shouted Beauchamp. "OK! OK!" He grabbed another two wads of notes and placed them on the table. "Now the prize is this much!"

That seemed to be enough to overcome their fear and people started closing in on Tessa again. But then the sound of two powerful rifle shots rang out from a long way off; then another two. There was a brief pause, followed by cries from the snipers. Two of them toppled over the edge of the buildings, making unpleasant *thumps* as they landed in the marketplace.

"Nice shooting," muttered Tessa.

"Nichts zu danken!" replied Müller in her earphones.

The crowd froze; she smiled.

"The Special Forces are here. Run everyone!" she yelled. "Run!"

Moments later, the square was filled with the cacophony of fast-approaching helicopters, no longer in stealth mode. Beauchamp knew things had taken a distinct turn for the worse. His deal was far from concluded; all the guns and the drugs he had been hoping to sell were still in the truck. His buyers grabbed their briefcases and started to rush back towards their vehicles. However, the ensuing chaos galvanised many of those surrounding Tessa to conclude that escape was unlikely, so they attacked her instead. Soon she was fighting furiously on all sides.

Beauchamp glared at his sister then ordered his people to get the merchandise to safety. The rear doors of the container slammed shut and, without the forklift, the truck started moving. Suddenly a streak of light shot across the sky as a missile was launched from one of the helicopters. Then the articulated truck exploded, showering the square with debris. Yelling expletives, Beauchamp leapt off the podium and headed for his car. However, it was hemmed in by the mêlée of panicking buyers attempting to flee. Beauchamp realised he would have to fight his way out and drew a pistol. Another missile arrived, destroying vehicles at the entrance, effectively blocking it. The marketplace was sealed and Special Forces agents appeared, abseiling down ropes from the helicopters.

Determined to follow Beauchamp as quickly as she could, Tessa wielded her swords with systematic brutality; mercy was not on her agenda. She was increasingly confident her Mission could be ended that night. There was frenzied fighting now throughout the square and a swathe of corpses littered her path. She slowly cut her way through the mob towards Beauchamp. She saw the angry flashes as he shot any Special Forces agents who closed in on him. But then she lost sight of him and shouted into her communicator. She knew Jones would still be airborne monitoring progress from above.

"Where's Beauchamp?"

"Three o'clock from where you're facing," came the crisp response. "He's heading towards the shops at the south side."

She immediately changed direction, but then the helicopter swung round and Jones lost sight of her. He anxiously prodded the pilot to change the helicopter's position.

Finally, Tessa found Beauchamp again. Two Special Forces agents had just caught up with him. But he turned his gun on them and fired; both men fell. He fired again, but there was no flash; the magazine was empty. He passed the gun to his left hand and drew a long knife. Desperate now, he ran towards a shop whose door stood slightly ajar. But then Tessa caught up with him.

"Stay where you are, Beauchamp!"

He stopped and turned to face her.

308

"Fuck you!" he yelled, throwing his knife at her. Although not a bad throw, she nonchalantly brushed it aside with her sword.

The two of them seemed to enter a time warp. No longer were they part of the pandemonium around them; for them this was purely a dispute between siblings.

"You said I had to be lucky all the time while you only needed to be lucky once," she mocked. "Well, it seems my luck has held and yours just ran out."

Suddenly she sensed an attack impending from behind. She spun round and slashed at the man creeping up on her. So strong was the blow that she barely noticed severing his sword arm before cutting deep across his chest. In a moment she was facing her brother again, swords re-sheathed. His gun was in his right hand again but she knew he hadn't reloaded it.

"It's over, Beauchamp."

"Hmm, you have changed," he observed, watching the dead man's body twitching. "You've developed some decidedly antisocial habits. Maybe you should see someone about those too?"

"Grow up! I'm only what you forced me to become."

"Perhaps. But I can't grumble. I've done an awful lot and had far more fun than I ever dreamed was possible. But, I have to admit, it is frustrating to think that all my life I've been trying to get rid of you, and still I haven't managed it."

"Oh, Beauchamp," laughed Tessa. "That's all irrelevant. You killed Crick and have just used a gun. There's no doubt you'll get the death penalty now."

Beauchamp slowly brought his arm up and aimed the pistol at her. She didn't move.

"It's empty, Beauchamp. Just like you."

He pulled the trigger, but there was only a metallic *click*. She shrugged and Beauchamp smiled. He let his pistol fall to the floor, lowering his arm slightly. Then he rocked his hand and a tiny dart shot out of his jacket sleeve. It struck Tessa's left thigh.

"Hah!!" he exclaimed gleefully. "Got you at last!"

"Congratulations, Beauchamp," she said, plucking the dart out. She pressed the wound to make it bleed as much as possible, but knew the dart had been poisoned. An unpleasant numbness had already started spreading up her body. "I hope you're satisfied."

She suddenly realised that while she was fed up with the emptiness of her new life, she definitely did not want to die. Hurriedly she opened the wound and thrust some moss and herbs into it from her waist bag.

Smiling, Beauchamp edged backwards towards the shop; Tessa followed.

"The pupils of a victim poisoned with this stuff dilate immediately, and I saw that happen in yours," he observed. "So I reckon it's curtains for you this time, *kiddo*. And, yes, that does make me happy. The poison is derived from Japanese puffer fish. Apparently it kills in minutes, but with a bit of luck it'll take longer for you. We can but hope, eh?"

As if in answer to his jeering, Tessa felt a stabbing pain shoot up her side. As it began to gnaw away at her left arm, an intense feeling of cold emanated from the wound.

"You really are a bitter and twisted bugger," she said. "You won't get away, regardless of what happens to me, and you've lost your empire and all your so-called friends. Is this really the epitaph you want?"

She was beginning to feel distinctly unwell. Whereas a few moments ago she had felt cold, she now felt unpleasantly hot. She could also sense her muscles stiffening. But still she stood in front of Beauchamp, looking him straight in the eye. Suddenly she heard a noise like a thunder crack going off inside her head, followed by an intense flash of light in her eyes. Her world spun unnervingly and she battled to maintain control.

"It is fun watching this, but I need to go," observed her brother, laughing. "Let's just speed things up, shall we?"

He took a step towards her and started lifting his arm again.

But this so enraged Tessa, she managed to tap some hidden energy reserves. She drew her Kimi sword and effortlessly sliced through his outstretched forearm. As his hand and wrist started to fall to the ground, she spun round and crouched down like a spinning top. She was worried that if she hesitated now she might not be able to stop him later. As she completed her turn, the sword struck Beauchamp on the back of his left shin. She expected the blade to sever the leg, but it didn't. Instead, it simply cut deeply into the bone and stopped with a dull *twang*.

To retrieve her sword, Tessa had to prise it roughly from Beauchamp's leg, causing him excruciating pain. As he screamed, clutching his wound, she stood up shakily and looked down at her sword, still wet with his blood. The blade wasn't ringing any more. She remembered what Lee had once told her. The sword would always ring as a reflection of her life force. It would only stop ringing if she were more dead than alive. She moved back, clumsily flicking the blade clean. Straining, she just managed to return it to its sheath. Her vision misted over and an annoyingly loud buzzing filled her ears.

"Beauchamp, you fool," she mumbled, but he wasn't listening. He hobbled a few paces and toppled over as his leg snapped. Then Tessa thought she heard something whistle over her head.

"Oh, you bitch!" he yelled. "Shit! You fucking ungrateful bitch." Then he rolled over, writhing in agony.

Tessa whispered weakly into her headset, "Jones, I've got a problem here … a big one."

But the words sounded weak and slurred to her. She had no idea whether they were intelligible to anyone. She thought, in the distance, she could hear Jones shouting orders. Hopefully, he'd be with her soon. The prospect of dying alone had always scared her. Collapsing to her knees, she looked up. She could see the stars which seemed to be tracing fine white circles against the dark sky.

"Oh, that's pretty," she mused. "Well, Penny, time for me to join you." The buzzing grew louder and Tessa started swaying, about to topple over.

So much for life flashing in front of you, she mused. Seems more like terrible tinnitus to me!

A wave of nausea engulfed her, but she didn't think she was strong enough to vomit. Briefly she thought how uncomfortable and undignified it was to die this way; but at least she had completed her Mission.

"Tessa, hold on!" she suddenly heard, as though from a long way off. "I'm here."

As she keeled over, she felt strong supporting arms grasping her.

"Tessa, fight it, look at me," demanded Jones.

She tried to turn her head to where she thought his voice was coming from, but it felt to her as if the whole universe were spinning. All the noises around her were mingling together and losing themselves in their own echoes. She felt Jones lay her down and straighten her legs. He was yelling for medical assistance. He gently pulled her chin round. She thought she could see him and smiled as, for a moment, a degree of clarity returned to her.

"You took your time," she whispered. He looked distraught. "Oh, dear, so much to say … so little time. Sorry, Gareth. Have you got him?"

"Yes, we've got him, it's all over. The medics are coming. Keep talking. Stay with me!"

"Poison dart, wicked stuff. Get my swords to Lee." For a moment she could see the stars again. "It's so beautiful up there," she whispered. She could see Jones shouting at her but she couldn't hear what he said.

Suddenly she heard another thunder clap inside her head, much louder than before. It was so violent that even in her state it came as a surprise, and she thought her whole body might have trembled. Then a wave of silent stillness swept over her. But not transient like before. This time it lingered and developed into all-consuming nothingness. Her heart felt as though it were being crushed in a vice and she found herself listening to the lengthening pauses between its beats. Then everything turned black…

CHAPTER 29

Gradually, Tessa became aware of a distant noise. Drip… Drip… Then she detected some metallic beeps too. The sounds grew louder and more frequent, soon forming their own macabre rhythm and rapidly becoming downright irritating. She struggled to remember what had happened. Hadn't she died, again? Suddenly, the prospect of opening her eyes seemed quite daunting. What would she see? But she couldn't keep her eyes closed for ever … could she?

Summoning all her powers of concentration and gathering her courage, she raised her eyelids a little; bright white light flooded in. Heavens! she mused, quickly concluding such thoughts were at best wishful aspiration. As her eyes grew accustomed to the light, she eased them open further. Her vision cleared and she saw a handsome young man, dressed in white.

"*Hallo, Frau Doktor, wie gehts?*" he asked.

"*Er … Nicht schlecht. Ich bin fest der Meinung das ich noch lebe,*" she replied.

"Oh! Most definitely," continued the doctor in English, smiling, "and I'm pleased to see you haven't forgotten your German. Can you feel and move everything – fingers and toes?"

"I believe I can," confirmed Tessa after flexing all her limbs.

"Good. I thought so. It looks as though you didn't sustain any permanent damage. You've been very lucky. I think you will make a full recovery quickly now."

"Wow!" exclaimed Tessa. "Wonders never cease. But the dart was poisoned, so how come I'm still alive? And, come to think of it, who are you?"

"I am Herr Doktor Bonn. The dart was poisoned, in fact, with sufficient toxin to kill several people. It seems two things saved you. That moss-like substance you pressed into the wound is quite remarkable. Perhaps you could tell me what it is later? It mitigated the effects of the poison which had not yet entered your blood stream,

313

and has since assisted the healing process. But your miraculous recovery is primarily due to your being immune to it. You ingested so much it gave your body a big shock, but eventually you managed to metabolise it. Have you been dosing yourself with fish toxins?"

"Not knowingly," she replied, then, smiling, "but I think I know who has."

"Well, your body has been toxin-free for several hours," continued the doctor. "I see no reason why you shouldn't leave tomorrow."

"Oh, excellent. No offence, but I've already spent too much time in hospitals. How long was I unconscious?"

"About twenty-four hours. But no more questions now. A few hours of natural sleep will make you feel much better."

Tessa realised she was very tired. Then a wave of apprehension hit her.

"Where are my swords?"

"They're here," said a familiar voice from behind the doctor. "Do you really think I would have dared separate you from them?"

Doktor Bonn smiled and stepped aside.

"Herr Jones has been with you since you were admitted. I will leave you alone for a minute, but I prescribe rest for you both."

Tessa and Jones smiled at each other.

"Hello, Gareth, how are you?"

"Oh, I'm fine. How do you feel?"

"Not at all bad, considering. I'm just surprised to be feeling anything... Look, there's something I need to tell you. Could you come a little closer, please?"

He moved alongside her.

"Sorry, closer."

His face was only a few inches from hers now.

"Thank you," said Tessa, and mustering all her energy, lifted her head and kissed him on the lips. Then she flopped back on to the pillow. He stood still for a moment, smiled and moved down to kiss her again.

"How about if we both follow the good doctor's advice and get some sleep?" he said. "I'll stay in my armchair over there and keep an eye on your swords for you. Just relax and rest."

"OK, but I'm afraid you'll have to give me my Kimi sword first. You can hold on to the other one, for now."

He chuckled, reverently brought her sword over and slid it into the bed with her as Tessa held up the covers. She put her hand on it and sighed with obvious relief. She already felt much better, and her expression showed it.

Jones smoothed the hair away from her eyes and patted her gently on the nose. Then he smiled and went back to his armchair in the corner of the room. He carefully tucked her other sword under his arms and closed his eyes. He felt better too.

"Gareth," she whispered a moment later, "we did get him, didn't we?"

"Oh, yes, we got him all right," he replied. "Well, you got him really. He was in no state to go anywhere."

Tessa sighed.

"I wish it hadn't come to that."

"I know… But I'm afraid the story doesn't end there."

"What do you mean?" she asked, her curiosity aroused.

"Well, Beauchamp was loaded into an ambulance with his severed hand. It had been packed in ice next to him; presumably they wanted to try and sew it back on. Anyway, they think that hand must have had a poison dart in it. He probably fired it at you just as you severed his wrist and it got stuck on the way. Suffice to say, nobody had noticed it. Anyway, he must have got hold of the dart and stabbed himself with it. He was nearly dead when they realised what had happened. He muttered something, but nobody could hear what, and to cut a long story short, he died. So, I'm afraid he's gone. Swindled the courts, and the media … and saved the taxpayer a fortune."

Tessa paused.

"Are you sure he stabbed himself?"

"Well, we've no reason to believe otherwise. Why do you ask?"

"I'm not sure, it's just... Did any of them get away?"

"Yes, a few."

"Hmm… So, was he under the impression I was dead?"

"I believe so. We all were, but as I helped load you into the ambulance, your hand twitched."

"You were stroking it at the time?"

"I was indeed," he replied, blushing. "Anyway, I didn't say a word to anyone and asked Doktor Bonn to bring you here in secret. We still weren't sure you'd make it, but either way it didn't seem a bad idea to let people think you hadn't."

"Poor Beauchamp," Tessa sighed. "He was always arrogant enough to believe it would be all right in the end, and then one day it wasn't. What a shame. But I'm not sure he'll be missed."

"Get some sleep," said Jones quietly. "We can talk later."

Tessa gripped her sword and slipped into a deep restful sleep.

It was early morning when she woke. Jones was snoring gently on the other side of the room holding her Bryani sword. Tessa felt her Kimi sword by her side and smiled. Then she again checked all her limbs were working. Encouragingly, it seemed the only deep wound she had sustained was the small hole where Beauchamp's dart had penetrated her Kevlar suit. Overall she felt fine.

Shortly afterwards Doktor Bonn came in and noticed Tessa watching him.

"Good morning," he said quietly. "How do you feel?"

"Very good, actually," she replied, jauntily.

"Well, let's see if I agree with your prognosis."

He gave her a comprehensive examination, checked her reflexes and stood back.

"You're right," he said. "I remain puzzled by the speed and completeness of your recovery, but I have to admit, you seem to be in excellent health."

"Clearly you've done an outstanding job," she replied.

He smiled sardonically.

"I frequently do, but on this particular occasion I have to admit I didn't do much at all. I'm sure you would have healed by yourself if I'd simply left your body to get on with it. All I perhaps did was nudge the process along a little."

"Well, thank you all the same. So, can I go?" she asked, hauling herself up and putting one of the pillows behind her.

"I don't see why not. Although I think you should eat something first, and maybe take it easy for a day or two."

Tessa smiled.

"That sounds very sensible. What may I have to eat?"

"What would you like? Some things might take a little more time, but we have a very competent kitchen."

"In that case, what I would really like is smoked salmon, scrambled egg, steamed rice, fruit, and a large pot of green tea. Would that be all right?"

Doktor Bonn raised his eyebrows.

"Hmm, probably, although I'm not sure about the green tea. But we'll see what the chef can find. Have you any idea what Herr Jones would like?"

"Oh, he's far more conventional. He'd like fried eggs, sunny side up, bacon, mushrooms, tomatoes, sautéed potatoes, toast, jam and coffee."

"And maybe some *bratwurst*?" added the doctor with a smile.

"What an excellent idea, I'm sure he would regard that as a welcome addition."

The doctor left and Tessa lay back, staring at the ceiling.

As her mind wandered, she remembered what Matsumoto had said. *Cheat death twice and you will remember everything.* Suddenly, a wave of distortion seemed to pass across the ceiling. She heard a rushing noise and, like snowflakes clearing, a misty curtain lifted within her mind. As the flood gates opened, she realised all the memories of her two training sessions with Matsumoto were returning. Tessa relaxed and let her past return to her mind. She grimaced with the enormity of what she remembered, but intriguingly she realised there were still some gaps. Then she began to consider the implications of what she had just recalled; they were remarkable, severe and far-reaching. For a long while she had felt as if her life was being manipulated by others; now her suspicions had been confirmed.

Three-quarters of an hour later a nurse arrived, pushing a trolley with their breakfasts on it. As Tessa took her tray, Jones woke up.

"Good morning," said Tessa brightly.

"Oh, hello, you're looking perky."

"Well, I had a bed to sleep in. How's the armchair?"

"Surprisingly comfortable, actually," he replied, inspecting his breakfast. "This looks good. Who ordered it?"

"Guess."

They both wolfed down their food, then Tessa had a long hot shower during which she removed the bandage over her wound. Only a small scab remained to mark the dart's entry point. Her newly cleaned clothes were returned, together with a fresh dressing to which Tessa added some herbs and moss. Then she put her Kevlar suit back on and slung her swords over her back. Just as she finished, Doktor Bonn came in and looked at her in surprise.

"Hmm. Quite a transformation."

"You don't approve?"

"Shall we just say I understand why the public mortuary is so full?"

"I'm sorry. But I've never hurt anyone by choice. On occasion someone has to stop those who would hurt others. Those whom I take on have killed many times before, and are always intent on killing me."

"Who am I to judge?" acknowledged Doktor Bonn. "After all, it was nearly you who died. But it's never easy when you spend your life trying to heal people, and see so much damage done to so many, by so few. Sign here and you can go."

She smiled and took the papers from him.

"Bad as this may be, I do believe it is better than guns and explosives."

"Yes, so do I," agreed the doctor, taking the papers from her. "But I think it would be even better if we had neither."

"Amen. The day we have peace, I will hang up my swords with pleasure. Thank you again, Herr Doktor."

She shook his hand and turned to Jones.

"Shall we go … somewhere?"

Just then Jones's phone rang.

"Morning, Potter. Yes, we're both fine, thanks… Oh, pretty much completely recovered by the looks of things. Yes, we'll be leaving in a few minutes." Then he listened for a while, smiled at Tessa and winked. "OK. No problem… Yes, good idea."

"What was that about?"

"Apparently the German media are making a big splash about Hochdahler Markt. It's been leaked that a Peacekeeper died, and they're poking around. We have been asked to return to the UK as soon as possible. A plane will collect us from the UNWP airfield near Duisburg."

"OK. But I don't want to go without the Bugatti."

"All taken care of, Potter's sending a transport plane. Where is the car anyway?"

"Oh, safe, and out of sight." Tessa looked at her watch. "Heavens, its guardian will be getting worried. We'd better phone him on the way. We'll need the GPS reference of the airfield, unless you know where it is?"

"Good point, I'll get Potter to send it to your car."

With Tessa wearing a white coat she had been given, Doktor Bonn led them into the corridor.

"You know," she said, to Jones, "this doesn't look much like a hospital."

"No. It wouldn't. The Orchid House is just up the hill from Hochdahler Markt. It's an exclusive, very well equipped, old people's home. The conflict drew a response from all medical facilities in the region. But it was Doktor Bonn who came to you, so we decided to bring only you here. It's helped make it difficult for anyone to track you down"

They climbed into the waiting taxi and Tessa spoke briefly to the driver, telling him where to take them. They moved off and she took out her phone.

"Guten morgen, Herr Schneider," she began. But he was so euphoric, she struggled to get another word in.

"Yes, I'm fine, honestly!" she laughed. "Yes, I know they said a Peacekeeper died, but it wasn't me… Yes, we'll be there in ten minutes. But, please, don't tell anyone I'm coming, this needs to stay low profile. The taxi will drop us at the bottom of the ramp. Could you open the garage door as soon as you see us? Thank you. See you shortly."

She smiled at Jones.

"He thought I'd been killed, and was wondering what on earth he should do about the car. He was my finance director … really nice man, you'll like him."

"So, you hid your car where you used to work?"

Tessa nodded. As soon as they arrived, the garage door went up.

"Hello," she said, smiling at Herr Schneider and going straight over to hug him. "Sorry I didn't call yesterday, but I was still busy. This is a colleague of mine, Herr Jones."

The two men shook hands and started to chat while she unlocked the Bugatti which politely informed them its defensive systems had been deactivated.

"Herr Schneider," said Tessa, after stowing her swords, "thank you so much for looking after the car, but I'm afraid we must go straightaway. I will come back to see you again soon." She kissed him lightly on the cheek.

Then she and Jones got into her Bugatti, and Herr Schneider pressed the button to reopen the door. A moment later, she reversed up the ramp and drove off. She spoke to the navigation system and set their destination.

"This isn't a car," exclaimed Jones, admiring the Bugatti's cockpit. "It's more like a comfortable jet-fighter."

"It is rather nice, isn't it? You wait until you see what she can do on the autobahn."

"Yes, well, I've already started worrying about that."

Two minutes later, the Bugatti rumbled on to the A3 autobahn and headed north towards Duisburg. On a remarkably empty road, they had soon reached 170 m.p.h. and were still accelerating strongly. Jones's eyes widened.

"Er, I don't think we need to hurry this much."

"I didn't know you were of a nervous disposition," she replied, laughing.

"Neither did I. But that was before the phrase *Concorde is grounded* took on a new meaning."

"Just relax and enjoy it..."

Two hours later they were back in London, driving away from Northolt.

Jones had been reading a newspaper he'd picked up at the airport.

"Hah, listen to this," he said. "The headline is: '*Trainee Peacekeeper honoured!* *The Special Forces have confirmed that Yoshino, the trainee Peacekeeper alleged to have contributed to the death of Major General Sinclair and the damage to Tower Bridge, has been completely exonerated. Apparently, previous announcements were part of an elaborate campaign of deception. Yoshino had in fact risked her life well beyond the call of her limited trainee obligations on several occasions. However, while recently active in Germany, Yoshino regrettably lost her life participating in what proved to be a decisive action against the Calver Cats..."*

Tessa sighed.

"So, I suppose I'm back to being Nariko?"

"Yep."

"Then all I have to do now is to work out how to become Tessa again."

"I doubt that'll be difficult," continued Jones.

"Maybe, but all my memories from training have returned. I'd been told it would happen if I cheated death twice, but it has still come as a bit of a shock. Mind you, it's amazing too."

"Sounds really strange to me," he replied. "You've always seemed to know what to do. What's the difference?"

She thought for a moment.

"Well, whereas before some knowledge would come to me if I needed it, now I have instantaneous access to the complete encyclopaedia."

"Hmm, how about telling me all about it over dinner?"

Tessa smiled.

"That would be nice. But I need to see Lee first."

"Fine. I should make an appearance at the office anyway. How about if I pick you up at seven-thirty?"

"Perfect, I shall look forward to that."

She dropped Jones off by a taxi rank and continued home. She gave both her swords a clean and then put them back on, together with her knives. She didn't make any attempt to hide the weapons; she didn't care what people thought. She was too angry.

CHAPTER 30

The students had already left when Tessa arrived at SKS. Lee had heard she was fine, but was surprised to see her so soon; especially combat ready.

"*Konichiwa*, Lee," she said tersely. "I'm still a bit hyped up. Would you mind wearing me out?"

He looked at her quizzically, sensing something was wrong. Nevertheless, he went to a weapons rack and selected a good sword.

He raised it and started a casual attack. Their blades clashed with a loud clang and Tessa nonchalantly brushed his weapon aside. Lee found her sword positioned an inch away from his neck, ringing menacingly. He looked at the blade, smiled and bowed.

She withdrew and he attacked again, faster and more aggressively this time. But seconds later, he again found her blade hovering menacingly close to his neck.

"Nariko-san, is something wrong?"

"What could possibly be wrong? Your plan has worked perfectly, hasn't it? Everything the Matsumoto wanted doing has been done, and neither you nor your brother had to get your hands dirty."

Lee pursed his lips.

"Ah, I see. Well, congratulations for remembering everything, but in that case…"

"Actually, not everything. But enough," interrupted Tessa, immediately initiating another brutal exchange of sword strokes.

As the fighting continued, Lee always found his efforts being expertly thwarted. Invariably her sword would finish perilously close to his neck, ringing confidently. For a long time, he had known he could only defeat her because she wouldn't be able to remember everything she had been taught when duelling a friend.

"Nariko-san," asked Lee, forcing a respite. "We are only sparring, aren't we?"

"Depends! You see, I need some answers from you, and I can

322

only think of one way to make sure I get the truth. So, stop me if you can, because otherwise I might just kill you for manipulating a Peacekeeper!"

Lee looked at her, wide-eyed.

"But…"

Not waiting to hear more, Tessa attacked, hard and fast. Again and again they parried, fought, and every time he lost. Soon, beads of perspiration were running down his forehead as he struggled to keep her at bay. At first he was convinced she wouldn't really hurt him, but after she'd expertly placed a shallow cut on both his arms, he wasn't so sure. As they continued to fight, she slowly backed him towards a wall; try as he might, he couldn't do anything about it. Then she put a long gash across the front of his tunic, then another a few inches higher, during which the blade of her Kimi sword passed so close he felt the draft of air across his chest.

The loud clangs brought Lee's wife into the room. She stood by the door, aghast. It was clear he was in difficulty.

Another vicious exchange of sword blows followed. It ended as Lee bumped into the wall behind him.

"Are you scared, Lee?"

"Getting there," he panted, beads of perspiration running down his forehead.

Before he could move, there was a loud *whoosh* and Tessa struck his motionless blade with the back of her Kimi sword. The resultant *clang* echoed round the room, followed by a brief *chink*. His sword snapped, leaving him holding the hilt. Before he had time to think, Tessa's sword was speeding back. He let go just in time to avoid the impact which catapulted the hilt across the room.

"That would do it," observed Lee.

He put his hands by his sides and stood motionless in front of Tessa, completely at her mercy. His wife ran across the practice room and knelt down where Tessa could see her.

"Nariko-san, please, don't hurt him," she pleaded in Japanese.

Tessa looked at her and smiled. Lee's wife had never spoken to her before and, for the first time, was not wearing a brightly patterned visiting kimono. Instead, she had on a more subdued narrow-shouldered type, with discrete logos displaying the Matsumoto family crest.

"Why shouldn't he suffer, after all he has put me through? I remember all my training and about the feud between the Matsumoto and the Fujiwara. You were only interested in teaching me so I could do your killing. You endangered my life to end your feud. I suppose Penny was allowed to commission this sword because you thought it would give me a chance of achieving what you didn't want to do yourself? Did you plan her death? Was Beauchamp just a happy coincidence for you? Did you and Master Matsumoto really have to ruin my life and turn me into something I never wanted to be? No wonder you never told me that you were related. You have been using me ever since I first came here. Now, I will not hesitate to use the power which you had me earn. Tell me the truth, all of it. Your life is at stake."

"Nariko-san, you have every right to be angry," conceded Lee. "But the truth is not as dark as you suggest. You have not been manipulated … at least, not by the Matsumoto. Although the Fujiwara have always tried proactively to end our feud, we have not. Our family swore an oath to the Emperor to that effect many generations ago. We have merely waited for fate to deliver an opportunity whereby, if we were fortunate, the feud might be ended in our favour. When your friend Penny, enrolled, I suspected such a time had come, but I could not understand why since she herself appeared not to be strong enough to play a part. Then she announced she wanted to commission a Kimi Amakuni sword. Of course, I knew such a weapon would be required to end the feud, but I also knew Yoshino herself would never be able to wield it sufficiently well. Her death was totally unexpected. But when you came and displayed your incredible prowess, I wondered whether Yoshino had known something I did not. Neither I nor Isamu helped you find the sword. It was your destiny to find it.

"Yes, when the opportunity arose we did train you to the best of our abilities. But, sooner or later, you would have learnt anyway. Sword-fighting is in your blood; that much has always been true, and will always remain so. It was truly remarkable that the Calver Cats and the Fujiwara came together, thus merging our feuds. But even with Kawasaki-Ku, Sinclair took care to offer you a way out. It was *your* decision to become involved…

"I am sincerely sorry, especially for the tragic deaths of so many whom you held close to your heart," sighed Lee. "But there was never any intention to make you into anything other than what your destiny decreed … and that, Nariko-san, has proved to be something of which you should rightfully be proud. It was your brother who inclined you towards Matsumoto's teaching, but it was you who chose to go. Yes, we are guilty of preparing you for the journey, but we did not force you to take it. We simply ensured you possessed the skills you would need to survive along the way. Fate dictated the rest. That is the truth, Nariko-san. There is nothing more I can say."

Tessa raised her sword.

"No! No! Please!" wailed his wife. "We are sorry, very sorry. He speaks the truth, Nariko-san. We knew this day would come. But we only cleared the path. It was your destiny that made you choose to follow it, not what our family has done to you. Please, please, don't hurt him!"

Tessa prepared to strike and Lee gritted his teeth and bowed his head. There was another *whoosh*, and she returned her sword to its sheath.

"I will consider what you said, Lee. But there are still some things which don't make sense to me. The most insulting part of it all is that you and Master Matsumoto hid this from me for so long. And tell your brother there is something to do with the camellias which I still do not remember … presumably, he will understand."

Then she walked out.

Back home, Tessa showered, changed and waited for Jones, thinking about what Lee had said. She didn't like to admit it, but even if she had known everything before now, she wasn't sure there was much she would have done differently. She had been manipulated, no matter how much Lee denied it, but given everything that had happened, could she really hold only the Matsumoto responsible?

At 7:30, there was a familiar knock at the door. For a while she and Jones sat on her sofa and talked. Tessa didn't mention anything about her exchange with Lee. She had been pleased to know that Jones had not been involved, and was even more pleased not to be alone tonight. Pre-dinner drinks helped them relax, after which they walked down to The Falcon for an excellent Italian dinner. After which she invited him in for a night-cap.

"That was a lovely dinner, thank you," he said, sipping a malt whisky.

"You're welcome. I enjoyed it too. Thank you for the company. I feel empty, on my own. So many of my friends have been killed."

"You're not alone," he said, putting his arm round her.

Tessa sighed and let him pull her towards him. She placed her hand on his chest and looked into his eyes. She knew he cared about her and she really didn't want to be alone that night. She smiled. Undoing one of the buttons on his shirt, she ran her hand through the hairs on his chest. He lifted her face and kissed her passionately. He didn't mention going home that night, and Tessa was glad…

The following morning they walked to Antonio's together. He greeted them with his usual histrionic display of euphoria and they were soon enjoying their breakfast. But in silence.

"Are you OK?" asked Jones quietly.

Tessa smiled.

"Yes, of course. I suppose it's just a bit soon after David's death, that's all."

"I understand. Sorry."

"Gareth, there's absolutely nothing for you to be sorry about," she replied, putting her hand over his.

"Good." He smiled, fondling her hand in return for a moment. "So, what will you do now?"

"I'm not sure. Presumably the Mission is completed?" He nodded. "Strange, really, it seems a bit of an anti-climax. Anyway, I shall retire. I'm not into this killing business. It offends me no matter how *deserving* the people are."

He looked at her with a wry smile.

"Well, I'll tell the authorities you're on a recuperative sabbatical."

"For the rest of my life."

"Yes, I hear what you say, but let's take it in small steps, shall we? Hopefully, it will be as easy for you to retire as you think. But just because you've decided to take a holiday of indeterminate duration doesn't mean the world's criminal fraternity has. We still don't know who sent that anonymous SMS and, don't forget, even though your Mission is closed bar the paperwork, there has been a resurgence of the Calver Cats in the UK. Some of the new gang might have been members of the old one. They may still hold a grudge against you."

"True. Maybe I won't relinquish my OCL just yet. But I am determined to give retirement a chance. I'm already changing the number-plate on the Bugatti. I shall focus my energy on building a new *Pennysview* on the land that David gave me. That should be fun. Maybe it will also give my life a more normal sense of purpose."

"Enjoy yourself, you've earned it," he replied, trying to decide whether he should have another piece of toast or not. "So, where is this land then?"

She didn't reply. Jones looked at her quizzically.

"Ah, I understand. Maybe it's a good idea if I don't know."

They continued chatting, but after a while he left and Tessa slowly wandered back to South Kensington, eventually deciding to go to SKS. She changed into a tracksuit and slung her sword case over her shoulder.

She arrived mid-morning and the practice room was packed with students practising. However, as she walked in, they stopped and turned to face her. In silence, they all bowed. Lee, meanwhile, stood up from his chair on the podium and bowed deeply as well.

"*Konichiwa*, Master Nariko,"

Tessa raised her eyebrows. Then she looked at the students.

"Well? What are you lot gawping at? Continue your training."

She walked over to the podium.

"*Konichiwa*, Lee-san," she said, bowing a polite depth.

"Nariko, yesterday's regrettably brief demonstration was truly masterful. It left me beaten and defenceless. It is a tradition in our clan that the chair is reserved for the most highly skilled fighter. That, of course, is why my younger brother sits in Matsumoto Castle. He was always the better warrior of us two. But now, this chair is yours, whenever you wish it."

"Hmm, thank you, but no thank you. You know how I abhor violence. Those who employ it invariably have it used against them. I would like to die of old age. Beauchamp is dead, my Mission and your feud are over. So I shall retire."

"Of course," said Lee, "we all try to retire at some stage, but alas it never seems to work. So, although I don't doubt you are committed to trying, I am also sure you will not succeed. If I am right, events will conspire to ensure you continue to use your God-given gifts. Would you care for some tea? I have something for you."

Tessa's eyebrows furrowed in puzzlement, but then she shrugged. Together they went into his lounge and sat down on *zabuton* in front of the low lacquer table. Shortly afterwards Lee's wife entered the room with a tray of *macha* tea equipment; she was followed by her father carrying two exquisite wooden boxes. Both of them bowed deeply to Tessa, prompting her to blush. Then, as Lee's wife whisked some green tea, the old man reverently placed the boxes on the table near Tessa. Shortly afterwards he and his daughter bowed and left.

Lee looked at Tessa and also bowed.

"Nariko-san, these are presented in acknowledgement of your considerable achievements."

He nodded towards one of the boxes, beautifully made from mahogany.

"That one is from me and my wife. The other," he continued, indicating a gorgeous walnut box, "is from my brother."

She looked first at the boxes, and then at him.

"This is most kind of you, but there is no need. I am retiring."

"Yes, I remember, you said. But these gifts are in appreciation of what you have *already* achieved. You have more than earned them. Fate will take care of the rest."

Tessa shook her head and smiled. She lifted the mahogany box and put it down in front of her. She opened it and found four fine throwing knives. She took one out and admired it.

"Oh! These are magnificent. Strong, beautifully finished and perfectly balanced. Are you sure?"

"Of course, Nariko-san. We hope you enjoy them. I noticed your Kevlar suit already has pockets for four knives; these should fit well."

Tessa bowed and thanked Lee profusely. Then she turned her attention to the walnut box. Inside she found six hardened-steel shuriken. They were traditional four-pronged Ninja throwing discs, finely balanced and incredibly sharp. They even had cutting edges projecting from their flat surfaces, to make it difficult for anyone inexperienced to pick them up. She carefully lifted one out, and smiled at Lee.

"These are wonderful ... just like the knives. Please convey my thanks to your brother."

"I will indeed. He sends his regards and congratulations," replied Lee, with a wry smile. "He also said you shouldn't worry about the camellia memories; apparently they have nothing to do with your training. You placed them in your subconscious yourself. So you won't recall them until the correct circumstances arise." Tessa looked at him in surprise, but Lee simply shrugged his shoulders. "That's what he said."

She chuckled and returned the shuriken to the box.

"Thank you."

Lee nodded and gestured for Tessa to drink her tea. For several minutes they sat in silence.

"What now?" he asked.

"I shall visit the land David left me and decide what to do with it. After that, I'm not sure."

"Well, I presume you understand you are always welcome here?"

"Even after yesterday?"

"Especially after yesterday. You have done nothing to be ashamed of. You deserved your explanations and I thought you extracted them rather effectively. A nicely balanced display of skill and aggression, sufficient to ensure you had everyone's attention, without really harming anyone… Nariko-san, the ravages of time are taking their toll on me. It is clear I am no match for you any more. My brother has taught you well. Very well indeed, in fact. So if, at some point in the future, you wish to spend time here, in whatever capacity, just come."

She smiled, carefully stacked the boxes on top of each other, and bowed.

"Thank you, especially for these wonderful gifts. Even in retirement, I value them greatly. But I shall go now. As you say, we should leave the rest to fate."

Lee nodded and they both stood up, bowing to each other.

After lunch, she packed a suitcase and got into the Bugatti. But she didn't start the engine; she couldn't decide whether to take her swords, or not. Finally she convinced herself she really needed to get used to being without them. She opened the garage door, started the engine, reversed out and stopped to watch the garage door close. Then, after a couple of choice expletives, she opened the door again and drove back into the garage. Laughing, she fetched her sword case. She would start getting used to being without them another day. She drove out of the mews, wondering what Lee would have said if he knew she couldn't even bring herself to spend a few days away from her beloved swords…

The first thing she did in Orkney was to take a bouquet of tulips, peonies, hyacinths and lilac to David's family crypt. There were too many tourists in the cathedral for her to linger, so she went instead to the ruins of *Pennysview*. Windswept and alone, she sat down amongst the rubble and talked as though David were still with her. She still missed him, but she knew he wasn't coming back.

Eventually, she went to her new island. It proved to be every bit as wonderful as she'd expected. When she found the moated manor house, overgrown and surrounded by trees, themselves unusual for Orkney, she was in raptures. She decided to renovate the building to its original form on the outside, but to equip the inside with modern technology and its own green power supply. She organised a ceilidh to introduce herself to the island's inhabitants, as "Miss Wood", and Alasdair McClellan was duly elected Island Chief. Then she retained some young farmers to clear and replant her gardens, and funded a project to rebuild the island's crumbling school and hire a teacher.

It was three weeks later when she finally returned to London. She met Gareth for dinner and again they spent the night together. However, Tessa began to worry that although she liked him a lot, their relationship owed more to her loneliness than any deep-seated desire to be with him. Nevertheless, during the next few days, they spent much of their free time together.

Furthermore, although Tessa tried to ignore it for a while, there was no denying that her life was not complete when she wasn't practising with her swords. She finally acquiesced and went to SKS. Lee was delighted to see her and didn't even mention her sudden reappearance. They soon agreed that, in exchange for teaching the advanced pupils, she could use the SKS facilities whenever she wanted…

Meanwhile, in Burma, the death of General Soe Gyi had prompted a marked shift towards democracy and the possibility of signing the Peacekeeper Treaty. However, this appeared to have been interpreted by some as the last opportunity they might have to eliminate the local branch of the UK Special Forces; largely because it was widely held responsible for the deaths of Bill Chalmers and General Soe Gyi. During the weeks after Hochdahler Markt, several of Htet's staff and one of his two cousins, were killed.

It soon became too dangerous for Htet to stay in Rangoon so he moved to the small guest house where he and Tessa had stopped for breakfast en-route to Thazi. He phoned Nyunt daily. However, one evening, she told him her grandparents had not returned from a trip to Kengtung. It was likely they had been detained, but he was sure they wouldn't say anything. They both had cyanide capsules and would chew on them if interrogated. But now he had to go to Nyunt. It would be a dangerous journey. He phoned his cousin to advise him of the situation. They decided the time had come to leave Burma, and agreed to meet at the hill station.

Htet left the following morning. The first part of his journey went well. However, the night after, he stumbled across a roadblock just past Taunggyi. His car had some armour plating so Htet decided to drive through. But the soldiers were quick to open fire, and somehow one of the bullets penetrated the passenger compartment. He winced as he felt the searing pain in his thigh. Although not immediately life threatening, he knew his situation had taken a significant turn for the worse. He drove on for a while, then stopped to bind his wound. His leg was a mess and even driving proved difficult. But he had to go on; getting Nyunt to safety was now his only concern, although he doubted he would be able to go with her.

Htet's cousin arrived at the hill station and Nyunt burst into tears when she heard that her father had been injured. She didn't need to see the severity of his wounds to understand what this meant. As soon as he arrived, he would destroy everything and the three of them would head south into Karen territory. She sat alone, sobbing. But then she had an idea…

Tessa and Jones had arranged to meet in Antonio's for lunch. While she waited for him, she idly watched the bustling street and congratulated herself on how comprehensively she had managed to repress Nariko's more violent character traits. She smiled as Jones came in.

"No swords?" he said, kissing her on the cheek.

"Of course not," she rebuked. "I'm retired."

"Just checking. Anyway, sorry I'm late, but I waited for this secure fax to arrive from Burma. It's handwritten and addressed to *Dr Wud*." He looked at her with arched eyebrows. "It's a bit strange, but maybe you know what it means. It's from someone called Nyant. Ring any bells?"

Tessa looked blank.

"*Nyant*, Burma…," she repeated quietly; then she remembered. "Nyunt! Of course! What does it say?"

Jones gave her a sheet of paper.

"Dear Dr Wud. Your friend that helps you is hurt bad. He is here soon. Army close. Grandparents not come back from market. He not know I right you. Please help us. Please. Nyant".

"Apparently, the originating comms station went dead shortly after it arrived," added Jones, questioningly.

Tessa looked at him wide-eyed and then cupped her head in her hands.

"Oh, no, no, please no! In the blink of an eye, how can this happen?" she moaned.

"Tessa, what are you talking about?"

She looked at him and sighed.

"Gareth, I just came out of retirement. I've got to go to Burma. Can you get me there in twelve hours?"

"What? No!" he shrieked, inappropriately loudly, glancing round to smile at those staring at him in surprise. "Not Burma!" he hissed. "You must be joking? Who is this Nyunt?"

"Well, you know Htet's the Head of UK Special Forces in Burma? He helped Sinclair a long time ago, and he helped me too. It's only because of him that I got out in one piece." Jones nodded. "Well, Nyunt is with him and I promised that if ever they needed help, they could contact me. Nyunt must have known Htet would never ask, so she did. Gareth, I owe him. I owe him big time. UK Special Forces owes him … I've got to go."

Jones sighed.

"Yes, but Burma is really difficult. And quite frankly, I doubt this fax would be seen as justification for anything, especially in a hurry. I do understand what you're saying, but you don't even have a Mission to hide behind."

"But Burma still hasn't signed the Treaty, so it wouldn't make much difference if I did."

"Yes, but they're in turmoil and many hope they will sign soon; personally, I'm not so sure. However, we don't want to do anything which might make them change their minds. I need some time."

"I don't have any. There are valuable lives at stake, I must try and save them."

She took out her *cbc*.

"Hello … this is Dr Tessa Pennington, Northolt International account number TPEN52374. I need a plane to go to Bangkok today … now. The fastest you've got. Yes, I know it's short notice, but it needs to leave as soon as possible."

During the brief pause, she smiled at an exasperated-looking Jones.

"Yes, no problem, that's fine. Charge it to my account. OK, then I'll make a transfer within the next few minutes to cover it. How quickly can the plane be prepared? Two hours would be fine. No, I won't be travelling myself, an armed Peacekeeper will be one passenger, and there may be one other. They have my full authority to charge any additional costs to my account… Sure, the plane can come straight back. OK, three-thirty departure. Thank you.

"So, are you coming?" she asked him, grinning.

"Oh, bugger! Do you think Antonio'll do my lunch to go?"

She leant over and kissed him.

"Thank you! There'll be food on the plane. Now, I think I can get myself into Burma, but I'll probably need some help getting out. A helicopter would be good, especially if Htet is hurt. Perhaps while I'm getting to him, you could organise one for me? I'll pay, and I'll take Potter's GPS watch with me so you'll know where I am. Think about it, I need to go. I'll meet you at Northolt, three-twenty latest."

Jones nodded.

"Are you sure this is a good idea?"

"Absolutely positive. Although Lee'll never stop laughing when he finds out!"

"OK," he said in resigned disbelief, "I'll see you later."

"You're a star, Gareth."

She kissed him again and left to run back to South Kensington, stopping at Floyds bank to arrange the money transfer to cover chartering the plane and to withdraw some cash for extras. Then she went home and changed into her dark bluish-purple Kevlar suit. She took out her new knives, but after admiring them for a moment, decided to take her old ones. If she used these knives in an open space she might not be able to recover them. Then she put her two swords in their case, took plenty of Matsumoto's herbs and mosses, grabbed a long black leather coat and went in search of a taxi.

She reached Northolt at three-fifteen. The taxi was directed to a smart three-engined executive jet where the two pilots were busy making their final checks. Despite seeing her sword case, they simply nodded to her, and continued working. A few minutes later a dark blue-grey limousine arrived. Jones and Potter got out.

"Hello, Potter," said Tessa cheerily.

"Afternoon, Nariko. Up to your usual tricks, I see."

"Can't imagine what you mean," she replied.

"Well, just in case, here's our latest GPS watch. It's also a two-way communicator. Jones can tell you how it works."

"Oh, thank you. Much appreciated. Ready to go?"

"Not really," moaned Jones.

Five minutes later the plane took off. When they reached cruising altitude, Tessa went forward to the pilots.

"Gentlemen, I have a favour to ask. Could you make a stop en-route, please?"

"We've filed a flight plan direct to Bangkok, miss" replied the Captain. "Where did you want to go?"

"I'd like you to drop me off discreetly in Northern Thailand, at Mae Sai. It's only a small airfield, but it should be large enough for this. Afterwards you can continue to Bangkok with my colleague."

"Well, we're not meant to deviate from our flight plan, Miss. But I do know Mae Sai, and it isn't far off our route. We would use more fuel."

"Of course, so how about this? At the last minute, you divert to Mae Sai and quietly drop me off. For your trouble, I'll give you both one thousand pounds cash together with a further thousand for fees and fuel. But I don't want anyone to know anything about this, ever.

Would that be acceptable?"

The captain smiled and looked at his colleague, who nodded.

"It's a pleasure doing business with you, miss."

"Excellent. Then please get me there as quickly as possible. People's lives are at stake."

She gave them the money and went back to Jones.

"I hardly dare ask, but what have you done now?"

"I'm getting off at Mae Sai, on the Thai side of the border. It'll mean I can get into Burma more quickly; they'll take you on to Bangkok."

Jones nodded and went in search of some food. While they ate, he explained how the GPS communicator worked. Later, as Tessa slept, he made some calls.

CHAPTER 31

The captain woke them an hour from Mae Sai.

"I have to say," observed Jones, drinking coffee while watching Tessa put on her sword harness, swords and knives, "I think this is complete and utter madness, even by your heady standards. Anyway, Curtis is going to meet me in Bangkok. I'll do my best to organise transport out for you; but even if we find a helicopter, we'll still need someone good enough and daft enough to fly it into Burma, illegally."

"I know, but I'm sure you won't let me down. Here's a credit card, charge whatever you need to it."

"You're lucky I read those Burma reports."

"Indeed. I'll switch the GPS tracker on if I'm in serious trouble, or when I start back."

"Final approach," announced the Captain, "buckle up, please."

They landed, and Tessa grabbed two bottles of water. No sooner had the plane's steps unfurled when a Burmese man came forward to meet them. He looked at Tessa, put his hands together and bowed.

"*Mingalabah*. I know where you go. Mr Curtis asked me to take you in. We must leave now."

"Thank you, Gareth," said Tessa, deducing who had briefed Curtis.

"For heaven's sake, be careful," he pleaded. "And whatever you do, don't *not* come back."

She smiled, and followed the Burmese man.

"No names," he continued as they walked through the terminal building towards a battered 1950's Chevrolet bus. "I go to Kengtung. You must hide in old carpet on roof, and stay still. I collect passengers, drive over border and stop by the path up mountain. You must find own way from there. You remember?" She nodded. "Good. I will make diversion for you to get off bus. You must not be seen."

"*Kyay zu tin bar de*," she acknowledged, bowing.

Tessa climbed up the ladder on to the bus roof and wrapped herself in the dirty, moth-eaten carpet. Then the man surrounded her with sacks of vegetables and baskets. Not long afterwards the bus rattled off. Inside the carpet it was stiflingly hot, stuffy and smelly; nevertheless, Tessa stayed completely still. The bus stopped a few minutes later to collect passengers and she drew one of her knives, just in case. More baggage was added around her, and eventually the bus moved off.

They stopped next at the Thai border. Tessa heard the formalities being completed and imagined the bus trundling across the bridge to Tachileik. Shortly afterwards it stopped again, for rather longer than she would have preferred. She could hear the compartment beneath her being comprehensively searched. Then someone climbed on to the roof, followed by her mysterious friend. She heard them talking and some sacks and boxes were moved. But the inspection didn't last long and she heaved a sigh of relief as the bus moved off. At least she was in Burma.

Some twenty minutes later, the bus juddered to a halt amidst a considerable commotion. A number of chickens had escaped from inside the bus on to the road and passengers flooded off to catch the hapless birds.

Tessa knew it was time for her to go. She carefully freed herself from the carpet, and delighted in being able to take a deep breath of fresh air. The bus had stopped with its roof concealed in the lower branches of a large tree which overhung the road. She smiled at the excellent planning of her friend and wished she could thank him. But he was busy directing the people chasing the chickens. She adjusted the carpet to hide the fact she had been there and clambered into the leafy tree. After a while the bus drove off and disappeared from view.

It was mid-morning, very quiet and a fine sunny day. Tessa dropped down onto the road. The path leading up the mountainside was nearby. She started climbing, stepping from stone to stone to avoid leaving footprints. She paused briefly to study the border crossing; it had been completely rebuilt and seemed to be operating normally.

In the trees near the top of the ridge, she drank some water and then started jogging towards Htet's house. She knew it would take her several hours to get there, and expected to arrive early in the afternoon. Hopefully, that would still allow them all to get back to the border before dusk. As she ran, she occasionally heard planes in the distance, but none came close.

She paused briefly by a stream, drank more water and washed her face. Eventually, she saw a suspiciously dark and dense column of smoke in the distance – far too visible to be normal. She stopped to look round and listen. Then she checked her weapons and took a deep breath... She stopped next behind the final brow and crawled to the edge, cautiously peering over. Near the house was the burnt-out wreckage of Htet's car, and the crumpled body of his cousin. Soldiers were milling around. All of them had guns and knives.

Htet was tied to a chair, well away from the house, facing in her direction. He'd been badly beaten and his right leg was covered in blood. She could see six soldiers, including the Major from the border crossing, standing behind Htet, and another had just entered the house. She wouldn't be able to get closer without them seeing her. Also, it looked as though someone was expected, but perhaps not quite yet. So, if she postponed making an entrance until dark, the situation might get worse. She elected to seize the moment.

She waited until she felt sure she knew the disposition of all the soldiers. Then she backed away and prepared herself. A minute later, at a fast but relaxed pace, she ran over the brow of the hill towards the hut. Htet saw her straightaway, but didn't react, so it was a while before the soldiers realised she was coming. The Major spotted her first. He drew his pistol and ordered a couple of soldiers to drag Nyunt out of the hut.

"Trap!" she screamed, earning herself a brisk slap across her face.

"Welcome, Nariko, we have been expecting you!" yelled the Major, grinning. "Now, stop where you are!"

Tessa slowed down and started walking towards him. She wanted to get as close as she could before she stopped moving.

"A trap, for me? How thoughtful. Who organised it?"

"No questions. Just stay where you are or I shoot this man," replied the Major clearly nervous.

Then he ordered two soldiers to disarm and handcuff Tessa.

"Htet, are you all right?" she asked.

He nodded and smiled, but made a point of moving his eyes towards Nyunt. Tessa smiled and gave a little nod of her head. She knew he meant that, in a conflict, he wanted Nyunt to be saved.

As the two soldiers approached her, Tessa took another couple of paces towards the Major. It improved her angle on the soldiers holding Nyunt. The men stopped wearily a few feet away from her.

"They'll kill us all!" yelled Htet violently rocking his chair, prompting the Major to pistol-whip him. But the momentary distraction was all she needed. Drawing her swords, Tessa moved towards the two soldiers and slashed them viciously across the chest, killing them both instantly. While the bodies were still falling, and before anyone else had time to react, she re-sheathed her swords, drew two knives and threw them at the soldiers restraining Nyunt. A moment later, her other two knives had hit the remaining soldiers, leaving only the Major standing. Panicking, he fired at Htet and yelled some orders. Two heavily armed men sprang up from the grass behind him. But Tessa had already somersaulted down between the bodies of the first two soldiers and taken their knives. She felt the heat of bullets passing perilously close, and one scored her Kevlar suit. Continuing to dodge bullets, she rolled away and threw one of the knives, then the other. Neither flew well, but both still hit their targets in the chest and the soldiers collapsed.

Swearing, the Major began firing at her. As more dust plumes kicked up around her, she struggled to her feet, drew her Bryani sword and threw it. A moment later, nearly ten inches of the blade was sticking out from the back of his skull. She quickly drew her Kimi sword and looked round expectantly. But all was quiet. Nyunt stood frozen by the entrance to the house, while blood dribbled down from Htet's mouth. Tessa ran over, cut him free and inspected his wounds. The little girl joined them uncertainly.

"Nyunt," said Tessa, smiling, "are you all right, dear?" The child nodded but glanced worriedly at her father. "Please could you go down the track a little way and check that no one else is coming? Don't go too far, and don't let anyone see you."

Htet nodded to the girl, and she ran off.

"Thank you for coming," he said to Tessa, clearly in considerable pain. "How did you know?"

"Nyunt sent me a fax," she replied, doing her best to stem the bleeding and bind his wounds.

"I am dying."

"Yes. I'm sorry. There's nothing I can do to stop that. I have bought you some time, but not much."

"This was very carefully organised. The UK Special Forces appeared to be the target, but really it was you. I couldn't find out who is behind it, but I do know there were two of them, neither of them Burmese. The Major told me your Peacekeeper name; maybe that helps. I didn't know about the camouflaged solders."

"Not to worry. We were just lucky there weren't any more of them," she replied, inspecting the threadbare tracks across her Kevlar suit. She was bleeding from one, but the wound was not serious and she pressed some healing herbs into it.

"Reinforcements will be nearby, and they'll have heard the noise," continued Htet. "You must leave now. I'm in no state to go anywhere, but Nyunt can. You'll have to take her."

"What?" exclaimed Tessa.

"There is no alternative, she must go with you. Her grandparents are dead, her cousins are dead, and soon the last of her parents will be dead. She has no one else. If you don't take her, she will be doomed to a dreadful life. If she survives today."

"But Htet, I can't! I have no experience … I'm … you see…"

He smiled and raised his hand.

"It's what's in your heart that counts. You'll be fine, and you two are already fond of each other. Please, promise me you will take her?"

He coughed up some blood and looked at Tessa, desperately pleading.

"Htet, you ask a lot."

"I don't think so. It will be good for you, and you'll enjoy it. Nyunt is a wonderful child, and I will die happy in the knowledge you will give her much more than I could ever have dreamed of giving her here. You said once if I needed your help for her, you would give it. Well, now I am asking. Give her a free life. Take her with you, please."

Tessa swallowed and looked at the little girl walking uncertainly back towards them, oblivious to the fact her future was being discussed.

"Htet, if she wants to come with me, I'll take her and do as much for her as I am able. But it is not going to be easy getting out of Burma. I don't have transport, and with Nyunt."

"Oh," he tried to laugh, "I'm sure you'll manage. Now, I will buy you some time. Go into the house and lift up the planks under the mat.

You'll find the munitions store there. Rig up a detonator for me. I will hold them off as long as I can, but when I am finished, I will blow the munitions. Now, ask Nyunt to come to me."

Tessa sighed.

"Nyunt, dear. Come and talk to your father."

As the young girl went to him, Tessa collected her weapons and went into the house. She found the munitions and used some hand grenades to make a detonator. Then she tied loaded automatic weapons by the windows and attached strings to their triggers. Afterwards she built a substantial barricade near the front door and laid several loaded rifles, a multiple-shot grenade launcher and a pistol behind it. Finally she rigged the detonator to a string which Htet could tension with his good leg. She would arm the detonator by pulling the pins on the hand grenades as she left. When he relaxed his leg, the munitions would explode.

As she worked, she watched Htet and Nyunt. After a while, Nyunt started crying and grasped her father's arm. When Tessa went back to them, it was with an empty feeling in her stomach and a heavy heart.

"It is done," she said sadly.

Htet nodded as Tessa knelt down in front of the little girl.

"Nyunt, would you like to come away with me or would you prefer to stay in Burma? I will not leave you alone; I will help you either way."

Nyunt's cheeks were wet with tears. She looked at her father, and then back at Tessa.

"My father want I go with you. I will try not to be problem… But can Pa Pa go too? Please!"

"Nyunt, you know I cannot," said Htet. "Don't make it difficult for Nariko. She will look after you. Go with her and have a good life."

Nyunt looked at him and started sobbing again.

"I don't want to leave you!"

"Nyunt," continued Tessa, realising that despite her best efforts her own eyes were beginning to water, "you may choose. You should only come with me if you want to. If you prefer, I will take you to someone else in Burma and only leave when you are safe."

"Nyunt," said Htet gently, but insistently.

Still sobbing, she gripped her father's arm harder and looked up at Tessa.

"If you willing take me," she whimpered, "I come. Please."

"Good girl," said Htet, wiping away her tears and straightening her hair.

"Now, help me into the house."

With Tessa supporting him, they struggled back inside the house. He lay down behind the barricade and Tessa handed him the strings to the guns.

"Left – one knot, right – two knots, back – three knots," she said, pointing to the three strings. "If you release the tension in this cable," she said, tying it to his foot, "grenades will detonate the munitions. I will pull the pins when we leave. OK?"

"I understand," replied Htet. "Nyunt darling, you must be very brave and remember what I said. Your mother and I will always be with you. We both love you dearly and will continue to love you, even when you cannot see us. Now be good, and do as Nariko says. When you leave, do not look back. You should look forward to your future with her. Now, go, both of you."

Distraught, Nyunt burst into noisy tears and hugged her father. But then, over the sound of her sobbing, the noise of powerful engines could be heard climbing the hill.

"Nariko," said Htet urgently, as tears started rolling down his cheeks. "That's two, maybe three trucks. You cannot fight them all. Take her! Please hurry. I must know she is safe."

Tessa swallowed and tensioned the detonator string with Htet's leg. Then she pulled the pins on the grenades. She activated her GPS watch and desperately hoped Jones would be able to come soon.

"Htet," she said quietly, cupping his hand in hers and with a tremor in her voice, "it has been an honour to have known you. May your spirit go in peace. Nyunt, we must leave now."

The child was screaming and sobbing uncontrollably, and tears started trickling down Tessa's cheeks too. As the noise from the trucks grew louder, Tessa looked at Htet. All three of them were crying. He reached up and kissed Nyunt – then nodded to Tessa. She gently prised the child away, and led her out of the house. As they walked, Nyunt, on the verge of hysteria, was screaming and struggling to go back. Tessa quickened the pace, and Nyunt was forced to start running. But still she looked back, almost stumbling. Tessa quickened

342

the pace again.

"Too fast!" shouted Nyunt. "I cannot."

"Sorry," replied Tessa, "I'll carry you."

"But I don't want to go!"

"Neither do I, Nyunt. But if we don't leave now, we will all die. We must hurry."

Tessa picked her up and started jogging towards Tachileik. It was all she could do to watch where she was going. Never had she so deeply regretted not arriving sooner. Meanwhile, Nyunt continued to look back, hoping against hope.

Eventually they heard the sound of a fierce fire-fight from around the house. Clearly Htet was determined to delay the soldiers for as long as he could.

Occasionally a loud bang echoed round the mountains as he worked his way through the grenades. With the sound of every exchange, Tessa shuddered and Nyunt whimpered.

Suddenly, the dreadful cacophony was replaced by an eerie silence. It seemed to last for ever. But Tessa knew Htet was tempting the soldiers to come closer. Suddenly there was an ear-shattering *whoomph!*

"Pa Pa-ye!!!" screamed Nyunt.

Tessa stopped and turned to see a thick plume of black smoke and wreckage rising into the afternoon sky. She sank to the ground and hugged Nyunt as tears rolled down both their faces.

"I'm sorry, Nyunt. I'm so, so sorry."

She did her best to console the child, but she knew the soldiers would be following them now. They were not quite half-way to Tachileik. She tapped the communicator.

"Jones, we're two and struggling! We need transport."

She didn't really expect a response, so she was almost euphoric when she heard his voice reply.

"Working on it. Keep going," he crackled.

Buoyed by this, Tessa looked at Nyunt.

"Come on, dear, we must keep moving."

She scooped up the child as she cried, and ran on. But the terrain became more difficult and Tessa's pace slowed. Furthermore, Nyunt couldn't be anything other than an awkward burden. Beads of perspiration started rolling down Tessa's brow.

Then she heard the sound of motorcycles and started looking for somewhere to hide Nyunt. Ahead to her right was dense jungle. It would slow her down if she went in there, while the army would be in their element.

"Two motorcycles come," said Nyunt suddenly.

"I know, dear," panted Tessa, continuing to run. "Tell me when they are very close, or draw their guns."

"Nearly here," said Nyunt worriedly.

Tessa put the girl down and pushed her round behind her own body. "If I move, keep directly behind me."

Bouncing along, the motorcycle riders drew pistols. They were still too far away for Tessa, so she watched carefully as one took aim. She saw his finger squeeze the trigger. Just before the gun spat a bullet at her, she dodged to her left and felt Nyunt follow. The bullet missed.

A moment later and the motorcyclists were close enough. Tessa quickly threw two knives. One hit a soldier in the centre of his chest, killing him. The other motorcyclist swerved to avoid her knife, and lost control. Catapulted off his bike, he landed roughly and lay still. She started towards his motorcycle but then it exploded and more soldiers with rifles appeared in the distance. Muttering expletives, Tessa scooped up Nyunt and started running again. She wished it wasn't such a clear day; although the sun had started to go down, both she and her adversaries could still see a long way.

Tessa was pleased and exhausted when they finally neared Tachileik. But her joy was short-lived. In the distance, she saw more soldiers come up the path from the road. Now there were soldiers in front, a steep drop to her left, dense jungle to her right, and soldiers gaining on her from behind. She was trapped.

She put Nyunt down and tapped her communicator.

"Sorry to bother you, but this is getting very difficult."

"Nearly there. Keep moving."

"Which way? Baddies north, baddies south, and cliffs east."

"West then!"

"Jungle? Great!" sighed Tessa, starting to run again.

Occasionally, soldiers would take pot shots at them; but for the time-being they were still too far away.

Then several plumes of dust rose up in front of Tessa. The soldiers were within range. As more shots were fired, she came to a depression in the ground and jumped in, quickly pushing some rocks up to the edge to help protect them.

"Stay down," she said to Nyunt, tapping her communicator.

"We're pinned down. Now would be really good!"

There was no reply.

The sound of rifle shots preceded several more plumes of dust rising around them. A bullet ricocheted off one of the nearby rocks. Tessa planned her final defence.

"Nyunt, dear, when the soldiers get here, I will fight them. You must run into the jungle. Don't look back, just keep going. Do you understand?"

Nyunt nodded and smiled, prompting Tessa to smile back and wipe the tears from the little girl's face. Then her communicator burst into life.

"You ordered a taxi, miss?" yelled Jones.

Tessa breathed a massive sigh of relief as she heard the sound of a helicopter speeding over the jungle, approaching out of the setting sun behind them.

The shooting stopped while the soldiers strained to identify the craft. Skimming across the tree tops, it flew over to where Tessa and Nyunt were crouching and gracefully swooped down. The door in the side was open and as Tessa looked up she saw Jones.

Soldiers started running down the hill towards them, firing. In moments their position would be overrun.

With the helicopter hovering only a few feet off the ground, Tessa stood up and threw Nyunt to Jones. Then, with bullets landing all around her, and some pinging into the helicopter, she jumped on to the landing skid and clambered into the doorway.

Suddenly Nyunt screamed. Tessa spun round and caught the knife which had just been thrown in. Jones looked down to see her holding the blade a few inches away from his chest.

"Go, go, go!" yelled Tessa, accompanied by a whining chorus of bullets.

The helicopter lurched sideways and upwards, hurling the three of them back from the doorway. Then it quickly moved away and the sound of gun fire receded.

CHAPTER 32

Tessa took a deep breath and knelt in front of Nyunt.

"Are you all right, little one?" she asked in concern, brushing some hair away from the child's eyes. Nyunt nodded. Tessa smiled and looked at Jones.

"Thank you. Impeccable timing as always."

"You're welcome," he replied. "Thank you for catching the knife."

She nodded and scrambled forward to the pilot.

"That was fancy flying, thanks."

The pilot winked at her.

"Hah! Hello, Curtis, what a lovely surprise," said Tessa, laughing. "Where did you learn to fly like that?"

"Basra and Helmand."

"Ah, well, you were brilliant. I hope this won't get you into trouble."

"I doubt it'll even be reported. Those guys were mercenaries and have already been disowned. It seems the Junta is more interested in gaining access to international aid and trying to avoid a war crimes tribunal. What about Htet?"

"He didn't make it."

"Oh, that's a pity. Is that his daughter?" Tessa nodded. "Hmm. We just entered Thai airspace."

Tessa clambered back and sat down next to Nyunt. She and Jones were eyeing each other with considerable suspicion.

"So, who exactly is this?" he asked.

"Oh, this is Nyunt. Nyunt, this is Gareth Jones, he's a nice man."

"He's not looking nice to me," grumbled Nyunt.

"Hmm," observed Tessa, "she's right, you know."

"Let me ask you again, Nariko. Who is this?" insisted Jones.

Tessa frowned.

"This is Htet's daughter. He…"

"And what's she doing here? It's one thing to try and save a Special Forces agent, it's another to abscond with a child."

346

"Jones!" exclaimed Tessa indignantly. "For years Htet risked everything in Burma for the UK. Now it's cost him his life, and those of his family, bar one. There is no one left to care for her now, so before he died, Htet asked me to look after her."

"Oh, another of your deathbed promises, is it? I suppose that makes it all right?"

"Stop it!" retorted Tessa. "Nyunt has been through enough. She doesn't need this, and quite frankly neither do I!"

"You cannot use an unsuccessful attempt to rescue a Special Forces agent," continued Jones pointedly, "as an excuse to start an orphanage for homeless Burmese."

Nyunt burst into tears, prompting Tessa to put an arm round her.

"Jones, she's not a bag of potatoes! She has just had to watch the last of her family being murdered. She's coming and that's final."

"Well, she's not coming with me."

"I know that. She's coming with me."

"Look, this is a young girl. How are you going to look after her? You wouldn't know where to start. You're a Peacekeeper."

"Retired! As for the rest, I'll work it out as I go along."

"Don't be ridiculous. She can't go to England!"

An awkward pause followed and Nyunt stopped crying, curious to hear Tessa's reply.

"Then I won't go either," she replied, smiling at the child. "I made a promise to Htet and Nyunt, and I'm going to keep it no matter how difficult. If I can't do it in England, then I'll do it somewhere else. But I am not sending her back to Burma to be killed, or worse."

"Er, sorry to intrude," said Curtis, calling back to them. "But I'm currently heading for the embassy. I presume that's…?"

"Thank you, Curtis. Just a minute, please," replied Tessa, butting in before Jones could say anything. She took out her *cbc* and dialled a number.

"Ah, good afternoon. It's Dr Pennington, may I speak to Mr Georges please…? Good afternoon, Mr Georges … yes, I'm very well, thank you. I hope you are too? …Good. Look, I'm sorry to call at short notice, again, but I desperately need a double room. Do you have anything, for a few days…? Oh, excellent. Thank you. Also, is the helipad still in operation…? Yes, please, we'll be landing in about forty minutes, if that's all right…? Indeed, thank you. See you shortly."

"Curtis," shouted Tessa, "take me and Nyunt to the Oriental Hotel, please. There's a helipad on top of the main building. You're expected."

"No. The embassy!" yelled Jones.

"Curtis, who's paying for this helicopter?"

"Ah! She does have a point, sir," he replied, looking at Jones.

"This is madness!" he grumbled. "All right, take her to the bloody hotel."

"Jones!" interjected Tessa. "Watch your language!"

He shook his head and started brooding.

Tessa smiled and gave Nyunt a gentle squeeze.

"Tessa, there are laws and procedures," continued Jones in a more conciliatory tone, "not even Peacekeepers can ride roughshod over them. Please, be reasonable."

"I know," sighed Tessa. "But what else could I do? It was awful, and would have got worse."

"Fine, let's meet tomorrow when we're all rested. We can discuss it then."

Tessa understood all too well what he meant, and how ill-prepared she was. However, as she looked down at Nyunt and their eyes met, she felt their spirits brush together. For a brief moment, Tessa was sure it would all work out fine. She smiled, but Nyunt burst into tears.

"Landing in five," interrupted Curtis.

Tessa took off her swords and remaining knives, and wrapped them in a blanket.

"I'll come to the hotel mid-morning with your sword case," said Jones, handing her the long coat she'd left on the plane.

"Thank you for organising all this," she said, "I really do appreciate it."

He nodded. Shortly afterwards, Tessa and Nyunt walked over to the hotel's welcoming staff, and turned to watch the helicopter lift off.

Twenty minutes later, they were alone in their room. Nyunt looked round, confused. Tessa offered her some of the fresh fruit from the basket on the table, and they both ate, and drank some water. Then Tessa went into the bathroom to run a hot bath, and telephoned down to reception. A few minutes later, staff from one of the shops arrived with a selection of clothes for her and Nyunt to choose from. Soon they were on their own again, with neat piles of clothes on the two beds.

"Right," said Tessa, "I think we both need a wash. Do you want to go first or shall I?"

"You first."

Tessa nodded and went into the bathroom. She was soon relaxing in a bath of steaming hot water, misty with fine salts. After a while, Nyunt came into the bathroom and sat on the stool, watching her. When Tessa finished, she rinsed the bath.

"So, do you want a go now?" she asked.

"Er, yes, please," replied Nyunt hesitantly.

Tessa smiled and ran the bath, checked the temperature and put some bath salts in.

"All yours, dear," she said, helping Nyunt to get in. Then she cleaned and dressed her wounds, none of which was serious, and started drying her hair.

When Nyunt got out, Tessa dried and brushed her hair, and helped her get dressed. Then the two of them went downstairs for dinner.

"Hello, Ice," said Tessa cheerily as they entered the Verandah Restaurant.

"It is good to see you again, Dr," he said, smiling at Nyunt. "Your daughter?"

"Er, well, yes," replied Tessa, not having thought about it quite like that before. "A quiet table by the river, please."

Tessa and Nyunt ate while watching the night-time activity on the Chao Phraya. But they were both exhausted and soon returned to their room for an early night.

Tessa stripped, had a quick shower and was soon sitting up in bed. Nyunt sat on the other.

"Your turn," said Tessa encouragingly. "I suggest you have a shower and then get some sleep."

Nyunt went into the bathroom, returning shortly afterwards looking embarrassed.

"No more water."

"Oh, I'm sorry, my fault, I should have shown you how," replied Tessa, chiding herself for not having realised that would be the case.

When Nyunt came back, she looked at both beds, thought for a moment, and then climbed into the empty one.

"Good night, dear," said Tessa. She switched off the lights and started drifting off to sleep, but she was soon roused by the sound of Nyunt sobbing. She got up, walked over to the other bed, climbed in and put her arm round the child.

"Oh dear, you poor thing. You've had a terrible time and now you've got to put up with my clumsiness. It will take me a while, but I do want to learn. Please be patient. I promise I'll look after you as well as I can."

Nyunt stopped sobbing for a moment and turned to look at her. Tessa brushed back her hair and wiped away the tears.

"I don't understand all you say."

Tessa smiled.

"Well, you're not the first to say that, so don't worry. We'll just teach you some more English and then you'll be able to talk to lots of people, as well as me."

"I want Pa Pa."

For a moment Tessa didn't know what to say and tears came into her eyes.

"I know. I wish he was here for you too, but we will be all right. We'll just take it step by step. Pa Pa didn't go away because he wanted to; he went away because he was a very brave man and willing to sacrifice everything for you. It is right to grieve for him, and you should never forget him. I won't."

Nyunt burst into tears again, and cried for most of the night. Tessa did her best to console her, but soon felt woefully inadequate.

Only as dawn approached did Nyunt finally fall asleep. Tessa crept carefully out of bed. She wanted to train as usual and got dressed as quietly as she could. She checked the child before leaving, and found she was watching her.

"Nyunt dear, I'm going across the river to exercise. I have to exercise every day to keep strong. You can stay here if you want, but if you would rather come with me, you can. What would you like to do?"

"I come," whimpered Nyunt sleepily.

Tessa smiled and helped her put on a tracksuit. Together they went across the river to the fitness centre. While Tessa sorted out the equipment she needed, Nyunt curled up on one of the mats; she soon fell asleep and Tessa covered her with some large towels.

When she'd finished her workout, she managed to scoop Nyunt up without waking her, and carried her to the jetty. Nyunt woke up as the boat arrived to ferry them back across the river. She smiled at Tessa.

"That's better," she said, looking into Nyunt's clear brown eyes. "And in case no one has said it to you for a while, you're very pretty."

Nyunt giggled and they returned to the hotel, eventually going down to the Verandah together for breakfast.

CHAPTER 33

Barely an hour later, Ice led Jones and Curtis to their table. This early arrival irritated Tessa since she and Nyunt were finally beginning to relax together.

"Good morning. May we join you?" asked Jones without smiling.

"Of course. Have you had breakfast?" asked Tessa.

They both shook their heads and looked longingly at the breakfast buffets.

"Well, help yourselves, gentlemen."

Jones put Tessa's sword case down next to her, and headed off in the direction of the various tables.

"He still not like me," grumbled Nyunt.

"Oh, he does really," replied Tessa. "He's just trying to do the best for both of us, that's all. He looks at you, and sees lots of paperwork. I look at you, and see the future… You didn't understand all of that, did you?"

Nyunt shook her head.

"Don't worry. Gareth is a good man. Just remember, no matter what happens, I will not desert you." Nyunt looked afraid at that, prompting Tessa to reach out and give her a gentle squeeze. "I promise."

"Can I get Burmese food?" asked the child.

"Probably. Have a word with Ice and see what he can find."

Nyunt got up and went in search of him. Tessa watched her go, pleased she was willing to venture off on her own. Jones and Curtis returned. At first little was said as they concentrated on their food. Nyunt came back, smiling.

"There is Burmese cook. I talk to him. Good food coming."

"Well done, dear. I look forward to seeing what we're getting," replied Tessa. "So, Curtis, I hear you've been promoted."

"Yes, and I understand you had a hand in that."

"Well, after yesterday, I'm doubly pleased I did what little I could to help. Besides, I'm sure you deserved it."

"Nariko," said Jones. "We need to have a word about, er..."

"See!" shrieked Nyunt.

"Nyunt," interjected Tessa pointedly, scowling at Jones.

"Yes, sorry. Anyway, could we talk in private please? Nyunt, would you excuse us for a moment?"

She looked at Curtis and nodded to Tessa.

"OK," said Tessa, "let's go and sit over there. Nyunt, if you're scared about anything, come to me straight away. OK?"

Nyunt smiled and picked up a piece of fresh papaya.

Jones and Tessa sat down at a nearby table. She checked no one could see, unfurled the blanket with her swords and knives in it, and put them in her sword case. She locked the cover and looked up expectantly.

"Tessa, please stop this foolishness," said Jones. "I don't believe it's right for you."

"Why on earth not?"

"Because you're a Peacekeeper, not a mother. You kill people for sport."

"Oh, for goodness' sake! I'm retired. And while I used to kill people, I have never killed for sport."

"And how long did your so-called retirement last? Nariko, you're ruthless, you…"

"Look who's talking!" she retorted on the verge of exploding. "You know I abhor violence. I only used my skills to end the Mission you and Sinclair manoeuvred me into, just after you lumbered me with the OCL. Remember?"

"In that case, if you're really retiring, you won't need your OCL any more, will you? So, if you're even going to try and keep her, you'd better pass me your sword case. Now, please."

Tessa looked at him wide-eyed, and swallowed. Then she glanced at Nyunt, who smiled and waved at her, now holding a piece of banana in her hand. Tessa had never expected to have to choose between a child and her own swords.

"Couldn't I just keep an RCL?"

"No."

She bowed her head and took a deep breath.

"Take it then, she's more important."

"All right." He reached over and pulled her sword case towards him. "But there's something else too. You weren't..."

"Careful, Gareth!"

"Look, somebody is going to say it, so it might as well be someone who knows you, respects you, and cares for you. Don't forget, I've proved it doesn't matter to me. But you haven't managed to kill off all baseless prejudice, so, it will matter to others. It'll come out eventually, you know it will, and..."

"Have you finished?"

"I didn't think I had," replied Jones with a wry smile, "but..."

"Well, if you wish to continue in a different vein, you may, but otherwise we're done."

"Tessa, just because you feel your life is empty, doesn't mean you have the right to fill it with hers. Is this some form of self-flagellation in order to honour a deathbed promise? Do you love Nyunt, or do you just feel sorry for her? Because if you don't love her, you shouldn't do this, it won't be in her best interests."

Tessa thought for several seconds.

"I think I love her, and I'm sure I'll grow to love her more. I suppose I do feel sorry for her and am obligated by my promise to Htet. But, most of all, I want to be a good mother and to give her more than her parents would ever have been able to give her in Burma."

Jones sighed.

"I still don't think you understand the enormity of what you're considering. If you start there will be no turning back. It will not only be your swords which you'll lose, it will be your freedom to do whatever you want. She will be dependent on you. If it went wrong, it would be an horrendous mess, and heaven only knows how it would be sorted out."

Tessa felt the immense pressure of long-term responsibility bearing down on her.

"I know," she replied weakly. "I understand what a massive change this will mean for me. I'll miss my swords dreadfully, but I've spent too much time destroying life; I don't want to do it any more. I want to make her the focus of my energy and help create a good person. It's something I've always dreamt of, but never expected to do. I couldn't forgive myself if I gave her to someone else. I would have failed Htet and abandoned Nyunt only because it's not convenient for me."

"But Burma is settling down. There really is no rumpus over what happened yesterday. Amazingly, the Junta is denying all responsibility and blaming the Calver Cats. I'm sure we could find some excellent parents for her in Burma. She would be amongst people of her own culture. You could still support her there if you wanted. Wouldn't that be a better way of honouring your promise to Htet?"

Tessa looked at him and was irritated to find tears welling up in her eyes. Choked with emotion, she looked down and found a tissue.

"I understand what you say, and I'm grateful you had the decency to say it. However, when I first met Nyunt there was a connection between us. I'm sure that spark will kindle a fire. This has been a terrible experience for her, she needs time to settle down and get used to feeling safe with me…"

At that moment Nyunt grabbed Tessa's leg.

"Thank you, dear, just what I needed," she said quietly, and lifted Nyunt on to her lap as some tears ran down her face. "Gareth, the fact is, I really want to look after her and I'll do everything in my power to make sure I give her a good upbringing. I am under no illusions as to how difficult it will be for me. I have a lot to learn, and I know I'll have to change. However, what you propose as an alternative is reasonable. I think Nyunt should be allowed to choose for herself. I leave it to you to put it to her."

"OK," he sighed. "Let's go back to Curtis."

Tessa dried her eyes and watched in silence as Jones picked up her sword case. Then she lifted Nyunt up and carried her back to the other table.

"Nyunt dear," she said softly, "Mr Jones wants to talk to you. Think carefully about what he says and then decide what you would like to do. If you don't understand something, ask him to say it again. There is no wrong answer; you should simply tell him what you want. All right?" Nyunt nodded.

Jones proceeded to explain the two options to her. Stay with Tessa, or let them find a family in Burma willing to look after her, with Tessa supporting her in any way she could…

"Do you understand the options?" he asked eventually.

Nyunt nodded.

"Are you sure?"

"Yes."

"Do you want me to say any of it again, or differently?"

"No."

"Do you have any questions?"

"No."

"OK. So, what would you like to do?"

Nyunt went quiet, clearly deep in thought. Tessa felt a huge knot tighten in her stomach and her mouth went dry… Suddenly, Nyunt smiled at Curtis and turned to Jones.

"I stay with Nariko … please."

"You're sure you don't want to go back to Burma?"

"I not go back. Nothing left for me."

"So be it," acknowledged Jones.

Tessa hugged Nyunt as more tears rolled down her cheeks.

"Thank you, dear. I will not betray you, or my promise to your father."

"Nariko," continued Jones, "this means you must apply for political asylum on behalf of Nyunt. And although your Peacekeeper status, and achievements, will help, you will still need to go through a formal UK adoption procedure if you want to bring her back to England."

"Fine," replied Tessa, struggling to clear her throat.

"Both processes are quite long-winded and for good reason, but adoption is the more complicated. That's because it's designed to give you both an opportunity to demonstrate you make a viable family unit. In particular you will have to demonstrate you are a good mother for Nyunt. However, asylum will need to be granted first."

"OK," murmured Tessa, hoping that was all.

"I haven't finished yet. Since we find ourselves in rather unusual circumstances, I have already asked the British Ambassador to speak with the Burmese authorities and they do not intend to object if Nyunt seeks asylum. I also had Potter liaise with the adoption authorities in England to see if it would be possible for you to adopt her *in principle* straightaway. At least then you would be able to take her home. Of course, you will still need to complete the process in England before the adoption becomes final. And, if the authorities aren't satisfied, the adoption will be annulled. Do you accept all of that?"

"Yes," she replied, wondering what she had let herself in for.

"Then the first step is to get two independent judgements of your suitability for this role. Fortunately for you, Potter and I have already done this."

Tessa looked up at him wide-eyed.

"I'd watch out for that right jab of hers if I were you, sir," said Curtis laughing.

Jones smiled.

"The next step is to identify some guardians, ideally a married couple who will be able to support you."

Tessa looked blank.

"You know, like godparents."

"Oh, I see."

"I took the liberty of suggesting Potter contact Lee and his wife. Suffice to say, you were right. When Lee heard what you'd done, it was indeed an awful long time before he stopped laughing. But he was delighted, and said he and his wife would be only too pleased to offer their support."

"That's wonderful of them, and you, and Potter," said Tessa gratefully. "But getting back to the point Curtis raised, why exactly did you just put me and Nyunt through an emotional wringer?"

"Because I had to be sure you both understood what you were committing yourselves to. Oh, and you'd better take this back, it suits you better."

He lifted her sword case and moved it back towards her.

"Very good, Jones," mused Tessa. "I'm impressed."

"Anyway," he continued, "the situation is still complicated by the fact that we don't have any formal means of identification for Nyunt. You know, passport, birth certificate, that sort of thing."

"I have," interrupted Nyunt.

Everyone watched intrigued as she rummaged in her tracksuit pocket, eventually producing an extremely scruffy passport which she proudly placed on the table.

"Father passport with me, he write my birth date," she announced proudly.

Tessa burst into laughter.

"Well done, dear. I think you got him there." She picked up the passport and looked at the elaborate characters all over it; a mass of squiggles formed primarily from two circles, one above the other. "Goodness me, what does all this mean?" asked Tessa, pulling Nyunt on to her lap. The two of them retreated into a private cocoon of peace and tranquillity as Nyunt explained the meaning of the groups of characters. Jones watched and a smile crept across his face; he winked at Curtis.

"Well, dear," said Tessa when Nyunt had finished, "I think you should teach me more Burmese and I'll teach you more English." Nyunt nodded enthusiastically. "Right, she's probably eight and a bit," continued Tessa. "She thinks she was born in Pagan before the Junta forcibly relocated their town, but we're still working on the precise birthday. Their calendar's different to ours."

"OK, but I'll need to take that with me," said Jones reaching out expectantly.

However, Nyunt grabbed it and shook her head.

"No. Mine. Pa Pa gave me."

"Ah," said Tessa. "Jones, could you manage with a copy? After all, you have seen the original."

"No, I'm afraid not. But how about if we get a photocopy for Nyunt, and return the original as soon as the legal people here have finished with it?"

"That sounds OK to me," said Tessa to Nyunt. "What do you think?"

Unenthusiastically she nodded and gave the passport to Tessa.

"Ice," said Tessa, seeing him close by. "Would you be able to arrange a couple of photocopies of this, please?"

"Of course," said Ice, taking the passport. "And your food will be ready shortly, miss." Nyunt looked delighted.

Ice returned a couple of minutes later with the copies. Tessa kept one, and gave the original and the other copy to Nyunt, whispering something to her.

"Thank you, Ice. Have you a pen Nyunt could borrow, please?" she asked.

Ice gave her a pen, and Nyunt handed the original to Jones.

"May I have a receipt ... please. Here is pen."

"Of course," replied Jones, chuckling.

"I promise I'll take good care of them, and Curtis will bring them back soon."

Nyunt nodded and watched him write the receipt.

"OK," he continued, as he handed the receipt and pen back to Nyunt. "So, names. Anything other than *Nyunt Pennington*?"

Nyunt looked confused.

"Oh, Pennington is my surname," interjected Tessa. "You automatically get that because we'll be living together, but have you any other names apart from Nyunt?"

"I don't think so."

"Right. Nyunt Pennington it is."

"Good, well, that's it for now," said Jones, with a satisfied look on his face. "I'll get the process started, but I'm going back to London tonight. I'm afraid you won't be able to return to the UK until the paperwork has been completed, but that should only take a couple of weeks. I'm sure you'll manage to amuse yourselves, and Curtis will be around if you need anything."

Ice returned to their table, smiled at Tessa, and much to everyone's surprise, whispered something to Nyunt. She giggled and returned his pen. Then a waiter came and put an ornate server on the table, leaving the shiny domed lid in place.

"They have chef from Mandalay," said Nyunt. "I asked for Burmese snack, very tasty."

Tessa smiled.

"Well, that sounds fun. What is it, dear?"

Ice lifted the lid.

"Oh, my!" exclaimed Tessa, aghast.

"Grilled locusts!" exclaimed Nyunt with delight. "They look good … they're big ones."

"Indeed they are," replied Tessa, in awe of the pile of black, charred locusts."

"Can I have one?" asked Nyunt enthusiastically.

"Er, well," said Tessa, swallowing, "you should offer them to our guests first, dear. Don't worry, gentlemen. I have it on good authority that they taste just like prawns, and are very nutritious."

"Really?" replied Jones, histrionically looking at his watch. "Thank you, Nyunt, they look wonderful, but I've just had breakfast and I really must get back to the office. Curtis can stay though."

"Ah, no, I'm afraid I can't stay either, sir. I, er, need to make sure you get back to the embassy safely, and I've still got a few things to sort out concerning the holes in the helicopter."

"Wonderful. Thank you for your support, boys," said Tessa despondently. "You tuck in, dear. I'll join you in a moment."

"OK," chirped Nyunt.

Grinning from ear to ear, Jones stood up.

"Shall I pop in this evening to let you know how things are going?" he asked.

"Good idea," replied Tessa. "Why don't you join us for dinner? You're welcome to come too, Curtis?"

"Thanks, but I'll pass if it's all right with you," he replied, looking first at the locusts and then at Jones. "But I'll drop you off on my way, sir, and organise a car to take you to the airport afterwards."

Tessa smiled at him, and then Jones.

"Well, thank you, both."

"You're welcome," replied Jones, nodding at the platter. "Enjoy!" He was interrupted by a loud crunch as Nyunt bit into a locust. "I have to admit, I suspect it's an excellent match..."

The next days passed quickly with Tessa and Nyunt thoroughly enjoying their time in Bangkok sightseeing. Tessa would point at something and say what it was in English, and then Nyunt would say what it was in Burmese. They both learnt a lot and Tessa was delighted by Nyunt's progress. This relaxing and fun holiday continued for just over two weeks. There were moments of friction; it wasn't going to be an easy transition for either of them. But together they were making an enthusiastic start on their new future.

One morning, while they were busy chatting, trying to decide what to do next, Ice brought Curtis to their table.

"Good morning, ladies," he said pleasantly.

They both smiled and Tessa gestured him to pull up a chair.

"Care for some breakfast?"

"Oh, yes, please."

As Curtis ate, Nyunt explained, in considerable detail, what they had been doing. She described the Grand Palace, the Temple of the Dawn and their breakneck trip through the *klongs* in a speeding longboat. As she impressed him with her much improved English, Tessa positively beamed with pride.

"Well," said Curtis when Nyunt finished, "the pair of you have clearly been very busy. And now I have some good news. First, Nyunt, here is your Burmese passport, safe and sound."

"Thank you very much, Mr Curtis," she said with a smile.

He raised his eyebrows.

"My pleasure. And, Nariko, here are the asylum papers, Nyunt's new passport and the temporary adoption documents. As Jones indicated, the adoption is *in principle* only, but effective immediately. However, it will be cancelled in the event that you fail to demonstrate to the UK authorities that all is well with the family unit."

Tessa nodded.

"So, now you can go back to England whenever you like. There's no rush, but if you could let me know when you intend to go, that would be good."

"Serious stuff, little one," said Tessa. "We've booked that Thai cooking course for tomorrow, and then there's the excursion to Ayutthaya and Sukhothai. When shall we go to London?"

"Well, could we go to the elephant farm after Sukhothai, and then to England?" asked Nyunt.

"Sounds good to me," replied Tessa. "That means we could pack on Thursday and travel on Friday."

"Fine," said Curtis. "If you like, I'll have our travel agents sort your tickets."

"Oh, thank you," said Tessa, "that would be most helpful. Two First Class seats please, or we'll go the day after. If the agent brings them over, I'll pay for them by credit card."

Curtis nodded.

"Right, well, thanks for breakfast. I'll leave you to enjoy the rest of your stay..."

CHAPTER 34

The weeks passed quickly as the two of them settled down to their new lives in London. Nyunt, unenthusiastically, had various inoculations and enrolled at a nearby school in Queensgate. Tessa drove her hard to catch up with the other pupils. But, she was very bright and soon started making excellent progress. Nevertheless, this gruelling academic pressure meant lengthy periods of intense study, to which Nyunt objected, vehemently on occasion. However, Tessa remained single-mindedly focused on satisfying the adoption authorities.

Occasionally she met Jones and Potter since they were concerned by the widely publicised resurgence of the Calver Cats in the UK.

"It seems they're trying to pick up from where the old gang left off," complained Potter. "There have been a number of violent robberies where calling cards have been left. For the moment the gang is only a shadow of its former self; but not for long at this rate. And we still don't know who's organising them."

Tessa's brow furrowed.

"Hmm. I presume the calling card's different? After all, it shouldn't have an Amafuji tiger's head – I've got the sword."

"Actually," said Potter, rummaging in his briefcase and unfurling a sheet of paper, "that's a very good point; there is a tiger's head, and the colours are different. We've been trying to work out their significance, but overall it's definitely the same logo. Perhaps they're just using the old cards?"

Reader, please note: The new Calver Cats logo is shown in the bottom left-hand corner of the back cover.

Tessa pursed her lips.

"Unfortunately, that is not the sort of thing even a criminal would dare misrepresent. It seems they've got another Amafuji-equipped fighter. That's bad. Also, although the logo has the same shape as before, the outer ribbons are black; perhaps funereal? And, unless I knew better, I'd say the centre C's are in Fujiwara vermilion."

Jones smiled.

"That's exactly what Maeda said. So, how about accepting a Mission to help us stop them?"

"Out of the question! I'm retired."

"I bet it's only another sabbatical," he replied with a wry grin.

"No, definitely retired. I have Nyunt to consider now. She's having a hard time of it, what with all the changes."

"Well, you are pushing her rather hard."

"Not unreasonably so," replied Tessa defensively. "It's important for her to catch up. And I've had to go back to school too. The adoption authorities run classes for new parents and I've been a diligent student. It's hard work being a single mum. So, I have neither the time, nor the inclination."

Jones looked doubtful.

"Seriously, I'm not doing it," she continued, studying the calling card. "Although something is clearly brewing out there, I don't want to be a part of it."

"OK," continued Jones, privately pleased she had declined the Mission, "but don't forget Htet never did identify the organisers of that Burma ambush. So maybe there is some truth in the Junta's claim that the Calver Cats were responsible. If that is the case, whoever it is will probably still be after you."

"I understand, but you'll have to find someone else to put at the sharp end."

Despite her determination to stay out of the limelight, Tessa knew she needed to be vigilant. She trained as hard as ever and always took her swords with her when she ran. She even varied the routes to ensure no one could predict her whereabouts. Furthermore, she never let Nyunt walk alone to, or from, school.

Everyone could see Tessa was trying her utmost to do her best for her adoptive daughter. But Nyunt was beginning to feel restless and frustrated; a situation exacerbated by missing her father and feeling increasingly homesick. Tessa sensed this, but wasn't sure what to do about it. Although the visits from the adoption authorities were going well, the tension between Tessa and Nyunt was building.

Tessa concluded that it might help Nyunt to have a tangible record of her parents. But getting hold of something proved incredibly difficult. Nevertheless, with help from Jones and Curtis, she eventually discovered that Htet had left a bag containing two photographs at the guest house north of Rangoon where they'd stopped for breakfast once. The pictures, one of him and one of Nyunt and her mother, were sent via a diplomatic bag to England. Since both were rather battered and faded, Tessa decided to have them restored professionally and framed before giving them to her on her birthday.

Meanwhile, Nyunt was also struggling to get used to her bedroom. Tessa had purposely left the guest room in her house, now Nyunt's room, decorated in western-style so her visitors were comfortable. But Nyunt found the bed too soft; she usually ended up sleeping with Tessa on a thin mattress in her bedroom, which was decorated and furnished like a room in a Japanese Samurai house. This didn't bother Tessa in the slightest, but it did compromise her social life. Although Gareth spent a few nights with her earlier on, Tessa could see this affected Nyunt adversely and as a result, she saw less and less of him. They remained close friends, but accepted that their relationship lacked longevity.

Then, three days before Nyunt's ninth birthday, as Tessa was adjusting her school uniform, the girl suddenly pushed her away.

"I'm not happy here," she announced, pursing her lips together.

Tessa counted to three and smiled at her.

"Well, I gathered that. But what exactly is making you unhappy?"

"Everything!" screamed Nyunt, bursting into tears. "I miss Pa Pa, I miss my friends, I miss Burma. I don't feel at home here, all I do is study! I hate school and … and …"

Her words petered out into desolate tears.

Tessa inwardly shrank. She'd been trying so hard, and thought they'd been making excellent progress.

"You started to say something, you might as well finish," she said levelly.

"And I hate you!"

Tessa felt as though an ice cold knife had been driven through her heart.

"That's very harsh, dear," she murmured. "Why did you say it?"

"Because you took me away from my home and brought me here, and you force me to go to school. All I ever do is homework … and, stuff."

"Well, I'm only trying to do what's best for you." Tessa knelt down and tried to reach out to Nyunt, who shied away. "I was worried that if I left you in Burma, you would have a terrible life and possibly be killed. I didn't want that so I thought it would be better to bring you here to live with me. Was that wrong?"

Nyunt sniffed and would not meet her eyes.

"And you keep calling me dear. It sounds patronising."

"Hmm, nicely put. I'm sorry, d…arling. I don't mean to be patronising, it's just me," she said, offering Nyunt a tissue. "Everyone has to go to school. I had to study hard too, and you are doing extremely well. I'm very proud of you, and your teachers are very pleased with you too."

"I'm still not happy here."

"So, what do you think we should do?"

"I want to go home."

Tessa baulked.

"I was hoping you would come to regard here as your home."

"No, I want to go *home*," repeated Nyunt, shaking with emotion.

"I see," replied Tessa, reeling inwardly. "But I wouldn't know where to take you. I don't think your home in Burma exists any more." Nyunt said nothing. "What you've said is very serious, but you have said it now. I suggest we think about it carefully and decide what to do after we've both had a chance to calm down. I understand what you've said, and I propose we talk it through this evening, just you and me."

"No homework?"

"No homework. But in the meantime, I would like you to go to school as usual, please. I promise we will talk about it tonight, and make a decision on what we should do. Is that OK?"

"Yes," whimpered Nyunt.

"Right, well, let's get you cleaned up and then I'll walk you to school."

As soon as she could, Tessa went to SKS and explained what Nyunt had said, to Lee and his wife. As they discussed the situation, Tessa became more and more agitated by the thought of being without the child, who she already regarded as her daughter. After a while she and

Lee had to take some classes, but later in the day Jones joined them. They sat in Lee's lounge drinking tea, with Tessa again describing her exchange with Nyunt. She was close to tears.

"It's probably nothing," said Jones, trying to console her. "Nyunt is bound to be disorientated by such a huge change in circumstances. It would be hard enough for someone who had just lived in Burma to start living here, never mind coping with everything else she's been through. You have been driving her hard ... I understand why, but it's a lot for someone so young to take."

Tessa dabbed her eyes.

"But she's a part of my life now. I wouldn't feel whole without her."

"Well, you're moulding her to be like you, so you shouldn't be surprised when she starts flexing her muscles. But I think this is just her blowing her top, not what she really thinks," he continued. "Anyway, on an entirely different topic, the pictures weren't quite ready so I asked Flood to collect them and bring them here later."

Tessa nodded. Not long afterwards there was a knock at the door. Flood came in, stooping to squeeze his enormous frame under the low ceiling.

"Good afternoon," he said pleasantly, looking in surprise at Tessa's watery eyes. He held out a package. "Um ... yours, I believe?"

"Thank you, Flood, it was good of you to bring it." She glanced at his sword. "Are you on duty?"

"Always, these days," he replied.

Tessa nodded and unpacked the parcel. She studied the framed pictures. Nyunt's true parents ... she doubted she could ever replace them.

"They've come out really well," she murmured, passing them round and reaching for the wrapping paper she'd bought. "I'd intended to give them to her on her birthday, but I think I'll let her have them tonight, as a peace offering."

Jones looked at her and smiled.

"You don't need to give her a peace offering. She's a clever girl; she'll work it all out for herself, given time. The two of you love each other, everyone can see that. I'm sure it will blow over, you wait and see."

Tessa looked at her watch.

"Oh, I haven't time to wrap them now anyway, I've got to collect her from school."

"Look," he said, "you wrap the pictures and I'll go and collect Nyunt. Flood can come and keep an eye on me. We'll bring her here, if you like?"

Tessa wasn't sure, but decided a change might do Nyunt good.

"OK, but be careful," she said, wondering what she meant.

Jones looked at Flood, carrying his sword, and smiled.

"I think we can handle it."

"Yes, of course. It's just that … I'm always worrying about her."

"Isn't that what mothers do?" Jones smiled at her. "Back shortly."

Ten minutes later, Tessa sat back to admire the neatly wrapped parcel.

"Very nice," said Lee, as his wife nodded and smiled. "I'm sure she'll be thrilled. Jones is right, Nariko-san, you shouldn't worry. Everything will be fine."

Tessa was just about to reply when her *cbc* rang with a particularly strident tone; the *Urgent Assistance Required* call. She looked at it.

"Jones is in trouble … Nyunt!"

She tossed the parcel to Lee and grabbed her swords. Barely before Lee understood what she meant, she had run into the practice room, taken two knives from the rack, and started sprinting up Barnaby Mews. To her amazement, she found queues of stationary traffic in Old Brompton Road.

Running as fast as she could, she zigzagged between the vehicles and went up Reece Mews into Harrington Road. When she turned right into Queensgate she could hardly believe the chaos. Cars were stopped at random angles completely blocking the road. Screaming mothers were grabbing their children and trying to get away from some two dozen people on the rampage, armed with swords. All were dressed in blue jeans and black fleece jackets worn with three-hole balaclavas covering their faces; the standard Calver Cats' uniform.

Tessa continued pounding towards the school. But off to her left, one of the attackers grabbed a mother who had just picked up her son.

"Yield," he yelled to Tessa, "or she dies!"

Tessa simply flicked one of her knives at the man. It struck him in the forehead and he fell backwards releasing the woman. For a moment she froze, trying to understand what had just happened;

then she realised she didn't care, and ran for safety with her child.

Suddenly Tessa saw Flood. There were several bodies nearby but he was surrounded and fighting furiously.

"Nariko!" he shouted. "Stop the van!"

But, on hearing the name *Nariko*, all the others turned on her. Tessa drew her swords as a dozen people converged on her. She also saw a separate group moving towards a black van parked facing up Queensgate with its back doors open.

"Nyunt!" yelled Tessa.

"Help!" came the muffled reply. "I'm here!"

Tessa realised her daughter was in the group nearing the van, and started moving in that direction. But her progress was blocked with surprisingly dogged determination. Inevitably, such conflicts were brutal but these assailants seemed to be possessed by a fanatical hatred, with no regard for their own lives. She couldn't help noticing that their pupils were slightly dilated.

Nevertheless, Tessa fought with consummate skill and merciless ferocity. Slowly, she worked her way towards the van; but she knew she wouldn't reach it in time.

"Nyunt!" she shouted desperately. "I will come for you!"

Shortly afterwards, the van doors slammed shut and it screeched off up Queensgate towards Hyde Park. Then Flood let out a loud cry and Tessa saw one of his two remaining attackers had stuck their sword in his side. He downed the other man, but the one who had wounded him raised his sword to deal a killing blow. Helpless, he staggered back against some railings.

Tessa slashed the men around her and momentarily moved out of the attacking mêlée. She tossed her Bryani sword vertically upwards and drew her second knife. She threw it at the man in front of Flood, hitting him in the temple. Then she caught her descending sword and continued fighting.

In the distance, she heard the ringing of another Amakuni sword and saw that Lee had joined the fray. She admired his relaxed precision; what he lacked in youthful vigour was compensated for by technique and confidence.

The conflict soon turned in their favour and the remaining assailants fell. When there were only two left, both facing Tessa, they realised all was lost and broke off their attack. One sprinted up Queensgate, with Tessa in hot pursuit, while the other headed towards Lee.

"Take him alive!" yelled Tessa.

She caught up with her fugitive just as he reached the busy Cromwell Road. He glanced back at her and then ran across. However, the traffic was still moving quickly there and he misjudged the distance between the vehicles. A large truck slammed into him. He died beneath the wheels. Exasperated, Tessa muttered an expletive and spun round. She ran back down Queensgate after the last man. She saw Lee nonchalantly throw a knife. It struck the man in the thigh and, with a yelp, he stumbled and fell. Out of the corner of her eye, Tessa noticed a dark blue-grey Special Forces car stop at the end of Queensberry Mews; presumably reinforcements had arrived.

She ran on towards the downed man, determined to get to him before he had time to think. He sat up clutching his thigh, apparently considering pulling the knife out. But then he relaxed and appeared to change his mind. Tessa stopped in front of him, but just as she was about to speak, a pistol shot rang out and a neat red hole appeared in the man's forehead. He flopped back, dead. Furious, Tessa spun round to find Lamper, a wisp of smoke rising from the barrel of his gun.

"You imbecile!" she shouted. "Why the hell did you do that? He might have known where they were going."

"I'm sure he did," replied Lamper, aiming his gun at her. "Now, I've just a couple of loose ends to clean up before I disappear. You first, then the old man. I wonder if you're fast enough to dodge a well-aimed bullet. Let's see, shall we?"

"Traitor," hissed Tessa, as she watched his finger closing on the trigger. Then another shot rang out.

Surprised, Tessa looked round to see who had fired. Potter stood nearby, gun in hand, eyeing the wide-eyed Lamper with disdain.

"You piece of shit!" he said disgustedly. Lamper collapsed to his knees, fell forward and died.

Tessa flicked the blood off her swords and re-sheathed them. She heard a helicopter lifting off in the distance, then the sound faded. As Potter issued some orders, she went over to Flood. He had slid down the railings and was sitting awkwardly on the pavement, clutching his side.

"Hi," she said, kneeling down beside him.

"Thanks," he groaned, nodding at the body of the man with Tessa's knife protruding from his head. She gently eased his hand away so she could look at his wound.

"You're welcome. Hmm, it's not too bad, but I bet it hurts like hell?"

He nodded.

"Potter," she shouted. "Flood needs an ambulance."

"On its way," said Potter, joining them. "So that bastard Lamper was our mole after all. He's done a lot of damage, and no doubt helped lure Sinclair to his death."

"Well, he's being judged now," she continued, looking around. "Flood, where's Jones?"

He smiled weakly.

"We were waiting for Nyunt, but as soon as she came out all hell broke loose. Jones issued the *UAR* and grabbed her while I tried to clear him a way out. We were soon surrounded so Jones took my handcuffs and locked her leg to his wrist; she had her arms round his neck at the time. Anyway, the thugs cornered him and bashed him over the head. They were really pissed off when they saw what he'd done, but they took them both."

Tessa looked at Lee.

"Who would go to all this trouble to get Nyunt?"

"I have no idea, Nariko-san," he replied, shaking his head. "But she was taken alive, so clearly they wanted to get your attention. We will have to wait for them to contact us."

"Sir, that's the ambulance," said a Special Forces man to Potter as a siren approached. "But we can't track the helicopter, it's flying too low. We've scrambled some police 'copters to try and find it. Their van was torched in the park, but we found this."

Potter nodded and showed the new Calver Cats calling card to Tessa.

"But if they wanted to get even with me by abducting Nyunt, why did Lamper say he wanted to kill both me and Lee?"

"Beats me," replied Potter. "But it seems something far bigger than any of us imagined has germinated right in our own backyard, and now they have Nyunt and the Head of UK Special Forces."

CHAPTER 35

Back in SKS, distraught, Tessa contemplated Nyunt's birthday present which was still lying on the table. Tears started trickling down her cheeks.

"If they hurt her," she wailed, "I'll hunt them to the ends of the earth."

"Don't say that," admonished Lee, quietly. "That's how feuds start, and we both know they're much easier to start than they are to finish. Focus on getting her and Jones back safely. Nothing more, nothing less."

She smiled weakly at him and nodded. His wife brought in some tea and they both cleaned their swords. Potter joined them.

"That is one hell of a mess," he said. "People were watching from the houses; cameras, mobile phones, the lot. I can keep your picture out of it, but the rest will be all over the media. We found their helicopter at a private airfield to the northeast of London. Apparently it landed and a small jet took off shortly afterwards. We're trying to track it, but it won't be easy. They're clearly determined to conceal their plane's flight-path."

For a long time, Tessa sat drinking green tea, broken-hearted and worried for Nyunt's safety. But then Lee's wife came into the room. She whispered in his ear and Tessa watched his expression change from concern to one of great satisfaction.

"We just called the Hayasaka to tell them what has happened," he said. "We got their answering machine."

"So?" queried Tessa, shrugging.

"Well, it seems the kidnappers have made a mistake. Neither Hayasaka-san nor I ever use our answering machines. If we are not able to answer our phones we simply let them ring. It is a code between us. If ever the other hears an answering machine, something is wrong."

Tessa looked up with a hard determined smile.

"Potter, I need to go to Japan. I might just be able to get Nyunt and

Jones back if we're quick."

"Japan!" exclaimed Potter. "Are you sure?"

She stood up.

"Yes. Somehow it feels right, it fits … although into what, I have no idea. I'm going home to collect some equipment. I'll organise transport on the way."

"Hold on, you can't just go to Japan fully armed. You need formal sanction," he remonstrated. "Hmm. Are you willing to accept a Mission to secure the safe return of the Head of UK Special Forces … and Nyunt, of course?"

"You bet!" she replied. She stood up and turned to Lee.

"Mitigating circumstances," she pleaded.

"Nariko-san, I couldn't agree more," he agreed, smiling.

"I'll try and make sure everyone at the castle is safe." She said, bowing.

He stood up and bowed back.

"Right," said Potter, "in that case, this is official business now. Well, it will be as soon as I've sorted the paperwork. But we'll worry about that later. I'll take care of the transport. It's high time I called in a favour from my old buddy, Air Marshall Boulding."

"Well, call me quickly if you run into any difficulties," replied Tessa, striding towards the door.

"Leave it to me. A car will collect you in fifteen minutes."

At home she quickly changed into her Kevlar combat suit. Then she slipped her new knives and shuriken into their leather carrying wallets and put them in a small rucksack. She had just added some fruit and a bottle of water when she heard a car reversing down the Mews. It screeched to a halt outside her house, and she saw a flashing blue light through the curtains. She grabbed her swords, the rucksack and her long black leather coat, and joined Potter in the back of the car.

"As quick as you can," he instructed the driver, "we'll pick up the escort in Old Brompton Road. Nariko, by the time we reach Northolt, a plane will be waiting. Where in Japan do you want to go?"

"Toyama. It's on the northwest coast," replied Tessa. "It's not a big place, but it does have a commercial airport. They won't be expecting me to come from there. Ask Maeda to arrange a car… Actually, on second thoughts, don't. I'll organise my own transport. That will add to the element of surprise."

"Look, I know you get on pretty well with Maeda," said Potter, "but don't you think we should at least tell him you're coming? His support for this would be very helpful."

"I know, but please don't contact him. The UK Special Forces had a high-level mole. There's probably one in Japan too. If you want, tell him after I've been in Japan for six hours."

Led by two police motorcycles with sirens blaring and lights flashing, the car lurched as it travelled at breakneck speed through London to Northolt. When it finally stopped on the runway, Tessa stared in amazement. Standing in front of them was a Eurofighter Typhoon III.

"Good grief, Potter!"

"Yes, well, I pulled out all the stops for this. It's not armed, it's a training craft. It's fitted out to take three, just. In this case you and two pilots. Apparently it won't be in the slightest bit comfortable, but it'll be damned fast! They'll have to refuel, but I'm assured they can do that while flying. Good luck!"

Tessa didn't know what to say.

"Go on!" he said, waving her out of the car.

She smiled, reached over and kissed him on the cheek.

"Thank you."

"Don't mention it. In fact, *please* don't mention it, ever, to anyone. Just try and get them both back safely."

"I promise."

Tessa got out of the car and was immediately handed a flying suit.

"Flown before, miss?" asked one pilot as his colleague completed the pre-flight checks.

"Not like this."

"Well, it's quite … exhilarating. We'll try not to scare you too much, but we understand you're in a hurry."

"A big hurry, so do your best to scare the living daylights out of me," replied Tessa donning the flying suit as Potter held her swords. "Fly like a bat out of hell!"

The man raised his eyebrows and smiled. A few minutes later they clambered into the plane and one of the ground crew helped Tessa stow her gear.

"Ready for the off, miss?" asked one of the pilots.

"Yep, go for it."

Shortly afterwards Tessa found herself being forced back in her seat as the afterburners cut in.

"All right, miss?" asked the pilot once they were airborne.

"Wow," she replied, struggling to talk. "I'll say! This is fantastic! Will it go any faster?"

She smiled as she felt another surge of power.

"Sir," said Potter's driver as the plane disappeared into the horizon, "we've been able to track the target for a few minutes. It had to climb to avoid bad weather over Iran. It does seem to be heading for Japan."

"Thank heavens for that," he replied. "Tell our guys to keep their eyes peeled. If it pops up again, we'll let our plane know."

Three hours later, Tessa's cogitations were interrupted by a voice in her ears.

"Excuse me, miss," said the pilot. "I have a message for you from a Colonel Potter. He says they've been able to track the target and it is heading for Japan, but probably a little south of where we're going."

"Perfect," replied Tessa.

"Still Toyama, Miss?"

"Yes, please... By the way, my name's *Nariko*."

"Welcome aboard, Nariko. I'm Squadron Leader Shields, and currently flying the plane is Squadron Leader Chudzik."

"Nice to meet you, gentlemen," replied Tessa. "Thank you for taking me to Japan."

"Oh, it's a pleasure. We don't often get an opportunity to take it out for a spin like this, so we're rather enjoying ourselves."

The plane refuelled over Kabul and sped on east. Tessa tried to get some sleep, but it was very noisy, cramped and uncomfortable.

The sun had almost set when the Typhoon gracefully swooped down and landed at Toyama airport. The plane spotters and control tower were stunned. They had been expecting a twin-engined executive jet. However, it quickly taxied out of sight, and the three occupants scrambled out.

"Gentlemen," said Tessa, discarding her flying gear before shaking the pilots' hands, "thank you very much indeed. I envy you, having

374

this machine in your garage. It was quite an experience."

"You're welcome, and good luck."

She smiled in acknowledgment, put on her leather coat, wrapped her swords in a blanket and grabbed her rucksack. Then she went in search of a taxi accompanied by a very nervous airport official...

Late that night, alone and unseen, Tessa walked out of Kanazawa's historic Higashi Chaya district across a wooden bridge and into dense forest. To make sure she arrived unannounced, she intended to walk up the hill. As she strode along the rough track, she had to work hard to control her anger. Being overly tense could result in her making a mistake, which would possibly be fatal, and not only for her. But the fact remained, she was livid.

After a while she stopped to meditate and eat some fruit. Then she took off her coat, put on both swords, and slid her knives and shuriken into the pockets on her suit. She put her coat in the rucksack and hid it under some rocks.

An hour later, she was peering through the bushes bordering the circular gravelled area outside the gatehouse. In the distance was the high stone wall which marked the perimeter of the castle grounds. The ornate roofed gatehouse with its substantial wooden doors was lit by two flickering lanterns. One door stood ajar, which would never have occurred in normal circumstances. Near one of the two wooden houses, she saw the crumpled body of one of the men who had previously opened the castle door for her. The other, presumably unconscious, lay motionless and tied up, close by. From her right came the sound of voices in Hayasaka's house. In the middle of the gravel circle stood two Calver Cats, laughing and joking.

OK, she mused. But who's running the show, and why?

The men were too far away for her to approach them over the gravel. So Tessa decided to use shuriken for her attack; they travelled further, faster and quieter than knives. She drew two and stepped silently out from between the bushes. She took aim and threw the first shuriken, hard, then the second, and immediately started walking forwards.

The first hit its target on the back of the neck, severing the man's spine as it sank in. The second struck the other man on the side of his head. There was a dull crack as it split his skull. Both men crumpled to the ground with barely a sound. Tessa retrieved her weapons and wiped them clean on the men's jackets. Then she walked over to Hayasaka's house, stopping short of the steps leading up to the door.

The house had been built hundreds of years ago when low ceilings were installed to make it difficult for someone to draw or wield a sword inside. She needed to decide whether she went in with both hands free for knives or with one of her swords ready, on the off chance someone inside had already drawn a sword. Then she heard Hayasaka's wife talking, sounding angry and scared. Suddenly she used the word "sword", and Tessa's mind was made up. She drew her Kimi sword and one knife, and went up to the door. She pulled it aside as noisily as she thought one of the guards might have done, and strode inside.

Across the room, Hayasaka's wife sat to the left of the low table, together with their three children. The younger boy and girl were by her side, looking terrified, while the older boy was nearby. A man dressed in Calver Cats uniform sat cross-legged at the head of the table. He looked round at Tessa but, before he had time to utter a cry, she threw her knife. It sank deep into his forehead and he keeled over backwards. The older boy jumped up and laid the body down quietly. Tessa drew another knife.

Hayasaka's wife nodded her head, forwards and over her shoulder.

Tessa raised a single finger in both directions, prompting Hayasaka's wife to nod. Tessa smiled, shaking her head at the older boy who seemed keen to take part. On hearing the sound of someone rummaging through a cupboard, she moved towards the bedrooms. The man in there shouted to his colleague, and, surprised not to hear any answer, popped his head out of the door inquisitively.

Tessa swung her sword down. There was a *ping* followed a moment later by a loud thud as his head hit the wooden floor.

Tessa spun round just as another man appeared in the doorway to the kitchen. He instinctively slid the door shut, but Tessa threw her knife anyway. The door was made from paper panels so the knife passed effortlessly through. She knew she'd killed him. The noisy clatter of pots as he fell confirmed it.

"Any more?" she asked.

"Only the two outside," Hayasaka's wife replied.

"There are none left outside," said Tessa, relaxing. "Are you all right?"

"Yes, we are fine, Nariko-san. They have captured the castle. Master Matsumoto and my husband are prisoners. I heard one of them say Matsumoto is hurt."

"Hmm. I bet that was a battle. Sorry about the mess."

"It is of no concern… I don't know who it is, we've been held here since they arrived, but I think they have your daughter. They are expecting you. But not until tomorrow."

Tessa nodded and retrieved her knives.

"I'm going to the castle. Revive your watchmen if you can, and get yourselves to safety."

Tessa left, walking across the gravel with a renewed sense of purpose. She strode through the open door into the castle grounds. As usual the camellia trees filled the night air with an intoxicating perfume. She stopped and took a deep breath.

Suddenly, a wave of distortion passed in front of the trees; as normality returned, so did her missing memories.

"Wow," she gasped in amazement. "Matsumoto-san, did we really do all that! Oh, my!"

She chuckled and took a camellia sprig with some fine white flowers on it, tucking it carefully into the top of her Kevlar suit. She looked round; now she understood why Matsumoto Castle felt like home to her. But then her expression hardened. She had some squatters to evict. She set off down through the forest, soon settling into a quick but relaxed pace, just as she had so many times before. She crossed the Kintai-style bridge and continued towards the castle. As she emerged from the swirling mist over the paddy fields, she found two guards standing by the bridge over the castle moat. They were talking, and neither of them heard or saw her approach. Barely slowing, she drew her swords and decapitated both men as she ran past. There were muffled thuds as their heads and bodies fell separately to the ground.

High on the castle rampart, Matsumoto smiled, while the person behind him grunted and retreated into the shadows of the Samurai house.

Tessa ran through the main gate, passed the chinthes and bounded up the steps. Security seemed lax, and she met no one else on her way to the top of the rampart. There, she looked round and, finding herself alone, continued under the high wooden arch through the avenue of trees. She stopped near the ornate roofed gateway to peer inside.

The courtyard was well lit so she had a clear view. Matsumoto was tied to a chair facing forwards at the bottom of the steps to the Samurai house; both his left shoulder and right leg were covered in blood. He looked pale and weak and had a nasty cut on his face. Gareth sat to his left, also tied to a chair, badly bruised but looking alert and defiant. Nyunt, who had clearly been crying, stood beside him clutching his right arm. Hayasaka, guarded by a single Calver Cat, was standing near the gateway with his hands tied behind him. Tessa turned away and leant against the courtyard wall. She breathed deeply, relaxed and gathered her strength.

CHAPTER 36

Suddenly, Hayasaka noticed Matsumoto smile. Then he heard a *ping*. The guard holding him twitched and his head shot into the air.

"*Ohayou gozaimasu*, Hayasaka-san," said Tessa, cutting the ropes binding him. "Your family is safe and unharmed."

The Calver Cats looked at her in surprise and annoyance, but made no move to attack.

"*Domo arigato gozaimas*, Nariko-san," replied Hayasaka, bowing. "We have a difficult situation here. Master Matsumoto is injured. I hope you didn't come on your own."

"You mean there are more?" asked Tessa lightly.

"Only the two in the house."

She nodded and stepped round him. There were bloody patches throughout the courtyard indicative of a vicious struggle, but twenty-three Calver Cats still faced her; surprisingly lightly armed though and, encouragingly, without guns. Furthermore, none of them was wearing a balaclava. So, not only did Tessa again notice their slightly dilated pupils, but their blank expressions too – had they been taking drugs of some sort?

She looked at Nyunt and winked, but received only a very scared look back.

As the opposing sides sized each other up, the eerie silence was broken by the sound of a toilet flushing. Tessa couldn't help but smile, and saw Nyunt was giggling too. A woman strode out of the Samurai house, wearing a vermilion-coloured kimono.

"I do hope you washed your hands," said Tessa loudly.

"Oh, very droll," replied her sister-in-law, momentarily taken-aback. "Thank God you're here. I was getting so bored in this hovel. I was going to start cutting things off people to pass the time. But I'll leave that for later now."

Tessa looked at Matsumoto and bowed. But, to Hayasaka's surprise, it was only an informal bow; not the deep bow of a student to their master. Matsumoto responded the same way, and smiled as Tessa adjusted her camellia cutting. Then she looked at Gareth; he cocked his head and mouthed, *"Retired?"*

"Well, Caprice," continued Tessa, "your husband defiled my life, and now you have defiled my family and my home. I warned you in London that I would not be so generous a second time. I trust you're prepared to accept the consequences."

"Hah!" she sneered. "The consequences of your dying are all good."

"Whatever. But why kidnap Nyunt?"

"Believe it or not, I want more than just your puny pathetic life. This seemed the best way of getting everything. My bullet only missed hitting you in Hyde Park because I needed to ensure that you finished some work for us first. After that, I simply wanted everyone where I could control them, and where better than this ramshackle pile of sticks and stones? Here, I can ruin your life by destroying those you love and then, only then, will you die together with the shame you have brought us. At the same time, I'll be able to stop this decrepit man and his wretched family from being such a nuisance. Revenge at last. Good, don't you think?"

"Sounds pretty bitter and twisted to me," retorted Tessa.

"No, it's focused. And so would you be if your family had been feuding for centuries."

"What?" asked Tessa incredulously? "You're a Fujiwara?"

"Absolutely! Before Beauchamp, I was married to Ryota Fujiwara."

"That buffoon?" replied Tessa, trying not to laugh.

Caprice went red.

"Careful! I'm quite willing to start the killing over here."

Tessa shrugged.

"That's better," continued Caprice. "Tonight I will go down in history as having ended the Matsumoto line, destroyed Matsumoto Castle and perpetuated the Fujiwara."

"Really? Together with the person still cowering in the shadows, I suppose?" mocked Tessa. "Well, good luck with that. But I'm surprised you view this beautiful place with such disdain. I love it."

"So do I!" yelled Nyunt, prompting everyone to look at her.

"Actually," interjected Jones, "I rather like it too."

"Oh! For goodness' sake, shut up!" hissed Caprice. "Is this really how you want to spend your last living moments?"

"Well," quipped Tessa, "look how you are spending yours!"

"Hardly something *I* need worry about. But since you ask, in my last few minutes on earth I'd be fighting for my honour; not that family honour means anything to the likes of you, of course. You brought nothing but disgrace on Beauchamp's family when you had all those operations in America..."

Unfortunately, this was the one topic Tessa could not abide being discussed. She immediately went from relaxed to furious and seriously considered throwing a knife at Caprice then and there. But killing her out of spite was not becoming of one who had sworn to uphold the law. Jones interrupted by bursting into raucous laughter.

"Caprice, you are joking, aren't you? Surely you're not saying this nonsense is all about your outmoded, twisted prejudices? Didn't you send your own son to America for major medical treatment? Get real!"

"That's different. She's disgusting," Caprice retorted, angrily.

"Rubbish!" he continued, amidst further bouts of laughter. "Sinclair and I knew about it all along, and, speaking from a deeply personal point of view, it's never been a problem for me." He finished speaking with a meaningful glint in his eyes.

Matsumoto looked at Tessa with raised eyebrows. She shrugged apologetically, adjusting the position of the camellia cutting.

"Hmm. Well, Nariko told me absolutely everything the first night she was here," added Matsumoto, smiling. "I thought it demonstrated considerable strength of character, focus and determination. All highly commendable qualities. What she was forced to do is certainly nothing to be ashamed of. Quite the opposite, in fact."

It was Tessa's turn to look at him with raised eyebrows.

"...and Pa Pa told me," shrieked Nyunt, keen not to be left out. "He told me how wonderful she is. And now I know he was right."

Though shocked her daughter knew, Tessa smiled lovingly at Nyunt. Caprice looked on, amazed and frustrated, incandescent with rage.

Tessa looked back at the Calver Cats. There were a lot of them, albeit very conveniently grouped; however, she would need to seize the initiative quickly, if conflict became inevitable.

"Caprice," continued Tessa, relaxed once more, "it seems you need to revise your opinions and try joining the modern world. My *conscience* is clear. However, I will demonstrate my *patience* one final time by asking you to release your captives, and surrender."

"Oh, piss off!" screamed Caprice. Then she looked at the expectant Calver Cats. "Kill …"

Tessa reacted immediately. She darted to her left, improving the angle, and threw two shuriken. The first skimmed across the necks of two men, severing their carotid arteries, before lodging in the wooden lid by the stone water urn. The second shuriken killed another Calver Cat, landing with a loud thump in a leg of Matsumoto's chair, narrowly missing him. He looked down and smiled. Tessa stepped sideways and threw two more shuriken. Each killed a Calver Cat, and helped open a path through the middle of the group. Tessa started quick handstands forwards, passing through the thugs, as a hail of knives headed to where she had just been standing; one nicked her arm, and another her leg. One of the Calver Cats rushed back to a fallen shuriken but screamed in agony as the flesh was shaved off two fingers in his clumsy attempt to pick it up.

Tessa finished upright near two men. She drew her swords and viciously slashed them. Then she re-sheathed her blades and threw the last of her shuriken, followed by two knives; more Calver Cats fell. She cartwheeled quickly to her right to avoid another volley of knives, but again one nicked her. She unsheathed her swords and dispatched the man closest. She engaged the others around her and started retreating towards the covered racks behind her as the remaining Calver Cats converged. She glanced quickly at Matsumoto; he nodded. She cleared some space, re-sheathed her swords, and threw her last two knives. Then she did three quick backwards handstands, ending by the first rack. She pulled off the cover histrionically to reveal a plethora of extremely unpleasant throwing weapons.

"Oh, shit," moaned one of the Calver Cats, as Tessa winked at them.

She drew her Bryani sword to defend herself and used her right hand to send a hail of missiles at her attackers. They always hit their target and the number of remaining Cats quickly dwindled. She hurled the last axe and there were seven men standing as she drew her Kimi sword. She took a deep breath and walked towards them.

The men had been well trained and took up an orderly U formation, determined to surround her. But by trying to attack together, they obstructed each other, and two soon fell. She herded the rest into a better position and, as two men tried to close in from behind, she squatted down and spun round, arms outstretched. In a moment she had severed the legs of both of them. As they toppled over screaming, she stood up and quickly thrust her swords into their chests. She turned her attention on the remaining three. Seconds later, two more were down. The last looked round at his fallen colleagues, gathered himself and raised his sword, beckoning her to attack. She smiled and swept her Kimi sword round and over, hard and fast. There was a pronounced *whoosh,* then a *clang* and a *chink.* The man looked down at his shattered blade.

"You could surrender?" suggested Tessa.

"That's not allowed," he replied, discarding the sword hilt and raising his fists.

Tessa shrugged, flicked the blood off her swords and re-sheathed them with a flourish.

Then she walked quickly towards the man. He tried to stop her with a strong right hook. But she nonchalantly brushed it aside with her left arm. So he swung at her with his left fist, but she dodged and punched him hard in the centre of his chest. The resultant abrupt *thump* echoed around the courtyard, accompanied by cracks from several of his ribs. Stunned and winded, the man staggered back; wheezing, and gasping for air. Tessa followed, carefully watching his pulsating arteries.

"Welcome…," she said, before punching him in the neck.

"To the true reward…," she continued, as she punched him again. This was such a powerful upwards blow into his diaphragm that it momentarily lifted him off his feet.

"…of crime!"

She turned away dismissively and walked towards Caprice. The man stood stock-still, eyes glazed, with his arms dangling by his sides. Then Tessa clicked her fingers, and, as a wry smile passed across Matsumoto's face, the man collapsed dead.

"Good grief!" murmured Jones.

Tessa winked again at Nyunt, and took some deep breaths. It had been hard work and she needed to recover; her injuries were minor, but there was more to do.

"Well, Caprice, it seems the odds have shifted in our favour. Do I get to meet your back-up now?"

"Don't flatter yourself. I don't need any *back-up* here. Everything is going completely according to plan. I'll tell our people where to come, when it's all over."

"Oh, so you're relying now on the one who can't be persuaded to come out of the shadows, are you?"

There was a relaxed-sounding chuckle from inside the Samurai house.

"Oh, I don't need persuading, Nariko-san. We simply wanted you to eliminate the last of the Calver Cats loyal to Beauchamp, first."

CHAPTER 37

A large man stepped confidently out of the shadows. He was dressed in full Samurai armour with a vermilion neck scarf.

"Hachiro-san," sighed Tessa, shaking her head. "I cannot tell you how disappointed I am to find you here."

"Stop talking Japanese, and get on with it," interjected Caprice impatiently.

"We have fought side by side," continued Tessa, still in Japanese, "I do not understand why you would want to fight me. Especially for this woman who understands and appreciates so little."

Not bothering to answer, he strode confidently down the stairs, past Matsumoto.

"Hachiro-san, please," pleaded Tessa as he stopped opposite her, "I do not wish to fight you. Can't we…"

But Hachiro interrupted her by drawing his sword; a fine Amafuji weapon which Tessa had never seen before. It bore a striking resemblance to her Bryani weapon. He gripped it with both hands and held it pointing downwards in front of him. Tessa smiled, even he didn't want to risk testing his draw against hers.

"So be it," she continued in English, "but I think you owe me an explanation first. Why are you doing this?"

"I was born the first son of the eighth generation of the Fujiwara clan. Not unusually, I was brought up in secret by others, but *I* am the rightful heir to the Fujiwara Empire."

"But … you stood by while your brothers and father were killed?"

"My brothers had enjoyed a good life at my expense. My time had come. Having someone else eliminate them all made it much easier for me."

"But Maeda, he trusted you?"

"He is just a blind fool!"

"Not as blind as Beauchamp! So, this is all about you, a Fujiwara, and Caprice assuming control of the Calver Cats? She re-established the UK Operation after I forced Beauchamp to leave, and you took control of the Asian Operations after I removed Bill Chalmers and Ryota. But you expected him to win, so when he lost you had to change the plan. That's why you said 'the best laid plans' to your father, and that's why he wanted to kill you rather than me. And in Cambodia, you hoped I would help you seize full control of the Calver Cats by killing or capturing Beauchamp and Ryuu."

Hachiro smiled. "We ensured events moved in our favour, and you carried on doing our killing for us. Who do you think sent the SMS telling you where to find Beauchamp? However, if the mercenaries in Burma had followed our instructions, you would have died there. But you got away. Now even that has been turned to benefit our cause."

"So did Beauchamp really commit suicide?"

"Of course not! He wouldn't have had the guts. The architect of his miserable demise is standing over there," retorted Hachiro, nodding towards Caprice who started laughing.

"Beauchamp had become a liability," she sneered. "He really did want to retire and I didn't want him around. But the *BCC* in the Calver Cats calling card never stood for Beauchamp Caradoc Caille … it was Beauchamp and Caprice Caille. He was just too stupid to understand I was controlling him. I couldn't risk him being in jail in England so I made sure Leiko could help him escape. Then you conveniently dispatched that little whore. Why else do you think Beauchamp kept on choosing to meet in places you knew so well? You've done well for us. But now it's your turn to die, and with you the age of the Peacekeeper. Meanwhile, this house and this man…," she gestured towards Matsumoto, "…are the only things of consequence that remains of our ancient rivals. We'll attend to Lee later. Tonight we finish things here."

Tessa shook her head in disbelief, still struggling to comprehend the enormity of what had been happening around her.

"But what about Penny?"

"Collateral damage. I needed her to fool the Matsumoto into believing the feud could be ended. That's why I prompted her into commissioning the Amakuni sword. All that took was a supposedly chance meeting over a cup of coffee. But that pompous idiot Collins-Clarke had Bill kill her, and you claimed the damn weapon. At first I was worried by you being so handy with it, but we soon managed to turn that to our advantage…"

"Enough!" interrupted Hachiro. "Now we fight, Nariko-san. I have watched your technique and gauged what you can do. You have travelled far and lack sleep, and you have already had to fight hard so you are tired. I know your limitations, and have forced you beyond them."

"Oh, boy," sighed Tessa, "it does hurt to know how we've all been manipulated."

"Not as much as this will," he retorted. "Are you ready?"

Tessa smiled at Nyunt, took a deep breath and drew her Amakuni sword. Gripping it with both hands, she held it out in front of her. The sound of its loud confident ringing filled the courtyard.

"You should never have kidnapped my daughter," she hissed.

A moment later their swords clashed with a mighty *clang*. More followed as they exchanged brutal blows and quickly took new positions. But Hachiro and Tessa were extremely accomplished duellers, so the fight took place in bursts of incredible speed and ferocity. They gyrated round the courtyard, each accumulating minor cuts. However, neither of them was winning or losing, and beads of perspiration started running down both fighters' foreheads. They fought on, not even slowing when others would have stopped completely. Frustratingly for Hachiro, Tessa showed no signs of exhaustion; she had no intention of letting Nyunt down.

Then he tried a bold, determined attack. Raising his sword, he rushed at Tessa, intending to strike a strong downwards-slashing blow. Sensing a window of opportunity, she raised her own sword high and almost horizontal in the conventional defence. Their blades met with yet another resounding *clang*, and he ran past her, spinning round quickly as he stopped. Tessa also turned, but positioned her right leg slightly further forward than necessary. This made it a difficult, but attainable, target for Hachiro; however, he would have to make a fast, low, right-to-left stroke. He was convinced she'd made a mistake and quickly prepared to deliver what he expected to be the decisive wound. Meanwhile, she knew her leg would have to stay vulnerable long enough to trap him, which meant she wouldn't be able to move it completely back to safety without stumbling. As he swung his sword down and round, she shuffled her leg as far out of the way as she could without compromising her stance. Hachiro's sword swept round and put a deep gash in the front of her thigh. It was a nasty cut, but not debilitating. Tessa didn't even flinch, instead moving her sword round to chase his and momentarily block its return.

Then, she let go of her Kimi sword with her left hand and quickly drew her Bryani sword. In a moment of horror, Hachiro realised he had just been seduced into committing the same error he'd made while they were practising in Cambodia. A split second later, Tessa's Bryani sword swept down and severed his exposed right arm. Grimacing in pain, he quickly tossed his sword at Tessa, forcing her to use her weapon to flick it away. Then he brought his left hand back in an effort to draw his short sword. He would fight on.

Seeing this, Tessa whirled both her swords round and brought them horizontal at shoulder height, pointing at him. She would need to strike with considerable force to penetrate his armour, and she didn't have much time. Her torso was completely unprotected and he had nearly drawn his short sword.

Carefully aiming between two scales in overlapping rows, she simultaneously thrust both weapons forwards. The blades jarred against his lower armour, buckling slightly under the pressure she exerted. But then they twanged straight and plunged through into his chest, piercing both lungs. A moment later several inches of each blade reappeared through his back. Tessa paused, and then withdrew her weapons. Hachiro gasped and sank to his knees. His left hand released its grip on his short sword and it slowly slid back into its sheath. Tessa flicked the blood off her own swords and returned them to their sheaths. He sighed and looked up at her as a trickle of blood ran from one corner of his mouth.

"So, now we know who is the better of us," he sighed, "and I must die without avenging the death of my wife."

"I haven't killed your wife," replied Tessa, nonplussed. "Have I?"

"Yes. She told me," said Hachiro, gesturing towards Caprice as he coughed and spluttered more blood. "When you first fought the Calver Cats in London. My wife was the beautiful blonde woman with the Amafuji sword you now wear as a trophy; the sword which I foolishly failed to recognise until Beng Mealea."

"Bryani?!" exclaimed Tessa. "She was your wife?"

"Yes, the swords are a pair, but you altered hers. It looks different now."

"Oh, Hachiro-san," rebuked Tessa, "I didn't kill Bryani. Yes, I fought her and won, but I didn't kill her. I wanted her alive so she could be questioned about Penny's death. One of the Calver Cats shot her, and while she was dying she made me promise to look after her sword. Bryani died in my arms. I had the weapon restored, that's why it looks so different. I swear I didn't kill her. Gareth was there, he saw it all."

Hachiro strained to look round at Jones.

"It's true," he said, "I was there. Nariko didn't kill Bryani. Caprice lied if she told you any different. In fact, I wouldn't be surprised if that woman ordered Bryani's death."

For a moment Caprice looked wrong-footed. Hachiro noticed it immediately.

"Oh, what a fool I've been," he groaned. "But soon I shall be with my wife again. Please forgive me, Nariko-san, and put my sword with hers?"

Tessa took a deep breath and drew her Kimi sword. She used it to flick his off the ground into the air. She re-sheathed her sword and caught his.

"Hachiro-san, I forgive you. But Bryani's sword is not a trophy, it was a gift and is my sword now. You have chosen to become a common criminal, betrayed your friends and brought the name of Peacekeeper into disrepute. Your weapon is disgraced, and shall be broken."

A tear ran down his face as, with a forlorn expression, he watched Tessa plunge the blade between two flagstones. Then she pulled the hilt over, hard. First it flexed and *twanged* in protest, then there was an abrupt *chink* and it snapped in two. Tessa used the hilt to flick the blade section up from between the stones. Then she hit it far out over the moat and threw the hilt after it. Only the *swish-swish-swish* of the pieces flying through the air disturbed the silence. Gradually the sound grew fainter, ending with a faint *splosh … splosh* in the water beneath.

Hachiro fell forward and died.

"You fucking bitch!" yelled Caprice.

Tessa, surprisingly pleased with herself, grinned as she savoured composing an appropriate reply. However, before she could say anything, Caprice threw a knife at her. It was an excellent throw, strong, fast and accurate. But Tessa nonchalantly plucked it out of the air, and prepared to throw it back.

"Don't do that," ordered Matsumoto quickly. "Enough people have died tonight. She should face justice more publicly."

For a moment, Tessa hesitated. Then she threw the knife. There was a *thump* as it stuck in the arm of Matsumoto's chair, severing the ropes binding his right wrist. He smiled, took the knife and started cutting the bonds to his left hand.

"Then see how you like this, asshole!" yelled Caprice. She raised her right arm and flexed her wrist. A powerful spring *twanged!*

Jones yelped as a small dart buried itself in the back of his neck.

Caprice moved her arm round to point it at Nyunt. But Matsumoto had already flicked his wrist. The knife shot towards Caprice and buried itself deep in her forehead. As she keeled over backwards, a second dart fired, landing harmlessly in the door frame of the Samurai house.

A moment later Tessa had plucked the dart from Gareth's neck and cut the ropes binding him. The dart looked to be of the same sort as the one Beauchamp had used on her. She opened the wound and pressed some of her mosses into it.

He looked up at her and smiled.

"Oh, dear, I'm not immune. But at least I'm not going to die tied to a chair."

"Your spirit could never be tied down," she replied, extending one hand to pull a shivering Nyunt towards her.

"Never mind, you and Nyunt are safe," he continued, "that's the main thing. You make a great pair, you know."

"He handcuffed himself to me so we wouldn't get separated," said Nyunt.

Tessa smiled.

"That was good of you, Gareth."

"Oh, not really. You'd have done the same, or something better. This place is magnificent. I can understand why you like it here so much."

Tessa nodded, cupped his right hand in hers and started stroking it.

"I did warn you it was dangerous, getting close to me," she whispered.

"Ah, but it was worth it." His voice became quieter and more strained. "Mind you, I'd like to hear you explain all this. Potter will help you, though, he's a good man."

Tessa moved closer. Holding his head between her hands, she kissed him goodbye. He looked up at her and grinned. Then the sparkle faded from his eyes and he slipped away. Tears trickled down her face as she continued to look into his eyes until she was sure his spirit had departed. She gently pulled his eyelids down and laid his head on his chest. Then she sighed and wiped away her tears, kneeling down in front of Nyunt.

"I'm sorry you had to see all this, little one. Are you all right."

Nyunt flung her arms around Tessa's neck.

"You came for me!"

"Of course. I promised I would."

Nyunt moved away slightly, her eyes watering.

"I was scared for a while. But Gareth was kind and protected me. He said I wasn't to worry because you loved me so much, you wouldn't rest until you'd rescued me. He was right, wasn't he?"

"Yes, darling, he was absolutely right. So, are you all right?"

"Yes, I am now."

Tessa lifted Nyunt up and turned to Matsumoto.

"And are *you* all right too, Matsumoto-san?"

"Oh, yes, I shall be fine," he replied, watching Hayasaka dress his wounds. "You fought well. Indeed, your use of HICA was exemplary. But I warned you it is dangerous to offer a limb to an opponent, especially one such as Hachiro. However, I have to admit, it did seem to work."

Tessa grinned and put Nyunt down.

"Go and talk to Mr Matsumoto while I collect my weapons."

Nyunt dutifully wandered over to Matsumoto, and he put his arm round her. She watched with interest as Tessa retrieved her knives and shuriken, cleaning them before putting them back into the pockets of her Kevlar suit.

When she came back, Hayasaka had just finished tending Matsumoto. Tessa sat down on the steps to the Samurai house and he walked over to her with the large box of healing mosses and herbs.

As he tended her wounds, Nyunt described everything that had happened. When she'd finished her story Hayasaka stood up, clearly satisfied with his handiwork. Tessa looked at the neat stitching.

"Very good, Hayasaka-san, thank you. So, Matsumoto-san, did you know Caprice had spoken to Penny?"

"No," he replied, shaking his head. "The first time Yoshino was mentioned to me was when she asked to commission the Amakuni sword. Her death came as a complete surprise and shock. It confused us, but we knew she had always intended to give the sword to another, so we waited. Obviously, Caprice did not know that. So, unwittingly, she became the architect of her own demise, and that of the Fujiwara clan. It makes one wonder who really started all of this... Anyway, your victory for the Matsumoto is at best Pyrrhic. Yes, the feud is over, but the Matsumoto line is also likely to finish. It seems the Chrysanthemum League will be carried forward into the next generation by the Amakuni, and maybe..."

He looked at Nyunt.

"Don't even think about it," retorted Tessa, quickly pulling her closer.

"Nariko-san. You should know by now that no one can alter another's destiny. That is dictated by a higher power. What one hopes will happen rarely does; but sometimes, as with you, what one does not consider likely suddenly occurs. That is what I have believed all my life and it has served us both well, has it not? You are alive and well, and so is your daughter. Also, whether you wanted it or not, you are a formidable Peacekeeper, and that is something of which you should be proud."

"Maybe. But where is Caprice's first born? And did Hachiro and Bryani have any children together?"

"Ah, now those, are indeed very interesting questions."

Tessa was about to continue when the sound of approaching helicopters interrupted.

"Oh, it sounds as though the Emperor's guard has been summoned. This mess is going to take some clearing up," observed Matsumoto, gesturing to the courtyard with a smile, "and there is the matter of Hachiro ... and perhaps Nyunt should not be introduced to all that just yet."

"I agree. But there's something else which needs to be done, isn't there?" observed Tessa. "If this location has been secret since the Emperor's purge of 1692, even from the Fujiwara, how did Hachiro know where to come?"

"Unfortunately you already know the answer, don't you?"

"I suppose so," sighed Tessa, "that is such a shame."

"Perhaps you and Yoshino should be on your way, and I will explain everything?"

Tessa nodded.

"You'll make sure Gareth is well looked after, and sent back to London?"

"Of course."

Tessa smiled at Nyunt.

"Come on, little one. It's time for us to leave."

"They're going to land near the chinthes," observed Hayasaka.

"Oh, dear," said Matsumoto, grinning at Tessa, "you'd better use the back door then."

"Oh, no, just my luck," she muttered, turning to Nyunt. "You're going to have to be very brave, darling. We're going to jump into the moat."

"OK," replied Nyunt cheerfully, apparently not in the slightest bit concerned.

"Aren't you scared?"

"No, why should I be?"

"Well, it's a long way down… It scares the living daylights out of me every time I do it."

"But you probably did it on your own before. I'll be with you now so it's OK."

Tessa laughed, scooped her up and kissed her on the cheek.

"Matsumoto-san, I do of course remember everything. Absolutely everything," she murmured.

"Of course you do," he replied, smiling at her with such a depth of emotion Hayasaka was amazed.

Tessa hesitated, unsure what to say.

"I'll need some time," she said quietly, glancing at Nyunt and back.

"Of course you will," he continued with a caring smile. "We both know there is not much in this world which is more important than the next generation. And when the time is right, you know the way."

Tessa nodded, sighed, and took one last look at Gareth; another man who should never have risked loving her. Then she turned and started walking. But as she passed Matsumoto's chair she stuck the fingers of her left hand down; and, just at the right moment, he raised his hand to meet hers. She paused for a fleeting instant as they touched. Then the moment passed and she carried on walking. Hayasaka watched, dumbfounded. Tessa stopped at the entrance to the Samurai house.

"Hayasaka-san, please have the car meet us at the Kenrouken Gate in two hours."

"I will do it now," he replied, snapping back to reality.

In the Samurai house, Tessa stopped to pick up a clean towel and a large polythene bag. A moment later they were in the garden.

"Oh, sorry," she said, putting Nyunt down. "There's something I've got to do before we leave."

She went to the well and raised a bucket of water. She poured it on a flourishing young camellia which had been planted in the ideal position to be seen from the house. Then she stood back briefly and smiled.

As the helicopters landed, Hayasaka turned to Matsumoto.

"She's still here."

"Yes, she's watering our camellia. She never could leave without doing that."

Tessa and Nyunt soon reached the door through the back wall of the garden. Tessa opened it, but it was still so dark that Nyunt couldn't see anything except the beginning of the plank leading away from the garden.

"Now then, darling, take off all your clothes and put them in this bag with the towel."

"What about you?" asked Nyunt as she stripped.

"Oh, I'll be all right, but we don't want you catching cold, do we?"

Tessa tied a knot in the top of the bag, and picked Nyunt up, wedging the bag between them. She stepped out on to the plank and reached back to close the door. Then she continued to the end, pausing for a moment some hundred feet above the moat.

"Who was Penny," asked Nyunt.

"She was a very close friend of mine who was very sadly murdered. It's a long story but I'll tell you later, if you want?"

Nyunt nodded.

"And why did Mr Matsumoto call me *Yoshino*?"

"Oh, that's part of the same story. He meant it as a compliment."

Momentarily distracted by the view, Tessa gazed into the distance. Dawn was imminent, birds had begun to sing and she could just make out the outline of the mountains in the distance.

"It's very pretty here," observed Nyunt, looking round.

"Yes, it is."

"Maybe we could come back some time?"

"Would you like that?"

"Yes."

"Good, so would I," replied Tessa. "Now, on *one*, I want you to cup your right hand over your mouth and hold your nose closed between your thumb and first finger. Then breathe out. On *two*, wrap your left arm round my neck, breathe in as deeply as you can and clamp your hand over your mouth. On *three* we'll go. I'll hold on to you all the time. OK?"

"I love you," whimpered Nyunt, overcome with emotion, "a lot."

"I know, darling," replied Tessa, smiling and kissing her on her forehead, "and I love you a lot, too."

"I know. Thank you."

"You are more than welcome. Ready?"

Nyunt nodded.

"One … two … three …"

CHAPTER 38

The Epilogue

Back in London, their lives quickly settled down again. Nyunt went back to school with renewed enthusiasm, and the adoption was finalised. Tessa gave up trying to retire. Instead, she continued teaching at SKS, and, albeit in the guise of Nariko, became one of the few people to attain legend status during their own lifetime. For a while, she kept a newspaper article from Japan reporting the death of Chief Inspector Maeda. It simply said that a serious error of judgement had been exposed and, to protect his family's honour, he had committed *seppuku* at Narita airport. A non-Japanese International Peacekeeper had acted as his *Kaishakunin*.

Tessa and Nyunt soon returned to Kanazawa. Nyunt made friends with Hayasaka's children and frequently slept at their house. However, Tessa always stayed at the castle with Matsumoto. It was the first of many such visits…

Five years later, Nyunt took up the sword and started training with Tessa at SKS. Eventually, she too became a Peacekeeper.

And the story concludes in Vol. 3, Bitter Legacy…

GLOSSARY

Throughout the Samurai Revival Trilogy, references to road names or places are fictitious, even if the name does exist. Furthermore, all references to brand names are intended as compliments.

Also, the author would like to thank the various public domain databases used while preparing this glossary, in particular, Wikipedia.

Angkor Wat (*lit. Temple City*) built by King Suryavarman II during the 12th century containing a temple mountain and galleried temple. Big and very beautiful, it is the world's largest Vishnu temple complex.

Arigato   Japanese for 'thank you.' (See Domo arigato)

Akzeptiert. Bitte warten German for 'accepted, please wait.'

Banteay Srei (*lit. citadel of the women*) is a 10th century temple dedicated to Shiva. Built of red sandstone, it is small but richly carved.

Beng Mealea of the same style, but smaller and less ornate, it is believed to have been the prototype for Angkor Wat. It is largely unrestored.

Bitte neue Address Angeben German for 'please enter a new address.'

Bratwurst   a German sausage - veal, pork or beef (*lit. pan-fired*).

Burma   (*also known as Union of Myanmar*) is a wonderful, predominantly Buddhist country south of China and west of Thailand on the Bay of Bengal. There have been numerous human rights abuses by the ruling Military Junta since independence from Britain in 1948. Recently, some concessions have been made to democratic activists.

Đà Nẵng   one of the major (South China Sea) ports in Vietnam.

Devatas   derived from Deva, the Hindu for deity; devatas are smaller more focused guardian spirits, or images thereof.

Dôbuku sugata is an unstandardized leisure jacket, possibly with sleeves, and wide, loose-fitting trousers – often worn by Samurai.

Domo arigato Japanese for 'thank you very much.' If 'gozaimasu' is appended, the thank you is even more generous and polite (pronounced 'Doe-moe Ah-ree-gah-toe Go-zah-ee-mahs').

Es freudt mich Sie kennen zu lernen German 'pleased to meet you'.

Guten abend German for 'good evening.'

Gleichfalls German for 'likewise.'

The Gondoliers the 12th comic opera (1889) by Gilbert and Sullivan.

Hallo, Frau Doktor, wie gehts? German for, 'hello, doctor (fem), how are you feeling?'

Hanko a personal seal/stamp used on official documents in lieu of a signature in Asian countries, including Japan. The Kanji characters comprising the author's Hanko (*shown in the bottom right-hand corner of the front cover*) are pronounced as Rheagan Greene and may be translated as 'Reason and hope – tools of dignity'.

Honmaru the innermost defended courtyard (bailey) within a castle, which contains the main donjon (*Eng. keep*).

Htet a Burmese name (male) meaning 'sharp'.

Ichi Japanese for 'one.'

In drei kilometre rechts einbieten, Ausfahrt Hilden nehmen the German for, 'in 3 km take the next exit right, follow the Hilden signs.'

Irabya a fictitious Middle Eastern country (see Bitter Legacy).

Kabuki (*lit. the art of singing and dancing*) is a classical Japanese dance/drama dating from the 1600s, performed with elaborate costumes.

Kaishakunin a trusted second acting for a person committing *seppuku*. Performing kaishaku (*decapitation*) should leave a slight band of flesh attaching the head to the body, so that the head may be hung in front as if embraced dakikubi (*lit. embraced head*). Due to the precision required for such a manoeuvre, the second would be a highly skilled swordsperson.

Kampai a common, sociable Japanese toast when drinking.

Kill Bill is the title to two excellent films (1 & 2 - 2003/4) directed by Quentin Tarantino and starring Uma Thurman.

Klong (or *Khlong*) is a (narrow) canal in Thailand. Many spread throughout Bangkok from the Chao Phraya river.

Konichiwa the Japanese for 'hello'.

Kyay zu tin bar de Burmese for 'thank you'.

Longyi a sheet of cloth (c. 6½ ft. by 2½ ft.) worn around the waist (male or female), held in place by folding fabric over without a knot.

Mingalaba(h) Burmese for 'hello'. Frequently used by foreigners, it was adopted as a greeting, mainly for schoolchildren, in the 1930s. It is considered a polite way to greet anyone (*lit. auspiciousness*).

Mǎhouq-pa Burmese for an abrupt 'no!' (adding '-bǜ' is more polite)

Nächste Ausfahrt in drei kilometre, bitte umkehren the German for, 'the next exit is in 3 km, please turn round'.

Naypyidaw is the new (2005) capital of Burma founded on a jungle site some 200 miles north of the old capital Rangoon (Yangon).

Nicht schlecht. Ich bin fest der Meinung das ich noch lebe the German for 'not bad. I do believe I'm still alive'.

Nichts zu danken! German for 'you're welcome/don't mention it'.

Nyunt a Burmese name (female) meaning 'blossom'.

Obi a sash for traditional Japanese dress, e.g. the uniform (*keikogi*) worn for martial arts, but commonly the wide 'belt' on a kimono.

OCL Open Carrying Licence. A fictitious construction to indicate a licence to carry a samurai sword, uncased, in public.

Ohayou gozaimas(u) Japanese for 'good morning'. The abbreviated form, 'ohayou', is the less formal form.

Pagan (Bagan) is an old (9th-13th century) Burmese capital some 430 miles north of Rangoon, famous for its 2000+ temple remains.

Pagoda like *stupa*, but later and usually of multi-tiered design.

Papa Edinsay a fictitious Orkney island.

RCL Restricted Carrying Licence. A fictitious construction to indicate a licence to carry a samurai sword, cased, in public.

-san   a common honorific signifying respect and formality (similar to 'Mr', 'Mrs' or 'Miss'), usually masculine, denoting familiarity if used with a first name. *NB Japanese honorifics are complex, so they have been simplified in this trilogy to just '-san'. Apologies to Japanese purists.*

Sayonara   Japanese for 'goodbye' (pronounced 'Si-o-na-ra').

Seppuku   is a form of Japanese ritual suicide by (left to right) disembowelment (lit. "*stomach-cutting*"). Originally reserved for Samurai, it was part of the bushido code of honour and was often used voluntarily to die honourably rather than fall into the hands of an enemy.

Siamovnt   a fictitious chain of hotels in Thailand.

Sashimono   a highly skilful fifteen hundred year-old Japanese technique of making wooden objects without using nails or glue.

Stupa   (*lit. heap*) a mound-like structure (often dome shaped), usually containing a Buddhist relic, used for religious worship.

Thanaka   a yellowish-white predominantly Burmese cosmetic paste made from ground bark, typically from the Murraya (thanaka) tree, with a fragrance resembling that of sandalwood. It is commonly applied to the face and sometimes the arms of women and girls.

Tower Bridge an iconic bascule bridge (built 1886–1894) over the River Thames, near the Tower of London. It comprises two steel framework towers clad in Cornish granite and Portland stone, joined at the top by two horizontal walkways which withstand the forces exerted by the bascules.

Thwa dau me the Burmese for 'goodbye.'

UNWP   (United Nations for World Peace) a revamped, credible and fully effective United Nations organisation – regrettably fictitious.

Vorgesehene Ankunft in ein und fünfzig Minuten German for, 'the programmed destination will be reached in fifty-one minutes.'

Vorgesehene Ankunft in vier und neunzig Minuten as above, but in forty nine minutes.

Vorgesehene Ankunft in vierzig Minuten as above, but forty mins.

Zabuton   a Japanese cushion, often highly decorated, generally used when sitting on the floor (tatami mats).